William Forsyth

Life of Marcus Tullius Cicero

Vol. 1

William Forsyth

Life of Marcus Tullius Cicero
Vol. 1

ISBN/EAN: 9783337332983

Printed in Europe, USA, Canada, Australia, Japan

Cover: Foto ©Raphael Reischuk / pixelio.de

More available books at **www.hansebooks.com**

CICERO.

FROM A BRONZE MEDAL STRUCK BY THE TOWN OF MAGNESIA IN LYDIA

To face Title-page of Vol. I.

LIFE

OF

MARCUS TULLIUS CICERO.

By WILLIAM FORSYTH, M.A., Q.C.,

AUTHOR OF 'HORTENSIUS,' 'NAPOLEON AT ST. HELENA AND SIR HUDSON LOWE,'
'HISTORY OF TRIAL BY JURY,' ETC.,
AND LATE FELLOW OF TRINITY COLLEGE, CAMBRIDGE.

IN TWO VOLUMES.—Vol. I.

WITH ILLUSTRATIONS.

LONDON:

JOHN MURRAY, ALBEMARLE STREET.

1864.

LONDON: PRINTED BY W. CLOWES AND SONS, STAMFORD STREET,
AND CHARING CROSS.

DEDICATION.

My dear Lord Brougham,

    I dedicate this work to you as a token of our friendship, and because a Life of Cicero cannot be more appropriately inscribed than with the name of one whose Eloquence and other splendid intellectual gifts, so conspicuously displayed and uniformly employed for the welfare of mankind, vividly recall to the minds of his countrymen the great Orator, Statesman, and Philosopher of ancient Rome. "Superest adhuc et exornat ætatis nostræ gloriam Vir sæculorum memoriâ dignus, qui olim nominabitur nunc intelligitur."

        Believe me,

           Very sincerely yours,

              W. FORSYTH.

The Firs, Mortimer, *December*, 1863.

PREFACE.

MORE than a century has elapsed since Middleton first published his 'History of the Life of Marcus Tullius Cicero,' which has during that period exclusively occupied the field in this country as the Biography of Cicero. It occurred to me that the time had come when another Life might be acceptable to the public. The advanced state of scholarship, which has made the history and literature of Rome so much better understood than when Middleton wrote—to say nothing of his defects as a biographer—justifies the appearance of a new account of the great Roman. The faults of his work are not inconsiderable. It is disfigured by a blind and indiscriminating tone of panegyric which is the language of flattery rather than of truth. It is almost entirely occupied with Cicero as a politician and an orator, and does not sufficiently enter into the details of his private and domestic life, which, in my opinion, form the chief charm of a biography. For as Madame Swetchine in one of her letters, alluding to the subject in the case of deceased friends, happily remarks,— "Tant que nous ne connaissons rien de leur caractère, de leur vocation, des actions de leur vie, ils demeurent pour nous à l'état d'abstraction; or, vous savez si ce sont les abstractions qui parlent au cœur." Middleton's work is also overlaid and encumbered with too much of the history of the time, so that the character of individuality is often lost. It is in fact, as the title seems to imply, an historical composition in which Cicero is the principal figure, but it is not the portrait of the man himself, with details properly subordinated as accessaries so as to form the background of the picture. Besides, the style is heavy and tedious, and I think that De Quincey is not far from the truth when he says that " by weeding away from it all that is colloquial, you would strip it of all that is characteristic; and if you should remove its slang vulgarisms, you would remove its whole principle of vitality."

My object has been to exhibit Cicero not only as an orator and a politician, but as he was in private life surrounded by his family and friends—speaking and acting like other men in the ordinary affairs of home. And the more we accustom ourselves to regard the ancients as persons of like passions as ourselves, and familiarize ourselves with the idea of them as fathers, husbands, friends, and *gentlemen*, the better we shall understand them.

It would be ungrateful in me not to acknowledge how much I am indebted to Abeken's most interesting and able work ' Cicero in Seinen Briefen '—an invaluable contribution to our right knowledge of his history —and to the ' Onomasticon Tullianum ' of Orelli and Baiter. I have also made much use of Drumann's ' Geschichte Roms nach Geschlechtern,' although I differ greatly from the estimate he has formed of the character of Cicero, and think him both prejudiced and unfair. I have derived most material assistance from the admirable edition of Cicero's letters by Schütz, where the correspondence is arranged in chronological order, and the difficulties are explained by clear and excellent notes. But for the convenience of reference I have always quoted the letters as they are given—most unmethodically it is true—in the popular edition of Ernesti. I have also referred to Brückner's 'Leben Cicero,' which has the merit of fulness and accuracy, but is a dull and unattractive book. It would, however, be mere pedantry in me to mention all the authorities of which I have made use. I believe that there is no author who has written on the subject whose work I have neglected. But after all, the great authority for the life of Cicero is Cicero himself, of whose works I have been, during a great period of my life, an assiduous student, attracted to them by the irresistible fascination of their contents and their style.

I had written much more than is printed in the following work, but as it would have swelled the volumes to an inconvenient size, I have been obliged very considerably to reduce my manuscript. For this reason I have omitted many details and translations of many parts of the speeches which I had prepared, and which I should have been glad to insert in the text. For the same reason also I have omitted a number of references in support of the opinions I have advanced, but if necessary they can be readily produced. I mention this merely lest it should be supposed that I have shunned pains and labor in the completion of my task. I can truly say that it has been with me a labor of love, and the most agreeable

relaxation I cared to find from the toils of my profession.   It is, no doubt, perilous to the interests of
lawyers to be supposed to occupy even their *horæ sub-*
secivæ with anything like literature.   But although
their profession has the first and foremost claims upon
their attention, it need not monopolize the whole, and
it can hardly be thought that they are less likely to
be qualified for the discharge of its duties if they make
themselves familiar with the models of ancient Eloquence and the Law of ancient times, than if they
confine themselves wholly to the study of technical
precedents and seek for inspiration only in the volumes
of Reports.

CONTENTS OF VOL. I.

ILLUSTRATIONS TO VOL. I.

ARPINO, NEAR WHICH CICERO WAS BORN.

THE LIFE

OF

MARCUS TULLIUS CICERO.

CHAPTER I.

THE BOYHOOD.

Æt. 1–16. B.C. 106–91.

ON the steep side of one of the Volscian hills, below
which the river Liris, now the Garigliano, flowed in
a winding channel to the sea, and on the northern fron-
tier of what has since been known as the Terra di Lavoro
in the kingdom of Naples, lay the ancient town of Arpinum. The banks of the river were thickly wooded with
lofty poplars, and a grove of oaks extended to the east,
where, not far off, the little river Fibrenus, now the Fi-
breno, in the midst of one of the loveliest of Italian land-
scapes, mingled its ice-cold waters with the waters of the
Liris. Before its confluence with the larger stream it
divided into two channels and rushed rapidly past a
small and beautiful island, now called the Isola di
Carnello ; and lower down at the point where the two
rivers met, another island was formed, now known as the
Isola San Paolo, or San Domenico, from a Dominican
monastery, which in later times was erected there and still
remains.

In this pleasant spot, at the point where the Liris and the Fibrenus met, amidst hills and rocks and woods, on the third of January, B.C. 106, Cicero was born.[1]

His family was old and respectable, but was of the plebeian and not of the patrician order. It was not *ennobled* —that is, none of its members had filled any curule office ; not even an ædileship, which was the lowest step in the ladder of rank that entitled a citizen to the honour of the ivory chair, and which, like all the other magistracies at Rome, was, at all events in the later centuries of the republic, open to plebeian and patrician families alike. It belonged to the equestrian class, and had long been settled in the neighbourhood of Arpinum. There was indeed a tradition at Rome that the Tullian *gens* was of royal descent ; and Plutarch alludes to it, saying, that some persons carried back the origin of the family to Tullus Attius, a king of the Volscians, who waged war not without honour against the Romans.

Cicero himself, like Napoleon, smiled at the efforts to make out for him an illustrious pedigree ; and, alluding to the funeral orations at Rome as a fertile source of the falsification of family history, said, that an instance of it would be an assertion by him that he was descended from Manius Tullius, the patrician who was consul with Servius Sulpicius ten years after the expulsion of the Tarquins.[2]

Arpinum had received the Roman franchise some time before, so that the inhabitants enjoyed the full rights of citizens of the Great Republic. The family name of

---

[1] The consuls for the year were C. Atilius Serranus and Q. Servilius Cæpio. According to the Julian reformed calendar the date of Cicero's birth would be October, B.C. 107.

[2] The word Tullius seems originally to have meant "spring" or "rivulet." Tullios alii dixerunt esse silanos, alii rivos, alii vehementes projectiones sanguinis arcuatim fluentis.—*Festus.*

Cicero was **most** probably derived, like those of the **Lentuli,** Fabii, Pisones and others, from the fact that some ancestor **had** been known as a successful **cultivator** of the humble vegetable called *cicer ;* but **another** less complimentary theory is that it **was** given in consequence of a personal defect in the face **of one** of his progenitors—in fact a wart or carbuncle **on the nose.**[3]   His paternal grandfather Marcus, **who** was still alive when Cicero **was born,** was no friend of innovation, and when his brother-in-law Gratidius, whose sister Gratidia he had married, **proposed** to introduce vote by ballot into Arpinum, he strongly opposed it.   Cicero mentions this story **of his** grandfather, and adds that Gratidius **was trying to raise** a tempest **in a cup (***excitabat fluctus** in simpulo*).   When Scaurus the consul **heard of old** Marcus's firmness, he much applauded it, and said, " I wish with such courage and virtue as you have shown, you had preferred the arena **of** a great metropolis to a provincial town."   **The** old gentleman hated the Greeks, and used to say that his countrymen were like Syrian slaves, the more Greek they knew, **the** greater rascals **they were.**

Marcus the grandfather and Gratidia had **another son** named Lucius, besides Cicero's father ; and, according **to** most genealogists, a daughter Tullia, **married to** Caius Aculeo, a Roman **knight.**   But **Drumann** asserts **that** he had no daughter, **and that Aculeo, who was a learned** lawyer **and** distinguished **orator, was married to Cicero's** maternal

---

[3] When Cicero as quæstor in **Sicily was about to make** an offering in a temple of some silver vessels which he had inscribed with his names **Marcus Tullius,** he told the silversmith **to engrave the** figure of a vetch (*cicer*) for the third name.   Had he lived in the days of heraldry, his *canting* arms would probably have had a vetch for the crest.   Plutarch says that when he was about **to enter into** public life he was advised to change his name of Cicero, but he proudly answered that he would make it **more glorious** than the **names** of the Scauri and the Catuli : and surely he kept his word.

aunt, the sister of his mother.[4] He was also the intimate friend of L. Licinius Crassus, who contested the
palm of eloquence wth Antonius, the grandfather of the
Triumvir, and Antonius himself was connected by marriage
with Lucius, the paternal uncle of Cicero.[5]

His father, who was also called Marcus, had weak health,
and he preferred to reside on his property and lead the
quiet life of a country gentleman, instead of engaging in
the struggles of ambition and mingling in the society and
bustle of Rome.   But he had also literary tastes, and seems
to have been a man of cultivated mind according to the
measure of his opportunities. He had enlarged the old
dwelling of the family, which appears previously to have
been little better than an ordinary farm house. The name of
Cicero's mother was Helvia, of whose family nothing more
is known than what Plutarch tells us, and this is comprised in the short sentence that she was a lady well born.
Cicero himself makes no allusion whatever to his mother
in all his numerous works.   One is curious to know whether
she was a woman of strong intellect, and an instance
amongst the many that could be quoted of mothers to
whom their sons have owed the mental powers which have
made them famous; and in such cases it will generally be
found that it has not been so much any brilliancy of ima-

[4] See Drumann, *Geschichte Roms nach Geschlechtern*, V. 213.
[5] The following genealogical table will be useful for reference :—

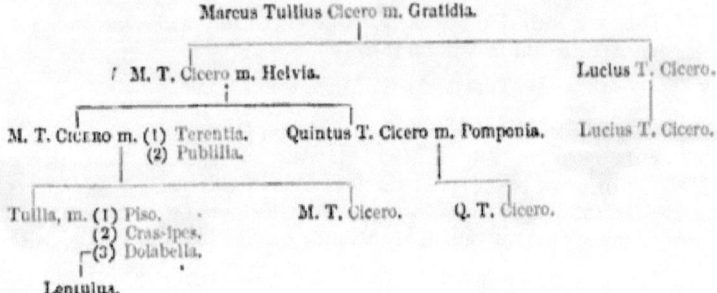

gination or accomplishment as native shrewdness and good sense, in fact, what we call mother wit, which has distinguished the mothers of celebrated men. An anecdote has been preserved of her as told by her son Quintus in one of his letters, which shows that she was a careful housewife and looked well after her domestic concerns. He says that she used to seal up all the wine jars in the house, even when they were empty, to prevent mistakes and discourage clandestine visits to the cellar.

Cicero, as for the sake of convenience we shall call the subject of this biography, although that was properly his surname, had one younger brother, named Quintus, but no sister. At the usual time, that is on the ninth day after his birth, he received what we should call the baptismal name of Marcus,[6] which, as it was afterwards given to his own son, was thus kept in the family for at least four generations. Of his childish years at the family residence near Arpinum no anecdote has been preserved. Plutarch indeed says that when he began to learn he was so distinguished by his abilities, that the fathers of his schoolfellows used to visit the school that they might see the young prodigy, and some of them were foolish enough to be annoyed because the boys when they walked together put Cicero in the middle as the place of honour. But this, if true, no doubt refers to the period when he had left Arpinum for Rome, as we shall see was the case during his

---

[6] This was called the *dies lustricus.* The full name, according to Roman style, would be written thus—

M. Tullius M. F. M. N. Cor. Cicero,

Marcus Tullius, Marci Filius, Marci Nepos, Cornelia, Cicero ; that is, Mark Tully Cicero, son of Mark, grandson of Mark, of the Cornelian Tribe. In order to enjoy the rights of Roman citizenship it was necessary to be enrolled in one of the thirty-five tribes ; and when the franchise was bestowed on Arpinum, its inhabitants were included in the Cornelian tribe.

boyhood, although the exact period is not known. He always had throughout life the greatest attachment to his birthplace, which he calls his cradle and ancestral home, and he seems to have loved its wild scenery with no ordinary fondness. Marius was a native of Arpinum, and just four years before the birth of Cicero had gained his brilliant victory over the savage hordes of Teutones and Ambones at Aquæ Sextiæ (the modern Aix) in the southeast of Gaul. This was followed next year by the complete and utter destruction of the Cimbri in a great battle fought near Verona, when Marius came to the rescue of the proconsul Catulus, hard pressed by the barbarians, and by their overthrow saved Rome from an attack which would have been more terrible than that of the Gauls three centuries before. We may well imagine when the fame of these victories reached Arpinum how proud the citizens were of the hero who had won them, and how they loved to talk in the forum and the market-place of his exploits, telling the tale to which the young Cicero must often, as he grew older, have lent a listening ear, and perhaps awakening in his mind that eager desire for distinction and applause which became the ruling passion of his life.[7] No memorial remains at Arpinum to mark the birthplace of the great Roman orator, but the fragment of an ancient altar built into the wall of a house on which are still seen the letters COS. VII., requires no name to show that it was erected in honour of Marius, for of him alone could it be said that he was seven times consul.

His parents must have soon observed that the young Cicero was a child of no ordinary promise, and this no doubt determined his father to take him and his brother

[7] There was a distant connexion between the families of Cicero and Marius in the following manner. A brother of Marius had adopted Gratidianus, the son of Gratidius, who was the brother-in-law of Cicero's grandfather.

Quintus to Rome, in order that they might there have the benefit of an education which it was impossible to procure at a provincial town. He therefore placed them both with their uncle Aculeo, who had a house in the street called *Carinæ*,[8] that they might join their cousins in the usual course of education pursued by Roman youths of good family.

There is a curious remark by Niebuhr that Cicero in his youth was without friends.[9] But for this he certainly had no authority. I should be inclined to believe that the direct contrary is the truth, and to say that few young men are likely to have had more. His amiable disposition and loveable nature, in which there was no coldness or reserve, to say nothing of his splendid talents and genial wit, must have made him one of the most companionable of men. Quick, warm, and impulsive in feeling, he was singularly fitted to form early friendships, and we need not doubt that he did so. But alas! how often are our early friendships buried prematurely in the grave. Who of us cannot from his own sad experience verify the mournful lines of the poet,—

> They, the young and strong, who cherished
> 　Noble longings for the strife,
> By the wayside fell and perished,
> 　Wearied with the march of life?

We do not know with any certainty whether Marcus the father left his sons under the care of their uncle and

---

[8] Drumann, *Gesch. Roms*, V. 213, assuming that Cicero's father had a residence in Rome, says that he lived in the Carinæ. It was one of the principal streets or perhaps "regions" of Rome. It lay between the Cœlian and Esquiline mounts, and was then a fashionable quarter. Pompey had a house there. Virgil, *Æn.* VIII. 361, speaks of *lautæ Carinæ*.

[9] *Hist. of Rome*, V. 30 (Ed. Schmitz). He in another passage qualifies this by saying " He seems to have passed his youth without any intimate friend; and it was only in his maturer age that a true friendship was formed between him and Atticus."

returned to his retreat in the neighbourhood of Arpinum, or whether he stayed at Rome to superintend their education. I think it is very probable that he sacrificed his inclination for a rural life to a sense of duty, and took up his residence, for a time at least, in the great metropolis, for Cicero speaks affectionately of the pains he took in instructing his sons, or in giving them the means of instruction (in nobis erudiendis) and calls him a most wise and excellent man.[1]

The two brothers stimulated by the reputation of Crassus, and perhaps at his recommendation, attended the lectures of the same professors or teachers whom he had used for the purposes of his own education. These seem to have been Greeks, and the object was not only to learn the language, with which Crassus was so familiar that it seemed to be his native tongue, but to acquire those branches of instruction such as rhetoric, grammar, and composition, which Greek teachers were alone at that period competent to impart at Rome. Cicero became very intimate, notwithstanding his extreme youth, not only with him but with Antonius, the grandfather of the Triumvir, who divided with Crassus the palm of Roman eloquence in those days ; and he expressly mentions that he used to apply for information from time to time to Antonius, and put questions to him as far as his boyish modesty allowed him to venture with so distinguished a man. We can well believe that both Crassus and Antonius took delight in gratifying the eager curiosity of so intelligent an inquirer, and must have felt respecting him what Lady Holland said to her husband, the first Lord Holland, of "little William Pitt," that he was "really the cleverest child she ever saw."[2] In alluding to these two eminent

---

[1] Optimi ac prudentissimi viri.—De Orat. II. 1. ;
[2] Lord Stanhope's Life of Pitt, vol. I. p. 4.

men at an advanced period of his life, Cicero says that
with regard to Greek literature the difference between
them was this; Crassus wished to have the reputation of
knowing it, but affected to despise it, giving the preference
in all things, including literature, in which the Latin language was up to that time miserably deficient, to the
native productions of Rome over those of Greece, while
Antonius, in compliance with that narrow-minded bigotry
which the Romans mistook for patriotism, pretended complete ignorance of both the language and literature of
Greece. But the object of both was the same. They
thought that the effect of their oratory would be lessened
before a Roman audience if they were supposed to be
admirers of a nation whom their countrymen so thoroughly
despised. Crassus therefore took care to vaunt his preference for everything Roman, while Antonius thought the
safer plan would be to have it supposed that he was wholly
ignorant of the exotic article.

There were two schools—we may almost call them
parties—of education at Rome in those days. The one
was the Latin, the other the Greek school.[3] The first
who opened a school for instruction in Latin literature
there, was Lucius Plautius, about the time when young
Cicero removed from Arpinum to the capital, and he
wished to become a student at his lectures, which were
well attended. But he reluctantly yielded to the advice of friends, who thought that he had better devote

---

[3] About half a century before Cicero was born the Senate passed a
resolution banishing philosophers and rhetoricians from Rome. The
then censors brought the subject again under the notice of the Senate,
saying that men who called themselves " Latin rhetoricians " had introduced a new kind of learning, and their schools were frequented by
young men who idled away their time there for whole days together (*ibi
homines adolescentulos dies totos desidere*). They declared that they did
not like the novelty, and called on the Senate to mark its displeasure
against both teachers and pupils. They were ordered to shut up their
" schools of impudence " (*ludum impudentiæ*).—*De Orat.* III. 24.

himself exclusively to Greek. Perhaps the wiser plan would have been to allow a boy of such industry and aptitude to study both, but if the choice lay between the two, beyond all doubt they acted rightly in giving preference to Greek, for Latin literature was then still in its infancy, and the language had not been enriched by the prose of Cicero, Sallust, Varro, and Livy, and by the poetry of Lucretius, Virgil, Catullus, and Horace. The only Latin poets who had then written, were Pacuvius, Nævius, and Ennius, and the only Latin histories were the dry and meagre annals of Fabius Pictor, Calpurnius Piso, and others.

Greek, however, had become at this time the fashionable study at Rome, and occupied something of the same position in a course of education that French does amongst ourselves. And Cicero tells us that the language was cultivated in Latium, or, as we should say, in the provinces, even more zealously than in the capital. It was considered the accomplishment of a gentleman, and Greek phrases and Greek quotations were everywhere current in good society. Even the sturdy Cato, the censor, who despised the nation and their effeminate character, and who had deemed their literature beneath the attention of a Roman, at last gave way to the prevailing Græco-mania, and according to a well-known story, applied himself in extreme old age to the study of the language. Cicero, as might be expected from his exquisite taste, was passionately fond of Greek literature, and his letters abound in expressions and quotations which prove his intimate familiarity with the rich treasures it contains. One practical reason for learning that language thoroughly was, that he might be able to converse with his Greek teachers, who seem to have been able to speak Latin only imperfectly, and in some cases perhaps not at all. Phædrus, the Epicurean, was one of his instructors, and he speaks of him in terms of peculiar regard.

He became also a pupil of the poet Archias. He was a Greek who had come to Rome from Antioch when Cicero was five years old, and, according to the usual custom of those days, resided in the house of a Roman patron, the wealthy Lucullus. His reputation as a poet depends exclusively on the speech which Cicero in later years delivered in defence of his former teacher and friend, for not a line of his verses has been preserved, but we know that he composed laudatory poems in honour of some of the noble families of Rome.

His intimacy with Archias may have awakened in Cicero the desire to be himself also a poet. We are told by Plutarch, that when very young he composed a poem called Pontius Glaucus, the hero of which was a fisherman of Bœotia, who having eaten a certain plant, went mad and sprang into the sea, where he was changed into a sea-god, the place from which he made the fatal spring being afterwards known as the Glaucus-leap. He translated also into Latin verse two Greek poems on astronomy or subjects connected with that science—the Phænomena and Prognostica or Diosemeia of Aratus, whose works were very popular at Rome. Although he had not the poetic faculty in the proper sense of the word, and frankly acknowledged this himself, he had great facility in the composition of verses, and amused himself with it at different periods of his life. Some of his productions were long poems such as the Marius, which seems to have been written during the life of that hero,[4] and was an epic celebration of his life and exploits ; and the poems on his Consulship (*de suo Consulatu*) and his own Times (*de suis*

---

[4] Drumann. *Gesch. Roms*, V. 221, ingeniously fixes the date of this poem as B.C. 87, when Cicero therefore was nineteen years old.

Temporibus). It was in one of these, most probably the Consulship, that the unfortunate lines occurred,

> Cedant arma togæ, concedat laurea laudi,[5]

and,

> O fortunatam natam me consule Romam !

the jingle of which provoked the ridicule of Juvenal, Quintilian and Seneca, as well as of the wits of his own day, who were never tired of laughing at him for them, and his enemies took care that nobody should forget them. He however clung to them with true parental fondness for a deformed offspring, and in his treatise *De Officiis* calls the verse beginning *Cedant arma togæ* "a capital line which I hear is attacked by the wicked and the envious." He must have heard of it often enough. Of his poem on Marius, Quintus Mucius Scævola the Augur had such a favorable opinion, that in some complimentary lines he declared that it would endure for endless ages, saying, "Canescet sæclis innumerabilibus." But the old lawyer was neither a poet nor a prophet.

When Rousseau once sent to Voltaire a copy of an ode addressed to Posterity, the sneering critic wittily remarked, *Voici une lettre qui n'arrivera jamais à son adresse,* and Cicero's epic has met with a similar fate. Both Plutarch and Pliny the younger lavish panegyrics upon his poetry, and Middleton goes so far as to declare that the fragments that time has spared us "are sufficient to convince us that his poetical genius, if it had been cultivated with the same care, would not have been inferior to his oratorical." He adds that "the world always judges of things by comparison, and because he was not so great a poet as Virgil

---

[5] Plutarch renders *laudi* by τῇ γλώττῃ, so that probably one version of the line was *concedat laurea linguæ*, which expresses more distinctly the meaning that military is inferior to civil glory. But there is more of alliterative jingle in the *laurea laudi*.

and Horace, he was decried as none at all." But Middleton is as extravagant in his praise as Cicero's detractors were unjust in their censure. He never could have been a great poet, for he had not the *divinus afflatus*, so finely expressed by Ovid in the line

> Est Deus in nobis, agitante calescimus illo !

without which there is no real poetry ; and he knew it, frankly confessing that his brother Quintus would have made a much better poet than himself. But he had a decided talent for vigorous versification, and the specimens that we find scattered amongst his writings, show that he was far superior in point of style and harmony, in choice of diction and facility of expression, to the poets who had hitherto written in the Latin language. Their compositions are full of the most uncouth barbarisms, from which Cicero's poetical works appear to have been wholly free, and I do not doubt that Roman poetry was indebted to him in no slight degree for the advance it made in the hands of Catullus, Virgil, Horace, and Ovid. It was no small service to weed away such monstrous words and expressions as deface the writings of Pacuvius, Nævius, Attius, and Ennius, who were the authors most in vogue when Cicero first exercised his youthful genius in the art of poetical composition.[6]

---

[6] One of the lines of Pacuvius was

> Nerei repandirostrum, incurvicervicum pecus.

The following is a list of the poetical works of Cicero, so far as they are known. 1. Translations of passages from Homer into Latin verse, scattered throughout his works. 2. The Phænomena of Aratus. 3. The Prognostica (Διοσημεῖα) of Aratus. 4-6. Alcyones, Uxorius, Nilus, poems of which nothing is now known bnt the names. 7. Limon—apparently a series of epigrams on distinguished men, in hexameter verse. Four lines are quoted by Suetonius in his Vita Terentii. 8. Marius. 9. De suo Consulatu. 10. De suis Temporibus, in three Books. 11. Elegia Tamelastis, mentioned by Servius in Virg. Eclog. I. 58. 12. Libellus Jocularis, quoted by Quint. VIII. 6. 13. Pontius Glaucus.

At the age of sixteen, according to the custom of the Roman youth, Cicero was with the usual ceremonies brought before the Prætor in the Forum; and there, in his presence, he formally laid aside the *toga prætexta*, his boyish dress, and assumed the *toga pura* or *virilis*, which indicated that he had arrived at the age of adolescence, and was introduced into public life. This, however, did not imply that his education was finished, any more than in the case of the change of dress so dear to an English boy when he assumes the dignity of a coat instead of a jacket; and Ovid expressly tells us with reference to such an occasion—

> Et studium nobis, quod fuit ante manet.

The change, however, in the case of a Roman boy was much more serious and important. It showed that he had reached an age when he might engage in the active business of life—the precise period when he began to do so of course varying according to his temperament and abilities. The *toga prætexta* which he had hitherto worn was a white robe with a coloured border, which was also the dress of the Roman magistrates, as distinguished from the plain robe which was worn by unofficial persons, and called the *toga pura*. And it is impossible not to notice the significance of the costume. The embroidered robe was symbolical of success in the struggle of life, and of the attainment of rank and station in the republic. We may well believe that the boy was clothed in it as a sort of uniform to awaken in his mind the stirrings of ambition, and point out the path to future eminence.

The custom was for the young man to be conducted by his father or other near relation to the Forum, when he was presented to the Prætor, whose tribunal or court was there, and the ceremony of the change of dress was performed. He then received the congratulations of his

relatives and friends who accompanied him, amidst the
applause of the surrounding crowd; for there never was
any lack of idlers in the Forum, and, indeed, so numerous
were they, that old Cato the Censor once proposed that
the ground should be paved with sharp stones to make it
a less agreeable lounge. After this the youth was conducted along the *Via Sacra*, which ran through the
Forum up to the Capitol, and a sacrifice was offered at
the altar of Jupiter, whose magnificent temple crowned
the hill. The rest of the day was spent in festivities at
home; and the hero of the hour, now no longer a boy but
a man, received presents as on a birthday amongst ourselves.

We have good reason to believe that whether Cicero's
father had returned to Arpinum or not after bringing his
sons to Rome, he was present on this interesting occasion,
for his son expressly tells us that immediately afterwards
he introduced Cicero to Quintus Mucius Scævola the
Augur,—the most profound lawyer of his day in Rome—
that he might have the benefit of his instruction, in the
science of which that accomplished jurist was so great a
master.

Chapter II.

THE STUDENT.

: Æt. 17-25. B.C. 90-82.

THE contrast between ancient and modern manners is so great that it is very difficult to realize it, and bring clearly before the mind's eye the usages of social life that belong to a remote antiquity. Law was taught in a very different manner in republican Rome from that to which we are accustomed in England. There were no chambers of pleaders or conveyancers, to which the young student might resort to copy precedents and answer cases, having first obtained admission there by the payment of an *honorarium*. Nor were there, so far as we know, public lectures on law like those of our inns of court, open to those who might choose to attend them. And yet there was a practice at Rome which bore a certain analogy to both these methods of instruction, and to a certain extent combined the advantages of both. It was this: those who aspired to fill the great offices of state knew that they could only climb the ladder of ambition by the suffrages of their fellow-citizens. The object, therefore, of every public man was to cultivate popularity, and there were two modes of cultivating it with success, both of which however might be, and sometimes were, combined. The one was by undertaking gratuitously the defence of the accused, and advocating causes in courts of justice; the other, by giving gratuitous advice on points of law to those who required their assistance. For this purpose the

house of a Roman jurisconsult was always open, not only
to suitors but to students, who came there to listen to the
responsa prudentum or legal opinions; which were delivered not in the stiff formal manner of a modern con-
sultation, but in the easy mode of familiar conversation,
sometimes during a walk in the *peristylium* of the house,
and sometimes during a saunter in the Forum. It was
thus that Cicero attached himself to Scævola the Augur
as a kind of pupil; and that so assiduously, that in his
own emphatic language he declares that he hardly ever
quitted his side. He used to take notes of his lectures,
and commit his maxims and sayings to memory; following
him to the courts when he pleaded as an advocate, and to
the Rostra when he harangued the people. He thus received practical lessons in eloquence and law, and formed
himself for the career which he had marked out for himself, and in which he was destined to acquire such death-
less fame. After the death of this great lawyer he transferred himself to another of the same family and name—
for he, too, was called Quintus Mucius Scævola, and was
the cousin of the Augur—who had filled the office of
Consul, and was Pontifex Maximus. He was the first who
attempted to give a scientific form to the Jus Civile, by
writing a systematic treatise upon it; and Cicero with
grateful enthusiasm calls him the most eloquent of lawyers,
and the most learned of orators. His time was now in-
cessantly occupied. He lost no opportunity of attending
the speeches of the different orators and pleaders in the
Forum and the courts; he watched the gestures of the
best actors, like Æsop and Roscius; and every day was
spent in reading, writing, and practising declamation.
Philosophy and oratory seem to have been the two chief
objects of his study; but if, of any man before Bacon
appeared, that might be said, which the great master of

modern philosophy claimed for himself, that he "had taken all knowledge for his province," it might be truly declared of the youthful Cicero. His appetite for knowledge was insatiable, and his desire for distinction boundless. No man ever lived to whom the hope of future distinction furnished a stronger motive for exertion.

Perhaps at no other place and at no other time, except at Athens in the palmy days of her great orators, have such opportunities been afforded for the study of eloquence as existed then at Rome. The constitution of the Republic imperatively required that those who looked to high office in the state should be practised speakers. The two great avenues of distinction were the Army and the Bar. And by the Bar I do not mean the profession of an advocate in the narrow and limited sense which it bears amongst ourselves; but every kind of display of eloquence in the Forum, whether in a speech in the courts of law before the Prætor, or in a *concio* or harangue addressed to the people. Even the successful soldier had to cultivate oratory to give him a fair chance of civic honours. Each of the successive steps in the ascending hierarchy of office, from the quæstorship to the consulship, could only be attained by securing the votes of the people under a system which amounted almost to universal suffrage; and to be able to speak well was then, as in all ages and times, the surest passport to popular favour. Pompey and Cæsar were both orators; and Cæsar indeed was considered one of the very best speakers of his day.

Cicero therefore devoted himself to the study of that art, of success in which he was soon to show himself the most splendid example. He diligently declaimed at home, and there noted down the passages which had most struck him in the Greek orators, or the speeches he had heard delivered; taking care at the same time to cultivate his

style by written composition, and the perusal of works of
rhetoric. But every kind of literature engaged his attention. I have spoken of his attempts in poetry ; and
rhetoric, dialectics, philosophy, and law by turns attracted
him, and occupied his busy hours. *Noctes et dies*, he says,
in omnium doctrinarum meditatione versabar.[1]

But he did not confine himself to the pursuit of studies
fitted to qualify him for success in the Forum and the
Senate. In his nineteenth year he quitted them for the
active life of the camp, and became for a time a soldier.
This was a most valuable part of the education of a Roman
gentleman ; and it was almost necessary in the case of
those who looked forward to high office. As one of the
great magistrates of the Republic, and especially as Consul,
he might have to command the Roman legions and conduct a campaign ; when, if he failed, and victory deserted
his standard, he was liable to be called to a severe account
by the sovereign people. It was therefore essential to
know something of the art of war, which can only be
taught by actual service in the field ; and the constant
quarrels in which the Republic was engaged both in Italy
and abroad gave ample opportunity for this. Rome was
rapidly accomplishing her destiny as the future mistress
of the world. The whole of Italy was subject to her sway ;
but the relation of the different towns and communities
there to herself, was anomalous and undefined. The inhabitants had not the rights of Roman citizens, except in
some special cases as in that of Arpinum ; and they were
looked upon rather as the dependants and tributaries of
the Republic than part of the Republic itself. This state
of things was of course galling to their pride, and they
chafed under a sense of injustice. They had to furnish
soldiers for the Roman armies, but could not vote in the

[1] Brutus, c. 90.

election of a Roman magistrate. The discontent at last
broke out into open war, which has been variously called
the Marsian, the Italian, or the Social War. It was
during this war that Cicero, then in his nineteenth year,
served in his first and only campaign, under the Consul
Cneius Pompeius Strabo, the father of Pompey the Great;
and in one of his speeches he mentions an incident that
occurred in his presence to show how courtesy may be
shown even to an enemy in the field.

A conference of the two generals took place midway
between the hostile camps, when Scato the leader of the
Marsians asked the brother of the Consul who attended
the meeting how he should address him, upon which
Sextus Pompeius replied "as a friend by inclination; as
an enemy from necessity."

About this time Philo, the philosopher of the school of
the Academy, came from Athens to Rome accompanied by
several distinguished Athenians, who had quitted their
country owing to the troubles occasioned by the war with
Mithridates. On his return from the Italian campaign
Cicero attached himself to him as a pupil, embracing the
study of philosophy all the more warmly, inasmuch as the
confusion that prevailed at Rome at this period during the
deadly struggle between Marius and Sylla seemed to have
annihilated the ordinary business of the courts of law.
But there was another mode of study of a practical kind
to which he did not fail to devote himself with a prescient
knowledge of its importance to his own future career.
The Forum resounded with the speeches of orators who
inflamed the passions of the people; and amongst these
Sulpicius the Tribune was pre-eminent as a popular demagogue. Amidst the crowd who listened to them as they
thundered from the Rostra, stood a tall thin youth with
outstretched neck and eager eyes, gazing with rapt at-

tention on the speakers, and learning from them the art
how to sway by the charm of eloquence the fierce democracy of Rome.   This is no fancy portrait, but one which
Cicero has drawn of himself in a most interesting passage
where he describes his own personal appearance, and
mentions how constant an attendant he was at the harangues that were then daily delivered in the Forum.[2]

During the reign of terror that ensued when Marius
and Cinna formed a coalition, and, amidst the horrors of a
proscription, slaked their sanguinary rage with the noblest
blood of Rome, it was as dangerous to have been a
public speaker as it was at Athens when Antipater demanded that the people should give up their orators, and
Demosthenes fled to Ægina to perish there by his own
hand rather than be dragged to execution.   Antonius,
Catulus, and Julius were put to death, and not long afterwards Scævola, Carbo, and Antistius met a similar fate.
Crassus would no doubt have fallen by the hand of the
executioner or the assassin if he had been still alive, but
he had died four years before.   In this terrible time Cicero,
who was still too young to attract the notice of the blood-
thirsty tyrants of Rome, quietly pursued his studies.   He
attended the lectures in rhetoric of Molo the Rhodian,
whom he praises as a consummate advocate and teacher;
and diligently laboured to improve his style by translations
from the works of Greek writers, amongst which he makes
special mention of the Œconomics of Xenophon.   Nor
does it seem possible for him to have adopted a better
method for the purpose he had in view.   It was that
which was recommended by one of the most illustrious of
English orators to his still greater son.

Pitt told the late Lord Stanhope that he owed greatly
whatever readiness of speech he possessed, and aptness in

[2] Brut. 91.

finding the right word, to a practice which his father had
impressed upon him. "Lord Chatham had bid him take
up any book in some foreign language with which he was
well acquainted, in Latin or Greek especially. Lord
Chatham then enjoined him to read out of this work a
passage in English, stopping when he was not sure of the
word to be used in English, until the right word came to
his mind and then proceed."[3]

Cicero also practised declamation at home, sometimes in
Latin but more frequently in Greek, in order as he tells
us to enrich his mind with the copious wealth of that
language; and also to have the benefit of instruction and
correction from Greek masters, who were present at these
exercises. The Stoic teacher Diodotus became an inmate
of his house, with whom he studied the rules of dialectics,
and who afterwards at a later period died under his roof.
And he now began to attempt prose composition, in which
his earliest work seems to have been the Treatise *de Inven-
tione*, but he spoke of it afterwards in disparaging terms
as a mere schoolboy performance.

He read and appreciated the letters of Cornelia the
mother of the Gracchi, lost alas! to us, which showed how
much of their education her sons owed to her; and he
found an agreeable relaxation in the charm of female
society. He mentions especially the ladies of one accomplished family, Lælia, the wife of Scævola the Augur, and
her daughters and granddaughters, whose conversation
contributed to refine and improve his taste.

By degrees quieter times succeeded. The fury of the
proscription had exhausted itself. Men like Curio, Cotta,
and the Lentuli, and others who had been banished or fled
from Rome, returned; and in the emphatic words of
Cicero, the course of law and the courts was reconstituted
and the Republic was restored.

[3] Lord Stanhope's Life of Pitt, I. 8.

1

THE ROMAN FORUM.

FROM A PHOTOGRAPH

Vol. i. p. 23.

Chapter III.

CICERO AT THE BAR.

Æt. 26–30. B.C. 81–77.

IT was at this juncture that Cicero **undertook his first cause**; or, as we should **say of an advocate, held his** first brief.

What this case was we cannot now ascertain. It is certain that it was not the case of Publius Quintius, for in his speech on that occasion he expressly tells us that he had been retained, and had spoken in several causes previously. But we may perhaps safely assume that it is the first of his speeches that have come down to us. It was delivered when he was twenty-five years old. The case is rather a complicated one, and affords us a curious insight into the mysteries of Roman law, of which some knowledge is required to be able to understand it. The argument of Cicero is clear and logical, showing that he was well versed in the technicalities of his profession, and fully able even at that early age to cope with such an antagonist as Hortensius, who was " retained " on the other side. But the facts are not of sufficient interest to make it worth while to detail them in this biography.

When he was in his twenty-seventh year, about the same age as that at which Demosthenes first came forward as a public prosecutor and delivered his speech against Androtion, Cicero made his first appearance in the Forum in a criminal trial for life and death, and defended Sextus Roscius of Ameria, who was accused of parricide, the pro-

secutor being Chrysogonus. 'He acquitted himself so well
on this occasion that he tells us that business began to
flow rapidly in upon him; and there was no cause too
important to be entrusted to his care. In fact, his speech
for Roscius—although his first in a public or state trial—
was the turning-point of his forensic career. We are
reminded by it of what is told of Thurlow's appearance in
the great Douglas case; and Erskine's defence in the
Greenwich Hospital case, when hastening home from
the court he exclaimed in triumph to his wife, " *Voilà !*
the nonsuit of cow-beef ! " Pasquier also, the great French
advocate of the sixteenth century, dated all his success
from a speech he made in defence of the University of
Paris, after he had toiled in thankless obscurity for fourteen years at the bar.

Sextus Roscius the elder was an inhabitant of the municipal town of Ameria, where he had considerable property
and was much respected. While making a short stay at
Rome he was murdered one night near the Palatine baths
as he was returning from a party of friends. The news
of his death was brought by a freedman of Titus Roscius,
at daybreak next morning to Ameria, a distance of fifty-six
miles. This T. Roscius, surnamed Magnus, as well as another member of the same family surnamed Capito, were
both natives of Ameria, and enemies of Sextus. The
latter left a son, also named Sextus, whose life had hitherto
been passed in the country, where he attended to the cul-
tivation of his father's estate, to which he was entitled
to succeed at the death of the latter. But the Roscii
were determined to deprive him of his inheritance, and
they induced Chrysogonus, one of Sylla's freedmen and
high in his favour, to assert that Sextus had died in
debt to him. Under pretence of liquidating this, the
property was seized and sold at a price miserably below

its value, and Capito and Chrysogonus became the pur-
chasers. The former bought for himself three of the
most flourishing farms, and took possession of the rest of
the estate and effects, under pretence of holding them for
Chrysogonus. Not content with this the two Roscii instigated Erucius to accuse the destitute son of having been
the assassin of his father, and Cicero had to defend him
against the charge.

The trial is a proof of the corrupt state of society at
Rome. There is no doubt that young Roscius was in the
most imminent danger of a conviction, and that Cicero
trembled for the result. And yet no charge was ever
more groundless, or supported in a court of justice by
more feeble evidence. This consisted almost entirely in
an attempt to show that the father disliked his son, of
which the only proof was that he kept him in the country,
and that he once had the intention of disinheriting him.
That such a case, so bare of even a presumption against
the accused, should have occupied a criminal tribunal for
a considerable time with a doubtful result, was an outrage
against common sense ; and can only be explained by considering the deplorable condition of the Republic, when
causes were decided not according to their merits, but
under the influence of bribery or fear. Sylla was all-
powerful in the state—Chrysogonus was his favourite ; and
Cicero knew that these were arguments against his client
which would go far to supply the want of facts. He made
a masterly and conclusive speech ; but much more elaborate, than, according to our notions of criminal jurisprudence, the case seemed to require, for not a tittle of
evidence was adduced to connect the son with the murder.
He was at Ameria at the time ; he had neither friends
nor influence at Rome ; not a shadow of proof was given
that he had ever seen or communicated with the assassins ;

nay, it was unknown who the actual assassins were. All the presumptions of guilt pointed towards the Roscii, Capito and Magnus, especially the latter, whose freedman had brought the first intelligence so rapidly to Ameria, and whose previous character and conduct subsequently to the murder justified the darkest suspicions. Under these circumstances we should imagine that the duty of the counsel for the accused would be simply to stand on the defensive, and challenge the other side to the proof of the indictment. Unless it could be shown that young Roscius was present at, or privy to the murder, there was an end of the case, and he might at once demand an acquittal. But Cicero did not venture upon such a course before the tribunal which he was addressing. He enters most minutely into the whole case; examines every possible view in which it can be presented; carefully balances the presumptions of guilt as they apply to the one party or the other; deprecates the idea of giving offence to Erucius or Chrysogonus; and artfully appeals to the compassion, and fears, and justice of the court.

Niebuhr says of his conduct on this occasion: "His defence of Roscius of Ameria, whom Chrysogonus wanted to get rid of, excited the greatest admiration of his talents, together with the highest esteem for his own personal character. It was an act of true heroism for a young man like Cicero, and still more so if we consider his family connection with Marius." About the same time Cicero seems to have defended Varenus, who was charged with the crime of murder and convicted; but we possess only a few fragments of the speech. Although he was now fairly launched in his profession, and notwithstanding the reputation which he had gained by his efforts as an advocate, he still did not consider his education for his profession as complete. And when his former preceptor

Molo came, in the year B.C. 80, as ambassador from Rhodes
to Rome, he placed himself again under his care, and took
lessons from the accomplished rhetorician.   It is an interesting fact, and shows how familiar had become the
knowledge of Greek amongst the educated classes at Rome,
that Molo addressed the Senate in that language to thank
them for the friendship they had shown to his native state.

The next cause in which Cicero was engaged, at least the
next of which we have any notice, although his speech
is lost, was one in which he was opposed to Cotta, one of
the most celebrated advocates of his day.   He appeared
against him on behalf of a lady of Arretium, whose right
to maintain her suit was contested on the ground that she
was not a Roman citizen.   And the trial had something
of a political character in it, and exposed Cicero to the risk
of offending the all-powerful dictator.   For Sylla had
deprived the citizens of Arretium of the Roman franchise,
which was so much coveted by the Italian towns ; and the
refusal to recognise their right to it had led to the deplorable conflict of the Social War.

But the incessant labours of the young advocate had
now begun to tell seriously upon his health.   He had
inherited a feeble constitution, and symptoms of consump-
tion began to show themselves.   We have described his
personal appearance, and his thin frame was hardly equal
to the wear and tear of his profession, which demanded
much more bodily exertion than we, with our colder and
less impassioned manners, can easily form an idea of.
With us a speaker, whether in parliament or at the bar,
knows little or nothing of the action and delivery of a
Roman orator.   The only motion we make is with the
hand, and too often that is confined to a see-saw monotony
of perpendicular action which justifies the satirical comparison by Moore of the speaker to a pump—

> " That up and down its awkward arm doth sway,
> And coolly spout, and spout, and spout away."

Very different, however, was it with the orator of Rome.
His whole body was instinct with the fire that burned
upon his lips, and the accents that trembled upon his
tongue found a corresponding expression in the move-
ment of his limbs. Cicero's gestures partook of the
excitement of his mind, and the meaning of his words
was enforced by the sympathetic action of his frame. He
tells us that he threw himself, heart and soul, into action
when he spoke, and spared no exertion of his limbs, while
he strained his voice to the utmost of its pitch in the open
air.

Can we then wonder at the consequences which followed? and that he soon suffered from

> " His fiery soul, which, working out its way,
> Fretted the pigmy body to decay,
> And o'er informed the tenement of clay."

He was obliged for a time to retire from the Forum and
the Courts, and quitted Rome for Athens, not, as Plutarch
says, through fear of Sylla—whose displeasure he had, as
we have seen, not shrunk from braving in the discharge of
his duty—but to seek, by change of air and scene, and
cessation from work, the restoration of his health. A visit
to Athens—"mother of arts and eloquence"—must have
had peculiar charms for Cicero. He was quite at home in
the language, and passionately fond of philosophy, which
still lingered in the groves of Academus, although oratory
had for ever fled from a city which was now nothing more
than the chief town of a Roman province, and filled with
busy idlers, as was the case a century later, when, as they
are described by St. Paul, "all the Athenians and strangers
which were there spent their time in nothing else but
either to tell or to hear some new thing."

The pleasure of Cicero's residence at Athens was en-
hanced by the society of relatives and friends. His brother
Quintus, his cousin Lucius, and his dear friend and life-
long correspondent, Titus Pomponius Atticus, were with
him there; and for six months they studied together and
enjoyed the recreations of the place.[1]   Antiochus of Asca-
lon instructed them in the philosophy of the Academy,
while from Zeno and Phædrus they learnt the tenets of
the school of Epicurus, to which Atticus, whose habits
were those of a refined and self-indulgent man, especially
attached himself.   Nor did Cicero, even at Athens, neglect
his darling pursuit—the art of oratory—which, like every
other acquisition and accomplishment, he knew could only
be obtained by pains and labor, although in his case it
was the labor of love, and eloquence seemed to have
settled on his lips in the cradle, as the bees were said to
have swarmed on the lips of the infant Pericles.   As
formerly he had studied under Molo, so now he took
lessons in rhetoric and elocution from Demetrius, a native
of Syria.

Leaving Athens Cicero travelled in Asia Minor, and
sought every opportunity of improving himself as a
speaker by soliciting instruction from the most celebrated
masters of rhetoric whom he met with on his journey.
He mentions the names of Menippus of Stratonice, Dionysius of Magnesia, Æsch·lus of Cnidus, and Xenocles of
Adramyttium, who contributed to the formation of his
style.   And as he passed through Rhodes, on his return
to Rome, Molo had the pleasure of welcoming his old
pupil, who did not disdain, for the third time, to place
himself under his tuition, and receive from him some

---

[1] Drumann thinks it is probable that Cicero while at Athens was
initiated into the Eleusinian mysteries. See the subject alluded to *de
Legg.* II. 14.

kindly corrections of what he himself described as the too
redundant and florid oratory of his youthful years. The
metaphor by which he characterised it was that of a river
that overflowed its banks; and to this his eloquence may
be compared to the latest period of his life. It arose,
no doubt, from his astonishing command of language,
which came pouring forth from his lips in a full and
inexhaustible torrent, and spread over his subject like an
inundation of the Nile.

At the end of two years Cicero returned to Rome. He
was now thirty years old. His health was completely
re-established, and, as he himself expresses it, he came
back almost a changed man. Sylla had died the year
before, and the leading advocates at this time in Rome were
Cotta and Hortensius, the latter of whom was eight years
Cicero's senior. He was *par excellence* an advocate;
confining himself chiefly to the courts of law and public
trials, and taking little part in the politics of the day.
But he rose through the usual gradation of offices to the
consulship, to obtain which it was almost essential to be a
popular orator, and to address the multitude from the
Rostra; unless, indeed, the candidate were wealthy enough
to bribe the suffrages of the people on an enormous scale,
and trust to the influence of gold rather than the influence
of eloquence. Corruption was now fast eating its way
into the heart of Roman institutions. Bribery was shame-
lessly resorted to, not only for political objects, but to
secure verdicts in the courts, where the *judices*, or, as we
may almost without inaccuracy call them, jurymen, prostituted their consciences and sold themselves to the highest
bidder. I am not now speaking of the prætorian or cen-
tumviral courts, where civil causes were tried, but the
public or state trials before judices, who at this time were
taken exclusively from the class of senators. It was a

long struggle between them and the knights as to which
body should have this important jurisdiction. Each
accused the other of corruption, and of selling verdicts for
a bribe, and each was, beyond all doubt, right in the
charge it made.

It was probably about this time that Cicero appeared as
the advocate of Roscius, the comic actor, in a civil suit,
and delivered a speech which, although it has come down .
to us in an imperfect state, enables us to understand the
subject-matter of the action and the argument.

Fannius Chærea had given up one of his slaves, named
Panurgus, to Roscius, on the terms that the latter was to
instruct him in acting, and they were afterwards to share
between them whatever he gained by his art. Panurgus
received the requisite instruction and went upon the stage,
but was not long afterwards killed—how, does not appear—
by a man named Q. Flavius. Roscius brought an action
for this against the latter, and the management of the case
was committed to Fannius. Before, however, it was tried,
Roscius compromised the matter, but only so far as regarded his own moiety, as he alleged, and Flavius gave up
a farm to him in satisfaction of damages. Several years
had elapsed, when Fannius applied to the Prætor for an
order that the accounts between him and Roscius might
be settled by arbitration. Calpurnius Piso was appointed
arbitrator. He did not make a formal award, but recommended that Roscius should pay to Fannius 10,000 sesterces (about 90*l*.) for the trouble and expense which
the latter had incurred in conducting the action against
Flavius, and that Fannius should enter into an engage-
ment to pay over to Roscius the half of whatever he
recovered from Flavius. Fannius agreed to this, and then
brought an action on his own account against Flavius for
the loss he had sustained by the death of Panurgus, and

got a verdict for 100,000 sesterces (about 900*l.*). Half
of this, according to agreement, ought to have been paid
over to Roscius, but Fannius not only retained it, but
commenced an action against Roscius for a moiety of the
value of the farm which the latter had obtained from
Flavius, on the pretext that Roscius had settled the former
action and obtained the farm on the partnership account.

Cicero maintained that his client owed Fannius nothing.
So confident was he of the strength of his case that he
offered to consent to a verdict against him, provided the
plaintiff could show that the debt now claimed was entered
in his ledger. He was willing to allow the entries of the
plaintiff to be evidence in his own favour; and in tender-
ing such an issue we may be very sure that he had good
information that he might do so with safety. But he
made a distinction between the ledger (*tabulæ* or *codex*)
and the day-book, or mere memorandum of account
(*adversaria*). Fannius wished to put the latter in evidence, but Cicero objected, and said that he could not
admit loose papers, full of erasures and interlineations, in
which, no doubt, Fannius had inserted the debt when he
determined to make his unjust claim. He seized the
opportunity of praising the skill and virtue of his client,
whose name as an actor has become so famous.

"Has Roscius defrauded his partner? Can such an imputation rest
upon one who has in him—I say it boldly—more honesty than he has
art; more truth than accomplishments; whom the Roman people consider to be a better man than he is an actor; who, though admirably
fitted for the stage on account of his skill in his profession, yet is most
worthy of being a senator on account of his modesty and decorum?"

The exact date of Cicero's marriage is not known, but
it is generally supposed to have taken place when he was
in his thirty-first year.[2] His wife was Terentia, a lady of

respectable family, whose sister Fabia was a Vestal virgin.
With her he lived many years happily, and, apparently,
with warm affection on both sides, until he quarrelled
with her for some mysterious reason, and the marriage
was terminated by a divorce.

Plutarch asserts that Terentia was a woman of violent
temper; and Niebuhr goes so far as to say that, "in his
marriage Cicero was not happy. His wife was a domineering
and disagreeable woman; and as, owing to his great sensi-
bility, he allowed himself to be very much influenced by
those who surrounded him, his wife also exercised great
power over him, which is the more remarkable because he
had no real love for her. It was she who, unfortunately
for him, led him to do things which drew upon him the
enmity of others."[3] I believe the description here given of
Terentia to be most unjust, and, unless I deceive myself,
the sequel of the biography will show that she was an
amiable woman and a most loving devoted wife.

that if it was in the year assumed in the text, it would follow that
Cicero's daughter was betrothed at the age of nine and married at the
age of thirteen.

[3] Hist. of Rome, V. 20.

Chapter IV.

QUÆSTOR AND CURULE ÆDILE.

Æt. 31-38. B.C. 76-69.

CICERO had now attained the age of thirty-one years; when, according to the Roman law, he was eligible for the first and lowest of the public employments of the state—the office of Quæstor. The ascending steps in the ladder of advancement were those of Quæstor, Ædile, Prætor—until they culminated in the Consulship, the highest object of ambition to a Roman citizen. Cicero was elected one of the quæstors and Hortensius one of the ædiles for the following year, and the province of Sicily was allotted to him, his immediate superior in the government of it being the prætor, Sextus Peducæus. He left Rome at the age of thirty-two, and spent a year in Sicily.

That island was then, and continued for many years to be, one of the most fertile of the dominions subject to the Republic. It was, in fact, called the granary of Rome, and the greatest part of the corn consumed in the metropolis was imported from Sicily and Egypt. It was divided into two provincial governments; one called Lilybæum, from the chief town in the district of that name—the modern Marsala—and the other Syracuse. The Romans were accustomed to determine the choice of almost all public employments by lot, and the chance of fortune gave Cicero Lilybæum as his province.

We possess few details of his quæstorship, but we know

SITE OF LILYBÆUM, NOW MARSALA.

Vol. i. p. 31.

that he discharged the duties of his office with scrupulous honesty and disinterestedness, and conciliated in a remarkable degree the good-will and attachment of the Sicilians. During his year of office there was a severe scarcity at Rome, but Cicero, whose especial duty it was to attend to the exportation of grain from the island, was able, by the measures he took, to alleviate the distress in the capital without inflicting any serious burden on the inhabitants. And he had an opportunity of exercising his profession as an advocate, for he successfully defended before his prætor some young Romans of good family who were accused of breach of military discipline, if not desertion from the service. During a visit to Syracuse he had the good fortune, while exploring the antiquities, to discover near the gate that led to Agrigentum, the tomb of Archimedes. It had been half buried amidst rubbish, and overgrown with brambles, so that the fellow-citizens of the great mathematician had forgotten its existence,

> " When Tully paused amidst the wreck of time
> On the rude stone to trace the truth sublime ;
> Where at his feet, in honored dust disclosed,
> The immortal sage of Syracuse reposed."

He knew that on the stone which marked the grave were sculptured the figures of a sphere and a cylinder, and observing these on a small pillar, the top of which peered out amongst the bushes with which the spot was overgrown, he at once discovered the tomb of which he was in search.

On leaving the island every mark of respect which it was in the power of the inhabitants to bestow was shown him by the grateful Sicilians. He tells us that extraordinary and unheard of honours were invented for him, but he does not specify their nature. He quitted the shores of Sicily leaving behind him the reputation of a disinterested and upright public servant, and carrying with him the good-will and confidence of the inhabitants, of which a striking proof was soon to be afforded.[1]

It was characteristic of Cicero's mind to dwell with self-complacency on his own merits. His foible was vanity, and he seldom lost an opportunity of praising himself where he thought that praise had been deserved. He was pleased with his own conduct as quæstor, and was in hopes that the fame of his administration had extended to Italy, and even gained him a reputation at Rome. But he good-humouredly tells us an anecdote to show how fallacious his expectations were, and how, like many others since his time, he mistook the small pipe of praise in a limited sphere for the trumpet of fame in the great world. In order to understand the point of the story we must bear in mind that there were two provinces in Sicily, the province of Lilybæum and the province of Syracuse, and the quæstor of the one was a distinct person from the quæstor of the other.

On landing at Puteoli, near Baiæ, which was then a fashionable watering-place, and crowded with visitors, he met a person, apparently an acquaintance, who asked him on what day he had left Rome, and what the news there was. "I have just come from my province," replied Cicero. "O! to be sure," said the other, "from Africa, I believe?" This was too much, and Cicero answered

---

[1] In his "Two Last Pleadings of Cicero against Verres" (London, 1812), Kelsall mentions that when he visited Marsala (the ancient Lily-bæum) he was told by his guide that he could show him the house in which Cicero lived when he was at Lilybæum. On arriving there he found it a white-washed house of a date not earlier than the 16th century. "*Questi, Signor*," said the honest Sicilian, "*fu la casa dove dimorava il Signor Cicerone quand il fu in Marsala.*" It turned out that this was the house where the guide's father had lived, who, like his son, was *Cicerone* of Marsala. It is curious that Cicero's name should have come to signify "lionizer."

angrily, "No; from Sicily." Upon which a bystander interposed, and turning to the questioner said, "What! don't you know that this gentleman has been quæstor in *Syracuse?*"

This little incident opened Cicero's eyes to the true state of the case. It was no use to be angry; and so, putting his dignity in his pocket—not that the Romans really wore pockets, which is an invention of modern civilisation—he mingled quietly with the crowd. But he also derived a useful lesson from the affront to his vanity. He saw the danger of absence if he wished for popularity, and determined from henceforth to keep himself before the people by actual presence amongst them; and from that time, to use his own words, he stuck close to the Forum—never allowed his hall-porter (*janitor*) to deny him to a visitor, not even when he had retired to rest.

On his return to Rome he betook himself afresh to the duties of an advocate, and was busily engaged in the Forum while the Servile War raged in Italy—the insurrection being headed by the bold and desperate leader Spartacus. He was killed in battle B.C. 71, and the revolt was finally extinguished by Pompey when he came back from Spain.

Five years must now elapse before Cicero would be of the requisite age—thirty-eight—to hold the office of ædile, the next public dignity open to his ambition. But having been quæstor, and possessing a sufficient qualification in point of fortune, he was eligible for admission into the Senate, and was accordingly placed by the censors on the list or roll of senators.

That during the next three or four years he was busily engaged in forensic labours we know from his own account of himself, but we do not possess a single speech, or even fragment of a speech, until B.C. 70, when, at the age of thirty-seven, he became a candidate for the ædileship.

I know not to what cause to attribute this blank in the records of his life. The very names of nearly all the speeches he delivered during this period have perished; but one of them, *pro M. Tullio*, is mentioned by Quintilian as extant in his time. Drumann thinks it belongs to the year B.C. 71. It seems that there was a quarrel between Tullius and Fabius as to the right to a certain house in Lucania; and the slaves of Fabius had attacked the slaves of Tullius, killed some of them, and pulled down the house.

It was Cicero's proud boast in after years that he had filled every public office at the earliest age at which it could legally be held (*anno suo*). His splendid reputation as an advocate made him at this time one of the most popular men at Rome, and he was unanimously elected Curule Ædile for the following year, coming in first of all the competitors, or, as we should say, at the head of the poll. But he did not rely merely upon reputation. He took care not to neglect any of the means whereby the favour of his fellow-citizens might be conciliated and their votes secured at future elections. At no time, and in no part of the world, not even in the United States, has canvassing been reduced to such a system, and carried on with such persevering assiduity, as at Rome in the days of Cicero. The aspirant to office had to practise on a large scale, and for a long period beforehand, all the arts which are resorted to in this country by the candidate for a borough or county on the eve of a contested election; and as the number of electors at Rome and in the provinces was enormous, and yet each elector expected some personal attention to himself, the neglect of which he could punish by refusing to vote, or by giving his vote to a rival, the candidates endeavoured, as far as possible, to become acquainted with the names and faces of the electors, and flattered them by civilities when they met them in the streets, the Forum, or the markets. For this purpose it was usual to employ intelligent slaves, whose duty it was to become familiar with the persons of the voters, ferret out information respecting them, and act in some respects like the ear-flappers in Swift's *Laputa* by directing the candidate's attention, as he walked along, to the different electors, and telling him their names. These useful attendants were called *nomenclatores*, and many amusing passages occur in the Latin writers about them. Of course one of the first acts of courtesy on the part of a candidate is to shake hands with the voter, and this was so universally the custom at Rome on such occasions that the expression "to shake hands" (*manu prensare*) came to be synonymous with beginning to canvass. But, as may well be supposed, all the arts employed were not so innocent as this. Bribery and corruption were resorted to on an enormous scale, and the venal voters found the exercise of their franchise a profitable trade, notwithstanding that law after law was passed to forbid and punish bribery. It was so systematically practised that particular names, such as *divisores* and *sequestres*, were given to the agents who distributed the money.[2]

It was during this year and as ædile elect that Cicero undertook one of the most celebrated cases in which he ever was engaged, and one of the very few in which he appeared as public prosecutor. This was the great Verres cause, which of all the trials of antiquity bears in many of its circumstances the nearest resemblance to the impeach-

---

[2] When Julius Cæsar was Dictator, he used to furnish the candidates whom he favoured, with tickets on which was written " Cæsar to such a tribe.—I recommend to you such a one, and hope you will vote for him." See Sueton. *Cæsar*.

ment of Warren Hastings at the latter end of the eighteenth century.

Caius Verres, whose name has become a bye-word for oppression and misrule, had, at the expiration of his year of office as prætor, B.C. 73, the island of Sicily allotted to him as his province, and he held the government for three years. Sicily at that time was a flourishing and prosperous country. The soil was fertile and well cultivated, and as we have seen, large quantities of corn were exported yearly from the island to Rome. The cities were adorned with splendid palaces and temples, the monuments of Grecian taste and magnificence; and costly treasures of art in the shape of statues, pictures and ornamental furniture, attested the wealth and luxury of the inhabitants. The government of such a province afforded a tempting opportunity for plunder, and Verres was not the man to neglect the opportunity which fortune had thrown in his way. It is difficult to credit the tales that are told of his rapacity, and we must search the dark annals of Oriental iniquity to find satraps like him. We might admire his passion for works of art, which amounted almost to insanity, were it not for the means he took to gratify it. But these were a series of cruel robberies.

He held the government for three years, and seems to have combined every quality of a bad man and unjust ruler. During that long period the wretched inhabitants were the victims of his rapacity, cruelty, and lust. He imposed heavy and unheard-of duties upon the produce of land and exports of commerce, and put the money into his own pocket. By violent interference with their contracts he reduced to beggary the farmers of the revenue. He plundered the towns of their works of art, sparing neither the temples of the gods nor the private dwellings of men. Statues and pictures and jewelled cups were torn from their

owners and appropriated to himself. To take one instance
alone ; he robbed the oratory of Heius, the Messanian, of
a marble Cupid by Praxiteles, two basket-bearers (Cane-
phori) by Polycletus, and a Hercules by Myron, and then
pretended that he had bought them. It was not safe to
seal a letter with a ring on which there was a well-cut
engraving, for if Verres saw the impression he made the
owner give him the ring.

But he was as cruel as he was rapacious. There was a
deep and dreadful dungeon at Syracuse, called Latomiæ,
formed out of a stone quarry by the tyrant Dionysius, and
used as a prison for malefactors. Into this Roman citizens
were thrown by Verres and kept in chains until they
were strangled by his orders. One unhappy man amongst
them, named Gavius, contrived to escape from the horrible
place and fled to Messana. Here he made no secret of
his intention to embark for Rome and impeach Verres
there. But he was seized by the magistrates, who at
Messana were the obsequious creatures of the governor,
and Verres happening to arrive the same day, condemned him to be first stripped and flogged naked in the
market-place and then crucified. While the poor wretch
was being scourged no sound escaped his lips except the
oft-repeated cry, *Civis Romanus sum !* as if, says Cicero, he
thought those magic words would have power to save him.
But in vain. Verres ordered a cross to be erected on a headland that commanded a view of Italy across the strait, saying
in savage mockery, that as Gavius called himself a Roman
citizen, he might have the opportunity of looking towards
his land. And there he was crucified and died.

This may serve as a specimen of the terrible charges
which Verres had to meet ; but to go through the long
list would be to transcribe whole pages of the orations
which Cicero had prepared, but which, owing to the sudden

and unexpected collapse of the defence, he had no occasion
to deliver.   A modern writer has indeed said that he will
" venture to raise a doubt whether Verres ought really to
be considered that exorbitant criminal whose guilt has
been so profoundly impressed upon us by the forensic arti-
fices of Cicero ; " [3] but making every allowance for rhetorical exaggeration as to the mode in which the charges
were "impressed" by the orator, there can be no doubt
that they were substantially true.   An attempt has been
made of late years to vindicate the character of Robespierre,
and when that has been successful—but not till then—we
may expect to see the memory of Verres rescued from the
execration of mankind.

To drag this great criminal to justice, a deputation from
all the principal cities of Sicily, except Syracuse, was sent
to Rome, and to whom would they so naturally turn for
help as to the man who lived in their memories as the first
quæstor of Sicily, and who was then in the zenith of his
fame as the most eloquent advocate of his day ?   They
applied to Cicero to come forward as the accuser of Verres,
and he readily consented to conduct the prosecution.   But
there was a preliminary difficulty to be got over.   Verres
had influential friends and connections, and was backed by the
support of the powerful families of the Scipios and Metelli.
As it was impossible for him altogether to avoid a trial,
the best plan for averting the danger seemed to be to make
the prosecution a sham, by employing a friend to conduct
it, or at all events some one who would betray the cause
he undertook.   This was a practice well known at Rome,
and called *prævaricatio*, that is, collusion with an adversary at a trial.   A creature of Verres, named Quintus
Cæcilius Niger, who had been his quæstor in Sicily, was
put forward to assert the right to be prosecutor, and Cicero

[3] De Quincey.   See his collected works, article Cicero.

had to contest this all important point with him at the
first stage of the proceedings, when he delivered his famous
speech *in Cæcilium* or *de Divinatione*, and triumphantly
vindicated his claim.

The preliminary question was called *divinatio*, because
the court decided it on argument alone without any evidence. The speech of Cicero on this occasion is a masterpiece of art. For cutting sarcasm and irony it has never
been surpassed. It suited his purpose to exaggerate the
merits of Hortensius as an advocate, in order to contrast
them with the deficiencies of Cæcilius. It would, he said,
be an *impar congressus;* and what more ludicrous effect
of the disparity between two opposing counsel can be
imagined, than an uneasy suspicion produced in the mind
of the prosecuting counsel by the speech of his antagonist
that the client whom that antagonist defends is innocent ?
Yet this is what Cicero suggests. Addressing Cæcilius he
said :—

"You yourself would begin to be afraid that you were prosecuting an
innocent man." He showed that the pretended enmity of Cæcilius towards
Verres was a sham. If they had quarrelled, they had been reconciled.
Besides, he had been mixed up with the frauds and oppressions of Verres,
and how could he accuse another of that of which he had been guilty
himself ? The character of his intellect unfitted him to conduct so great
and difficult a case. It required a man who could not only speak but
attract the attention of his audience. If he had learnt Greek at Athens
and not at Lilybæum, and Latin at Rome and not in Sicily, it would
still be difficult for him to undertake such an important cause. He had
neither the industry, nor the memory, nor the eloquence which it required. And then with well-affected modesty he alluded to himself.
"You will say perhaps, 'Do *you* then possess all these qualifications ?'"
"I wish indeed I did! but at all events it has been my constant study
from my earliest youth to endeavour to possess them . . . . Even I,
who, as everybody knows, have had such practice in the Forum and the
courts, that none or few even of the same age have undertaken more
causes—and who have devoted all the time I could spare from the cases
of friends committed to my care to make myself more apt and ready for
forensic business—I, I say, so help me, Heaven! when the day ap-
proaches on which I shall be called upon to defend a client, am not only
disturbed in mind, but tremble in every limb."

He went on to say that he was not afraid of Hortensius
as an opponent.   He knew all his arts and style of speaking, for he had often encountered him as an antagonist.
But what would become of Cæcilius ?   Hortensius would
so puzzle him and perplex him with dilemmas, that which-
ever way he turned he would be caught.   His mind would
get into a pitiable state of confusion, and the very gestures
and action of the great orator, to·say nothing of his eloquence, would so confound him that his wits would desert
him.   But there was an easy mode of testing his capacity.

"If you, Cæcilius, to-day," said Cicero, "can answer me; if you can
venture to change a word of that written speech which some school-
master has composed for you, made up of scraps of other men's orations,
I shall think you not unfit for the conduct of the prosecution, and able
to do your duty in the cause. But if in this rehearsal you cannot cope
with me, what must we think will become of you in the real combat
with your fierce and eager adversary ? "

Addressing the court in conclusion he said :—

"You must determine which of us two you think is most fitted to
undertake a case of this magnitude with good faith, with industry, with
skill, and with authority. If you prefer Cæcilius to me, I shall not deem
myself lowered in estimation ; but take care that the people of Rome do
not suspect that so honest, sincere, and thorough a prosecution as I
should conduct, was not to your liking nor agreeable to your order."

The point being settled in his favour, Cicero was allowed
one hundred and ten days to collect the evidence and prepare the case. Accompanied by his cousin Lucius, who
afterwards assisted him at the trial, he went to Sicily, and
worked so assiduously, that in fifty days he was ready to
open the impeachment. At Syracuse and Messana alone
did he meet with any difficulty in procuring evidence.
But he soon overcame the opposition of the Syracusans,
and was able to induce them to erase from the city records
a complimentary decree which Verres had extorted from
their fears. He was invited to meet the Senate in the
town hall, and addressed them in Greek. They asked

him why he had been shy in coming to Syracuse to prosecute his inquiries, and he told them that he had expected
little assistance from a city which had sent a deputation to
Rome to support Verres, and which had a gilt statue of
him in its public hall. At Messana he was thwarted by
the new prætor Metellus, the successor and friend—perhaps relative—of Verres, and the inhabitants were forbidden
to afford him any assistance. But Cicero had evidence
enough, and armed with a mass of documents, and attended by a crowd of witnesses, he crossed over to Velia,
on the Bruttian coast, and there, to avoid the brigands who
then as now infested that part of Italy, took ship for Rome,
where he arrived nearly two months before he was expected.

The great object of Verres and his friends now was
delay. If the trial could be put off, or rather spun out until
the following year, the chances were that he would escape.
Hortensius was already consul elect. He would enter
upon office in January. The Metelli were fast friends of
Verres, and instead of Glabrio Marcus Metellus would
be praetor at Rome, and Lucius Metellus prætorian governor of Sicily. Many of the members of the court (*judices*)
as now constituted would be disqualified from sitting by becoming tribunes or holding other offices; and by repeated
challenges Cicero had at last obtained a jury on whose
honesty he thought he could rely. The witnesses would
be tampered with by bribes or terrified by threats. The
impeachment would drag its slow length along and men
would begin to get tired of it, as was the case with the
trial of Warren Hastings. The business days during the
remainder of the present year were few, owing to the frequent interruptions caused by festivals and games. If
then the prosecution were conducted in the usual manner,
with long speeches continued from day to day, it would be
easy for Hortensius to prevent the case from being finished

within the year. But Cicero was determined not to be so baffled. He was thoroughly in earnest, and cared less to distinguish himself as an orator than to convict the criminal. He therefore abandoned the idea of opening the case in the usual manner, and resolved to bring forward his witnesses at once and let the evidence tell its own tale.

The judices were at this period taken exclusively from the senators. This jurisdiction had been restored to them after a cessation of fifty years, during which it had been transferred to the knights. The court met in the Temple of Castor, and Glabrio, the city prætor, a just and honest man, was president. It was an exciting and memorable scene. " From the foot of Mount Taurus, from the shores of the Black Sea, from many cities of the Grecian mainland, from many islands of the Ægæan, from every city or market-town of Sicily, deputations thronged to Rome. In the porticoes and on the steps of the temple, in the area of the Forum, in the colonnades that surrounded it, on the house tops and on the overlooking declivities, were stationed dense and eager crowds of impoverished heirs and their guardians, bankrupt *publicans* and corn-merchants, fathers bewailing their children carried off to the prætor's harem, children mourning for their parents dead in the prætor's dungeons, Greek nobles whose descent was traced to Cecrops or Eurysthenes, or to the great Ionian and Minyan houses, and Phœnicians whose ancestors had been priests of the Tyrian Melcarth, or claimed kindred with the Zidonian Iah, 'all these and more came flocking' and the casual multitude was swelled by thousands of spectators from Italy, partly attracted by the approaching games, and partly by curiosity to behold a criminal who had scourged and crucified Roman citizens, who had respected neither local nor national shrines, and who boasted that wealth would yet rescue the murderer, the violater, and the temple-robber from the hand of man and from the Nemesis of the Gods."[4]

The trial began on the 7th of August, and the speech with which Cicero opened the case is known by the name of *Interrogatio Testium*, because it was in fact merely a short introduction to the appearance of the witnesses on whose evidence he relied.[5]

In it he complained bitterly of the attempts made by Verres to compel the jury to stifle the prosecution. He hinted intelligibly enough that a bribe had been offered to himself. He spoke boldly and openly of the shameful extent to which judicial bribery was carried, mentioning cases that were notorious, and amongst others that of a senator who had taken money from the accused to be distributed amongst his fellow-jurors for a verdict of acquittal, and money from the prosecutor to give, himself, a verdict of guilty. Well then might he exclaim, *nulla in judiciis severitas, nulla religio, nulla jam existimantur esse judicia*. He warned the court that on the issue depended whether the senators should retain their judicial jurisdiction, and contrasted the state of things when the knights had that jurisdiction with what it was now, declaring that then for fifty years there was not even a suspicion of a bribed verdict. He told them that so confident were Verres's friends that he would get off if the trial could only be procrastinated until the following year, that when Hortensius was declared consul elect and was returning from the Campus Martius escorted by his supporters, Curio ran up to Verres and embraced him, crying out, " I congratulate you, fear nothing ;—to-day's election has secured

---

[4] Art. Verres in Smith's Gr. and Rom. Biography.

[5] The other five Verrine orations which we possess were written but not delivered by Cicero. They were published after the condemnation, and remain an imperishable monument of his industry, ability, and eloquence.

you an acquittal." There never was, he said, a tribunal since courts existed in Rome composed of such august and illustrious members as the present. If it failed in its duty, as it would be impossible to find in the whole body of senators men more fit for the office, the conclusion would be that the jurisdiction must be transferred to some other class. The usual course in a prosecution was, he admitted, to have all the speeches first, and hear the witnesses afterwards, but he intended now to produce the evidence on each article of charge separately, and he concluded by formally stating that which he brought forward first.

"We say that Caius Verres, whilst he has in many things acted rapaciously and cruelly towards Roman citizens and our allies, and nefariously towards gods and men, has besides carried off from Sicily forty millions of sesterces contrary to law."

The examination of the witnesses lasted nine days, but the defence broke down at once. Hortensius seems to have been a bad hand at cross-examination and lost his temper. He put only a few questions and then abandoned the case. It was during the contest that Cicero made one of his sarcastic jokes. Hortensius (in violation of the Cincian law which required the services of advocates at Rome to be gratuitous) accepted as a present from Verres a valuable image of the Sphinx, one of the spoils he had brought from Sicily, and while cross-examining a witness he said, "You speak in riddles; I cannot understand you!" "Well!" interrupted Cicero, "that's odd, for you have a sphinx at home to solve them."

Verres soon saw that the evidence was too strong for him to get over, and he slunk away from Rome on the third day after the trial began. He was condemned to banishment and a heavy fine was also imposed upon him. He retired to Marseilles with a large portion of his ill-gotten wealth, and the works of art he had carried off from Sicily; and we are told that Antony afterwards placed his name in the proscription list because he would not part with some Corinthian vases which the Triumvir coveted.

In the following year Cicero entered on the office of Curule Ædile, which gave him the right to the curule chair (*sella curulis* [6]),—a seat of ivory like the Lord Chancellor's marble chair in Westminster Hall in former times, —and also to the *jus imaginum* or privilege of placing his bust in wax or marble in his hall, which was the heraldic emblazonment of ancient Rome, and in fact ennobled the family of the magistrate who was entitled to the honour. A Roman family was as proud of the number of busts of ancestors — some of them blackened by age — which it could show in the *atrium* or hall of the house, as in modern days an English family is of the quarterings on its shield.

The duties of Curule Ædile are detailed by Cicero in one of his orations against Verres. The nearest equivalent to such an office in this country is that of First Commissioner of Public Works, and in some points the functions are analogous. They were two in number, besides two "plebeian" ædiles, whose duties were so nearly the same, that it is hardly worth while to point out the difference. They had the care of the public buildings (*ædes*) and especially the temples, also of the streets and markets, and superintended the police of the city. They also provided for the celebration of the great religious festivals at Rome, and exhibited the annual games in honour of different deities of which the Romans were so passionately fond. This of course entailed considerable expense, and it

---

[6] Aulus Gell. Noct. Att. III. 18, derives the word *curulis* from *currus* because, as he says, certain magistrates in the early times of the Republic used as a mark of honour to be carried to the senate-house in a carriage (*currus*) in which was a seat called *curulis*.

does not appear that there was any salary attached to the office, or any fund upon which the ædile could draw except his own resources. But just as mayors in corporate towns in England differ in the frequency and cost of their entertainments during their year of office, so the ædiles of Rome differed in the outlay they lavished upon the public shows. It gave those who were ambitious an admirable opportunity of buying popular favour, with a view to the higher honours of the state. Many men ruined themselves by the profusion and extravagance of the spectacles and games they exhibited, incurring an expense of which it is hardly possible in these times to form an adequate conception. Amongst those whose names have been handed down to us as conspicuous for the magnificence of their shows while filling the office of ædile are Atticus,[7] Julius Cæsar, Lentulus Spinther, and Æmilius Scaurus. It was customary during the festivals of the year, for the ædiles to adorn the Forum with all possible splendour, and for this purpose they borrowed from friends and others works of art, such as pictures and statues. Thus Cicero mentions that Caius Claudius borrowed a famous Cupid in marble by Praxiteles, from Heius, a wealthy native of Messana in Sicily, and contrasts his conduct in borrowing and restoring it, with the conduct of Verres, who plundered Heius's sacristy or chapel of the same Cupid. Verres lent to Hortensius and Metellus, when they filled the office of ædile, the statues which he had carried off from Sicily, and a magnificent display they must have made. Plutarch tells us that the Sicilians assisted Cicero in many ways during his ædileship, out of gratitude for his services, and in memory of his conduct as their quæstor at Rome.

---

[7] Cicero says that Atticus ransacked all Greece and the Greek islands for works of art to give *éclat* to his ædileship.—*Pro Domo*, 43.

He exhibited the usual shows and games, but could rely upon other sources of popularity, and avoided unnecessary expense. He says himself that his ædileship did not cost him much. At the same time it was necessary to do the thing on a liberal scale.[8] The people did not like to be baulked of their spectacles, and a stingy ædile would have a poor chance of the consulship.

In the mean time Cicero did not neglect his profession as an advocate. He defended Fonteius in a criminal case, and Cæcina in a civil action, and we possess both the speeches he delivered—but the former only in an imperfect shape.

Fonteius had held the prætorian government of Gaul for three years, and was accused of extortion and corruption by the inhabitants of the province. Cicero challenged the other side to produce a single trustworthy witness or piece of evidence to substantiate the charge. Gallic witnesses were not to be believed upon their oaths. Could they give credit to the testimony of men who belonged to a nation which retained to thr, day the horrid and barbarous custom of human sacrifices? Were they to be frightened by the threats of those "cloaked and trousered" (*sagatos et braccatos*) foreigners who swaggered in the Forum, declaring that there would be a fresh Gallic war if Fonteius were acquitted? These were the men whose ancestors had pillaged the Oracle of Delphi, and besieged the Capitol of Rome. It would be a disgrace and shame if the news reached Gaul that Roman senators and knights gave their verdict, not because they believed the evidence of Gallic witnesses, but because they were terrified by their threats. One of the charges against Fonteius was that he had accepted bribes to relieve some of the provincials from the

---

[8] Quanquam intelligo in nostrâ civitate inveterasse et jam bonis temporibus ut splendor ædilitatum ab optimis viris postuletur.—*De Off.* II. 16.

burden of making roads, or to take no notice if they were
badly made ; but this Cicero disposed of by showing the
orders which Fonteius had given to his lieutenants on the
subject, and the way in which those orders had been
obeyed. Another charge was that he had exacted illegal
duties upon wine ; but that part of the speech in which his
advocate dealt with this, is lost. He quoted numerous
instances in which the testimony of Roman nobles of the
highest character had been discredited, because they were
supposed to be influenced by personal enmity against the
accused, and argued that *a fortiori* the evidence of men,
such as the Gauls who hated Fonteius, ought to be disbelieved. These were not times when Rome could afford
to lose a man like him. He pointed to him as he stood
before them, with his mother and vestal sister clinging to
his embrace. Other women might become wives and
mothers, but to Fonteia, a vestal virgin, her brother was
the only being on whom she could lavish her affections.
Let them take care that the everlasting fire that burnt
upon the altar, kept up by her nightly vigils, was not
extinguished by her tears. It concerned the honour of
the Roman people that it should not be said that the threats
of Gauls had more influence with them than a Vestal's
prayers.

It would be impossible to make the next case, in which
he appeared for Cæcina, interesting. The question turned
upon the point whether illegal force had been used in
ejecting Cæcina from some landed property which he
claimed in right of his deceased wife, who had left him her
heir.[9]

---

[9] To this period most probably may be referred the speeches *pro Ma-*
tridio and *pro Oppio*. The latter is chiefly known from a few fragments
found in Quintilian. Oppius was quæstor of Aurelius Cotta, governor of
Asia Minor, and seems to have drawn his sword upon the proconsul.

Chapter V.

CORRESPONDENCE AND DOMESTIC LIFE.

Æt. 39.   B.C. 68.

THE year following his ædileship, B.C. 68, is that in which Cicero's extant correspondence first begins. It is a rich mine of information, and furnishes the best materials, not only for his own biography, but a great part of the history of the time. Nowhere else do we find such a vivid picture of contemporary events. We seem to be present at the shifting scenes of the drama, as the plot unfolds itself which involves the destinies of Rome. We hear the groans of the expiring Republic, which had been mortally wounded during the long civil wars of Marius and Sylla, and was fast sinking under the flood of social and political corruption which is sure to follow in the train of civil war. At one time we watch with eager impatience the arrival of a courier at Tusculum, with a letter from Atticus telling his friend the news of the day, and in Cicero's reply we read all the fluctuations of hope and fear which agitated him during the momentous crisis of his country's fate. At another we contemplate the great orator and statesman in the seclusion of his villa, as a plain country gentleman, busying himself with improvements on his estate, building farm-houses, laying out and planting shrubberies, and turning watercourses, or amusing himself with pictures and statues, and the various objects which interest a man of refined and cultivated taste. At another we find him at Rome sick, weary, and disgusted with the din of strife, mistrusting everybody where no one seems worthy of trust, and harping ever on the vanity of ambition and the worthlessness of popular applause. We see him at one moment exalted to the summit of human glory when saluted in the Senate by the proud title of *Pater Patriæ,* and at another sunk in the lowest depths of despair when he is a wandering fugitive exile from Rome, and tells his wife that while he writes he is blinded by his tears.

There is a charm in these letters to which we have nothing comparable in all that antiquity has spared us. To say nothing of their exquisite Latinity, and not unfrequently their playful wit, they have a freshness and reality which no narrative of bygone events can ever hope to attain. We see in them Cicero as he was. We behold him in his strength and in his weakness—the bold advocate, and yet timid and vacillating statesman—the fond husband—the affectionate father—the kind master—the warm-hearted friend. I speak not now of his political correspondence, written with an object in view, and with a consciousness that it might one day be made public, but his private letters to his relatives and friends, in which he poured out the whole secret of his soul, and laid bare his innermost thoughts, yearning for sympathy and clinging for support. To quote the words of De Quincey:[1] "In them we come suddenly into deep lulls of angry passion—here upon a scheme for the extension of literature by a domestic history, or by a comparison of Greek with Roman jurisprudence; there again upon some ancient problem from the quiet fields of philosophy." They show that he was a man of genial soul, and of a most kind and amiable disposition—what Dr. Johnson would have called a thoroughly " clubable " person. He is never more at home than when he is indulging in a little pleasant banter and irony, as when he

---

[1] Collected Works, article Cicero.

makes fun of Trebatius the lawyer, who had left the atmosphere of the courts, to turn soldier and serve under Cæsar
in Gaul. But he is always the scholar and the gentleman ;
and no one had more of that refined polish which the
Romans described by the expressive word *urbanitas*. I
do not think that in the whole of his correspondence a
single coarse word or vulgar idea occurs. It is not so in
his speeches. There he often indulged in language which
is, according to modern notions, offensive to good taste and
even decency, as when he attacked Piso and Gabinius and
Antony. But that was the fault of the plain-speaking
time in which he lived, rather than of the man ; just as the
occasional coarseness of Shakespear must be attributed to
the age in which he was born, and not to his own gentle
nature.

How pleasant it is to hear him giving his friend Atticus
a message from the little Tullia, or Tulliola as he often
calls her—making use of the endearing diminutive so
significant in the ancient Latin and modern Italian—to
remind him of his promise to make her a present, and
afterwards telling him that Tullia had brought an action
against him for breach of contract; or to find him speaking of his only son " the honey-sweet Cicero," that " most
aristocratic child," as he playfully styles him, who was
with his sister in his youthful days the pride and delight
of his life. We see him lounging on the shore at his villa
near Antium, and there penning a letter to confess that
he is in no humour to work, and amuses himself with
counting the waves as they roll upon the beach. We
would not willingly exchange that letter to Atticus, in
which he says of himself that he knows he has acted like a
" genuine donkey " (*me asinum germanum fuisse*), for
the stiffest and most elaborate of his political epistles.

From his villa at Formiæ he writes to complain of the

visits of troublesome country neighbours, and says he is so
bored by them that he is tempted to sell the place ; and,
therefore, while they annoy him there is a capital opportunity for a purchaser.

His fondness for books amounted to a passion. He tells
Atticus, that when his librarian Tyrannio had arranged his
books it seemed as if his house had got a soul; and he is
in raptures with a book-case when ornamented with the
gay colours of the parchment-covers (*sittybæ*) in which
the precious rolls were kept. We find him at one time
begging his friend to send him two of his assistant
librarians to help Tyrannio to glue the parchments, and to
bring with them a thin skin of parchment to make indexes.
He tells Atticus on no account to part with his library, as
he is putting by his savings (*vindemiolas*) to be able to
purchase it as a resource in his old age. By "library"
Cicero means the copies of manuscripts which Atticus was
having made at Athens by some of his clever slaves ; and
what would we not now give to possess one such set of
manuscripts as were put on board a trireme at the Piræus
and consigned to Cicero in his Tusculan villa? In the
midst of all his anxiety and disgust at the state of public
affairs, when it was evident that the old Republic was
tottering to ruin, he says that he supports and refreshes
himself with literature, and would rather sit in a well-
known seat at his friend's country house, with the bust
of Aristotle over his head, than in a curule chair. At
another time he says, that he does not envy Crassus his
wealth, and can despise the broad acres (*vicos et prata*) of
others, if he has it only in his power to purchase books.

In one of his letters he playfully finds fault with his
freedman Tiro for an inaccurate use of a Latin adverb,
fideliter. In another he defends himself against a criticism
of Atticus, and maintains that he was right in putting the

preposition *in* before *Piræa*, but admits that *Piræum*, as the accusative case, would have been more correct.   Now and then he indulges in a pun, as when he tells Atticus, who thought some of the windows of his house on the Palatine Hill, which had been made by his architect Cyrus, too narrow, that he was perhaps not aware that he had been finding fault with the *Cyro*pædia.   How true is the picture he draws of the contrast between the hollow friendship of the world and the calm and sober happiness of domestic life.   Amidst the crowd that thronged his hall, and attended him, as was the custom, to the courts, begirt as he was with " troops of friends," he complains that there is not one with whom he can joke freely, or to whom he can unburden his soul in sorrow.   In other words he expresses the same sentiment as Bacon, that " a crowd is not company, and faces are but a gallery of pictures, and talk is but a tinkling cymbal, where there is no love."

How were these letters sent ?[2]   There was no post-office in ancient Rome : and the only mode of conveying them was either by couriers called *tabellarii*, who were despatched express for the purpose ; or by friends who happened to be going to or near the residence of the person to whom they were addressed.   We find Cicero frequently complaining that he had no trustworthy person at hand to whom he could confide an important letter without danger of its being opened and its contents read ; and he mentions one instance where he lost a letter from Atticus owing to the friend who had charge of it being

[2] Before a letter was despatched five things were requisite, four of which are enumerated in a line of Plautus (*Bacch.* IV. 4, 64), " Stilum, ceram, et tabellas et linum." To these must be added the seal. The *tabellæ* were thin tablets of wood smeared with wax, and with an elevated rim or border. These when written upon, *i. e.* scratched with the *stylus*, were bound together by a packthread, and the knot of the string was sealed with wax and stamped with the signet-ring.

attacked and robbed near the burial ground (*bustum*) of Basilius.

I propose to notice a few of these early letters to Atticus somewhat in detail, for they will give us a good idea of Cicero's style and habits of thought, and also show the cordial friendship that existed between these two eminent men—a friendship as frank as it was sincere, which never varied during all the vicissitudes of their lives, and was terminated only by death.

In the first letter written in the latter part of the year to Atticus in Epirus on the western coast of the Adriatic, where, in the neighbourhood of Buthrotus, he had recently purchased an estate, Cicero begins by alluding in feeling language of affectionate sorrow to the death of his cousin, or, as he calls him, *brother* Lucius—the only son of his uncle Lucius—who had, as we have seen, been associated with him in the prosecution of Verres. Cicero greatly deplored his loss, and speaks of him as a man endowed with every excellence, and distinguished by great sweetness of disposition. He next refers to a subject which was a fertile source of domestic annoyance for many years—the unhappy disagreement between Quintus and his wife Pomponia, who was a sister of Atticus. Quintus was a man of hasty temper, easily vexed, but soon appeased, and Pomponia seems to have been a lady rather apt to take offence, and jealous of her imagined rights—what we may call *touchy*, and inclined to stand on her dignity. A little anecdote which Cicero relates of her in one of his letters, and which will be afterwards mentioned, exhibits her in a sulky and unamiable mood. Terentia also and Pomponia did not get on very well together. The frequent quarrels of the ill-matched pair Quintus and Pomponia caused great distress both to Cicero and Atticus; Atticus naturally took his sister's part, and his displeasure at his brother-in-law's conduct was most probably the reason why, at a later period, he abandoned the idea he once entertained of accompanying Quintus, in the capacity of quæstor, to his prætorian government in Asia Minor. Cicero was not at all blind to his brother's faults, but he also knew the many good points of his character ; and it is pleasant to read the kind and affectionate terms in which he always speaks of him, until unhappily they quarrelled many years after, as I shall have occasion to relate in a subsequent part of this work. In the letter to which I am now alluding, he tells Atticus that he might appeal to Pomponia herself to say how earnestly he had endeavoured to induce her husband to treat her with proper affection. Quintus was displeased at this interference, and Cicero says that he had written to him to appease him as a brother, to admonish him as a junior, and to reprove him as an offender.

Other topics in the same letter are two matters of business in which Atticus was interested, but about which nothing certain is now known. Cicero takes occasion also to correct his friend in a point of law, and tells him that the doctrine of adverse possession has no application in a case of trust or question of guardianship, which is very much what an English lawyer would say at the present day. Atticus had asked him to employ his good offices in reconciling Lucceius to him, for they had had a quarrel ; and Cicero assures him that he had done so, but to little purpose. He next congratulates Atticus on his recent purchase in Epirus, and begs him to remember to get anything which may be suitable for his own Tusculan villa ; " for there," he says, " in that place alone do I find rest and repose from all my troubles and toil." This is the first mention that occurs in Cicero's writings of his favourite villa at Tusculum, which he seems to have bought only a short time before. He concludes the letter by telling Atticus that Terentia is suffering a good deal from rheumatism in the limbs; and that she and his darling Tulliola send their best compliments to him, and his sister and mother. The last words are, "Be assured that I love you like a brother."

In the next letter, which is short, Cicero promises that Atticus shall not again have to complain of him as a negligent correspondent, and begs his friend who has plenty of leisure to copy a good example. He mentions that Fonteius has purchased the house of Rabirius at Naples, which Atticus had had some thoughts of buying; and says, that his brother Quintus now seemed to be on good terms with Pomponia, and that they were both staying at their country residence near Arpinum.

The manner in which he communicates the next piece of intelligence is disappointing, if we accept the usual reading. It is the death of his own father, and all he says on the subject is this: "My father died on the 25th of November."[3] He then turns off to ask Atticus to look out for appropriate ornaments for his Tusculan villa. This looks, to say the least, cold and unfeeling; and yet Cicero was the very reverse of being either cold or unfeeling. We have seen that he deplored in the language of genuine sorrow the loss of his cousin Lucius, and we learn that his grief for the death of his daughter Tullia was so excessive that he was derided for it by his enemies. We are therefore surprised to find him noticing so shortly and dismissing so summarily the death of his excellent father.[4] But the truth is that what we call *sentiment* was almost wholly unknown to the ancient Romans, in

---

[3] *Pater nobis decessit a. d. VIII. Cal. Decembris.*—Ad. Att. I. 6.

[4] I strongly suspect that the true reading of the sentence is *Pater nobis discessit*, not *decessit*, that is, "My father left me," probably to return to Arpinum. This is the conjecture of Madvig, *de Ascon.* Comm. p. 71, quoted by Drumann, *Gesch. Roms*, V. 213, who approves of it.

whose writings it would be as vain to look for it as to look
for traces of Gothic architecture amongst Classic ruins.
And this is something more than a mere illustration.   It
suggests a reason for the absence.   Romance and sentiment came from the dark forests of the North, when Scan-
dinavia and Germany poured forth their hordes to subdue
and people the Roman Empire.   The life of a citizen of
the Republic of Rome was essentially a public life.   The
love of country was there carried to an extravagant length,
and was paramount to and almost swallowed up the
private and social affections.   The state was everything ; the individual comparatively nothing.   In one of
the letters of the Emperor Marcus Aurelius to Fronto,
there is a passage in which he says that the Roman
language had no word corresponding with the Greek
φιλοστοργία, the affectionate love for parents and children.
Upon this Niebuhr remarks that the feeling was " not a
Roman one ; but Cicero possessed it in a degree which
few Romans could comprehend, and hence he was laughed
at for the grief which he felt at the death of his daughter
Tullia."[5]   His divorce from Terentia appears to be a
violent exception to the general rule of his character ; and
we shall have to consider hereafter whether he can or cannot be justified for his conduct on that occasion.

   In these first letters we get a few glimpses of his domestic life.   He tells Atticus that his daughter Tulliola,
his darling (*deliciæ nostræ*), is betrothed to Calpurnius
Piso Frugi.   This event, which we should have thought
full of interest to him, he mentions in the most laconic
manner—*Tulliolam C. Pisoni L. F. Frugi despondimus.*[6]

---

[5] Hist. of Rome, III. 30.   Niebuhr translates φιλοστοργία, "the tender
love for one's *friends* and parents."   But I doubt whether στοργὴ is ever
applied to any other than family affection.   It is especially used to denote
the love of one's offspring.
   [6] *Frugi* means "abstinent" (frugal), and Cicero, in *Verr. de Signis*,

The young lady was then only nine, or at the most eleven, years old.   Atticus had promised her a present, and Cicero tells him that she looked upon her father as bail for the performance, but he intended rather to forswear the obligation than make it good.   In another letter he says that Tulliola has brought her action (*diem dat*), and summoned bail.

I have noticed the first mention in Cicero's letters of his Tusculan villa, in the furnishing and adorning of which he was at this time so much engrossed, and it may be interesting to describe it so far as we are able after the lapse of twenty centuries.

About twelve miles across the Campagna to the east of Rome, on the slope of the Latin hills which form as it were the framework of the landscape, and which now sparkle with the villas of the Roman nobility who resort there during the heats of the summer and autumn months, stands the modern town of Frascati.   The terminus of the railway which connects it with Rome is in the plain a mile below the town.   About two miles beyond Frascati, and almost at the summit of the hill that rises above it, is the site of the ancient city of Tusculum, the *arx* or fortress of which crowned the top.   A lovelier walk than that which leads to this spot can hardly be imagined.   The path winds with a continuous ascent through woods, and past villas and convents, " bosomed high in tufted trees," until it strikes into a narrow road or rather lane, paved with ancient polygonal blocks of flat stone.   This is the

puns upon the name and that of Verres (brush or besom), contrasting the conduct of *Verres*, who had *swept* Sicily clean of its works of art, with the *abstinence* of *Frugi*, who, when prætorian governor of Spain, having broken one of his gold rings, ordered a goldsmith of Corduba (Cordova) to attend him in the market-place, where he publicly weighed out gold and had a new ring made in the presence of bystanders, to prevent the possibility of its being said that he had plundered it.   This certainly looks like a caricature of caution.

identical road which led up in ancient times to Tusculum
from the plain below, and along which Cicero must often
have walked or been carried in his *lectica* on his way from
Rome to his country-seat. Following this lane the
traveller reaches a romantic spot, where are the remains
of a small amphitheatre; and a little further on to the
right, on a grassy platform jutting out on the south-west
side of the hill and commanding a glorious view, is the
site of Cicero's villa. In the distance across the Campagna and right opposite glittered the walls and roofs and
towers of Rome; beyond were the blue waters of the
Mediterranean; on the right lay Tivoli; and on the left
the Alban lake, embosomed, however, and hidden from
sight by its surrounding hills. Antiquaries who throw
doubt upon every thing tell us that there is no certainty
that this *is* the real site of Cicero's villa, and some call it
the villa of Tiberius. But very possibly the Emperor
may have become the owner of the villa, just as Sylla was
before Cicero bought it.[7] Some writers place the villa
in quite a different locality. After describing the walks
round the Alban lake, Eustace mentions a shady alley in
the woods which led to the town of Marino; and says,[8]
"The same alley continues to Grotta Ferrata, once the
favourite villa of Cicero, and now an abbey of Greek
monks. It stands on one of the Tumuli or beautiful hills
grouped together on the Alban mount. It is bounded on
the south by a deep dell, with a streamlet that falls from
the rock, and having turned a mill meanders through the
recess and disappears in its windings. This stream, now
the Marana, was anciently called Aqua Crabra, and is

[7] When I visited the spot in the autumn of 1859 a solitary workman
was employed by the Aldobrandini family, to whom it belongs, in ex-
cavating chambers and pavements, which I saw just as they were disinterred from their sleep of ages.

[8] Classical Tour through Italy, II. 258.

alluded to by Cicero. Eastward rises a lofty eminence
once crowned with Tusculum ; westward the view descends,
and passing over the Campagna fixes on Rome and the
distant mountains beyond it ; on the south a gentle swell
presents a succession of vineyards and orchards, and behind it towers the summit of the Alban Mount, once
crowned with the temple of Jupiter Latiaris. Thus Cicero
from his portico enjoyed the noblest and most interesting
view that could be imagined to a Roman and a Consul ;
the temple of the tutelary divinity of the empire ; the seat
of victory and of triumph ; and the theatre of his glorious
labours—the capital of the world

'Rerum pulcherrima Roma!'"

But it is surely an insuperable objection to this theory
that Grotta Ferrata is fully three miles from the ancient
Tusculum ; and if Cicero's villa really occupied the site
where it is supposed by Middleton, Melmoth, Eustace,
and other writers to have been, it never would have borne
the name of Tusculanum.[9]

The villa itself was arranged as closely as possible on
the model of the Academy at Athens, so as to resemble it
in miniature. In fact, Cicero used playfully to call it his
academy, and he added to it a *palæstra* or exercise ground,
a *gymnasium* (which perhaps was the same as the *aca-
demia*), and a *xystus*, a colonnade or corridor with open
pillars like that which may still be seen on the south side
of the Capitol at Rome, by the side of the modern road
which leads up from the Campo Vaccino (the Forum) to
the Campidoglio. It was here that Cicero and Atticus
passed many delightful hours together away from the noise
and bustle of Rome, communing together on lofty themes,

---

[9] After all we must be content to guess in such matters where certainty is impossible, and say with Livy, " Famâ rerum standum est, ubi
certam rebus derogat antiquitas fidem."

and enjoyed those conversations in retrospect of which each
might say to the other—

> " I've spent them not on toys, or lusts, or wine,
>   But search of deep Philosophy,
>   Wit, Eloquence, and Poetry—
> Arts which I loved, for they, my Friend, were thine !"

The neighbourhood of Tusculum was a favourite resort
of the old Roman nobility.[1] On the declivity of the hill
were scattered the villas of Balbus, Brutus, Catulus,
Metellus, Crassus, Pompey, Cæsar, Gabinius, Lucullus,
Lentulus, and Varro, so that Cicero was in the midst of
his acquaintances and friends ; but he thought his own
villa lay a little out of the road, as it certainly did.[2]

Above all things Cicero's passion was a library. To
add this to a house was, as he expressively termed it, to
give the house a soul ; and in nothing was he more urgent
with Atticus than in entreating him to send him books,
which of course in those days meant manuscripts. He
begged him never to lose an opportunity of picking up
for him works of art to ornament his villa and grounds ;
and great is the joy he expresses at the arrival of a Herm-
athena,—a double-headed bust of Mercury and Minerva,
on a square pedestal—and he mentions statues or pictures
from Megara, and figures of Mercury in Pentelic marble
with bronze heads, some of which may perhaps yet be
discovered and add to the treasures that are contained in
the Museum of the Vatican. He tells Atticus not to be
afraid of the expense,—it was his hobby (*genus hoc est
voluptatis meæ*)—and he would take care and repay him.

Besides his house at Rome and residence at Tusculum,
Cicero had many other villas, of which the principal were

---

1 " Hic Brutus sociique aderant; hic Attice, Tulli
       Gaudebas sermone tui ; ingentesque procellæ
       Conticuere fori, et raucæ fragor abfuit urbis."
    Cicero cum Familiaribus.— *Oxford Prize Poem*, 1829, by Sir Eardley Wilmot.
2 Devium ἀπαντῶσι et habet alia δύσχρηστα.—*Ad Att.* VII. 5.

situated on the west coast of Italy. Following the direction from north to south, they lay respectively near the following towns:—Tusculum, Antium, Asturia, Sinuessa, Arpinum, Formiæ, Cumæ, Puteoli, and Pompeii. Besides his villa near Antium, he had a house in the town, which he purchased in the year 45 B.C., from M. Lepidus, only a short time before his death. Antium (now Porto d'Anzo) was situated on a headland looking down upon the blue waters of the Mediterranean, and Cicero enjoyed the cool breezes and .quiet retirement of the spot. He had here a good library, and many of the manuscripts which were saved when his villas at Tusculum and Formiæ were plundered by the satellites of Clodius at the time of his exile, were brought to his country-seat at Antium. His Asturian villa lay in an island which was formed by a river that here emptied itself into the sea. It was surrounded by a thick wood of shady trees, in the solitude of which he used to pass whole days alone while mourning for the death of his daughter. Formiæ was not far from Cajeta (*Gaeta*) and the modern town or village of Castiglione. His villa there was laid in ruins by Clodius, but afterwards restored by Cicero, and it was in the adjacent park that he was murdered by the emissaries of Antony. He purchased his country residence near Cumæ on the hill above the town after his return from banishment. It was not far from Baiæ, the favourite watering-place of the fashionable world of Rome, and amongst his neighbours he mentions the names of Pompey, Varro, and Marcus Brutus. At no great distance from this was Puteoli (*Puzzuolo*) on the sea side, where he had a villa of considerable size. Annexed to it was a building to which, as at his Tusculanum, he gave the name of Academy, and here he once entertained Julius Cæsar on his way to Rome after his return from the east. He was much attached to this residence,

Sketched by Ainslie.

CICERO'S VILLA, FORMIÆ.

but it had one drawback. The neighbourhood was populous, and he complained that he had too many visitors. After his death the villa became the property of C. Antistius Vetus, and it was here that the Emperor Hadrian was buried.

His Pompeian villa lay a few miles from Naples, close to Pompeii, and was so called of course from the city which has been disinterred after the lapse of twenty centuries.

The question naturally occurs, from what sources did Cicero derive the wealth which the possession of so many residences implies, and how was he able to bear the cost of keeping up so many establishments? He inherited the Arpinum villa, but all the rest were purchased by him. We know from Plutarch that all the fortune he got by his wife Terentia was a myriad of *denarii*, equal to about 3500*l*., which was by no means sufficient to support such an expense. And he made it his boast that he took nothing for his services as an advocate. How then did he become so rich as to be the proprietor of fourteen or fifteen different villas, all furnished with exquisite taste and adorned in many instances with master-pieces of Grecian sculpture and Roman art?

There were no cotton lords at Rome, and commerce flourished to only a limited extent. But Cicero could have derived no benefit from either commerce or manufactures. His career was that of an advocate and statesman, and in neither capacity was he directly paid. The most certain mode of acquiring wealth to a public man at Rome was a provincial government.[3] This followed, as a

[3] De Quincey says, "Almost the only open channels through which a Roman nobleman could create a fortune (always allowing for a large means of marrying to advantage—since a man might shoot a whole series of divorces, still refunding the last dowry, but still replacing it by a better) were these two—lending money on sea risks, or to embarrassed municipal corporations on good landed or personal security with the gain of twenty, thirty, or even forty per cent.; and secondly, the grand resource of a provincial government."—*Collected Works, Cicero.*

matter of course, the possession of the office of Prætor or Consul, and the frequent instances of accusation of ex-governors charged with oppression and extortion, show with what unscrupulous avarice the pro-prætorian and pro-consular powers were too often exercised. Cicero, however, declined a pro-prætorian government, and he declined also to take either of the provinces allotted to him and his colleague Antonius when he laid down the office of Consul. He did not assume a pro-consular go-vernment until after his return from exile, some years after his consulship. It could not therefore have been from this source that he derived that wealth which enabled him to be the possessor of so many estates, and to live in such affluence and luxury at a much earlier period. But there were two other modes of becoming rich, and Cicero participated largely in both. Rome was rapidly advancing to the position of mistress of the world, and her leading men were the masters of Rome. It therefore was the policy of distant kings and commonwealths to conciliate their favour and support, and for this purpose presents of enormous value were transmitted to them. We can hardly call them bribes, for in many cases the relation of patron and client was avowedly established between a foreign state and some influential Roman ; and it became his duty, as of course it was his interest, to defend it in the senate and before the people. For instance, Cicero mentions Dyrrachium as a place of which he was patron, and whose interests he had always defended. Such a custom opened no doubt the door to corruption, for money was lavished to buy the votes of the senators, and agents were employed at Rome to distribute it. The purity and disinterestedness of Cicero's character makes me believe that he never accepted such presents as a bribe, nor allowed his public conduct to be influenced by any

regard for money; but he undoubtedly did receive presents
from foreign suitors, and we can easily imagine that they
were large in amount, for they must have been most
anxious to secure the good-will and propitiate the favor
of the matchless orator and foremost man of Rome.   The
other and unobjectionable mode of acquiring wealth was
by legacies, which in ancient, as in modern times, has
always been deemed an honorable source of riches, provided no unworthy acts are resorted to for the purpose of
influencing the testator.   In the second Philippic he makes
it a matter of boast that he had received upwards of twenty
million sesterces (about 178,000*l.*) from legacies left him
by his friends.[4]

But he also borrowed without scruple, and after his
return from exile was almost constantly in debt.   Before
he went to Cilicia as proconsul Caesar had lent him a
sum of 800,000 sesterces, equal to about 7000*l.*   The
purse of Atticus seems to have been generally open to
him, and he freely availed himself of it.   The money,
however, was supplied not as a gift but a loan, and in
some cases his friend became security for him when his
credit was low and he wished to borrow from others.
But on the other hand he lent money largely to his
friends, the repayment of which was often in arrear, and
his embarrassments were thereby increased.   Drumann
says that he did this for the sake of the interest, and to
lay men whose services might be useful under obligations
to him.   But this writer throughout his elaborate work
does all he can to produce an unfavorable impression of
the character of Cicero.   He never gives him credit for a
single disinterested action, and attributes the most selfish
and unworthy motives to his conduct.   He is as much

[4] Ego enim amplius sestertium ducenties acceptum hæreditatibus
retuli.—*Philipp.* II. 40.

prejudiced against him as Middleton was in his favor, and neither of them can be trusted as a biographer when the subject in question is not a matter of fact but of opinion affecting Cicero's character. It is not clear that he lent money at interest at all, and at all events we may well believe that his object was to do a kind action and not to put money in his pocket, or make use of the services of his debtors. Political motives may have perhaps had weight with him in inducing him to advance a very large sum to Pompey at the outbreak of the Civil War, but he was probably quite as much influenced by the exaggerated feeling of gratitude which, as we shall see, he entertained towards him for conduct which little deserved it.

Chapter VI.

THE PRÆTORSHIP.

Æt. 40-41.   B.C. 67-66.

CICERO became Prætor elect at the age of forty—
B.C. 67—and under circumstances which prove that
his popularity at that time was very great. The times
were stormy, and the assembly of the people in their centuries for the election of prætors was twice interrupted by
tumults before the legal formalities were completed, so
that it became necessary to hold a third meeting to choose
those officers. The occasion of these tumults was the
attempt to pass several obnoxious laws. The first was a
bill brought forward by the tribune Aulus Gabinius, and
known as the Gabinia Lex, to invest Pompey with an
extraordinary commission and supreme command in the
Mediterranean to extirpate the pirates whose vessels
swarmed in that sea, and ravaged the coasts almost with
impunity. Their audacity struck terror into the heart of
Rome. They had captured ambassadors on the high seas,
and actually seized and destroyed a Roman fleet in the
port of Ostia. The bill, however, was strongly opposed
by Hortensius, Catulus and other leading senators, on the
ground that it conferred unconstitutional powers on Pompey, and they pointed to the example of Marius and Sylla,
as showing the danger of bestowing such extraordinary
commands on the generals of Rome. The friends of
Lucullus, who had the conduct of the war against Mithridates, took an active part in the opposition to the bill,

which they alleged was an encroachment on his authority, because the chief haunts of the pirates were in the Levant, which might be considered as part of his province. To counteract this, and render him popular with the mob, Gabinius had a picture made of the magnificent palace which Lucullus was then building, and displayed it in the Forum, while he addressed the people to make them believe that Lucullus was enriching himself at their expense.

The second bill was proposed by Lucius Otho, and though of much less importance, excited still more clamor and violence. Its object was to assign separate rows of seats in the theatres to the equestrian order next to the senators, for the knights had hitherto sat indiscriminately with the rest of the spectators. This was, as might be expected, a most unpopular measure in a republic like that of Rome, and gave rise to tumults which may be compared to the O. P. riots at Covent Garden in the early part of the present century. It was, however, with some difficulty carried, and Otho became, as we shall see, extremely unpopular in consequence.

Caius Cornelius, another of the tribunes, was the author of the third bill, and the opposition to it reveals the extent and depth of political corruption in high places at Rome. It was a bill for punishing with the severest penalties bribery at elections, and enacted, that those who were guilty of the offence should be incapable of public office or a seat in the senate. It was strongly opposed by the senators, but was extremely popular with the masses. The excitement was so great that the consuls were obliged to protect themselves by a military guard; business was suspended, and the election of magistrates was put off. The result was that the bill was withdrawn and another, less stringent in its nature, was brought forward by the Consul C. Calpurnius Piso, and, ultimately, became law.

In one of the earliest of his extant letters to Atticus, written about this time, Cicero gives a lively idea of what a candidate for public office had to go through at Rome, telling him that there was nothing like a canvass to bring a man into contact with every kind of rascality.[1] In the same letter he expresses his disgust at the state of affairs in the city, which, he says, were growing worse with incredible rapidity; and he turns with delight to the thought of his Tusculan villa, and the library he had formed there, begging his friend to keep carefully for him some books which Atticus had purchased for him at Athens.

Although, owing to the confusion that prevailed, the comitia for the election of prætors was twice adjourned without any definite result, Cicero, who had seven competitors against him, was on both occasions chosen Prætor Urbanus by the unanimous votes of all the centuries. And when at last, on the third attempt, a valid election did take place, the same result followed, and he was still at the head of the poll.

Next year, B.C. 66, at the age of forty-one, Cicero assumed the office of Prætor Urbanus, or City Prætor. The most important part of his duties was of a judicial nature ; and it was usual to determine by lot what particular jurisdiction, civil or criminal, each prætor should exercise during his year of office. Cicero happened to get as his division of labor the criminal courts ; or, at all events, had to preside at trials of magistrates accused of extortion, embezzlement, and other offences in their provincial governments.[2] This formed no inconsiderable part of the criminal business at Rome, and required in the judge both

---

[1] Scito nihil tam exercitatum esse nunc Romæ quam candidatos omnibus iniquitatibus.—*Ad Att.* I. 11.

[2] Postulatur apud me, prætorem primum, de pecuniis repetundis.—*Pro Cornelio Fragm.*

firmness and honesty, for the culprits were generally men of powerful influence and great wealth. He had soon an opportunity of displaying both these qualities in an important case. Caius Licinius Macer had, while holding the prætorian government of Asia Minor, been guilty of great oppression and extortion, and, being accused by the provinces which had suffered under his misrule, he was put upon his trial before a body of *judices*, over whom Cicero presided. Macer was a relation of Crassus, and, relying upon his support, he so confidently expected an acquittal that he did not even assume the mourning dress (*toga sordida*) which it was usual for persons under prosecution to wear in order to excite sympathy and compassion. He was, however, convicted, and was so overwhelmed with shame at the result that he either destroyed himself or died of grief.[3] Writing to Atticus, Cicero tells him that his own conduct on the occasion had won him golden opinions from the people; and he adds—what would startle us to hear said of an English judge—that the credit he gained by Macer's conviction was of more value to him with the populace than any benefit that could have flowed from the offender's gratitude if he had been acquitted. This shows how much the result of the trial was thought to be in the power of the presiding prætor, although the judices, or jurymen, alone had the right to pronounce the verdict.

[3] Plutarch says that he took to his bed and died; but according to Valerius Maximus, he watched the close of the trial from a balcony, and when he knew that he was convicted, and saw Cicero, the presiding judge, take off his robe (*prætexta*), or as we should say, put on the black cap, he sent a messenger to tell him that he died accused but not condemned, and therefore his property would not be confiscated. He then instantly suffocated himself by forcing a napkin into his mouth. This reminds us of the *peine forte et dure*, the punishment formerly in this country for standing mute, which was sometimes endured by prisoners when they dreaded a conviction to be followed by forfeiture of lands and goods, if they pleaded to the indictment and were found guilty.

It is never right, nor in **good** taste, to make a jest on a personal infirmity, but Plutarch mentions a sarcasm **which** fell from **Cicero** on the **bench on** an occasion that almost **justified an** exception **to the rule. To understand** the **point** we must remember that a **short thick neck, like that of** a bull, **was** thought by the Romans the **sign** of an impudent unscrupulous character. Vatinius, a rude and insolent man, whose neck was swollen with tumours, came before him, when **sitting** as prætor, with some petition or request which Cicero **said** he would take time to consider. Vatinius replied that if *he* were prætor he would **make no** question about it. **Upon** which Cicero retorted, "Yes; but you **see I have not got** so much neck," we should say *cheek*, **"** as you have."

Although filling the office **of a criminal judge** Cicero **was not** debarred from the exercise of his profession **as an** advocate. He defended M. Fundanius in a speech **now** lost; and also Aulus Cluentius Habitus, **who was** accused of murder and tried before Q. **Naso**, Cicero's own colleague **in the prætorship.** The indictment **seems also to have comprised the** charge of conspiracy to procure the condemnation **of a man** named Oppianicus.

The case discloses a melancholy tale of wickedness; and Sassia, the mother **of** Cluentius, might almost **contest** the palm of pre-eminence in guilt with Lucrece **di** Borgia. Not long after her husband's death her daughter married her first cousin, **Aurius** Melinus, **for whom** the mother soon conceived an adulterous passion. She employed all **her** arts to alienate his affections **from his** wife, and at last **succeeded** in inducing him **to** divorce her. She then flew **to the arms of** her son-in-law and openly married **him. By and by,** however, Melinus, having incurred the enmity of Oppianicus—against **whom** there was the strongest suspicion that he had poisoned his own wife and brother, and procured the murder of a near relative of Melinus—was, through the interest of Oppianicus with the tyrant Sylla, included in one of his lists of proscription, and put to death. This murder of her husband attracted the love of Sassia; and Oppianicus, being equally smitten, paid his addresses to her and offered her marriage. She at first refused, on the ground that he had three sons alive and she did not wish to be encumbered with such a family. Oppianicus understood the hint, and in the course of a few days caused two of them to be murdered. The scruples of Sassia were now removed, and she married Oppianicus—wooed and won, as Cicero says, not by nuptial presents, but the deaths of murdered children.

The career of Oppianicus was one of the most abandoned villany; and, having unsuccessfully attempted to take off Cluentius by poison, he was put upon his trial for this crime, and, being convicted, was sentenced to banishment. He had endeavoured to bribe his judges, and for that purpose had distributed amongst some of them a large sum of money, which they took, but, notwithstanding, pronounced a verdict of guilty. For this offence they were afterwards put upon their trial and convicted. Oppianicus died in exile five years after his condemnation; and three years after his death, Sassia bestowed her daughter in marriage upon his son by a former wife, and urged him to accuse her own son, Cluentius, of having caused her deceased husband, Oppianicus, to be poisoned. It was on this occasion that Cicero defended Cluentius, and delivered one of the longest of all his speeches, but it is also one which least admits of abridgement. It revealed a shocking history of crime, murder, incest, and subornation of perjury. But as it consisted chiefly in an elaborate examination of the facts, it would, after the narrative already given, be merely repetition to attempt to condense the argument.

With respect to part of the accusation, which charged Cluentius with having entered into a conspiracy to get Oppianicus convicted, it seems, strange to say, that the law made this a criminal offence only in the case of a senator, which Cluentius was not. When, therefore, he applied to Cicero to defend him he told him he was safe, as the law did not touch him, and he would at once take the objection which would secure his acquittal on that charge. But Cluentius entreated him, with tears, not to do so, declaring that he was more anxious about his character than his safety; and Cicero says that he complied with his wishes and abandoned the point of law in his favor. but for this reason,—he saw that on the merits the case admitted of a complete defence.

The advocate on the other side was Attius, and he had quoted a passage from one of Cicero's speeches in a case where he was prosecuting counsel, and in which he had urged the jury to give an honest verdict, and had cited instances of perverse acquittals which had brought justice into contempt. But Cicero refused to be bound by the opinions which he merely expressed as an advocate. It was, he said, a great mistake to look for his real sentiments in his forensic speeches. They were adapted to the exigency of the occasion; and he mentioned, apparently with approval—certainly without censure—the startling saying of Antonius, that he never liked to have any of his speeches written down in order that he might, when an inconvenient passage from them was quoted against him, be able to deny that he had uttered the words. Clearly he would have been no friend to Hansard! Cicero seems to have been more struck with the folly than the immorality of the remark, for he adds, "just as if men did not remember what we have said or done unless we have committed it to writing."

The language in which the orator described the in-
cestuous marriage of Sassia with her son-in-law is worth
quoting. "That nuptial couch which two years before
she had spread for her daughter on her marriage she bids
them adorn and prepare in the same house for herself,
while her daughter is turned away an outcast. The
mother-in-law weds her son-in-law with no religious ceremonies, with no one to give the bride away, amidst the
dark and gloomy forebodings of all."[*]

Cicero this year delivered one of his finest speeches in
support of a bill brought in by the tribune Manilius for
superseding Lucullus in the conduct of the war against
Mithridates and conferring the supreme command upon
Pompey, then in the zenith of his fame. The campaigns
of Lucullus in the east had at first been brilliantly successful, but of late the tide of fortune had turned, and his
soldiers had mutinied in the field. It appears, at first
sight, strange to find Julius Cæsar also giving his support
to this measure, the obvious effect of which would be to
increase the power and exalt the reputation of the only
man at Rome who was likely to stand in the way of his
ambition. Various reasons may be assigned for this.
Pompey was a favorite with the people, and the proposal
was so popular that Cæsar may not have liked to oppose
it. Some writers think that his object was to see a precedent set for the grant of such ample powers as he hoped
one day to have conferred upon himself. But this, perhaps, is too refined a view, and gives Cæsar credit for too
long-sighted a policy. A more Macchiavellian theory, but
not the less probable, is, that he may have wished Pompey
to be exposed to the chances of failure, or the obloquy and

---

[*] The result seems to have been that Cluentius was acquitted, as
Cicero afterwards boasted that he had " thrown dust " in the eyes of the
jury (tenebras offudisse judicibus) at the trial.—Fragmn. See Onom.
Tull. II. 165.

envy which follow the possession of power.   The measure
was at first strongly opposed by Catulus and Hortensius.
Catulus asked the people, in a speech he addressed to them
from the Rostra, upon whom they could rest their hopes if
they persisted in trusting everything to Pompey, and he
was carried off by a mischance?   The people, with a loud
shout, exclaimed, "Upon you!" and this so pleased him
that he ceased to struggle against the bill.

The speech is interesting, independently of its merits,
as the first *concio*, or political harangue, which Cicero
delivered from the Rostra.   He says in it, that hitherto
his modesty had deterred him, and his incessant occupations as an advocate had prevented him, from addressing
the people there, but he was now emboldened by the
unmistakable evidence of their favour, as shown by their
unanimous election of him, three times repeated, as prætor.
He showed how necessary it was that Rome should put
forth all her strength to protect her possessions in Asia
against the attacks of two such powerful kings as Mithridates and Tigranes; for not only did their allies implore
their help but their own revenues were in the utmost
danger.   Their arms had suffered a reverse, on which, he
said, he would not dwell, but rather pass on to the question, who was the commander most fit to carry on the
campaign?   There ought to be four qualifications to make
up the character of a distinguished general—military
genius, virtue, authority, success.   He showed that all
these qualities were united in Pompey.   He drew a
splendid portrait of him as a warrior, and praised to the
skies his disinterested self-denial.

"No feeling of avarice ever turned him aside from his destined course
to think of booty; no licentiousness attracted him to pleasure; no delights to self-indulgence; curiosity never tempted him to explore cities,
however famous, and in the midst of toil he shunned repose. The works
of Grecian art in the Asiatic towns, which other generals thought they
might carry off, he did not even allow himself to look at!"

His nature was gentle; he was affable and accessible to
all. His exploits in war had been so remarkable that no
one even ventured to ask of Heaven in his prayers such
success as had been bestowed on Pompey. They must not
be misled by the authority of Hortensius, who opposed the
bill, but remember that he had also opposed the bill of
Gabinius for appointing Pompey to the supreme command
in the Mediterranean against the pirates, and what would
have become of the Roman empire if his authority had
then prevailed? As to the bugbear with which Catulus
tried to frighten them, of the danger of concentrating so
much power in the hands of one man, his answer was, that
this had been often done before—in the case of Scipio
Africanus, of Marius, nay, of Pompey—with the full ap-
probation of Catulus himself. The honor of Rome required that the commander in Asia should be not merely
a good soldier but a good man. "For," said Cicero, "it
is difficult to express the odium in which we are held by
foreign nations on account of the oppression and rapacity
of the governors who have gone out from us of late years."
He declared that they respected nothing, either sacred or
profane; not even the sanctity of a private dwelling.
They should choose, therefore, a general who would not
plunder their allies, nor attack the virtue of wives and
daughters, nor pillage the towns of their works of art and
the treasuries of their gold. Such was the picture which
a Roman orator drew of the conduct of those who were
invested with command in the distant provinces of the
empire, and he appealed to the opponents of the present
measure whether he did not speak the truth. He concluded
by calling Heaven to witness that he supported the bill,
not to curry favour with Pompey, or obtain any advantage
for himself—on the contrary, he knew well that he exposed
himself to enmity, alike open and concealed—but because,

out of gratitude for all the honors the people had conferred upon him, he was determined to prefer their wishes,
the honor of the commonwealth, and the safety of the
provinces and their allies, to any private interests of his
own.

Even now, amidst all the bustle of active life, and distinguished as the leading orator of Rome, he found time
for, and did not disdain to profit by, if we may believe
Suetonius,[5] the lessons of a rhetorician named Gnipho. At
the mature age of forty-one he was still content to be a
learner in the art of which he was considered by all other
men to be the greatest living master.

During this year his brother Quintus became a candidate for the ædileship of the ensuing year, and was successful.

Two or three days before the expiration of Cicero's
office, Manilius, whose measure in the senate he had so
vigorously supported, was brought before him and charged
with peculation. It was the usual custom to allow ten days,
at least, before the trial took place, in order to give the
accused time to prepare his defence, but Cicero appointed
the following day. This was considered harsh, and incensed the people, with whom Manilius was a favourite,
and who thought that he was prosecuted because he was
the friend of Pompey. The tribunes summoned Cicero to
give an account of his conduct before the people, when he
explained that he had always shown humanity towards the
accused, so far as the law allowed, and as he did not wish
to act otherwise towards Manilius he had purposely appointed the only day on which he would sit as prætor to
try him; adding significantly, that those who wished to
help Manilius were not likely to do so by getting him
tried before another judge. The people loudly applauded

---

[5] De Illustr. Gramm. 7.

him, and called on him to undertake himself the defence
of Manilius. This he consented to do; and accordingly,
says Plutarch, "taking his place before the people again,
he delivered a bold invective against the oligarchical party
and those who were jealous of Pompey."

At the close of his prætorship Cicero was entitled to
claim a provincial government, which was looked forward
to at Rome as one of the best prizes in the lottery of ambition. It afforded the most certain means of rapidly
accumulating wealth; and, even if a man were virtuous or
cautious enough not to go the length of a Verres or an Antonius, and provoke an impeachment by his avarice, there
were numerous modes by which he might enrich himself
in the command of a province, and yet keep himself within
the pale of the law.

Cicero, however, at the close of his prætorship declined
the glittering temptation, and refused to accept a provincial government. He is entitled to the praise of disinterestedness in this so far as the love of money is concerned, for, had he been an avaricious man, he would have
taken care not to let slip such a golden opportunity of
amassing wealth; but it would be a mistake to suppose
that contempt of riches was the cause of his refusal. He
was covetous indeed, but covetous of honor, and he might
truly say,

> " And if it be a sin to covet honor,
> I am the most offending man alive."

He candidly tells us that, with the consulship in view, he
did not dare to leave Rome. Two years must elapse before
he was qualified by law to attain that supreme dignity,
but in the mean time he must actively prosecute a canvass
amongst the immense body of electors, both at Rome and
in the rest of Italy, and he could not afford to hazard a
year's absence and incur the risk of verifying the proverb,

"Out of sight out of mind." He did not belong to one of the old aristocratic families whose ancestors had been senators, and who seemed to think themselves entitled to a monopoly of office, looking upon it as a kind of hereditary right.[5] He had no statues or pictures in his hall to show that his forefathers had been seated in the curule chair. He was, in fact, a *parvenu*—or, to use his own term, a *novus homo*—and he had all the difficulty to contend against in struggling upwards which is felt in England by those who have to make a position for themselves, and run the race of ambition against competitors who start with the enormous advantage on their side of an historic name and family influence.

Perhaps, also, there was a nobler feeling than mere ambition which influenced his resolution not to leave Rome. The state of affairs was eminently critical. He saw, and feelingly deplored, the tremendous evils to which his country was a prey. Let me quote what Niebuhr says on this subject. "To comprehend the occurrences of this time it is essential to form a clear notion of the immensely disordered condition of Rome. There never was a country in such a state of complete anarchy : the condition of Athens during its anarchy bears no comparison with that of Rome. The anarchy of Athens assumed a definite form ; it occurred in a small republic, and was quite a different thing altogether. Rome on the other hand, or rather some hundreds, say even a few thousands, of her citizens, who recognised no law and no order, had the sway over nearly the whole world, and pursued only their personal objects in all directions. The " Republic was a mere name, and the laws had lost their power."[7]

---

[5] Namque antea pleraque nobilitas invidiâ æstuabat, et quasi pollui consulatum credebat, si cum quamvis egregius, novus homo adeptus foret.—Sallust, *Bell. Cat.* c. 23.

[7] Hist, of Rome, V. 15.

Chapter VII.

CANVASS FOR THE CONSULSHIP AND ELECTION.

Æt. 42. B.C. 65.

TO obtain the consulship was the next great object of
Cicero's ambition, and although he could not be
elected until the following year, he announced himself as
a candidate at the *comitia tributa* or assembly of the
people in their tribes, held in the Campus Martius for the
election of Tribunes, on the 17th of July, B.C. 65.

This was done not in the form of an address to the
" free and independent electors " according to modern
usage, but in an equally plain and intelligible manner.
He tells Atticus that he intends on the day mentioned to
begin shaking hands with the voters (*initium* PRENSANDI
facere), which was as well understood at Rome as it is
in an English borough or county on the eve of an impending dissolution of Parliament.

It was during his canvass that his brother Quintus addressed to him that interesting letter or essay known as
De Petitione Consulatus. It may be called a Manual of
Electioneering Tactics for Ancient Rome, and proves that
he was a man of much shrewdness and ability. It throws
some insight into the state of society and customs of the
time; and is as if at the present day an account were
given of the best mode by which an aspirant to Parliament
could secure a seat in the House of Commons. But the
limits of the present work will not allow me to do more
than refer the reader to it. A nobler mode of winning

the favor of the electors than a resort to such arts as
Quintus recommends was the display of eloquence in the
Forum, and Cicero gained great reputation this year by
a splendid defence of the ex-tribune Caius Cornelius, who
was accused before the prætor, Q. Gallus, of having violated the constitution (*crimen majestatis*). Cornelius had
been tribune, and the offence with which he was charged
consisted in his having proposed a law which we should
think in the highest degree equitable, but which gave
great offence to the Senate. This was that no one should
be absolved from the obligation of obeying the law except
with the consent of the supreme power in the state, that
is the people at a meeting duly assembled. The Senate
had taken upon itself to exercise a dispensing power;—
thereby reminding us of the conduct of James II., so bitterly
resented by Parliament in his reign—and treating therefore the measure as unconstitutional, they waited until
Cornelius had laid down his office, during the tenure of
which he was *sacrosanctus* and could not be impeached,
and then put him upon his trial. The prosecution was
conducted by the leading men of the Senate, such as Catulus, Lucullus, Hortensius, Metellus and Lepidus;—a
formidable array—but Cicero defended him, and he was
acquitted. The speech is unfortunately lost. It lasted
four days, and is mentioned by Quintilian in glowing terms
of praise. He says that Cicero defended Cornelius, not
only with powerful but brilliant weapons.

As may well be supposed the people in whose interest
the measure had been framed were on the side of Cornelius,
and they loudly applauded the successful advocate. In a
subsequent speech against Vatinius, Cicero declared that his
defence of Cornelius was of great use to him in his canvass
for the consulship; and he needed every aid that eloquence
and ability could supply. For practically all Roman citizens

not belonging to the hereditary aristocracy had been excluded from the two highest magistracies—the consulship
and the censorship. "After the case," says Mommsen,[1]
"of Manius Curius, no instance can be pointed out of a
consul who did not belong to the social aristocracy, and
probably no instance of the kind occurred at all." The
great curule houses kept the appointment to themselves,
and looked with the utmost jealousy upon the attempt of
any "new man" to force his way to that proud pre-
eminence. The time had gone by, as Mommsen truly
remarks, when it was any longer possible to take a small
farmer from the plough and place him at the head of the
community; for Rome was not now merely the capital of
a limited territory, or the chief power of an Italian con-
federacy, but was rapidly becoming the mistress of the
civilized world. She held the east and west in fee : Africa,
Egypt, Syria, Greece, Spain, Gaul, Sicily, and Sardinia
were her tributaries, and she governed them by her officers
as completely as any part of Italy.

In a letter written this year, the date of which apparently is some time in June, and addressed to Atticus who
was then at Athens, Cicero tells him the names of those
who he expected would be his competitors. One indeed,
P. Galba, was already in the field, but Cicero calls his a
premature canvass (*præpropera prensatio*), and says that
he met with flat downright refusals from the electors in
old Roman style,[2] who told him without ceremony that
they did not intend to vote for him but for Cicero. The
others who were certain to be candidates were Antonius

---

[1] *Gesch. Rom.* Bk. III. c. 11. He gives a list of the *gentes* which
furnished patrician consuls and curule ædiles for about 200 years down
to B.C. 173, from which it appears that 16 houses supplied 140 consuls
and 32 curule ædiles : of these the lion's share fell to the Cornelian and
Valerian *gentes*.

[2] Sine fuco ac fallaciis more majorum negatur.—*Ad Att.* I. 1.

and Cornificius; and, possibly, Cæsonius and Aquillius might stand.   But besides these there was Catiline, over whose head there was then impending a trial for pecuniary corruption in his provincial government of Africa.   He had held that command for two years, and was now impeached by the provincials.   Clodius was the prosecutor; and Catiline was disqualified to become a candidate unless and until he was acquitted.   But Cicero was so confident of his guilt and of his conviction, that he uses the strong expression : " Catiline will be a competitor provided that the jury decide that the sun does not shine at noon." [3]   In other words, " Catiline can only be declared not guilty by a jury which is ready to declare that the sun does not shine at mid-day."   In point of fact, however, Catiline was acquitted, for Clodius the prosecutor was tampered with.   He took money from Catiline to betray the cause; and the jury were also bribed.

But here a difficulty occurs which has puzzled many learned men.   Fenestella, a grammarian who wrote shortly after the death of Augustus, declares that Cicero defended Catiline in this impeachment.   Asconius Pedianus, who lived about a quarter of a century later, and is one of the most useful of all the commentators on Cicero, says that he did not ; and I think the arguments are convincing to show that Asconius is right.   But in the very next letter of Cicero that we possess, we find the remarkable passage : " At this moment I contemplate undertaking the defence of Catiline *my competitor*.   We have just such a jury as we wished to get, and have the best possible understanding with the prosecutor.[4]   I hope, if he is acquitted, that he will be more disposed to coalesce with me in the can-

---

[3] Si judicatum erit, meridie non lucere, certus erit competitor.—*Ad Att.* I. 1.   It is extraordinary how this passage has been misunderstood by several writers.

[4] Summâ accusatoris voluntate.—*Ad Att.* I. 2.

vass; but if it turns out differently I shall be able to bear
the disappointment." This proves beyond all doubt that
Cicero at that time meant to defend him; and it is on this
letter that Fenestella, and those who follow him, rely to
prove that he did defend him in the case of the impeachment by the Africans. But what is the date of the letter,
and to a defence in what case does it refer?

The letter begins by informing Atticus of the birth of
Cicero's son—"*L. Julio Cæsare, C. Marcio Figulo consulibus.*" But they were not consuls until the year *after* Catiline had been tried and acquitted on the African charge. It
is clear, therefore, that the intended defence here spoken of
cannot refer to that charge, unless we adopt the hypothesis
that Cicero, in mentioning the names of the consuls, means
consuls elected but not actually in office. This would get
over the chronological difficulty, for we may then conclude
that the letter was written in the same year as the former
one, and before Catiline's trial for embezzlement had taken
place. I am not, however, aware that any other instance
can be found of a Roman writer dating an event by the
names of consuls *elect.* The universal custom was to mark
the year by the consuls for the time being; and, besides,
Cicero speaks in this second letter of Catiline as an actual
competitor. But I have already mentioned that he was by
law disqualified from standing while his trial was pending.
Some writers try to get over the difficulty by relying on
the fact that in the course of these two years Catiline was
twice tried under two different prosecutions for different
offences. The first trial was for embezzlement in Africa,
the second was for illegal violence, if not murder, alleged
to have been committed in the time of Sylla;[5] and they
assume that it is to this second trial, as then impending,
that Cicero refers when they say his intention was to

---

[5] Dio Cass. 37. 10. Cic. pro Sullâ, 29. 91.

appear as Catiline's advocate, although it is all but absolutely certain that he did not.

But there remains a great difficulty, which I have not seen adverted to by any other writer. In the same letter which bears the date of the consulship of Lucius Cæsar and Figulus, Cicero tells Atticus that he is very anxious for him to come to Rome to exert his influence with his friends amongst the nobility, who it was generally believed *adversarios honori nostro fore*. Now the obvious meaning of these words is "who will be opposed to my election as consul;" and it was natural that Cicero should wish to have the benefit of his friend's assistance during the canvass. And he goes on to say, "Take care, therefore, and be in Rome in January, as you originally intended." If then this letter was written in the year B.C. 64, when Cæsar and Figulus were actually consuls, the January here referred to must be the January of the following year, B.C. 63. But the contest would before that time have been decided, as the election was to take place in the course of the year B.C. 64, and Atticus could be of no use at Rome *then* as a canvasser, or give Cicero any help in an election which was over. Upon the whole I am inclined to believe that the hypothesis is right which assumes that the letter was written in the year B.C. 65, when Lucius Cæsar and Figulus were consuls elect. Atticus appears to have complied with the request of his friend, and to have resided at Rome for the next two or three years, for during that period there is a blank in their correspondence, and it is not renewed until the second year after Cicero's consulship.

The chief interest in the question is independent of the fact whether Cicero did actually defend Catiline or not. It is enough that we find him seriously contemplating the intention, and using language with respect to the approach-

ing trial (whatever the charge may have been) which
implies that a packed jury had been secured. How could
he think of appearing in defence of such a man as Catiline
whom, as we shall see, he soon afterwards bitterly attacked?
If the profession of an advocate in ancient Rome had been
the same as it is in England there would be no difficulty
in the matter, for the modern advocate does not concern
himself with the guilt or innocence or moral character of
his client. His duty is merely to deal with the legal
evidence, and to show if possible that it fails to bring the
charge home to the accused. And, except in some rare
cases, he is by the very fact of his profession understood to
be under an implied obligation to undertake the defence of
the accused if his assistance is required. But at Rome
it was different. The advocate there was conceived to
have a much wider discretion than we allow, and it was
optional with him to appear or not in any case as he
thought fit. His services were gratuitous, and he generally practised in the courts with a view to qualify himself
to become a successful candidate for public office. It is
therefore remarkable that we find Cicero not only ready to
defend Catiline at his trial, but ready to make common
cause with him in canvassing for the consulship. Are we
to adopt the explanation at which Cicero seems to hint in
his speech in defence of Cælius at a much later period of
his life? He there, in order to relieve Cælius from the
odium arising from his former intimacy with Catiline,
declares that he himself had formerly been deceived in his
estimate of that man's character, and had thought him a
good citizen and a firm and faithful friend. But it is
difficult to reconcile this view with the fact that not very
long after he had told Atticus that he intended to defend
Catiline, and if he was acquitted hoped to have him as an
ally in his canvass, he delivered a speech in the Senate,

known as the oration *in Togâ candidâ*, in which he furiously attacked him and upbraided him with all the infamy of his past life. The truth is, that we must not look for perfect consistency in Cicero, nor be surprised to find that with a political end in view he was not as scrupulous as he ought to have been about the means. I believe him to have been one of the purest and most virtuous of the ancients, and in some respects to approach nearest to the character of a Christian gentleman ; but I am far from thinking him faultless, and the highest Pagan morality, when "darkness covered the earth, and gross darkness the people," was something very different from Christian principle.

In the same letter in which he announced his intention of becoming a candidate and commencing his canvass for the consulship in July of this year, he told Atticus that he should perhaps take the opportunity of what we may call a legal vacation [6] to go into Cisalpine Gaul (the modern Piedmont and Lombardy) and stay there from September to January under the pretext of being Piso's lieutenant, in order to canvass electors and secure votes.

The same letter shows how anxious he was at this time to stand well with every one and offend nobody. Cæcilius, the rich and miserly uncle of Atticus, had, as he alleged, been cheated by Varius out of a large sum of money. Varius made a fraudulent assignment of his goods to his brother Satrius ; and Cæcilius brought an action (something like our action of trover) against Satrius and wished Cicero to be his counsel. But Satrius was on intimate terms with Cicero, and had been of considerable use to both him and his brother Quintus at other elections. And, besides, he was a friend of Domitius Ahenobarbus, a wealthy and influential nobleman—upon whom Cicero says

---

[6] Cum Romæ a judiciis forum refrixerit.

he chiefly depended for attaining the object of his ambition. He pointed this out to Cæcilius and begged to decline the retainer; but the old usurer was much offended, and showed his displeasure by dropping for a time the acquaintance. Writing to Atticus, Cicero excuses himself for not appearing against Satrius in his uncle's case, and puts it on the ground that he did not like to be counsel against a man who was his friend, and in distress; but conscious that Atticus would guess the true reason, he goes on to say: "If you like to take a harsher view, you will think that reasons of ambition prevented me. Well! even if this be so, I think that I may be pardoned, since it is no bagatelle that I strive for. For you see what a race I am running, and how necessary it is for me not only to retain but to acquire the good-will of everybody. I certainly am anxious to do so."

Assuming that I am right in the date of the letter which has reference to Cicero's intended defence of Catiline, it was during this year that his only son was born.[7] For that letter commences thus: *L. Julio Cæsare, C. Marcio Figulo consulibus filiolo me auctum scito, salvâ Terentiâ.* It is certainly a stiff mode of announcing such an event to an intimate friend: "know that in the consulship of Cæsar and Figulus I have had an increase to my family by the birth of a son, and Terentia is doing well." He then passes on to talk of Catiline and his own prospects of the consulship.

The consuls for the next year, B.C. 64, were Lucius Julius Cæsar, and Caius Marcius Figulus, who had assumed that name on adoption, according to the Roman custom. His original name was Thermes, and in a letter to Atticus, written in the previous year, Cicero had ex-

[7] Middleton places the birth in the following year, when Lucius Cæsar and Figulus were actually consuls.

pressed a hope that Thermes would be Lucius Cæsar's colleague; because, if not, he foresaw that he would be a formidable competitor to himself on account of his popularity arising from his completion of the Flaminian Way, of which work he had the superintendence. This Flaminian Way is now known as the Corso, the principal street of modern Rome. It runs north from the Capitol to the Piazza del Popolo, at the extremity of which is the Porta del Popolo, the old Flaminian gate, through which in after years the Via Flaminia passed and crossed the Tiber over the Milvian bridge, the modern Ponte di Molo. But in the time of Cicero there was no Flaminian gate, which did not exist until the Aurelian wall was built, embracing a much wider circuit than was occupied by the city in the days of the Republic. It is perhaps hardly necessary to mention that modern Rome is almost wholly confined to what was the Campus Martius, then a green and grassy plain, with a few monuments and public buildings, and where some years afterwards M. Agrippa erected the stately Pantheon, and Augustus placed that beautiful Mausoleum for the ashes of his family, the first occupant of which was the young Marcellus, so beloved and so lamented by the whole of Rome.

Cicero was now actively in the field, and had six competitors. These were Catiline and Galba, both of patrician rank, and C. Antonius Hybrida (a younger son of the deceased orator), L. Cassius Longinus, Q. Cornificius, and C. Licinius Sacerdos, all of the plebeian class. But both Antonius and Longinus belonged to the class of *nobiles*, that is their families had held offices of state entitling them to the curule chair; and Cicero was the only candidate whose family was of the equestrian order, and could boast of no public dignities. This placed him at a great disadvantage, owing to the jealousy felt by the proud

nobles against the pretensions of one whom they looked
upon as an upstart, and he well knew the means they had
in their power of defeating his election. For they were
wealthy and influential, and wealth and influence had all
but omnipotent sway amongst the electors. On such
occasions unblushing bribery and corruption of all kinds
were freely resorted to. And it must be remembered that
the voters were not merely the populace of Rome. The
Italian towns that possessed the franchise contributed large
numbers, all of whom might be practised upon by his
opponents.

Julius Cæsar and Crassus openly espoused the side of
Catiline and Antonius, who had formed a coalition and
fought a common battle for the consulship. Antonius was
a man of bad character, and his name had been erased from
the list of senators by the censors.[8] So unscrupulous was
the agency at work to influence the election, that the
Senate was called upon to interfere. A measure was
proposed to give more stringent effect to the laws against
bribery and corruption, but the tribune Orestinus interposed his veto. This gave occasion to Cicero to deliver
a speech known as "the oration in the white robe,"
because as a candidate he wore, according to the usual
custom, a white toga (intended perhaps to be emblem-
atical of purity of election). It is unhappily lost, and
we possess only a few fragments preserved by Asconius.
In it he attacked his two principal competitors with unsparing severity, and thus laid the foundation of the bitter
hatred which Catiline felt towards him, and which, as we

---

[8] The censors had this power. P. Lentulus, after having been consul
B C. 71, was expelled from the senate by the censors on account of his
dissolute course of life. There is an instance in English history of a peer
being deprived of his dignity by act of Parliament on the ground of
poverty. By a statute passed in 17 Edw. IV., George Nevil, Duke of
Bedford, was for that reason deprived of his peerage.

shall see, culminated afterwards in an attempt upon his life. They had, he said, on the previous night, together with the agents they employed to bribe the electors, met at the house of a man of rank notorious for the part he took in that kind of corruption.[9] And he alluded to Catiline's alleged criminal intercourse with Fabia, a vestal and the sister of Terentia, contriving at the same time to damage his opponent and save the honor of his sister-in-law, by saying that Catiline's conduct was such that his very presence raised a suspicion of guilt even where there was nothing wrong.

This speech was delivered only a few days before the *comitia centuriata,* or meeting of the centuries, was held in the Campus Martius, to determine the election of consuls, which was conducted in the following manner :—

The people assembled in the Campus Martius were told off into their centuries, and it was then decided by lot which century should vote first. A narrow passage fenced off on each side, and called *ponticulus,* led into an enclosure called *septum,* "barrier," or *ovile,* from its likeness to a sheep-pen, and each of the voters passed along it. As he entered it he was furnished by officers, called *diribitores,* with tickets on which were written the names of the candidates. At the other end were placed urns or boxes into which he deposited the name of the candidate or candidates for whom he wished to vote, and when all the members of the century had voted the tickets were taken out by scrutineers called *custodes,* and the numbers were pricked on a tablet most probably smeared with wax. The result was then announced, and the majority of the individual votes determined the vote of the century. That which came first was called the *prærogativa centuria,*

---

[9] According to Asconius it was either Cæsar or Crassus who was here pointed at.

and its vote generally determined the fate of the election. The vote of the first century chosen by lot was taken as an indication of the wish of the majority of the people,[1] and the other centuries generally followed suit. The number of the centuries was ninety-seven, and the election depended upon the votes of the majority of the whole.

So great, however, was Cicero's popularity, that the electors, instead of resorting to ballot, proclaimed him consul by loud and unanimous shouts.[2] Antonius had the next greater number of votes, beating Catiline by a small majority, and the rest of the competitors appear to have been nowhere. Cicero therefore and Antonius became the consuls elect for the following year, although they did not actually assume office until the first of January. The triumph of Cicero was greatly to the credit of the people. His only claims to their suffrages were his splendid abilities and his unsullied character. He was opposed by men of rank, and wealth, and power, who were ready to buy votes as freely as they bought merchandize, and against such a temptation he could only rely upon popular gratitude for his services as an advocate and a statesman, and his fame as an orator. Bad as was the state of society at Rome, utterly bad as was the tone amongst the upper classes, demoralized by long years of civil strife, it is impossible not to believe that the heart of the people was in some degree sound, which could thus respond to the call of genius and virtue and reject the bribes that were freely offered.

Most probably Cicero had been too busily occupied with his canvass and the excitement of his election this year to

---

[1] Pro signo voluntatis futuræ.—*In Verr.* I. 9.

[2] Me cuncta Italia, me omnes ordines, me universa civitas non prius tabellâ quam voce priorem consulem declaravit.—*In Pisonem.*

find much time for the duties of an advocate. At all events we know of only one trial in which he was engaged, and that was when he defended Q. Gallius the prætor of the preceding year, who was accused of having obtained his office by illegal means, in other words, by bribery and corruption. The speech is lost, but it was successful, and Gallius was acquitted.

Chapter VIII.

THE CONSULSHIP.

Æt. 43.   B.C. 63.

CICERO had attained the summit of ambition. He was Consul of Rome. As such he was entitled at the expiration of his year of office to the government of a province, an honorable and lucrative preferment which was naturally much coveted ; and it was usual for the two consuls on the day of their inauguration to draw lots for the provinces which each was to obtain. Cicero, however, in the first speech that he made in a crowded Senate on the very day he assumed office—the first of January—publicly declared that he sought neither a provincial government, nor honor, nor advantage, nor anything which it would be in the power of a tribune of the people to oppose. And he made this noble promise, "I will, Conscript Fathers, so demean myself in this magistracy as to be able to chastise the tribunes if they are at enmity with the Republic, and despise them if they are at enmity with myself." This was, indeed, as he himself declared at the time, the only way in which the office could be discharged with dignity and freedom, but it was not the less praiseworthy in him to commit himself to such an act of self-denial, and look solely for his reward in the approval of his own conscience and the regard of his fellow-citizens. Sallust says that he had already won over his colleague Antonius, by agreeing to resign to him the province that might fall to his lot, in case it were better worth having than the one which Antonius obtained. Afterwards, when the lots were drawn and Cicero got Macedonia, a tempting prize, he at once made it over to Antonius, and contented himself with Cisalpine Gaul. This, however, he did not retain, but voluntarily gave it up and exerted himself to get it assigned to Q. Metellus Celer.

At the very outset of his new career he distinguished himself by three remarkable triumphs as an orator. The first of them is characterised by Niebuhr as "one of the most brilliant achievements of eloquence." A bill called a *lex agraria* was brought forward by the tribune P. Servilius Rullus, the object of which was to create ten commissioners, called Decemvirs, for five years, with power to dispose absolutely, with a few exceptions, of the whole of the public lands of the State, and out of the proceeds of the sale to purchase other lands in Italy on which to settle colonies from Rome. They were also to have the entire control over all the prize or booty taken in war, except such as was already in the hands of Pompey, and if we may trust the account which Cicero gives of the measure in his impassioned argument against it, they would become in fact the uncontrolled masters of the whole revenues of the Republic. He first opposed the bill in the Senate in a speech of which a great part is lost. He challenged Rullus and those who supported him to meet him in the Forum, and let the people decide between them. They deemed it more prudent not to accept the challenge, but Cicero harangued the multitude from the Rostra in two speeches, the first of which is remarkable for its ability and power. He had a difficult part to play, for the measure professed to be one of relief for the populace of Rome, and the multitude that thronged the Forum that day must at first have listened with unwilling ears to a speaker whose object was to make them relinquish a proffered boon.

But he succeeded, and by a simple method. He told the
people that the proposed Decemvirate was nothing more
nor less than tyranny in disguise. The ten commissioners
would be ten kings, the name most hateful to Roman ears.
From first to last he impressed this upon his hearers, and
drew a startling and no doubt an exaggerated picture of
what would happen if the bill passed into a law.

He began by thanking the people for placing him in the
proud position in which he stood, and declared that he was
not opposed to the principle of an agrarian law as such.
He was not one of those, he said, who thought it a crime
to praise the Gracchi, whose measures and wisdom had
been of such service to the State. When, therefore, as
consul elect, he first heard it mentioned that the tribunes
intended to frame an agrarian law, he was anxious to be
admitted into their counsels and assist at their delibera-
tions. But they declined his co-operation, and concocted
the measure in darkness and secrecy. At last he heard
that it had been published, and immediately sent to have
a copy taken and brought to him. He declared that he
began to read it with a full determination to support it if
it were a bill beneficial to their interests, and one which a
consul who was in the right sense of the word a liberal
(*re non oratione popularis*) could readily and with honor
defend.

"But," he continued, "from the beginning of the first chapter to the
end I find that nothing else is intended or done than the creation of ten
kings, who, under the name and pretence of an agrarian law, are made
the masters of the public treasury, the revenues, all the provinces, the
whole republic, the kingdoms, the free nations—in short, the whole
world. I assure you, men of Rome, that by this specious and popularity-
hunting agrarian law nothing is given to you, but all things are conferred on a few individuals; a show is made of granting lands to the
Roman people, but in fact they are deprived of their liberty—the wealth
of private persons is increased, but the public wealth is drained; in
short—what is the worst feature in the whole scheme—by means of a

tribune of the people, whom our ancestors intended to be the protector and guardian of freedom, kings are established in the state."

Having struck this chord he rang the changes upon it throughout his whole speech, and to make the proposed appointment more invidious, described the regal retinue which the commissioners were to have as "the ministers and satellites of their power." He drew a ludicrous sketch of Rullus going to Sinope and sending a summons to Pompey, who was then pursuing his career of conquest in the East, to attend him while he put up to sale the lands which the great general had won by his sword. And with reference to the object of all this, namely, the purchase of lands in Italy to be colonized by citizens of Rome, he showed how contemptuously Rullus had spoken of them in the Senate, quoting the expression he had used when he declared that "the populace was too numerous, and must be drained off," as if forsooth, said Cicero, he were speaking of a sink or sewer, and not of a class of excellent citizens. Would the people like to abandon all the pleasures and delights of Rome, its liberties, its franchise, its games and its festivals, and be settled in the arid plains of Sipontium, or the pestilential marshes of the Salapini? It was not safe to trust to these men the power of choosing sites for colonization. The policy of their ancestors had been to plant colonies as a protection against danger, and to regard them, not as mere towns of Italy, but bulwarks of the empire. Such is a very brief outline of the argument of the speech which Cicero delivered.

Rullus and his colleagues did not venture to answer him on the spot, but they spread abroad the report that the reason why he attacked the measure was because he wished to secure the soldiers and partisans of Sylla in possession of the lands which had been assigned to them by the dictator, and feared lest they might be deprived of them by the operation of the proposed law. He was, therefore, called upon to speak at another meeting, when he briefly showed the absurdity of the charge by pointing out that the bill expressly confirmed the title of those settlers, and that therefore he could have no motive on that account for opposing it. He ended with these words, "They are preparing an army against you, against your liberties, and against Pompey; Capua against Rome; against you a band of desperate men; against Pompey ten generals. Let them come forward, and since they have summoned me to address you at a public meeting, let them now speak themselves." The result was that the bill was rejected.

The next measure on which he exerted the marvellous power of his oratory was one which was in itself eminently just, but at the time inexpedient, and he therefore opposed it. Sylla had not only proscribed individuals and families who were the objects of his vengeance, but had confiscated their property, and by a most iniquitous law decreed that their descendants should be incapable of holding any public office and disqualified from becoming candidates. Never had men a juster title to civic rights, not forfeited by any crime or fault of their own, but torn from them by the strong arm of a tyrant. They were numerous and influential, belonging, as many of them did, to the first families in Rome. It seemed to be an act of only common justice to take off the ban under which they lay, and they were actively prosecuting a petition to the Senate, the object of which was to have their civic *status* restored. But what is just in politics is not always expedient, or at all events is not always thought so. In the present case there was danger lest if the men who had suffered under the tyrant's law got power into their hands they might use it for purposes of retaliation, and intestine strife would be the con-

sequence. Cicero, therefore, made a speech in opposition
to their claim, and actually by his eloquence persuaded them
to abandon it. ;'

Almost immediately afterwards he succeeded in quelling
a popular tumult in the same way. The people had
never forgiven Otho for the law of which he was the
author four years before, and by which particular seats
were reserved for the equestrian class at the theatres and
public shows. Whether there had been a delay until now
in giving effect to the law, or whether Otho, conscious of
its unpopularity, had hitherto abstained from appearing in
the theatre, I know not; but it so happened that when he
entered it at the beginning of this year he was received
with a storm of hisses. The knights clapped their hands
and applauded him. A serious riot ensued, and Cicero was
sent for. He invited the people to follow him to the neighbouring temple of Bellona, and there addressed them in an
extempore speech—known as that *pro L. Roscio Othone*, but
now unfortunately lost—by which he completely appeased
the anger of the crowd, and restored them to good humour.
The only hint we have of anything he said is what Macro-
bius tells us, namely, that he upbraided them for making
such a noise and disturbance while Roscius was acting.

History can record few such triumphs of eloquence as
these; and well might the elder Pliny in allusion to them
exclaim with all the fervor of enthusiastic admiration, that
Cicero was the first who had deserved a civil triumph and
the "laurels of the tongue."[1]

His next important speech was that in which he defended the senator Rabirius, who was prosecuted by the
tribune Labienus for the alleged murder of Saturninus,
in a popular tumult seven-and-thirty years before. The
speech we have is imperfect, so that it is hardly fair

[1] Hist. Nat. VII. 30.

to criticise it; but it seems to have been by no means
one of his happiest efforts. Saturninus was a tribune of
the people, and a seditious demagogue. He and others
had seized on the Capitol and held it with an armed
band of followers, when the Senate authorized the consuls to use the whole power of the state and crush the
insurrection. An attack was made on the Capitol, and
Saturninus was slain in the conflict. A slave named
Scæva came forward, and avowing himself the author of the
deed claimed a reward. Thirty-seven years had passed
away since then, and the affair must have been well-nigh
forgotten, when Attius Labienus accused Rabirius, then an
aged senator, of having killed Saturninus, whose person as
tribune of the people was inviolable, and he was put on his
trial before two special judges appointed by the prætor called
Duumviri. These were Julius Cæsar and Lucius Cæsar.
He was defended by Hortensius, who denied that his client
had killed Saturninus. Rabirius however was found guilty.
He was condemned to death, and sentenced to be crucified
in the Campus Martius like the meanest slave. He then
appealed to the people, and Cicero was his advocate before
the multitude assembled in the Campus Martius. By one
of those capricious acts of power which the tribunes possessed and so often abused, Labienus limited the speech to
half an hour, but Cicero adroitly turned this to the advantage of his client. He said it was a proof that Labienus thought that so short a time was more than enough
for so clear a defence. So far as we can gather from what
remains of his speech, the argument was simply this:
capital punishment was odious, and death by hanging
ought never to be the sentence against a Roman citizen.
He was sorry he could not assert that Rabirius had slain
Saturninus, for Hortensius had denied it; but he had
armed himself for the purpose, and that was just as bad if

it was a crime at all.   But it was no crime, as Saturninus deserved his fate, and Rabirius did right in obeying the call of the consuls to assist in putting down the sedition. When he declared that he wished he could claim for Rabirius the honour of having killed Saturninus the enemy of the Roman people, he was interrupted by shouts, and stopping suddenly, he exclaimed: "That clamor does not disturb me; but it comforts me, since it shows that there are some ignorant citizens, but not many.   The Roman people who stand here silent would never, believe me, have made me consul if they thought I should be disconcerted by your clamor.   How much less noisy you have already become !   Why do you keep back your voices, which are a sign that you are foolish and a proof that you are few?"

The people, however, were unfavorable, and Rabirius would have been again condemned had not Metellus Celer, who was augur this year as well as prætor, bethought himself of an expedient to save him.   There was almost always some mode of stopping the business of a public meeting at Rome, where such reverence was paid to legal formalities and superstitious observances.   It seems that the *comitia* could only go on while a flag waved on the Janiculum hill on the other side of the Tiber.[2]   Metellus pulled down the flag, and this broke up the assembly.   Labienus afterwards abandoned the prosecution ; the judgment of the *duumvirs* was tacitly allowed to go for nothing, and Rabirius was saved.

Cicero also in the course of the year defended C. Calpurnius Piso, who had held the proconsular government of Gaul.   He was a stern and severe ruler.   Cicero praises him in a letter to Atticus as "the pacificator of the

---

[2] The origin of this no doubt was that in early times the flag was hoisted as a signal that all was safe on the Etruscan side.   If it was hauled down it gave notice that invaders were approaching.   The observance of the custom long outlived its necessity.

Allobroges ; " but it was pacification much in the same
sense as the well-known saying, " order reigns at Warsaw."
He was accused of extortion, and also of having unjustly
punished one of the Gauls who were subject to his sway.
Cæsar, who was their patron at Rome, conducted the prosecution, and Cicero undertook the defence. The speech
is lost; but we know that Piso was acquitted.

The crisis of Cicero's destiny was now approaching, for
he had to deal with the great Catiline conspiracy.

Lucius Sergius Catilina was born b.c. 106, in the same
year as Cicero himself.[3] He belonged to one of the
oldest of the patrician families in Rome. The Sergian
gens traced its proud pedigree back to Sergestus, one
of the companions of Æneas. His grandfather was M.
Sergius, a soldier of distinguished bravery. In the second
Punic war he received twenty-seven wounds and lost his
right hand, but like Götz von Berlichingen in Goethe's
drama, he supplied its loss with an iron one. Catiline
was a bold and desperate man. He was steeped in
murder from his earliest youth. In the civil wars of
Sylla he killed with own hand his brother-in-law ; and
tortured to death Marius Gratidianus, a kinsman of
Cicero, and carried his bloody head through the streets
of Rome. He was suspected of an intrigue with Fabia,
the sister-in-law of Cicero, and a vestal virgin. She was
tried on the capital charge, for the penalty of such an
offence in a vestal was death, but she was acquitted. He
is said to have murdered his own son in order to marry
Aurelia Orestilla, who objected to having a step-son in
her family. Niebuhr says of him, " he was so completely

[3] It may be interesting to mention that Augustus Cæsar was born in
the year of Cicero's consulship.

diabolical that I know no one in history that can be compared with him; and you may rely upon it that the colors
in which his character is described are not too dark,
though we may reject the story of his slaughtering a
child at the time when he administered an oath to his
associates." Cicero declared that there never before was
seen on earth such a monster made of opposite and con-
tradictory characters, and that he himself at one time was
almost deceived by the better qualities of his nature—

> Thus with each gift of nature and of art,
> And wanting nothing but an honest heart.

He was of immense stature and prodigious strength. Like
Saul, "from his shoulders upwards he was higher than
any of the people." Sallust has drawn a picture to the
life of the brawny giant tortured with the stings of his
guilty conscience: his pallid cheeks, his bloodshot eyes,
and his unsteady step showed how remorse was preying
on his soul. He gathered around him the dissolute youth
of Rome, and became the pimp and pander of their licentious pleasures, exacting from them in return the use of
their daggers whenever he had an enemy whom he wished
to murder.[4] He was elected prætor, and after the expiration of his office became governor of Africa. He was then
accused by Clodius of extortion and embezzlement, and
tried on the charge but acquitted. Cicero had, as we
have seen, already crossed the path of his ambition; and
he knew that in him as consul he would find his most
resolute opponent. His plan was to obtain the consulship,
and then by means of armed violence make himself master
of Rome. For this purpose he had been gradually collecting, by means of his emissaries in different parts of

---

[4] For the character of Catiline see *pro Cœlio*, c. 5, 6; *in Cat.* II, 4;
Sallust, *Bell. Cat.* 5 & 15; Plut. *Sall.* c. 32; Flor. IV, 1; Vell. Pat. II,
34; Liv. Epit. 102.

Italy, a band of needy and disaffected men, ready for any desperate enterprise. The place of rendezvous was Fæsulæ (the modern Fiesole), a town that commanded the northern pass of the Apennines, and looked down from its lofty height upon the valley of the Arno. On the other side of it farther towards the north is still pointed out the site of the camp of Hannibal, where tradition tells us that the Carthaginian leader halted on his march to Rome before the battle of the Thrasymene lake. Fæsulæ was occupied by one of his creatures, Caius Manlius, a veteran centurion of the old army of Sylla, under whose orders the motley groups as they arrived were directed to place themselves, and there await the signal for revolt.

Catiline's chief chance of success in his canvass for the consulship lay in the unscrupulous use of bribery; and to prevent this, if possible, Cicero brought forward and got the people to pass a law which punished the offence with banishment for ten years, and enacted that it should not be lawful for a candidate for public office to exhibit any gladiatorial shows during the period of two years before the election, unless he was called upon to do so by the will of a testator whose property he inherited. The object of this no doubt was to deprive candidates like Catiline of the excuse of keeping in their pay bodies of armed men to overawe the election, and create tumult and disorder. He knew that the new law was levelled at himself; and frantic with rage, he hired assassins who were to attack and murder Cicero in the Campus Martius, at the meeting held for the election of consuls. The day fixed for the comitia was the 26th day of October, but the consul was warned in time. On the previous day he discovered in the Senate the plot against his life, and getting the comitia put off challenged Catiline to appear next day, and answer him to his face. Catiline came, and, with the reckless audacity

of his nature (*ut semper fuit apertissimus*, says Cicero),
avowed his design, saying that there were two bodies in
the state (meaning the Senate and the people), one of
which was infirm with a weak head, the other was strong
but had no head. He would, however, take care that
while he lived, it—a head—should not be wanting. Hearing his bold avowal, the Senate in alarm immediately armed
the consuls with full power to take such measures as they
deemed right, by passing the well-known resolution—*ut consules viderent ne quid detrimenti respublica caperet*. The
comitia were held the next day, and Cicero putting on a
breastplate of glittering steel that all might see the reality of
his apprehension of the danger that threatened him, went to
the Campus Martius surrounded by a body of armed attendants. Catiline was there with his band of ruffians, but did
not venture to attack the strongly-guarded consul. The
election took place without a riot, and Catiline was again defeated. Junius Silanus and Licinius Murena were declared
the consuls elect. This second repulse made Catiline
furious; and that very night he and his fellow-conspirators
met at the house of Porcius Læca, and planned the destruction of the city by fire and sword. The great obstacle
in their way was Cicero, and he must be got rid of. Two
of the party whose names are differently given by different
authors[5] undertook to murder him next morning, by gain-
ing admission to his house under the pretence of an early
visit to pay their respects according to the Roman custom.
Fulvia, the mistress of one of the conspirators, got intelligence of the plot just in time to put him on his guard.
When the two assassins reached his house in the gray dawn
of the morning they found it closely barricaded, and were
denied admittance. Cicero summoned the Senate to meet

---

[5] Sallust mentions C. Cornelius and L. Vargunteius; Plutarch, Marcius
and Cethegus; Cicero (*pro Sullâ*, 6) names only Cornelius.

him next day, the eighth of November, in the temple of Jupiter Stator, the ruins of which are still seen in the Forum. The news of the nefarious plot got wind, and when Catiline showed himself in the hall he was received with an ominous silence; not an acquaintance spoke to him, and when he approached his seat the senators who were near moved away and left their places.

It was then that Cicero rose and burst forth with that passionate appeal: [6]—

"How long, Catiline, will you abuse our patience? How long will that fury of yours baffle us? To what lengths will your unbridled audacity extend? Do you stand unmoved at the sight of the guard that garrisons the Palatine at night—the watches that patrol the city—the terror of the people—the concourse of well-affected citizens—this strongly-defended place of meeting for the Senate—the looks and countenance of all those around you? Do you not feel conscious that your plans have been discovered? Do you not see that your conspiracy is known to all here? Which of us, think you, is ignorant of what you did last night and the night before, where you were, the persons you met in conclave, the plot you formed? What times we live in! What a state of morals is disclosed! The senate is aware of all this—the consul sees it, and yet this man lives! Lives, do I say? Aye! even comes to the senate; takes part in the council of the nation; marks out and designates with his eyes each one of us for slaughter. We, on the other hand, brave men that we are, fancy that we do our duty to the Republic if we manage to escape his fury and his weapons. Long ago, Catiline, you ought, by the consul's order, to have been led forth to execution; and on your head ought to have been hurled the destruction which you have long been plotting against us all."

And so he went on in a strain of indignant eloquence. He reminded the Senate how the Gracchi and Melius and Saturninus and Servilius had been put to death for conspiracy against the state, and said he almost reproached himself for allowing Catiline to live. But his apology was this: if Catiline was prematurely dragged to the scaffold,

---

[6] The dates of the Catiline orations are these :—The first speech was delivered in the Senato on the 8th of November; the second to the people on the following day; the third to the people on the 3rd of December; the fourth in the Senate on the 5th of December.

the roots of the conspiracy would remain. **His** punishment must overtake him when, with his accomplices in crime, he joined the camp **of** Manlius in open and undisguised rebellion. He therefore called upon him to rid the city of his and their detested presence; and if he wished to **justify** the cry which sent **him away an** exile from Rome, he would hasten to **the brigands who were** his associates and levy war against his country. **Face to** face he upbraided him with the infamy of his past career; and alluding to the murder of his son by his own hand, said that he would not be more explicit, lest it should be known that so terrible a crime had been committed in Rome, or that the criminal had not been punished.

At the **end** of this **terrible invective** Catiline rose and attempted to speak. He **began by** imploring the Senate **not to** judge him hastily **or harshly, and reminded them that he** was sprung from a family which had rendered **many** services to the state. **It was** not likely that he, **a** patrician, should be the destroyer **of the** Republic; and a man like Cicero, a mere provincial,[7] **its saviour.** Here, however, his voice was drowned by loud cries of "Traitor! Parricide!" which **assailed him** on all sides. He stopped, and glaring furiously **around** exclaimed, "**Since then I** am driven **headlong by my** enemies, I will **extinguish** the conflagration **of which I am** the victim, in the common ruin of all." He **quitted the Senate house, and** after conferring at his own house with the **chief** leaders of the conspiracy, and assuring them **that he would** soon be at **the** gates of Rome with an army, **he** that night left the city **with a** few associates **and made** for the camp **of** Manlius. There we will follow him after mentioning **the** events **that occurred at** Rome.

---

[7] *Inquilinus*, a **tenant or occupier of** a house as distinguished from **the** owner.

The next day Cicero addressed the people at a public meeting in the Forum. He began by congratulating them on the flight of Catiline, and said he only regretted that so few had accompanied him. His prayer was that the rest would follow him. "I will point out the road," he said: "he has gone along the Aurelian way; if they wish to make haste they will overtake him this evening." He excused himself on the same grounds as he had alleged in the Senate the day before for letting Catiline escape. The catastrophe that would overwhelm the traitors was imminent and certain. Abroad Rome was at peace with the whole world, and she had now only to contend with an internal foe. Some said that he had acted harshly, and pretended to believe that Catiline would consider himself in banishment and go quietly to Marseilles. If so, they might say of him what they liked; he was content to be charged with driving Catiline into banishment, but he prophesied that in three days they would hear of him at the head of an army of rebels. He then described the character of the partisans of Catiline who were still left in Rome, and again urged them to go. They would find no sentries at the gates; no ambuscades to attack them on the road. If, however, they chose to stay, let them beware. If they stirred in their nefarious plot they would find the consuls and magistrates and Senate prepared; and would expiate their guilt in that prison which their ancestors intended to be the scene of the punishment of open and notorious crimes. He concluded by calling on the people to pray to the gods who so visibly preserved them to continue to protect the city, now that all external enemies were overcome, against the wicked attempts of abandoned citizens.

Catiline and Manlius were immediately declared public enemies by the Senate, and a certain time was given to

the rebel forces to lay down their arms or incur the
penalties of treason. The great object was to obtain
legal proof to warrant the arrest of the chief conspirators
who remained in Rome. This was by no means easy, for
such was the fidelity of the conspirators to each other, and
so closely was the plot concealed, that notwithstanding a
large reward was offered for the discovery, not an informer
came forward. But an opportunity soon occurred of which
Cicero dexterously availed himself. There happened to be
at this time in Rome some envoys from the Allobroges,[8] a
people whose territory was nearly identical with the limits
of modern Savoy: and the conspirators thought that if the
flames of war could be kindled in Gaul beyond the Alps, a
useful diversion might be made in their favour. They
therefore sounded the ambassadors through Umbrenus, a
Roman freedman, who had been in their country, and was
probably personally acquainted with them. The result
was that the whole plot was disclosed to them, and they
promised to aid it to the utmost of their power. But
whether they intended treachery from the first, or were
frightened at the idea of compromising themselves, or
wished to curry favour with the Senate, they, after some
little hesitation, revealed the secret to Q. Fabius Sanga,
who was the patron of their nation at Rome, and he immediately communicated the information to Cicero. This
he afterwards declared, in addressing the people from the
Rostra, was nothing less than the finger of Providence.
" For who could have expected the ambassadors of a rest-
less and discontented people like the Gauls to resist the
splendid offers made to them by patrician nobles, and
prefer the safety of Rome to their own advantage ?"

The advice he gave was that they should pretend to
enter heartily into the plot, and entrap the conspirators by

[8] Plutarch says they were only two.

obtaining written evidence of their guilt. With this view
they, at the next meeting, asked for papers which they
might show to their countrymen at home, as credentials to
vouch for the truth of the story they would have to tell.
Letters were accordingly written, and, amongst them, two
which bore the seals of Lentulus and Cethegus. Furnished
with these the ambassadors prepared to leave Rome. One
of the conspirators named Vulturcius was to accompany
them and introduce them to Catiline as they passed through
Etruria. Cicero was kept informed by them of all that
was going on, and he took his measures accordingly. The
envoys were to set out on their journey at nightfall, and
he directed two of the prætors to take a guard with them
and post themselves in ambush, in two parties, at each end
of the Milvian bridge (now the Ponte di Molo), about a
couple of miles from the old city walls, across which the
Allobroges would pass. When they came up to the spot
the soldiers rushed forward, and, after a scuffle in which
swords were drawn on both sides, made them prisoners.
They were brought to Cicero's house just as the day was
beginning to dawn, and the letters they carried were taken
from them. The news of the event soon spread, and the
consul's house was filled by an eager and anxious crowd of
enquiring friends. They advised him to open the letters
before bringing the matter before the Senate, lest if their
contents turned out to be of no importance he might be
censured for rashness in causing such a commotion without
good grounds. He of course knew that there was no fear
of this, and told them that in a case of public danger he
would lay the matter as it stood before the public council.
He immediately summoned a meeting of the Senate, and
sent messengers to invite four of the principal conspirators
—Gabinius, Statilius, Lentulus, and Cethegus—to come
to his house. They came, little knowing that he held in

TEMPLE OF CONCORD.

RESTORED BY CAV. CANINA

Vol. I. p. 115.

his hands the damning proofs of their treason. At the same time, on a hint from the ambassadors, he directed the prætor Sulpicius to go to the house of Cethegus and search for arms, and a great quantity of swords and daggers were found there all ready for instant use.

The Senate had by this time met in the Temple of Concord, and were impatiently waiting for Cicero's arrival. He took with him the envoys and the four conspirators, and passed through the crowded streets attended by a strong guard of citizens. It is easy to imagine the procession as it approached the temple:—the consul with his lictors and their fasces in the midst of the throng, his look elate, and his face flushed with the consciousness of coming victory ; the uncouth Gauls in their barbarian attire; the guilty conspirators affecting unconcern, but weighed down by the fear of some terrible discovery. The temple was guarded by a body of armed knights, with Atticus at their head, and Cicero entered it accompanied by Lentulus and Cethegus who were senators, but the rest were left in custody outside. He unfolded the tale he had to tell, and Vulturcius was called in to be examined. By order of the Senate Cicero offered him a free pardon if he would tell the truth and discover all he knew, and after some little hesitation Vulturcius made a clean breast of it. He confessed that Lentulus had furnished him with a letter and instructions to Catiline, urging him to arm a body of slaves and approach the city, in order to cut off the fugitives while fire and slaughter were raging within the walls. The ambassadors were next brought in. They told the Senate that the conspirators had given them the letters and a written oath which was found upon them ; that they were instructed to send a body of cavalry into Italy ; that Lentulus had assured them it was written in the Sibylline books and foretold by augurs that he was to be king of

Rome ; and that there was a dispute as to the time when
the city should be set on fire and the massacre begin.

A letter was then shown to Cethegus, with its seal un-
broken and thread uncut. He acknowledged the seal to
be his, and the letter was opened in his presence. In it
he promised the Senate and people of the Allobroges that
he would make good what he had told the ambassadors,
and entreated them to perform what those ambassadors had
undertaken for them. Up to this time Cethegus had put
on a bold front, and when asked to explain the discovery
of arms in his house, had answered that he was fond of
collecting choice weapons. The production of the letter,
however, confounded him, and he sat silent.

Lentulus was next asked whether he recognised his seal.
He said, Yes ! It bore the likeness of his grandfather ;
and Cicero upbraided him for using it for such a purpose.
Its dumb significance ought, he said, to have deterred
him from so great a crime. The letter was to the same
effect as that written by Cethegus ; and he was told he
was at liberty to speak in his own defence. At first he
refused to say a word, but at last he rose and began to
cross-examine the ambassadors and Vulturcius, pretending
to be ignorant of the object of their visits to his house.
Suddenly, and to the surprise of all, instead of denying
what they alleged he avowed it ; and at that moment
another letter was produced which Vulturcius declared had
been given to him by Lentulus for Catiline. Lentulus
admitted his seal and handwriting, but showed visible signs
of consternation. · The letter was short and guarded, without any signature. It urged Catiline to collect forces from
all quarters, even of the lowest rabble. Gabinius was now
brought in, and he too at first, like the others, denied his
guilt, but ended by admitting it. Statilius also made a
full confession ; and they were all separately handed over

to different persons, who became answerable for their safe
custody.   There was a difficulty about dealing with
Lentulus, who, as prætor, could hardly be held in arrest,
but he relieved them of it by abdicating his office, and he
was assigned to Lentulus Spinther, one of the ædiles and
a relative, Cethegus to Q. Cornificius, Statilius to Julius
Cæsar, and Gabinius to Crassus.   Orders were also given
for the arrest of five others ; and Cicero mentions it as a
proof of the clemency of the Senate, that it was content
with the punishment of these nine men out of the numbers
who were implicated in the wide-spread conspiracy.
According to Sallust, Catulus and Piso tried hard to induce
Cicero to suborn evidence to accuse Cæsar of being a party
to the plot, but it is needless to say that he refused to lend
himself to so foul a scheme.   Sallust adds, that as Cæsar
left the temple, some of the knights approached him and
threatened him with their swords.   They were, however,
prevented from attacking him ; and Plutarch says that
the consul threw his cloak round him and hurried him
away.[9]

It was now late in the evening, and from the Temple of
Concord he crossed over to the Rostra, which was only a
few paces distant, and addressed the people.   He told

[9] An attempt was made to implicate Crassus in the conspiracy, but
failed.   A man named Tarquinius, who had been just apprehended on
his way to join Catiline, was brought before the senate, and he declared
that he had been sent by Crassus to tell Catiline not to be disheartened
by the arrest of Lentulus and the rest, but to hasten to Rome and take
measures to rescue them.   But the senators refused to believe the tale,
and with cries of indignation insisted that it was false.   Sallust insinu-
ates that some of them did believe it, but there were too many who
were under private obligations to the wealthy noble.   They resolved,
however, on the motion of Cicero, that the information was false, and that
Tarquinius should be imprisoned until he disclosed the name of the
person who had suborned him to give the evidence.   Sallust adds that
he heard Crassus afterwards declare that the author of the calumny was
Cicero himself—an accusation which we are at liberty entirely to disbelieve.

them all that had been done; and fearing that he might be reproached for letting Catiline escape, took pains to show that if he had remained in Rome things might have had a very different issue. Catiline would not have been such a fool as to fall into the trap which had been set for Lentulus, Cethegus, and the rest. He would never have set his seal to letters which contained such manifest evidence of his guilt. In what had happened they should recognize the hand of Jupiter Optimus Maximus, whose statue, by a singular coincidence, was erected in the Capitol on that very morning, while the conspirators were conducted through the Forum, and looking down upon the senate-house saw the whole machinations of the plot unravelled and disclosed. But while piously attributing his success to the guidance of heaven, Cicero did not forget himself. And if ever pride or even vanity was justifiable, this was a moment in which it might fairly be allowed. He asked, however, from them no mark of honor, no reward, no monument to his glory, but the everlasting memory of that day. He wished all honors and rewards to be summed up in their simple gratitude. "In your memories, men of Rome," he exclaimed, "my fame will live; it will be the subject of your private talk; it will be perpetuated and endure in the annals of literature; and I feel that the same day, which I trust will never be forgotten, is consecrated to the safety of the city and the recollection of my consulship." He called on them to be his protection against the enemies his conduct had provoked, and dismissed them to their homes, as it was then already dark, with an admonition to worship Jupiter, the guardian of Rome's safety and their own, and to relax nothing of the vigilance which they had hitherto displayed. It would be his care that this should not be long required, and that they should enjoy lasting tranquillity.

He then retired, escorted on his way by the cheering crowd to the house of a friend, for his own was occupied by women who, with Terentia and the vestal virgins, were celebrating the mysteries of the Bona Dea, of which I will speak more hereafter, and upon which no man might venture to intrude. Plutarch says, that soon afterwards Terentia came to him and informed him of a portent that had just happened. As the fire on the altar was dying out, a bright flame had suddenly leaped forth from the ashes, and the vestals declared it was a good omen to encourage him to execute what he had resolved for the good of his country. He adds that Terentia, " as she was otherwise in her own nature neither tender-hearted nor timorous, but a woman eager for distinction," excited her husband against the conspirators, as also did his brother Quintus, and Publius Nigidius, one of his intimate and most trusted friends.

Rewards were given to the Allobroges envoys and to Vulturcius, and in the Senate Catulus bestowed on Cicero the glorious appellation of " Father of his country." Lucius Gellius also declared his opinion that he was entitled to a civic crown.

A public thanksgiving to the gods was decreed for the services he had rendered " in preserving," so ran the resolution, " the city from conflagration—the citizens from massacre—Italy from war." An unheard-of honor, which hitherto no civilian had enjoyed, it having been reserved exclusively for military success.

There were no reporters in ancient Rome, although stenography was well known, and while the accused were under examination, Cicero directed four of the senators to take down the questions and answers, and the statements of the informers. These he had copied by a number of hands, and distributed to the people. He also sent copies all over Italy, and to the distant provinces.

The next question was how to deal with the conspirators under arrest; and on the following day, the 5th of December, the Senate met to determine it. Cicero, as consul, brought the matter before them, and called on Silanus, one of the consuls-elect for the following year, to speak first. Silanus gave it as his opinion that they should be put to death. Julius Cæsar then rose, and in a long speech declared that he would vote for any punishment short of death. He proposed that the conspirators should be distributed in dungeons amongst certain Italian towns, and there kept in close imprisonment for life; that those towns should be responsible for their safe custody under severe penalties; that their property should be confiscated; and that no one should be allowed to propose hereafter a remission of their sentence. Cicero seems to have risen next, and in a speech of consummate art, while affecting to hold the balance evenly between the two opinions, and summing up the arguments on both sides with almost judicial fairness, he took care to impress upon his hearers that no punishment was too great for the crime, and to show that he as consul was quite ready to execute their sentence, whatever it might be.[1] For what might happen to himself he cared not;—he believed that he was safe, and walled round, as it were, by the gratitude of his countrymen—but if he fell a victim to the attacks of his enemies, he commended his youthful son to their care, who would find not only safety but honor in their recollection that he was the child of the man who, with danger only to himself had been the saviour of them all. He called upon them to decide quickly and firmly. The question was one that concerned the safety of the Senate, of the Roman

---

[1] Mr. Merivale (*History of the Romans under the Empire*, I. 137) says that "Cicero himself demanded a sentence of death." But this is incorrect. The utmost that can be made of his speech is to say that it showed no disinclination to the capital sentence.

people, their wives and children, their altars and their hearths, their shrines and temples, the salvation of the city and of Italy, their freedom, their empire, in short the whole commonwealth. They had in him a consul who would not shrink from obeying their decree, and who would defend it as long as his life lasted.[2]

A great number of senators followed, whose names are given by Cicero in one of his letters to Atticus at a later period, and they all inclined to the opinion of Cæsar, until Porcius Cato rose and gave a new turn to the debate. He spoke vehemently in favor of the capital punishment, and said that as the conspirators had confessed, they should be treated as men convicted of capital crimes and suffer accordingly.

His speech decided the fate of the criminals. The Senate voted for death. This sentence seems to have embraced only five of the conspirators, Lentulus, Cethegus, Gabinius, and Statilius, whose letters had been found on the Allobroges ambassadors, and also Cæparius. Cicero, as chief magistrate, lost not a moment in putting it into execution.

On the left hand facing the Forum, at the north-east extremity or corner, and on the southern face of the Capitol, are two subterranean chambers or vaults, one below the other, into which the visitor now descends by stone stairs. This is the Mamertine Prison. It was and still is a terrible place. Anciently there were no steps leading down to the lower dungeon, but the unhappy victims were let down into it through a hole in the roof, which still exists. It is difficult at first sight to make out whether these dungeons are cut out of the solid rock, or built of enormous blocks of stone in the style of Etruscan

---

[2] Sallust makes no mention of Cicero's speech. He hated him, and endeavoured to detract as much as possible from his fame.

architecture. At all events there is no doubt that they are an Etruscan work; and they are generally attributed to Ancus Martius. But others think that Servius Tullius ought to have the credit of being the builder or rather digger of this horrible gaol. Probably it was commenced by the first-named king, and finished or enlarged by the second, from whom it took the name of *Tullianum*, for it was not called the Mamertine until the middle ages, and for what reason it is difficult to say. It was in the lowest of the two dungeons that Jugurtha the Numidian king was starved to death. On being let down into its gloomy depth he cried out, either in madness or in irony, "How cold, Romans, is this bath of yours!" The small church of S. Giuseppe dei Falegnami stands above it, on the ground which in the lapse of ages has been heaped up against the declivity of the hill. But formerly stairs called Gæmoniæ used to lead up to the mouth of the prison, from which criminals were thrown and killed.[3]

The house in which Lentulus was confined stood on the Palatine hill, opposite to the Temple of Concord, and thither Cicero went (Plutarch says with the Senate) attended by a guard. He took him from the custody of his relative Lentulus Spinther, and returned along the Via Sacra through the crowded Forum nearly to the foot of the Capitol, when turning off to the right he crossed over to the Mamertine prison, and there delivered him to the gaoler. The other four condemned conspirators were brought by the prætors to the same place,[4] and all were

---

[3] According to Roman Catholic tradition St. Peter was confined in the lower dungeon in the reign of Nero. The story is that the apostle here converted the gaoler and several of his fellow-prisoners, and that in order to obtain water to baptize them he created a miraculous spring in the floor of the vault. Whatever may be thought of the legend, the spring —and its water is delicious—still exists.

[4] Plutarch says that each of the conspirators was brought separately

strangled in the gloomy vaults. Cicero waited until the executions were over, and then turning to the multitude who stood in awe-struck silence below, he announced the doom of the traitors by crying out in a loud voice "*Vixerunt!*" "for so," says Plutarch, "the Romans, to avoid inauspicious language, name those that are dead."

He descended into the Forum, and returned to his own house. The people thronged round him with acclaiming shouts, and it was perhaps then that Cato, as we are told by Appian, hailed him father of his country. "A bright light," says Plutarch, "shone through the streets from the lamps and torches set up at the doors, and the women showed lights from the tops of the houses in honor of Cicero, and to behold him returning with a splendid train of the principal citizens."

He always looked back to this as the proudest moment of his life, and yet it was the beginning of infinite sorrow and trouble to him, for, as we shall see, his exile from Rome and the ruin of his fortunes may be distinctly traced to his conduct on this day. He had put to death Roman citizens without a trial ; and this was the accusation which was henceforth to be the watchword of his enemies, and to overshadow the rest of his life.

It cannot, I think, be doubted that the Senate in decreeing instant death as the punishment of the conspirators made a great mistake. When the National Convention of France in 1793 voted for the death of Louis XVI., he had already been tried and convicted (however infamous the trial was), and the only question left was the nature of the sentence. Lentulus and his associates had not been tried at all. The Senate was not a judicial tribunal, and had no power given it by the constitution to inflict the penalty of

by Cicero to the prison, but this is not very likely ; and another account assigns that duty to the praetors, as stated in the text.

death. This was the sole prerogative of the sovereign people, and was expressly provided for by law.

I cannot, therefore, understand how Niebuhr is justified in saying, as he does, "There is no question that the conspirators were lost according to the Roman law, and the only thing required to make their execution legal was to prove the identity of their signatures."[5] It is true, indeed, that the consuls had been invested with supreme authority—and, perhaps, this gave them the absolute power of life and death—but we must remember that by referring the question to the Senate, they in fact abdicated the power, and threw upon that body the responsibility of the decision.[6]

Let us now turn to Catiline. On quitting the city he joined Manlius in Etruria, and when he heard of the arrest and execution of the conspirators in Rome he prepared to march with his rebel forces, not less than twenty thousand strong, into Gaul, crossing the Apennines by the pass of Fæsulæ. But Q. Metellus Celer, who was one of the prætors this year, lay with a considerable force in the Picenian territory, not far from Rimini, and crossing rapidly to Fæsulæ, he took possession of the heights with his legions, so as to bar the passage in that direction. The command of the army that was to advance from Rome against Catiline had been entrusted to Antonius, while Cicero remained in the city. He marched into Etruria on the track of the conspirators, and Catiline was

---

[5] Hist. of Rome, V. 25.

[6] Mommsen, who depreciates Cicero in every possible way, and hardly ever speaks of him except in a tone of contempt, says (*Gesch. Rom.* bk. V. chap. 5), "the humorous feature, which is seldom wanting in an historical tragedy, was that this act of the most brutal tyranny should be consummated by the least self-possessed and most timid of all Roman statesmen, and that 'the first democratic consul' was raised to that post to destroy the palladium of old Roman freedom—the right of appeal to the people."

thus placed between two fires. Metellus closed the avenue of escape to the north by Fæsulæ, and Antonius was coming up from the south. On his right lay the Apennines, and in that direction, towards the east, there could be no hope of safety. He therefore turned to the left, and marching along the north side of the broad valley of the Arno, made for Pistoria (the modern Pistoia), intending to force his way to the west across the Apennines, whose wooded ranges rise above the town, and so escape with his companions into Gaul. But the Roman legions came up with the rebels at the foot of the ascent, close to Pistoria, and he was compelled to stand at bay. Antonius, who no doubt did not like the idea of destroying the man who had been formerly his friend, and was his colleague in the contest for the consulship, had just then a convenient fit of the gout, and gave up the command to his lieutenant Petreius, a brave and veteran officer. A desperate struggle ensued, in which Catiline and his followers fought like lions, but were defeated with terrible slaughter on both sides. When Catiline saw that the day was lost he rushed into the thickest of the enemy, and fell covered with wounds. His body was afterwards found far ahead of his own soldiers in the midst of a heap of slain. He still breathed, and his countenance wore in his dying moments the same stern and fierce expression which was habitual to him. He was probably buried where he lay ; at all events no man knoweth the tomb of Catiline to this day.[7]

It is a striking proof of the elastic energy of Cicero's mind that, at the very moment of the explosion of the conspiracy, and in the midst of the most awful danger, he was able to deliver in defence of one of his friends a

[7] When I was at Pistoia I saw a street there which bears the name of *Tomba di Catilina.*

speech distinguished chiefly by its light wit and good-humoured raillery. I allude to his speech *pro Murenâ*, the tone of which Niebuhr tries to explain by a curious and rather fanciful theory. He says,[8] " It is very pleasing to read Cicero's oration for Murena, and to see the quiet inward satisfaction after his consulship in which he was happy for a time. This speech has never yet been fully understood, and no one has recognised in it the happy state of mind which Cicero enjoyed at the time. If a man has taken a part in the great events of the world, he looks upon things which are little as very little ; and he cannot conceive that people to whom their little is their All and their Everything should feel offended at a natural expression of his sentiments. I have myself experienced this during the great commotions which I have witnessed. Thus it has happened that the sentiments expressed in the speech for Murena have for centuries been looked upon as trifling, and even at the present day they are not understood. The stoic philosophy and the jurisprudence, of which Cicero speaks so highly on other occasions, are here treated of as ridiculous ; but all this is only the innocent expression of his cheerful state of mind." But the historian forgot that the speech was delivered before the end of Cicero's consulship, and in the very crisis of the conspiracy. Catiline had just quitted Rome, and his associates were, as Cicero well knew, left behind in the city to carry out their infamous scheme.[9]

The circumstances of the case were these. Lucius Murena and Decimus Silanus had this year, after a severe contest, been elected consuls for the ensuing year. One of the competitors was Servius Sulpicius, the well-known lawyer, who immediately after his defeat accused Murena of having employed bribery and corruption to carry his

---

[8] Hist. of Rome, V. 29.   [9] See *pro Murenâ*, c. 37.

election. This had been made illegal by the Calpurnian law, which punished the offence by disqualifying for public office the party who was guilty of it; but during this very year Cicero was, as we have seen, himself the author of a law which inflicted the additional punishment of exile for ten years. The prosecution was conducted by Servius Sulpicius, assisted by three *subscriptores*, as they were called, who " were with him in the case "—M. Cato, Cn. Postumius, and a son of Sulpicius. On the other side for the defence were, Hortensius, Crassus, and Cicero, three of the most brilliant advocates of Rome.

We must call to mind the circumstances of the time, and the position and character of the parties at the trial, in order to appreciate the admirable speech which Cicero delivered on this occasion. The copy which we possess is, unfortunately, imperfect, but enough has been left to justify the praise of Manutius, who calls it *jucunda in primis oratio.*

The trial took place early in December, and in the following month the new consuls would enter upon their office. Sulpicius, the defeated candidate, was a lawyer; Murena, the successful one, a soldier; Cato, who took part in the prosecution, had recently been elected one of the tribunes of the commons, and he was a follower of the cold and stern philosophy of the Stoics. Cicero spoke last, after the charge against his client had been investigated and repelled by Hortensius and Crassus, and the following is a brief outline of his argument.

The plan of attack had been, first to throw aspersions upon Murena's character; next to contrast his claims to the honor of the consulship with those of his opponent; and, lastly, to establish the charges of bribery. Cicero, therefore, followed the same order, and, in a brief review of his client's life, showed that he had honorably won laurels in the campaign against Mithridates, and contributed some spoils of the enemy to his own father's triumph. But Cato pretended that he was corrupted by the effeminate manners of the East, and said that Murena was "a dancer!" "Nay, but, Cato," said Cicero, "a man of your authority ought not to pick up names in the street, nor use the scurrilous language of buffoons. You ought not lightly to call the consul of the Roman people a dancer; but consider what other faults such a character must have, to whom that epithet can be justly applied." Adverting to the personal qualifications of the two candidates, he playfully rallied Sulpicius upon his profession as a lawyer, and contrasted its obscure drudgery with the dashing exploits of Murena as lieutenant of Lucullus in Asia Minor. He seized the opportunity of pointing out the superiority of eloquence over case-law, and showed how often legal opinions and decisions are upset by a clever speech from an advocate; adding, with affected modesty, "I would say less in its praise if I were a proficient in the art: as it is, I speak not of myself, but of those who are or have been eminent orators." He then alluded to other reasons which accounted for the greater popularity of his client, his good fortune in having obtained as prætor the office of administering civil justice; whereas his rival had to discharge the odious duty of conducting criminal enquiries against those who embezzled the public money. Besides this, Sulpicius seems to have made up his mind from the first that he must be defeated in the contest; and while engaged in his canvass to have determined upon the prosecution of his competitor.

"But this is not the way," cried Cicero, " to succeed. I like a candidate for office—especially such an office as the consulship—to go forth to the Forum and the Campus Martius full of hope, and spirit, and resources. I disapprove of the getting up of a case against an opponent —the sure herald of defeat. I like not solicitude about evidence rather than about votes; threats rather than flattery; virtuous indignation rather than courteous salutations; especially since the fashion now is for the electors generally to call upon the candidates at their houses and judge by the countenance of each how far he feels confident, and what are his chances of success. 'Do you see,' says one, 'him there with the downcast and gloomy look? He is dispirited : he has lost all heart and thrown up the cards.' Then this rumour begins to be whispered about :—' Are you aware that so and so meditates a prosecution, is getting up a case, and looking out for evidence against his rivals? I'll vote for some one else, since he shows the white feather, and despairs of success.' The most intimate friends of candidates of this kind are disheartened and lose all zeal, and either abandon a cause which seems as good as lost, or reserve their support and interest for the subsequent trial which is to take place."

In dealing with the speech of Cato he artfully warned the court against the danger of being overawed by that illustrious name, and quoted examples to show that in former times the overweening power of the accusers had proved the safety of the accused. He next attacked the Stoic philosophy, upon which he threw the blame of Cato's severity ; and this is, perhaps, the cleverest part of the speech. In some portions we might almost fancy we were reading the defence, amongst ourselves, of a member of parliament, whose seat was contested before an election committee of the House of Commons, on a petition containing allegations of bribery and treating.

Cato, as a disciple of that rigid school which held all offences to be equally criminal, and regarded the man who unnecessarily twisted a cock's neck as equally guilty with one who strangled his own father, had professed to be shocked at the idea that Murena had employed solicitation and the usual electioneering arts in his canvass. Crowds had gone out to meet him on his return to Rome, while he was a candidate for the consulship—

"Well," said Cicero, "there was nothing extraordinary in this. The wonder would have been if they had stayed away. 'But a band of partisans followed him in procession through the streets.' What then? Prove that they were bribed to do it, and I admit that it was an offence. Without this, what have you to find fault with? 'What need is there,' he asks,

' of processions?' **Do** you ask me what need there is of that which has always **been a** custom amongst us? The lower classes have only this one opportunity of our election contests for earning gratitude or conferring obligation. Do not, therefore, deprive them, Cato, of the power to do **us** this **service.** Allow those **who** hope for everything from us to have **something** which they can give **us** in return. They cannot plead for us in the courts, or give **bail** for us, or invite us to their **houses.** All this **they** ask at our hands; **and they** think that these **benefits** cannot be repaid by them **in any other** way than by displaying their **zeal as** partisans. ' **But shows were** publicly exhibited, and dinner-invitations were promiscuously **given.'** Now although **in fact this was not** done by Murena **at all, but only by** his friends according to usual **custom;** yet I **cannot help recollecting how** many votes we lost owing **to inquiries** which these things occasioned in the senate.

"Cato, **however, joins issue** with me like a stern and Stoic philosopher. He denies the **proposition** that it is right that good-will should **be conciliated by good dinners. He** denies that in the choice of magistrates the **judgment should be** seduced by pleasure. Therefore, if any candidate, with a view to his return, **invites** an elector **to supper, he** shall be condemned as a **violator of the law.** ' Would **you, forsooth,'** says he, ' aim **at power and office, and aspire to** guide **the helm** of the state by fostering **the sensual appetites of** men, and corrupting their minds? Are you asking for **some vicious indulgence from a** band of effeminate youths, or **the empire of the world from the Roman** people?' This is a solemn way **of putting it** indeed, **but** such language **is opposed** to our habits and **customs, and to the very** constitution itself."

As he approached the close of his oration Cicero adopted a more serious tone. He eloquently described the dangers which threatened the commonwealth from the attacks of Catiline, and appealed to the compassion of the jury to save his client from the ruin with which an adverse verdict would overwhelm him. Murena was acquitted, and Cato good-humouredly remarked, " See what a witty consul we have ! " [1]

Besides the law affixing new penalties to bribery, of which he was the author, Cicero got another measure passed this year which was directed against the abuse of what were called *liberæ legationes.* When a senator

---

[1] Cicero says (*de Fin.* IV. 27) that he **had** laughed at the Stoic philosophy in his speech *pro Murenâ*, as he **was then** addressing the vulgar, and wished to amuse the crowd. "Apud imperitos tum illa dicta sunt : aliquid etiam coronæ datum."

wished to travel in Italy or the provinces on private business he used to apply for, and generally obtain from the senate, a commission which entitled him to assume the privileges of an ambassador. The name given to this was *libera legatio*, and it was burdensome and oppressive to the inhabitants of the towns through which he passed, or in which he stayed; for he could claim at their expense provender for his horses and entertainment for himself and his retinue. And the period seems to have been of indefinite duration, for the reform introduced by Cicero merely limited it to a single year.

The end of his consulship had arrived, and on the last day, the 31st of December, he intended, according to the usual custom, to address the people from the Rostra on laying down his office. But he had soon a foretaste of the troubles that awaited him. One of the newly-elected tribunes, Q. Cæcilius Metellus Nepos, who had entered upon office on the 10th of December, interposed his veto, on the ground that a man who had condemned Roman citizens to death without a trial, or allowing them to speak in their own defence, ought not to be allowed himself to speak to the people. Cicero says that no such insult was ever offered to a magistrate before. According to Plutarch, Metellus acted in concert with Julius Cæsar, who had just been elected one of the prætors, with Cicero's brother Quintus as his colleague. But he turned the interruption to good account. No harangue that he could have delivered would have served his purpose better than the few simple words he uttered when forbidden by the tribune to speak. Taking advantage of the moment when the usual oath at the close of a magisterial office was administered to him, he raised his voice, and in a tone loud enough to be heard by the multitude, he swore that in his consulship he had saved the Republic from destruc-

tion. The people, with applauding shouts, cried out,
"You have spoken true!"[2] It was a noble tribute of
spontaneous gratitude to the retiring consul, and one to
which, in after life, he often referred with feelings of par-
donable exultation.

[2] Dio Cassius, XXXVII. 38, says that the people would not suffer
Cicero to make a speech. This is simply false, and need be mentioned
only as one instance out of many of Dio's malignant attempts to injure
his memory.

CHAPTER IX.

VIR CONSULARIS.

Æt. 45.   B.C. 62.

CICERO was now a Consular—*Vir Consularis.* He had
filled the highest dignity which it was in the power of
the Republic to bestow, and henceforth he must live in Rome
as a private senator. He was indeed entitled to the
government of a province, but this, as we have seen, he
had at the outset of his consulship declared he would not
accept. He resigned Macedonia to his colleague Antonius,
who proved to be a most oppressive and extortionate governor, and he contrived to get the other province of Cisalpine Gaul, which had fallen to the lot of Antonius, handed
over to Metellus Celer, who, as prætor, did good service
against Catiline, by preventing his escape in the direction of Fæsulæ.

This Metellus was the brother of Metellus Nepos the
tribune, who had interposed to prevent Cicero from addressing the people on laying down his consulship. Nepos
had quitted Pompey in Asia Minor, where he was serving
under that general and devoted to his interests, in order to
hurry to Rome and become a candidate for the tribuneship.
He was elected, but the senatorial or conservative party
exerted itself successfully to get Marcus Porcius Cato
chosen as his colleague for the purpose of counteracting
any mischief he might have in view, and the two were
installed in office as wild and tame elephants are yoked
together in the East. The tribune made no secret of

his hostility to Cicero, who, anxious to keep on good
terms with him both for the sake of his own safety and
out of regard for Nepos's brother Metellus Celer, tried
to get Claudia, Celer's wife, and Mucia, who was Pompey's
wife and sister of the two Metelli, to persuade him to
behave more amicably, and give up the design of attacking him. But this was in vain. Before he interfered on
the last day of the year to prevent Cicero from addressing
the people, he had at a public meeting declared his intention to do so, and he lost no opportunity of flinging the
charge against Cicero that he had violated the constitution
by condemning Roman citizens to death without a trial.
The point he made was that the man who had punished
others without allowing them to speak, ought not to be
permitted to speak himself. " Thus," says Cicero in one
of his letters, " putting on a par and deeming worthy of
the same sentence of punishment those whom the Senate
had condemned as guilty of a conspiracy to burn down the
city, put the senators and magistrates to the sword, and
light up the flames of civil war, and the man who had
prevented the senate-house being turned into a shambles,—
who had saved Rome from conflagration and Italy from war."

On the first of January of the new year (B.C. 62), Cicero
rose in the Senate and made a speech directed against
Metellus, letting him know that he was on his guard and
would not allow himself to be attacked with impunity.
Two days afterwards Metellus spoke, and openly threatened Cicero, addressing him by name, and making use of
very violent language. This called up Cicero, who delivered a speech full of biting invective and sarcasm, which
seems to have produced considerable effect. It is unfortunately lost, but it is that *Oratio Metellina* to which he
refers in one of his letters to Atticus, where he says that
he will send him a copy of it with some additions.

Metellus Celer, who was then governor of Cisalpine Gaul, heard of this, or most probably read a copy of the speech, and he wrote to Cicero to complain of the attack he had made upon his brother, declaring that although he commanded a province, was at the head of an army, and had the conduct of a campaign, he felt grieved and humiliated. The reply of Cicero to this letter is a masterpiece of composition, and a model of what such an answer should be to an irritated friend.

The tribune's next move was made no doubt in concert with Pompey, with whom he kept up intelligence; and it was perhaps the chief object he had in view when he returned to Rome and stood for the tribuneship. He brought forward a bill in the Senate enacting that Pompey should be recalled from Asia Minor at the head of his army in order to restore the violated constitution. This effected a double purpose. It gratified Pompey and aimed a blow at Cicero, for by violation of the constitution Metellus meant the measures taken by him in his consulship. It is not certain whether Cicero spoke on this occasion, but the probability is that he did not, for he nowhere alludes to such a speech, and seems rather to imply the contrary.

The Senate, however, was strongly opposed to the bill. Cato spoke against it, and a sharp altercation took place between the two tribunes. The bill was rejected in the Senate, but Metellus, insisting on his right as tribune to bring it before the people without the preliminary sanction (*Senatus auctoritas*), convoked a meeting for the purpose. He relied not only on the influence of Pompey's name, but also on the support of Cæsar, who was then prætor, and who, strange to say, was in favour of a measure, the immediate effect of which, if carried, would be to make Pompey dictator and master of Rome.

On the morning of the appointed day Metellus filled the

Forum with his supporters, and blocked up the avenue
with an armed rabble to prevent the opponents of his bill
from interfering. Cato, however, accompanied by another
tribune, Minucius Thermus, and a few friends, with difficulty made his way to the tribune's seat, which he found
occupied by Metellus and Cæsar, who thus openly abetted
Metellus in his violence. Cato forced himself between
them, and when the clerk or officer put the usual question
to the meeting whether they accepted or rejected the
bill, he interposed his veto and forbade the matter to
proceed further. But Metellus was determined not to be
thus baffled. He took the bill out of the hands of the
officer and began to read it aloud; but Cato snatched it
away from him, and when he began to repeat it from memory Thermus put his hand over his mouth to prevent
him. During this indecent scene the crowd below had
remained quiet and no doubt astonished, but on a signal
from Metellus, his hangers-on made an attack upon the
opposite party, who, notwithstanding the precautions taken
to exclude them, had forced their way into the Forum,
and the wildest uproar immediately ensued. The Senate
was at the moment sitting in the neighbouring Temple of
Concord, and to quell the riot they hastily invested the
consuls with summary authority by the usual formula,
Videant Consules ne quid detrimenti Respublica capiat,
which gave them for the moment despotic and absolute
power, and had the same kind of effect that a proclamation
of martial law would have with us. Murena, one of the
consuls, took instantly a body of soldiers to the Forum
and restored order, arriving just in time to rescue Cato
and Thermus from the hands of the mob. Metellus made
another effort to get his bill carried at the same meeting,
but the opposition was too strong, and he and Cæsar
withdrew from the place.

He lost no opportunity, however, of denouncing Cicero to the populace, and harped constantly on the string that he had condemned Roman citizens to death without a trial.

At last he quitted Rome and went back to Pompey, pretending that he required his protection, and that the sacred office of tribune could not shield him from the attacks of his enemies. And I am much mistaken if we do not find in the facts that have just been related, a key to the explanation of much of Pompey's conduct when he returned to Rome.

It has been already mentioned that he was by the Gabinian law (Lex Gabinia) invested with the command of the army of the East, with full power to carry on the war against Mithridates, and that he conducted it with brilliant success. The last decisive battle was fought during Cicero's consulship, and Pompey sent an account of his victories to the Senate in a public despatch, which was most probably encircled with laurel leaves (*literæ laureatæ*), according to the Roman custom. At the same time he wrote to Cicero, but in a formal and indifferent tone; at all events Cicero thought so. Possibly Pompey was too much occupied with his own achievements to pay much attention to what was passing at Rome. Cicero, however, felt hurt, and in his letter in reply did not scruple to say so, alluding to his own services to the State in a way which, according to modern notions, would be thought to be in rather bad taste.[1] He told Pompey that he had expected from him a more explicit acknowledgment of them, and said he wrote openly on the subject as his own natural disposition and their common friendship required.

---

[1] It must, however, be remembered that an acknowledgement of his services from a man in Pompey's position would have been invaluable to Cicero, and he had a right to expect it.

He hinted that the warmth of his own regard was not reciprocated, and expressed a hope and belief that their friendship would be like that which existed between Scipio Africanus, to whom he says Pompey was far superior, and Lælius, to whom he himself was not much inferior. Pompey was ungenerous enough to take offence at this letter. He was inflated with the success of his arms, and thought it almost an insult that Cicero should speak of his own civic glory in the same breath that he mentioned the exploits of the conqueror of Mithridates.

We now turn to matters of more private interest. When Sylla's proscription had driven numbers of families from Rome, and silence and desolation reigned in their former abodes, Crassus had become the purchaser, or at all events the possessor, of many of the houses that were hastily abandoned by their former inmates. One of these was a noble residence on the Palatine hill, overlooking the Forum, which had been originally built by the tribune M. Livius Drusus, who was assassinated B.C. 91. It joined a portico which had been erected by Q. Catulus out of the spoils taken from the Cimbri in that decisive battle when he and Marius destroyed their army, and it occupied the site of a house which had belonged to M. Flaccus, put to death by order of the Senate for sedition, and which had been razed to the ground.[2] Cicero now bought this house from Crassus for the sum of three and a half millions of sesterces (about 30,000l.) and he was obliged to borrow money at interest to pay for his purchase. He says jokingly in one

[2] The architect told Drusus that he would build the house so that no one should overlook him and see what he was doing. "Nay," he replied, "if you have skill enough, build it so that all the world may see what I am doing."—Vell. Pater. II. 14. Lepidus, who was consul in the year of Sylla's death, erected the most splendid mansion that had up to that time been seen in Rome; but within thirty-five years afterwards it was eclipsed by the superior grandeur of at least an hundred dwellings. Plin. Hist. Nat. XXXV. 24.

of his letters that he was so much in debt that he was
ready to become a conspirator if he could be taken into a
plot, but he found he was too much distrusted to be admitted an accomplice.   Niebuhr thought that he had discovered the site of Cicero's house on the Palatine, "that
is to say," he observes, "I know the place within about
fifty feet where the house must have stood, and I have
often visited the spot."[3]   The vast ruins which astonish
the gaze of the traveller on the south-east side of the
Palatine belong to a later period.   They are the gigantic
substructions of Nero's golden palace, a wilderness of
masonry, in which it is impossible to trace the chambers
or decipher the plan.

> Cypress and ivy, weed and wallflower grown
> Matted and massed together, hillocks heaped
> On what were chambers, arch crushed, column strown
> In fragments, choked up vaults, and frescoes steeped
> In subterraneous damps, where the owl peep'd,
> Deeming it midnight : Temples, baths, or halls?
> Pronounce who can.[4]

A scandalous report about this time disturbed Cicero's
equanimity.   His former colleague Antonius had, as we
have seen, got as his provincial government Macedonia,
and he continued there the malpractices which had formerly made him infamous when, as prætorian governor of
Achaia, he had been guilty of oppression and extortion.
On the present occasion a trial was impending over him
for his conduct in Macedonia, and it was expected that
Cicero would defend him.   But it appears that Antonius
had implicated Cicero in the matter, and while plundering
the province had given out that he was to have a share of
the spoil.   Nay, more, he had declared that a freedman of
Cicero, named Hilarus, who was in the employ of Antonius,

---

[3] Hist. of Rome, V. 41.   [4] Childe Harold, canto 4.

and a great rascal, had been sent by Cicero into Macedonia
to take care of the money to be squeezed out of the province. This rumor naturally caused much annoyance to
Cicero, and we find him complaining of it in a letter to
Atticus in terms of indignation. I do not believe that any
such corrupt bargain existed between them. It is utterly
inconsistent with Cicero's whole character, and ought not
to be believed without strong proof, of which there is none.
The tone in which he speaks of the rumor to Atticus
shows that he was innocent, and I do not doubt that if it
was true he would have said so in confidence to his intimate friend, from whom he really seems to have concealed
nothing. Besides he alludes to it in a letter to Antonius
himself, in a way inconsistent with the idea of guilt.[5] But
at the same time I agree with Wieland and Abeken that
there is evidence, although obscure, of the existence of
some pecuniary transaction between Antonius and Cicero,
and that Antonius owed him money, which he was very
dilatory in paying.[6] As to the origin and nature of this
debt we know nothing whatever, and it is both unfair and
uncharitable to attribute it to so corrupt a cause as a bargain for a share in the plunder of a province which he had
voluntarily resigned to Antonius. It must, however, be
admitted that his conduct was inconsistent with regard to
this man. An impeachment was hanging over his head,
and, in a letter to Sextius, Cicero says that he had defended
him in the Senate, *gravissime ac diligentissime*, although
everybody felt that Antonius had not behaved towards him
as he ought. But, writing to Atticus, he told him that he
was informed that Pompey was determined on his return
to Rome to get Antonius superseded in his government,

[5] Ad Div. V. 5.

[6] Ad Att. I. 12. This depends] upon the assumption that the name
Teucris, which occurs in several of Cicero's letters to Atticus, means Antonius. I believe that it does.

and he declared that the case was so bad that he could not
in honor nor without loss of credit defend him. Moreover, he said he had no inclination to do so, on account of
the calumnious rumours he had set afloat respecting
himself.[7]

Although Catiline and most of his accomplices were
dead, the ramifications of the wide-spread conspiracy still
remained to be disclosed. Cæsar himself was not free
from the suspicion of having been privy to the plot.
Lucius Vettius accused him before the quæstor Novius
Niger, and Q. Curius impeached him in the Senate, claiming the reward which had been offered to the first disco-
verer of the conspiracy. Vettius avowed himself ready to
produce the most damning evidence of his guilt—a letter
written to Catiline by his own hand—and Curius declared
that his information was derived from Catiline himself.
Whether Cæsar was guilty or not cannot now be either
affirmed or denied with certainty, at all events he was too
crafty or too powerful to be caught. He appealed to
Cicero in the Senate, and proved from his lips that he had
himself at an early period volunteered to give information
about the conspiracy. This was no doubt a strong presumptive proof of innocence, and so completely turned the
tables upon Curius that he was held not to be entitled to
the reward he claimed as the first informer about the plot.
As to Vettius, he was almost torn to pieces by the mob
while addressing them in the Forum, and Cæsar had him
thrown into prison. He also got the quæstor imprisoned
for allowing a superior magistrate (Cæsar was then prætor)
to be summoned before him.

---

[7] Ad Att. I. 12. If the letter to Sextius was written after the one to
Atticus, quoted in the text, that is if Cicero, notwithstanding what he
said to Atticus, did after all defend Antonius, the case would be much
worse. I have followed the order in which Schutz and Abeken place
the correspondence.

Several others of high rank were however found guilty
and banished. Amongst them was Autronius. He had
been Cicero's schoolfellow and friend in boyhood; his colleague in the quæstorship; and he now came to him, and
over and over again with tears besought him to defend
him; but Cicero refused, and appeared as a witness against
him.[8]

Next came on the trial of P. Sulla. The accusation
against him was that he had been implicated in two separate conspiracies with Catiline. Against the first of these
charges he was defended by Hortensius, and against the
other by Cicero. The prosecutor was Lucius Torquatus.
He twitted Cicero with inconsistency in appearing as
the advocate of a man who was accused of taking
part in the conspiracy which *he* had crushed with such
severity; of defending Sulla, and giving evidence against
Autronius, who was one of the conspirators. But the
answer was easy. Autronius he said was guilty, and
Sulla was innocent. Cicero admitted that there were
some crimes, such as that of treason, or, as he called it,
parricide against one's country, of which a man might be
so notoriously guilty that no advocate would be bound or
ought to defend him. But he denied that there was a
tittle of evidence affecting Sulla. Apparently all that
Torquatus relied upon was a statement by the Allobroges
ambassadors that they had asked Cassius when he was
trying to engage them in the plot what Sulla thought
of it, and he answered "I don't know." Torquatus
argued that this was a proof of guilt, for Cassius did not
exculpate him! Of course Cicero had no difficulty in
dealing with logic like this. He said that the question in

---

[8] Two years afterwards, during the consulship of Julius Cæsar and
Bibulus (B.C. 59), Autronius was put upon his trial, and Cicero did then
defend him, but without success.

a criminal trial was not whether the accused was excul-
pated, but whether the charge was proved. He showed
also that during the progress of the conspiracy Sulla was
not at Rome but at Naples, thus establishing what we
should call an *alibi;* and he declared that during his
consulship he had never discovered, nor suspected, nor
heard anything that compromised or affected him.

In the course of his speech he defended himself against
a personal attack of Torquatus, who had the hardihood to
charge him with having falsified the public records and
altered the evidence given in the Senate by the informers.
It shows how low was the tone of morality at Rome when
so monstrous an accusation was possible; and the sur-
prising thing is that Cicero does not seem to have mani-
fested anything like the indignation at the charge which
we should have expected. I need not say that he triumphantly vindicated himself, although one would have
thought that no vindication was required.

The rest of the speech consisted chiefly in an appeal to
the past life of his client as evidence of his innocence.
Surely he had had misfortune enough in having the consulship to which he had been elected torn from him, when
all his hopes were dashed to the ground, and his joy was
changed to mourning and tears. But his own sorrow at
the thought of Sulla's misfortunes he declared overpowered
him, and he would say no more. He left therefore the
case in the hands of the jury, with an earnest hope that
they would, like him, show compassion on innocence as
they had shown severity towards guilt, and by their verdict
that day relieve both himself and them from the false
charge of cruelty.

Chapter X.

MYSTERIES OF THE BONA DEA AND TRIAL OF CLODIUS.

Æt. 44–45.   B.C. 62-61.

GREAT as had been Cicero's popularity, and glorious his triumph over the enemies of the state, it was not to be expected that such measures could be taken, and such a conspiracy be crushed, without creating bitter enemies against himself. The ramifications of the plot were so extensive, and the social and moral condition of Rome was so corrupt, that numbers of the young men connected with the aristocracy, against whom there was no positive proof, were accomplices in the design; or, if not, were at all events disappointed that Catiline had failed. And of course they looked upon Cicero as the sole cause of his failure, and hated him accordingly. But it was not from disappointed conspirators or jealous rivals that the storm which shattered his fortunes arose. The blow came from a different and unexpected quarter, and it was on this wise it happened.

Amongst the numerous rites and solemn festivals of religion at Rome, there was one of a peculiarly sacred and mysterious character in which women alone took part, and which had never been profaned by the eye of the other sex. This was the service in honor of the Bona Dea— the goddess who gave fruitfulness in marriage—which was celebrated on the first of May, at the house of the first consul or the first prætor, and at which prayers were offered up for the safety of the whole Roman people (*pro salute populi Romani*).   No lodge of freemasons ever excluded the presence of women more carefully from its ceremonies than the votaries of the Bona Dea excluded the presence of men.   Not even a sign or token of their existence was allowed to be seen.   Statues were covered up, and pictures were veiled which exhibited the form of the male sex; and it was sacrilege of the worst kind in a man to venture to cross the threshold while the rites were going on.

We may imagine therefore the consternation of the Roman citizens in the beginning of May B.C. 62, when the rumour ran like lightning through the streets that a man had been discovered disguised as a woman in the house of Cæsar the prætor, during the celebration there of the mysteries of the Bona Dea.   It was too true.   One of the most profligate young patricians of that profligate age, Publius Clodius Pulcher, had introduced himself dressed in woman's clothes into the house at night, and had dared to profane the sacred ceremonies by his presence.   He contrived to escape by the help of a maid-servant from the infuriated matrons,[1] and as his face was muffled up he hoped that his identity would not be known.

Scandal declared that his object was to carry on an intrigue with Pompeia, Cæsar's wife, but this is almost incredible.   No time or place can be conceived less favorable for such a purpose, and Clodius must have been mad to choose the mysteries of the Bona Dea as an opportunity for a love affair.   No doubt he sought only to gratify

---

[1] According to one account Aurelia, the mother of Cæsar, permitted him to escape. *Aurelia pro testimonio dixit suo jussu eum esse dimissum.* Schol. Bobiens. *in Orat. in Clod.* If so, it was probably with a view to hush the matter up and prevent scandal.

a prurient curiosity, and his past life and character were
in unison with the exploit. He had already seduced his
own sister Clodia;[2] his intrigue with Mucia, Pompey's
wife, was the cause of her divorce from her husband; and
he was notorious for every kind of debauchery and vice.
Graceful in person, eloquent in speech, and nearly related
to many of the first families in Rome, he had already made
himself infamous by his immoralities. He was a younger
son of Appius Claudius, and a direct descendant of that
Appius Claudius the decemvir, who gained such a bad
notoriety in the case of Virginia, whose father stabbed her
to death in the Forum to save her from dishonor. His
elder brother, whom Niebuhr calls "a good-natured but
superstitious and little-minded person," had obtained the
highest honors in the Republic; and he had three sisters,
one, the infamous Clodia or Quadrantaria,[3] that is, "Halfpenny," as she was nicknamed, married to Metellus Celer,
another to Marcus Rex, and the third to Lucullus. He
belonged in fact to one of the highest patrician families
at Rome, and no doubt presumed upon its wealth and
influence to screen him from the consequences of his
crimes.

The matter seems to have been for a time hushed up,
and probably Clodius thought that no further inquiry
would be made, as the year passed away without any steps
being taken. But early in January, at the commencement
of the new year, B.C. 61, Q. Cornificius, who was then

---

[2] Mr. Merivale (*Hist. Rom.* I. 167) says "the odious charge that he
had lived in incest with his sisters can only be regarded as a current tale
of scandal, the truth of which it would be preposterous to assume." I
fear it is neither preposterous nor incredible. It was at all events firmly
believed at Rome.

[3] The *quadrans* was a small coin at Rome about the value of a farthing,
and was the price of a public bath. Clodia used to frequent these baths
as if she were one of the "labouring classes," and hence the nickname.

Princeps Senatus, brought the question before the Senate.
By them it was referred, as a matter affecting religion, to
the College of Pontiffs, who declared it to be an act of
sacrilege.   Upon this the Senate resolved that the consuls
should propose a bill in an assembly of the people to bring
Clodius to justice, and to authorise a departure from the
ordinary form of trial.   The bill enacted that instead of
the *judices* or jurymen being chosen by lot, which would
give Clodius a chance of escape, as the jury might happen
to be composed of men easily accessible to a bribe, the
prætor should select a certain number of jurymen for
whose character he would of course be responsible.   This
led to violent opposition.

In the mean time, after five years' absence from Italy,—
five years of unparalleled military renown—Pompey had
just landed at Brundusium, with the main body of his
army which he had so often led to victory.   If he had
possessed the ambition and the boldness to make himself
Dictator of Rome, he might have marched upon the capital ;
and in the state of parties at the time he would have
probably succeeded almost without a struggle.   So general
was the opinion that such was his design, that, according
to Plutarch, Crassus withdrew himself with his children
and property from the city, which he believed, or affected
to believe, was about to throw open its gates to the conqueror, and receive him as its master.   But Pompey
adopted a course which surprised everybody.   He dismissed his soldiers to their homes, and attended only by a
small escort travelled towards Rome with hardly more
state than if he had been a private gentleman.   When he
reached the walls he stopped, for as he claimed a triumph
he could not enter the city.   Outside the gates he addressed the people in a speech which Cicero, who probably
heard it, described as distasteful to the poor, spiritless to

the wicked, unpleasing to the rich, and trifling to the good.   It therefore fell flat upon the audience.[4]

Piso the consul then suggested to Fufius, a tribune, and a man whom Cicero calls *levissimus*, that he should introduce Pompey to the people in the Circus Flaminius, where, it being market day, there was a considerable crowd, and ask him publicly his opinion whether the prætor should choose the jurymen for the trial of Clodius, as the Senate had proposed by the bill.   Pompey, however, evaded a direct reply.   He, as he always did, tried to trim between the contending parties.   He did not like to oppose the Senate; but he was also afraid of offending the mob, amongst whom he knew that Clodius was popular and had many active partisans.   He therefore spoke, as Cicero calls it, very "aristocratically," praising the Senate in general terms, and professing his respect for its authority; but he took care not to commit himself to any distinct opinion on the question that had been put to him.

Soon afterwards, when his demand for a triumph had been granted, Pompey entered Rome; and, when he took his seat in the Senate, the consul Messala asked him what he thought of the alleged sacrilege and the bill then before the people.   He rose and made the same general kind of speech as before, eulogising the Senate but avoiding a direct answer to the question.   Cicero was close beside him, and Pompey, when he sat down, told him that he thought he had made a sufficient reply.   The speech seems to have been applauded, as was natural it should be by an assembly which the great man had just flattered by his praise; and Crassus then rose.   Cicero, who never could get the merits of his own consulship out of his head, tells Atticus that Crassus saw that Pompey had been well

---

[4] Non jucunda miseris, inanis improbis, beatis non grata, bonis non gravis: itaque frigebat.—*Ad Att.* I. 14.

received, because the Senate believed that he approved of
the acts of that consulship. This we may be permitted to
doubt. Most probably Pompey was cheered because the
Senate was glad to believe that they had found in him a
champion ; and they gave credit to his professions of respect
and devotion to their order. However, Crassus rose and
delivered a most complimentary panegyric on Cicero,
praising his consulship to the skies, and declaring that he
owed it to Cicero that he was still a senator, a citizen, a
freeman ; nay, that he owed to him his life ; and as often
as he regarded his wife, his home, his country, he felt the
force of all his obligation to him.

While Crassus was speaking, Cicero, who was sitting
next to Pompey, watched him closely, and says his emotion
was visible. Perhaps, he adds, this was because Crassus
had thus seized an opportunity of showing good-will to
him while Pompey had shown indifference ; or, because
he saw how favorably the Senate listened to the praise
which Crassus had bestowed.

Cicero rose next, and it is amusing to read his own
account of his speech. He says he was determined to
show off before Pompey, who now heard him for the first
time ; and he exhausted every rhetorical artifice, as he
descanted on the well-worn theme of the Catiline conspiracy, and urged the necessity of concord between the
Senate and the knights, and the union of Italy in the common cause. " *Quid multa?* " he says, " *clamores.*" He
sat down amidst thunders of applause.

But to return to the affair of Clodius. Everything
depended on the question how the tribunal that was to
try him should be constituted. Clodius and his friends
left no stone unturned to prevent the jury from being
selected by the prætor. Of the two consuls Piso sided
with them, and did his utmost to get the bill rejected ;

but Messala on the contrary was strongly for it. Cicero confesses that he himself, who had at first been a very Lycurgus in the matter, was beginning to take a more lenient view; and yet in the same breath he avows his fears that the case of Clodius, defended as it was by the bad and neglected by the good, would be the cause of great mischief to the state. Cæsar seems to have taken no active or open part on either side; but he divorced his wife Pompeia, using according to Plutarch the memorable words, "Cæsar's wife ought to be above suspicion." The Senate, however, stood firm, so much so that Cicero calls it a very Areopagus; and it was determined that the bill should be submitted to the people, and if possible carried.

At last the day of the assembly came, and in one of the letters to Atticus we find a lively description of the scene. The voting on the question of a law took place in the same manner as when magistrates were chosen, and has been already described. Bands of youths headed by the younger Curio, whom Cicero contemptuously calls a girl (*filiola*), flocked early in the morning to the meeting to support Clodius; and went about amongst the crowd urging every one to vote against the bill. Piso himself, whose duty as consul it was to propose it, did the same. Slaves and retainers of Clodius filled the narrow passages (*pontes*) through which the voters had to pass to give their tickets. And the trick was resorted to (not unknown at elections in France at the present day) of furnishing only voting tickets in the negative marked with an A (for *Antiquo*), and none in the affirmative or *Uti Rogas*. Cato flew to the platform and attacked Piso in a well-timed speech. He was followed by Hortensius, Favonius, and others on the same side, but Cicero was silent.

The meeting broke up without coming to any decision.

The Senate was then summoned, and notwithstanding the opposition of Piso and the abject entreaties of Clodius, who threw himself at the feet of the senators, it was moved that the consuls should address the people and urge them to accept the bill.   Cicero proposed as an amendment that there should be no such resolution ; but only fifteen divided with him, while four hundred voted for the motion.

The Senate further resolved that they would transact no public business until the bill was carried.   Hortensius, however, fearing that the tribune Fufius Calenus would interpose his veto if the bill was passed by the people, and so render it a dead letter, proposed that Fufius himself should bring forward a bill declaring, like the other bill, that Clodius's offence was sacrilege, but providing that the jury should be chosen by *lot* out of the decuriæ. This was intended as a compromise, for it limited the number of persons out of whom the jury could be formed, and so diminished the chances of having a needy and corruptible set, and yet preserved at the same time the principle of fairness in not selecting the names.   But Hortensius felt so confident that Clodius must be convicted, that he was indifferent as to what kind of tribunal tried him.   His expression was that Clodius's throat would be cut by a sword of lead.   Cicero, however, was of a different opinion : he feared that the men who tried Clodius would be poor and open to a bribe, and he knew that the other side was rich and unscrupulous.   The event proved that he was right.

The proposal of Hortensius was carried, and the day of the trial at last came.   Lentulus, or according to Valerius Maximus, three of that family came forward to prosecute. Of the jury, several were challenged by the accused and rejected ; others were challenged by the prosecution amidst the wildest uproar.   The jury were fifty-six in number, and

Cicero describes them as finally empanelled. With few exceptions he says a worse set never sat round a gambling table : disreputable senators, needy knights, and insolvent tribunes.[5] The few respectable men amongst them whom Clodius had not been able to set aside by his challenges sat sorrowful and ashamed, blushing at the company in which they found themselves. At first, however, all seemed to be going well. The forms of a criminal trial were duly observed : the points as they arose were decided unanimously in favour of the prosecution with almost stern severity, and all that the prosecutor asked was granted. Hortensius chuckled at the thought of his own sagacity, and the universal opinion was that Clodius would be found guilty.

For his defence he relied upon an *alibi*. His case was that he could not have been in the house where the mysteries of the Bona Dea were going on, for at that time he was at Interamna, fifty miles distant from Rome. But Cicero came forward as a witness. Instantly there was a tremendous clamor. The whole court rose and surrounded him as if to protect him from assassination. Such a mark of respect, he says, was more honorable than Xenocrates received when his oath was dispensed with at Athens, and he gave evidence unsworn ; or Metellus (surnamed Numidicus), when on his trial the jury refused to look at his accounts when they were handed to them.[6]

---

[5] Maculosi senatores, nudi equites, tribuni, non tam ærati, quam, ut appellantur, ærarii.—*Ad Att.* I. 16. It is difficult to know the precise point of contrast here between *ærati* and *ærarii*. Several explanations have been attempted, but I believe I have given the real meaning.

[6] A somewhat parallel case once occurred in Scotland. A chest containing the muniments of title of the Maitland family in Scotland had been buried for safety during the civil war in the 17th century. On the return of more peaceful times it was taken up, but the deeds were found to be illegible from damp and decay. It happened, however, that the first Lord Lauderdale, who was the son of Baron Maitland of Thirlestane,

Such a reception struck terror into the hearts of Clodius and his friends. Cicero deposed that on the very morning in question in his own house he had an interview with Clodius. This if true was decisive, and it was unlikely that the evidence could be disbelieved. The court adjourned, and the next morning a crowd attended Cicero at his house, like that which had attended him when he laid down his consulship. The jury declared they would not meet again unless they had the protection of a guard. The question was brought before the Senate, and a guard was ordered. The magistrates were directed to see to it, and the jury were complimented on their behaviour.

But Clodius and his friends were busy in the interval, and to some purpose. The wise rule of English law which secludes a jury, when once empanelled in a criminal case, from the outer world, and isolates it from all the temptations which might beset it to swerve from the path of duty, was unknown at Rome. A gladiator slave was employed as an emissary to visit the jurymen at their houses, or send for them, and bribe them. And with what? Not merely with money, but the promise of the embraces of abandoned women, and, to use the words of Lord Macaulay in another case, "abominations as foul as those which are buried under the waters of the Dead Sea."[7]

At last came the moment of the verdict. The Forum was crowded with a rabble of slaves. The respectable citizens kept away. Twenty-five voted for a conviction,

Chancellor of Scotland, and died in 1595, had made long before a calendar or *précis* of his deeds, and so high was the opinion entertained of his integrity, that the Scotch parliament directed that this calendar should be accepted as evidence, and ordered the clerk-registrar to authenticate it accordingly. See Crawford's *Peerage of Scotland*.

[7] Noctes certarum mulierum atque adolescentulorum nobilium introductiones.—*Ad Att.* I. 16.

thirty-one for an acquittal, and Clodius was declared Not Guilty![8]

It has been supposed by some, and, indeed, is asserted by Plutarch, that Cicero's motive in coming forward as a witness against Clodius was to quiet the suspicions of his wife, Terentia, who was jealous of his attentions to Clodia, Clodius's sister, the wife of Metellus Celer. And Wieland says that it would be ridiculous to attribute Cicero's conduct to conscientious motives. But I entirely disagree with him, and also entirely disbelieve Plutarch's story. There is not a tittle of evidence in support of it, and it is belied by the whole conduct and character of Cicero. Without challenging for him a higher degree of morality than may be claimed by one of the most virtuous of the Romans in an age of disgraceful profligacy, I think we may rely on two facts to show that the insinuation against him is false. In the first place there is not a hint or trace of the faintest kind throughout the whole of his private correspondence that his wife was jealous of him, or that he ever gave her cause for jealousy. In the next, the language in which he always speaks of Clodia, giving her the nickname of βοῶπις, or "ox-eyed"—not, however, an uncomplimentary epithet, as witness Homer, who thus characterises the regal Juno—and alluding to her abandoned life in the most offensive terms, is quite inconsistent with the idea that he had loved her. And why should it be "ridiculous" to suppose that Cicero, who was conscious that a frightful scandal had been committed, shocking to all sense of decency and propriety in the Roman mind, and who knew that the defence set up by the perpetrator was a lie, should feel himself compelled, by a regard for

[8] Catulus sarcastically asked one of the jurymen afterwards, "What did you want a guard for? Were you afraid lest you should be robbed of your bribe?"

truth, and in the interest of religion, to which, amidst all
the scepticism of that age, the multitude clung, to come
forward, from conscientious motives, to bear testimony to
a fact which, perhaps, he alone could prove? Wieland
says such an assumption is contradicted by Cicero's conduct a few years later, when he defended another young
profligate, Cœlius, and certainly then showed that he took
a lenient view of youthful immorality. But the cases were
entirely different; and it is really idle to suppose that
there was any analogy between them. He was then plead-
ing as an advocate, who was bound to do the best for his
client, and it would be hard indeed to suppose that because
in such a case he extenuated the follies of youth, he was,
therefore, indifferent to vice. The result of the trial gave
rise to the darkest forebodings in Cicero's mind. He tells
Atticus that the Republic—the preservation of which his
friend attributed to his counsels, but he, Cicero, attributed
to Divine wisdom—was ruined by the verdict, if verdict it
could be called, when thirty men, the meanest and vilest
of the people, were bribed to trample under foot every
law, both human and divine. In another letter he declares that the constitution was overthrown by a verdict
purchased by bribery and lust.[9]

He preserved, however, a bold front externally, and
exposed with unsparing severity in the Senate the infamy
of the court which had acquitted Clodius. Before the
trial took place he had been roused from the apathy into
which he confesses he was in some danger of falling on
the subject, by attacks made upon him by Clodius at mob-
meetings in the Forum; and thus provoked, Cicero thundered against him, and Piso, and Curio, and the rest of
his followers in the Senate, in a way which, he tells
Atticus, he should have liked him to behold. On the 15th

[9] Emto constupratoque judicio.

of May, after the trial was over, being called on by the consul to speak, he rose, and dwelt at some length on the gravity of the crisis, and the danger which such an acquittal threatened to the state. Turning then to Clodius, who, as a senator, was present, he addressed him, and said, "Clodius, you are mistaken; the jury saved you, not for Rome, but for a prison. It was not that they wished to retain you in the state, but to deprive you of the privilege of banishment. Be then of good courage, Conscript Fathers, and preserve the dignity of your order." In this strain he proceeded for some time, and sat down. What followed? It is a curious illustration of the tone and temper of that august assembly, which we are apt to regard as the most serious conclave the world ever saw, and also of the tone of Cicero's mind, to find him the next moment engaging with Clodius in a quick fire of repartee and puns, in which each tried to make the sharpest and wittiest retort upon his adversary, while the Senate vociferously applauded. Some of the jokes are now obscure, and have lost their point, and some are not fit for explanation. As a specimen, however, of the kind of wit that so delighted the senators of Rome, I will quote one or two of the passages. "You have bought a house," said Clodius. "One would think," replied Cicero, "that you said I had bought a jury." "They did not believe you on your oath," exclaimed Clodius. "Yes," retorted Cicero, "twenty-five of the jury did believe *me*, but thirty-one did not believe *you*, for they took care to get their money beforehand." This last blow seems to have floored Clodius, for Cicero says, although he is hardly a fair reporter of his own wit, that, overpowered by the cheers that followed this sally, he became silent and crestfallen.

During the progress of the Clodian affair Cicero's vanity

had been hurt by a slight put upon him in the Senate by
the consul Piso.

The senators of consular rank had the precedence next to
the consuls in the Senate, and were first called upon to
deliver their opinions. But it was in the option of the
consuls to call upon them in such order as they thought
fit, and we can easily imagine how often personal or party
considerations influenced their choice. Since he had
ceased to be consul Cicero had enjoyed the honor of
precedence in speaking; but Piso was determined to
affront him. When, therefore, at the beginning of the
year, it became his duty, as one of the new consuls, to put
the question in the Senate, he passed over Cicero, and
called upon his own relative, C. Calpurnius Piso—who was
afterwards consul—to give his opinion first. Cicero came
next; Catulus third, and Hortensius fourth. Cicero, however, was gratified by hearing murmurs of disapproval
amongst the senators, and he consoled himself with the
reflection that, by the affront, he was relieved from the
necessity of keeping on terms with Piso, whom he paints in
no flattering colours, and that, after all, the second place in
the Senate was one of almost as much authority as the first.

It was a leading object of Cicero's policy to uphold
the dignity and authority of the equestrian order, and
secure, as far as possible, a good understanding between it and the Senate. Sometimes he went too far,
and in his anxiety to prevent a rupture and conciliate the
knights, he defended them in cases where he knew and
confessed that they were wrong. He seems to have acted
here on the dangerous principle that the end justifies the
means, and to have advocated or opposed measures, not
because they were right or wrong in themselves, but
because he feared that their rejection or adoption would
irritate the equestrian body.

After the scandalous acquittal of Clodius the Senate most properly resolved that an inquiry should take place as to the alleged corruption of the jury. The *judices* were composed of three classes:—1. Senators; 2. Knights; and 3. *Tribuni Ærarii.* Such an inquiry, therefore, was directed quite as much against the Senate as the Knights, and conveyed no imputation upon the one more than the other; yet, strange to say, the Knights took offence at the proposal, and Manutius assigns for this the extraordinary reason that they did not consider themselves within the purview of the law which made it punishable for jurymen to take bribes.[1] As if they could set up the disgraceful privilege of being entitled to violate the plainest principles of morality and justice! It happened that Cicero had not been present in the Senate when the resolution was passed appointing the inquiry, but when he observed the discontent of the equestrian class—who, however, did not venture to make any open complaint—he took the Senate to task, and blamed it severely in a set speech, exerting all the powers of his eloquence in defence of a claim which he himself characterised as indecent. It is impossible to justify this. Cicero's conviction—as that of every honest man—was, and must have been, that the Knights were flagrantly in the wrong, and no political consideration ought to have induced him to support them in such a case. In the result the tribunes interposed their veto and the inquiry was not proceeded with.

About the same time another cause of dissension between the two orders arose, owing to a caprice of the Knights, as Cicero calls it,[2] which he says he not only tolerated, but even justified and applauded.

[1] Manut. *in Orat. pro Cluentio.*
[2] Ecce aliæ deliciæ equitum vix ferendæ, quas ego non solum tuli, sed etiam ornavi.—*Ad Att.* I. 17.

The facts were these. The Knights were the farmers of
the public revenue—a kind of middlemen between the
tax-payers and the state. They entered into contracts for
the payment of certain fixed sums into the exchequer,
which they were of course bound to make good. It happened that some of them had made what turned out to be
a bad bargain, for the revenues of the province of Asia
Minor. In their avaricious eagerness, as they themselves
confessed, to get the contract, they had made too high a
tender, and they now wanted the terms of their contract
to be altered. Cicero says that the case was full of odium,
and the demand shameful, and yet he supported it. His
reason was, the danger lest, if they gained nothing, they
might be wholly alienated from the Senate. He exerted
himself to have their claim heard in a crowded house, and
there, at the beginning of December, he spoke for them on
two consecutive days. But Metellus, the consul, and Cato
opposed them, and their petition was rejected.[3] It is
worth while to notice the terms in which Cicero spoke of
these two occurrences afterwards. "What was more just
than that those should be put on their trial who had
received bribes in a case they had to try? This was
Cato's opinion, and the Senate agreed with him. The
Knights declared war on the house—not on me—for I
dissented. What was more impudent than the conduct of
the farmers of the revenue in claiming a remission of their
contract? Yet I had to throw the die in their favor for
the sake of not alienating the whole body."

Writing, however, at the end of the year which had just
closed—the year I mean in which Piso and Messala were
consuls, B.C. 61—he says, that it had seen the overthrow

[3] When Julius Cæsar was consul one of his first acts was to get the
contracts reduced to the extent of one-third. By this politic concession
he of course conciliated the good-will of the Knights.—*Dio Cass.*
XXXVIII. 7.

of two strong supports of the constitution erected by himself alone; it had witnessed the weakening of the authority of the Senate and the disruption of the union of the two orders.

In the month of September this year Pompey celebrated his third triumph; and it was such a triumph as had never before been seen in Rome. For two days the populace gazed with wonder at the trophies of his victories as the stately procession wound its slow course along the Sacred Way to the Capitol. Brazen tablets were carried on which were engraved the names of the countries he had conquered—Pontus, Armenia, Cappadocia, Paphlagonia, Media, Colchis, Iberia, Albania, Syria, Cilicia, Mesopotamia, Phœnicia, Palestine, Judæa, and Arabia. They proclaimed that he had captured one thousand fortresses and nine hundred cities, destroyed eight hundred pirate ships, and founded thirty-nine towns; that he had raised the revenue of his country from fifty millions to eighty-five millions, and that he was now pouring into the treasury the value of twenty thousand talents in the shape of money, gold and silver plate, jewels, and ornaments. A long array of prisoners of war followed the chariot of the conqueror. There were to be seen Zosime, the wife of Tigranes, king of Armenia, and his son, with his wife and daughter; Aristobulus, king of Judæa; the sister of Mithridates and her five sons, with women from Scythia, and hostages of the Iberians and Albanians, and of the king of Commagene.

It is very important to ascertain what was Cicero's real opinion of Pompey, upon whom, more than upon any man, next to Cæsar, depended the fate of Rome. For this purpose we must not look to his public speeches, in which it might be politic to flatter the successful and popular general, but to his private correspondence, and

observe the sentiments he expressed **in all the confidence**
of friendship. **We** have seen **what he said** of **his first**
appearance **on the scene of politics** after his return from
the East, and we shall find the true state of the case **to be**
that *Cicero always mistrusted Pompey, and Pompey disliked Cicero.* Cicero soon discovered the weakness of his
character, and was quite aware that ambition and not
patriotism was the **ruling** principle of his **conduct. But**
at the same time he knew that he was the only statesman
at Rome who could make head against the rising reputation of Cæsar, and counteract the designs of that dangerous
and unscrupulous man, into which he himself seems to have
had from the first a tolerably clear **insight.**

   To **preserve** the constitution as it had **been** handed
down from their forefathers—to maintain the authority
of the Senate and keep up the aristocratic element as a
breakwater against the wild sea of democracy which was
surging around them—was the leading object of **Cicero's**
policy. For most of the senators, and especially for **the**
young nobility, he had a profound contempt. **Cato,**
indeed, **was** an exception, for he was **a man of sturdy**
honesty, and as true as steel. **But then he was Utopian**
and impracticable, and, with the **best intentions, sometimes**
did mischief. **At least Cicero, whose motto certainly was**
not *frangi non flecti,* **thought so;** and **he** said **that Cato**
spoke as if he were in the republic **of** Plato, **and not**
amongst the rabble of Romulus.[4] As to the aristocracy
generally, they were enervated by luxury and **given** up to
frivolous amusements. He describes them as men who
thought they were in paradise if they got tame fish to
come to their call and eat out of their hands; " fools
enough to believe," he adds, with bitter scorn, " that even
if the constitution were destroyed their fish-ponds would

[4] *Ad Att.* II. 1.

be safe." But his own personal safety required that he
should have some powerful support against the attacks of
his enemies, who had already shown that they were determined, if possible, to destroy him. He therefore determined to ally himself as closely as possible with Pompey,
and courted his friendship while he kept himself on his
guard. To make this clear I will quote one or two passages from his letters, which will, I think, fully bear out
the view I take of the relations between these two eminent
men—the one, at that time, the greatest soldier, and the
other the greatest orator of the Republic.

Writing to Atticus about the Clodian affair, he says,
"But that friend of yours (though you know whom I
mean),"—he meant Pompey; Atticus took care to be
friends with everybody—"about whom you wrote to me,
and said that he began to praise when he found he did
not dare to blame, professes to show great affection for
me—embraces, loves me secretly—but it is plain enough,
he is envious of me. There is in him nothing of courtesy—
nothing of sincerity—nothing of political honesty—nothing
grand or generous—and no steadiness."

Shortly afterwards, when Clodius had been acquitted,
he tells Atticus that, "the mob-speech-loving leech of the
public treasury, the wretched and hungry *canaille*" [5]—in
such terms Cicero spoke of the lower orders at Rome—
"thinks that I am an especial favorite with him, surnamed the Great; and faith! we are on such terms of
close intimacy that those riotous and revelling conspirators
of ours—those downy-bearded youths—call him in their
talk Cnæus Cicero. Therefore, in the theatre and at
gladiatorial shows, we receive astonishing applause without a single hiss (*sine ullâ pastoriciâ fistulâ*)."

At a later period of the same year he tells his friend—

---

[5] Illa concionalis hirudo ærarii, misera ac jejuna plebecula.

"I am on the most friendly terms with Pompey. I know what you say. I will be on my guard where caution is required."

Next year he writes, "I have allied myself so intimately with Pompey that each of us is thereby strengthened in his own line of policy, and stands on firmer ground." But very soon afterwards—in fact, in the next letter—when he is replying to some friendly caution which Atticus had given him, he says that he agrees with him, and does not intend to put himself in the power of another, "for he to whom you allude " (meaning Pompey) " has nothing in him great or elevated; he does nothing but stoop to court popularity."

He defends himself to Atticus for ingratiating himself with a man whom he so distrusted, on the ground that it was for the public interest they should be friends, for if they quarrelled there would be nothing but disorder in the state. And he flattered himself with the idea that by allying himself with Pompey he could steer his own course and Pompey would follow in his wake, so that no harm but good would result from their friendship. Fatal delusion! into which he was the more easily led, because Pompey, well-knowing his weak side, took care to flatter him about his famous consulship, and declared that *he* might have served the Republic well but that Cicero had saved it. "That he should do this," says Cicero, " may or may not be advantageous to me : it certainly is advantageous to the state."

Of Cicero's domestic and private life during the last two years we have only a few glimpses. He resided chiefly in Rome, and was busied in politics. But he felt wearied and disgusted at the state of affairs. He had no confidence in most of the public men ; and in the midst of the Forum and the Senate felt himself almost alone.

M 2

In one of his letters to Atticus he says :—"I am so abandoned by all, that the only repose I enjoy is in the society of my wife and daughter, and my honey-sweet Cicero. For the hollow friendships of ambition have a certain show and glitter externally; they give credit in the Forum but confer no home-felt happiness; therefore when my house is filled with visitors in the morning—when I go down to the Forum attended by troops of friends—I cannot find a soul in all the crowd with whom I can freely joke, or into whose ear I can breathe a sigh." But his love for Atticus increased more and more. He draws a beautiful picture of their friendship in one of his letters;[6] and frequently enquires about his *Amaltheum*—a name which Atticus had given to a room in his house near Buthrotus (probably a library)—wishing to know how it was furnished, and saying that he had a fancy for making a similar one at his country seat near Arpinum.

He alludes, in feeling terms, to the death of one of his slaves, Sositheus, who was an *Anagnostes* or reader, for the Roman gentry used often at their meals to have books read to them by an attendant, as was the custom in monasteries in this country, amongst the ruins of which may sometimes be seen the gallery where the reader was stationed.

He alludes also to some domestic annoyances, about which he cannot be more explicit, as he does not like to mention them in a letter confided to the care of an unknown courier. But to relieve Atticus from anxiety, he expressly adds, that they are of no great moment.

[6] *Ad Att.* I. 17.

Chapter XI.

THE FIRST TRIUMVIRATE.

Æt. 46. B.C. 60.

THE consuls of the new year (B.C. 60) were Lucius Afranius and Q. Metellus Celer. Afranius was one of Pompey's creatures, who had made every exertion to get him chosen consul-elect in the preceding year, but, as Cicero says, did not rely for that purpose upon his influence or popularity, but on the means to which Philip of Macedon alluded when he said that any fortress could be taken into which an ass could enter laden with gold. In other words, Afranius's election had been carried by wholesale bribery; and it was the current report that the consul Piso kept in his house the agents who worked the machinery of corruption. The scandal was so great that on the motion of Cato and his brother-in-law Domitius Ahenobarbus, the Senate passed two resolutions, the one authorizing a judicial inquiry into the subject before the ordinary magistrate, and the other (directed no doubt against Piso the consul) declaring that whoever kept in his house agents for the purpose of bribery (*divisores*) was guilty of an offence against the State. Cicero had a perfect contempt for Afranius. He says that he was such a noodle that he did not know the value of what he had bought—that is the consulship: it was a choice which would make any one who was not a philosopher groan.

One of the first measures of the new year was an agrarian law, brought forward by the tribune Flavius.

He proposed that part of the public lands should be distributed amongst the disbanded soldiers of Pompey's army. Pompey of course was the real author of the scheme, which Cicero says had nothing popular in it but his name. Its principal feature was that the lands should be purchased by setting apart, for five years, for that purpose, a portion of the revenues acquired by Pompey's conquests.

The Senate was opposed to the whole plan, looking upon it as a scheme for the further aggrandisement of Pompey. Cicero, however, was willing that the law should pass, with certain modifications. He spoke in its favor, but strongly insisted that the right of present possessors should be respected; and proposed that some of the lands which Flavius had included in his bill should be excepted. He thought that the measure thus altered might be beneficial, and he was glad to have an opportunity of gratifying Pompey. The city would thereby be relieved of a needy crowd, and many uninhabited tracts in Italy would be peopled.

The question excited a lively interest at Rome, where faction ran so high that Flavius the tribune actually threw Metellus the consul into prison. Dio Cassius says that the Senate followed the consul to the gaol determined to share his imprisonment, but Flavius put his back against the door and kept them out. What an extraordinary instance of the audacity of the tribunes; and what a picture of the lawlessness of the times! Pompey however interfered, and Metellus was released. But the measure did not become law. A more serious matter diverted public attention from the subject, and it was allowed to drop. Ever since the capture of Rome by the Gauls the city had dreaded nothing so much as a Gallic invasion. News reached Rome that the Gauls were in arms, and that the

Helvetii had already attacked that part of Gallia Narbonensis which was called *par excellence* the Province, and
which so long retained its ancient title under the name of
Provence. It was, therefore, no time for civic squabbles
when such an enemy was bestirring himself. The Senate
at once decreed that the two consuls should each assume
the government of one of the Gallic provinces, the one
taking Gallia Cisalpina, the other Gallia Narbonensis;
and they ordered a levy of troops, and cancelled all fur-
loughs. They also determined to send ambassadors into
Gaul to induce the various tribes not to join the Helvetii
in hostilities. As usual the choice of these ambassadors
was to be decided by lot, and it happened that Cicero's
name was drawn first out of the urn, but the Senate
unanimously exclaimed that they could not part with him,
and he must stay in Rome. The same thing happened in
the case of Pompey; so that, says Cicero, they two were
retained as if pledges for the safety of the State.

At this time an incident occurred, trivial enough in
itself, but fraught with important consequences to Cicero.
Ever since he had appeared as a witness against Clodius
on his trial for violating the mysteries of the Bona Dea, he
had been the object of that man's bitterest hate; and he
had taken no pains to propitiate him, attacking him in the
Senate, not only in solemn harangues, but with bitter and
offensive jests. And when he met him in the streets he
did not cease to tease him with his jokes. Some of them
are really not fit to quote. It will be sufficient to say that
they allude with grim pleasantry to Clodius's alleged incest
with his own sister! He seems at this time to have
despised Clodius too much to be afraid of him; but he did
not know the character of the man, who possessed

"—— the unconquerable will
And study of revenge—immortal hate;"

and it is impossible not to be struck with the ingenuity with which he conceived and the tenacity with which he pursued his plan of vengeance. To get Cicero into his power and strike the blow with effect, it was necessary that he should be clothed with some great magisterial office; and no magistrate at Rome could vie in authority and power with a tribune of the people. But none but a plebeian could be such a tribune, and Clodius was a patrician. That difficulty, however, might be got over by adoption into a plebeian family or *gens*, and to accomplish this object he devoted all his energies. The legal mode of accomplishing an adoption was by getting a special law passed at the *Comitia curiata*, a meeting of the people voting in their curiæ, but Clodius feared that if the thing were attempted in a legal and regular way he might not succeed, for in the curiæ the aristocratic element preponderated. He therefore got the tribune Herennius to propose that the question of Clodius's adoption should be decided by the votes of the whole body of the people in the Campus Martius.[1] This would of course give an opportunity for riots and bribery, and all the tricks by which a tumultuous body may be persuaded to vote. Pompey supported the proposal, but the other tribunes interposed their veto. The consul Metellus, Clodius's own brother-in-law, opposed it, and the matter for the present dropped.

In the mean time Cicero pursued the most conciliatory line of conduct towards the young nobility of Rome, who, deeply implicated as many of them had been in the Catiline plot, dissolute in morals, and overwhelmed with debt, long

---

[1] It is curious to notice the way in which Cicero introduces the name of Herennius to Atticus. "There is a man called Herennius, a tribune of the people, whom perhaps you do not even know; and yet you may know him; for he is one of your own tribe, and Sextus, his father, *used to distribute bribes amongst you!*"—*Ad Att.* I. 13.

felt incensed against him for the part he had taken in
crushing the conspiracy. He so won them over by his
affability that he became quite a favorite with them, and
they showed him the utmost respect. But he knew that
he stood on slippery ground. Catulus, one of the best and
noblest of the senators, died this year; he of whom Cicero
said that neither the storm of danger nor the favoring
breeze of honor could ever divert him from his course,
either by hope or fear.[2] Since his death he hardly put
faith in any one at Rome. He said that the well-affected
had no steadiness of principle, and the disaffected hated him.
There was not a statesman amongst them. Crassus was
afraid to say a word that might endanger his popularity,
and Pompey sat silent in his triumphal robe.[3] He therefore remained upon his guard, distrusting his new-born
friendships, and having constantly in his mind a line of
Epicharmus worthy of Machiavelli—

Νᾶφε καὶ μέμνησ'ἀπιστεῖν· ἄρθρα ταῦτα τῶν φρενῶν.

"Be wary and mistrustful : the sinews of the soul are these."

Writing to Atticus shortly afterwards, he for the first time
mentions Julius Cæsar's name, and the expression he uses
is remarkable. He had just been defending his policy in
allying himself with Pompey, on the ground that he thereby
made him a better citizen and statesman; and he added,
"what if I also make Cæsar (*whose breezes just now
are very favorable*) a better man? Am I doing much
disservice to the state?" Cæsar had not then returned
from Spain, which he held as his prætorian government,
and where he had gained great military reputation, but he
was expected in Rome in a couple of days, and Cicero was
then to have an interview with him.

In the course of this year Cicero defended P. Scipio

---

[2] *Pro Sextio*, 48.

[3] Pompeius togulam illam pictam silentio tuetur suam.—*Ad Att.* I. 18.

Nasica, who was accused of bribery by Favonius, " Pompey's ape," as he contemptuously calls him, but the speech is lost.

But in the midst of his public occupations, he still found leisure for literary pursuits. He composed a history of his consulship in Greek and sent it to Atticus, begging him to criticise it and point out any mistakes he might have made in grammar or style. He promised also to send a Latin history of the same period if he completed it, which he afterwards did, and told Atticus that he might expect a poem also on the same subject, that he might not omit any kind of panegyric upon his own exploits.[4] He added that if others wrote on the consulship he would send Atticus their works ; but somehow or other the perusal of his book made them reluctant to begin. " I have," he says in a tone of triumph to his friend, " I have confounded the Greek nation ; those who used to urge me to give them something to polish and touch up have ceased to trouble me. If my book pleases you, take care that it circulates in Athens and the other towns of Greece." His vanity in fact was something wonderful. He was never tired of speaking or writing about himself ; and it is amusing to see the *naïveté* with which he confesses his foible. He goes on to tell Atticus that if there was any subject in the world preferable to his consulship, by all means let it be applauded, and he would be content to bear the blame for not choosing that topic for his praise. But Atticus had himself about the same time written in Greek an account of the consulship and sent a copy to Cicero, so that the books crossed on the way. Cicero thought the style of his friend's work rather bald, and told him so : it was probably not florid nor complimentary enough to satisfy him, but he had the grace to add that it was " when un-

---

[4] Ne quid genus a me ipso laudis meæ prætermittatur.

adorned adorned the most;" and in that respect like women
—the sweeter that it had no perfume. His own composition
was very different; and he confessed that he had emptied on
it all the "scent-boxes" of Isocrates and his school, and had
given it a touch of the colors of Aristotle. About the
same time he made a collection of the speeches he had
delivered while consul, and called them his 'Consular
Orations.' He told Atticus that Papirius Pætus (one of
his friends and correspondents) had made him a present of
a library. Pætus seems to have been one of his clients,
and he said jokingly, that he had consulted their common
friend Cincius whether, under the terms of the Cincian
law, which forbade an advocate from receiving any re-
muneration for his services, he might legally accept the
books. They were at Athens, and he begged Atticus to
employ his "friends, clients, guests, freedmen, and slaves,"
so that not a sheet of the precious manuscripts, whether
Greek or Latin, might be lost, declaring that he grew
daily more and more fond of devoting all the time he could
spare from the labors of the Forum to literature.

In the course of the year he wrote an admirable letter,
or rather essay, on the duties of a provincial governor,
addressed to his brother Quintus, who had obtained the
prætorian province of Asia Minor. It does credit to his
head and heart; and we shall see that when he was himself proconsul of Cilicia he took care to practise the equitable doctrines he had preached.

Cæsar returned from Spain to Rome in June, flushed with
victory and saluted *Imperator!* by his soldiers, to demand
a triumph and the consulship. But to obtain the triumph
he must remain without the walls, and to obtain the
consulship his presence was necessary within the city.
The Senate was unwilling to dispense in his favor with
the existing law, and therefore, finding that the two objects

were incompatible, he **gave up** the triumph and stood for the consulship. But he wanted **money** to bribe the electors, and to **get over** the difficulty he made common cause with Lucceius, who was **wealthy** and ambitious, on the condition that Lucceius should bribe for both in their joint names. The Senate was alarmed at the idea of having Cæsar consul, with a tool like Lucceius for his colleague, and they therefore put forward Bibulus as their candidate. But as they well knew that without bribery he had no chance, they subscribed amongst themselves to enable him to bid as high as his competitors. Even **Cato**, the incorruptible Cato, approved of this, and contributed money for the purpose, thinking that it was for the interest of the State, and all fair to fight the enemy with their own weapons. The plan was successful, and Bibulus was elected. It will be seen hereafter that the Senate was not mistaken in their man, and that while he held office as the colleague, he was the constant antagonist of Cæsar.

When he left Rome to assume the prætorian government of Spain Cæsar was, in point of fortune, a ruined man. He had squandered unheard-of sums on his ædileship, determined to buy popularity at any cost. His creditors, therefore, threatened to detain him; but he got some of his friends, and the wealthy Crassus amongst them, to be his bail, and went off. On his return he found Pompey the foremost man at Rome; between whom and Crassus there was an ill-concealed antipathy. Each was jealous of the other and bent on his own aggrandisement. Cæsar saw at once that if he could reconcile the two, and make them join him, he would be master of the situation. He knew that a "threefold cord is not quickly broken," and that he would be more than a match for them both in the game he resolved to play. He could use the influence of Pompey and the gold of Crassus for his own purpose, and with this view he laboured to form that famous **triple alliance** which is known in history by the name of the First Triumvirate.

Not that this implied any organic change in the constitution. **The** Senate and the People were still the two' **great** estates of the realm, with the machinery of consuls and tribunes and the other magistrates **still** apparently working as before; but a new motive power **was** applied by the coalition of the three most ambitious and influential men at Rome.[5] The vessel of the State began to drift in a direction very different from her former course, and no one saw this more clearly than Cicero. Cæsar had some difficulty in overcoming the mutual repugnance of Pompey and Crassus, and getting them to act together, for they had **never been** friends since **the** time **of their joint** consul **ship.** **Both,** however, assisted **him now in his** canvass for the consulship—Crassus with his money and Pompey with **his** influence. Pompey was anxious to have his actions in **Asia** ratified by a *senatus consultum*—a sort of bill of indemnity for the past—and this both Crassus **and Lu-** cullus opposed; but Cicero, with politic dexterity, supported it. Pompey felt what **an** advantage it would be to have on his side **a man so** popular **in** the Forum, **of such** weight in the Senate, and such influence with the Knights, as Cicero. **And** there was much to tempt him **to** join the alliance. Cæsar professed the utmost deference **to** his **views,** and, by a union **with** the three, he **had** the prospect, to use his own words, **of** "reconciliation with his enemies, peace with the multitude, and repose for his old age." But then what would become of his political principles? Was he to abandon the cause of the Republic and **the** course he had followed from his youth to make

---

[5] Societatem cum utroque (Cæsar) iniit, ne quid ageretur in republicâ quod displicuisset ulli e tribus.—Sueton. *Cæs.* 23.

himself an instrument in the hands of others, and sur-
render his free will to theirs? He said he was determined to take as his motto the noble line of Homer—

Εἷς οἰωνὸς ἄριστος ἀμύνεσθαι περὶ πάτρης.

And in this mood he addressed to Atticus, in the month
of December of the closing year, a letter in which, after
expressing his views on politics, he tells his friend that he
expects him at Rome on the day before the festival of
Compitalia, and will have a warm bath ready for him.
Terentia invites Pomponia, and he will ask Atticus's
mother to join the party. And Atticus is not to forget
to bring with him Theophrastus on Ambition!

Such then was the state of affairs at the opening of the
new year. Cæsar, Pompey, and Crassus, had formed a
coalition, and every effort was made to induce Cicero to
join them. But he held aloof, determined to temporise,
and not commit himself to an alliance which, it was his
firm conviction, threatened ruin to the Republic. He did
not, however, wish to break altogether with three such powerful men, whose hostility he would have to encounter almost
alone, for he could count on no effective support in his own,
that is, the conservative party. This gave his conduct the
appearance of vacillation; but it may well be doubted whether
he could at this juncture have acted more wisely than he
did. Had the aristocracy of Rome cared less for their
fish-ponds and more for the interests of the State—had
they numbered amongst them many such men as Catulus,
and Cato, and Cicero—a party might have been formed
which would have been strong enough to resist, and perhaps counteract, the policy of the Triumvirate. But
whether, even then, the Republic could have been preserved is another question, which is not so easily answered.
I believe that its knell of dissolution had been struck, and

that nothing could have prevented its final overthrow.
We must remember that at Rome the whole effective
power was in the hands of the people. Not through the
medium of representative institutions—that great secret
for reconciling liberty with order which was never discovered by antiquity—but the people in the most direct
and primary sense. The Senate could not pass a single
law binding on the whole community. It might pass a
consultum or an *auctoritas*, which, within certain limits,
had authority, but neither was equivalent to what we
should call an Act of Parliament. And in what state was
the people that reliance could be placed on it to maintain
the constitution? The wars of Marius and Sylla, and the
intestine disorders which had so long preyed upon the
commonwealth, had demoralised the masses, and also the
aristocracy. The result of the Social War had added
enormously to the constituency by throwing open the
franchise to the Italian towns; and the increase of
numbers, by diminishing the sense of responsibility, had
made the electors more accessible to corruption. The
wealth of conquered provinces had given ambitious and
successful generals and governors the means of wholesale corruption, which they unsparingly exercised, and it
was in vain that law after law was passed, each more
stringent against bribery. We have seen that even
Cato thought it right to secure the election of Bibulus
by bribery, because in no other way would he have a
chance of making head against Lucceius, who was patron-
ised by Cæsar. The simplicity and virtue of old times
had passed away. The people demanded the most profuse expenditure on shows, and games, and festivals, as
the passport to their favor and their votes. The immorality of private life was frightfully on the increase. There
was hardly a public man in Rome, except Catulus, and

Cicero, and Cato, of those whose names still float on the stream of time, whose youth was not branded with the deep stain of profligacy: Catiline, Clodius, Curio, Dolabella, Antonius, Pompey, and Cæsar, were all guilty of vices which in our day would have incapacitated them from playing leading parts as statesmen—or at all events would, by the mere force of public opinion, have deprived them of all public influence. Was it not then a chimera to suppose that the Republic of other days could be preserved? And yet this was the dream to which Cicero clung, even to the last. Blinded by his attachment to ancient forms—an ardent lover of temperate liberty—conservative in all his views—he could not bring himself to believe that the old constitution was worn out, and that, while the form remained, the spirit and the life were gone. Those who move with the tide are hardly conscious of the rate at which the tide is flowing, and come upon the rocks before they are aware.

Are we then, with some modern writers, to suppose that Cæsar was actuated by patriotic motives in overthrowing the Republic and making himself master of Rome? That he saw that a change was necessary, and made himself the instrument of that change out of pure love for his fatherland?

That he was one of the greatest of soldiers—and all but one of the greatest of orators—a consummate statesman— a wise ruler when he had attained the summit of his power—magnanimous and humane towards his enemies when he could afford to despise them, though pitilessly cruel when he had an object to gain—all this we may freely admit; but it ought not to alter our opinion as to his nefarious plot against the constitution and liberties of Rome, nor blind our eyes to the fact that he was unscrupulously and selfishly ambitious.

Pompey was weak and vainglorious; utterly unfit to stand against his giant competitor or confront the dangers which overwhelmed the sinking State. No man could do this who was not gifted by nature with a genius for military command—for the sword must ultimately decide the struggle—and in the hour of trial it was found that, whatever reputation he might have gained against the barbarians of Spain—the half-civilized forces of Mithridates—or the pirate-hordes of the Mediterranean—he was deficient in the great qualities of a soldier, and was as feeble in the conduct of a campaign as he was infirm of purpose in the Senate.

In January or February Cicero defended Antonius, who was tried for malversation in his provincial government of Macedonia and condemned. Having in the course of his speech made some remarks on the state of the times, his words were immediately *mis*reported to the triumvirs. This so enraged them that, with indecent haste, they that very day hurried on Clodius's adoption; and Pompey, who was then augur, took the auspices while the meeting of the people was held, and so sanctioned the ceremony. In this act of adoption there were several irregularities, owing to which, as we shall see, Cicero afterwards contended that it was illegal. Amongst other objections P. Fonteius, the adopting party, was a minor.

Disgusted with late events Cicero left Rome early in the year, and passed several months at some of his villa residences in the country. The first letter we have was written to Atticus from Tusculum. His friend had been urging him to undertake a work on geography, and had sent him a book on the subject by Serapio of Antioch, of which Cicero candidly confesses he did not understand the thousandth part. Very probably Wieland is right in his conjecture that Serapio's work was full of mathematics or physics, a branch of study to which Cicero had never applied himself. He thanked Atticus, however, for the book, and said that he had given an order for the payment, as he did not wish to put him to the expense of it as a present. He seriously thought of writing a geographical work, and collected materials for the purpose, but he seems to have been deterred by its difficulty (*magnum opus est*, he says), and never to have carried out the idea. He was at this time weary of politics, and glad to exchange the bustle of Rome and strife of the Forum and Senate for his villas and his books. And yet it is amusing to observe his inconsistency. In the same breath that he asks who are to be the new consuls he declares that he has little curiosity to know, for he has determined no longer to trouble himself with politics. But all his letters show how anxious he was for public news, and how little he could content himself with the idea of retirement. Charles V. in his convent of St. Yust took, as we now know, a lively interest in the politics of Europe, and Cicero in the country was never satisfied unless he heard constantly from Atticus the gossip of Rome. In his next letter, written from his villa near Antium (Porto d'Anzo), he says that he either amuses himself with his books, of which he had there a pretty good collection, or with counting the waves on the beach, for the weather was not fine enough for fishing. As to writing he was in no mood for it at all. He tells Atticus he would rather have been a *decemvir* (a sort of mayor) in the petty provincial town of Antium than consul at Rome. "Only think," he exclaims, "of there being a place so near Rome where there are numbers who have never even seen Vatinius! "(a noisy and troublesome tribune of the people devoted to Cæsar) "where nobody except myself cares whether any of their Twenty Commissioners are alive and well—where no one catechises me, and all love me."

This allusion to the Commissioners refers to a measure which to ingratiate himself with the people Cæsar had proposed for making a distribution of the public lands in Campania. To execute the scheme twenty Commissioners (*Vigintiviri*) were to be appointed, and two who accepted the office were no less persons than Pompey and Crassus. Cato strongly opposed the measure, and so also did Bibulus the other consul, saying, "It is not the bill that I fear, but the recompence that is expected for it." When however it came before the people, he was so roughly handled and pelted by the mob that his life was in danger; and Cæsar enraged at his conduct had the audacity to throw his colleague into prison, from which however he almost immediately released him. Owing to the opposition the bill encountered it did not pass for several months, and after it became law a place in the commission was offered to Cicero in July, but he peremptorily refused it. Nothing, he says, could have disgraced him more in the eyes of his countrymen, nor would it have been a prudent step on his part to take, for the whole body of commissioners was unpopular, at least amongst men of the right stamp.

A more tempting opportunity of employment soon engaged his attention. As Cæsar and Pompey found they could not secure his active support, they seem to have wished to remove him from Rome on the honorable pretext of an embassy. Alexander III., King of Egypt, had been dethroned by his subjects, and Ptolemy Auletes made king in his stead. He was befriended by Pompey, whom he largely bribed; but he was an oppressive ruler, and the Egyptians soon became discontented with

him. Pompey wished to gain for him the title of friend
and ally of the Roman people, and Cæsar backed the
attempt, which was opposed ·by the other consul Bibulus
who advocated the cause of the Egyptians. In the mean
time there was a talk of proposing to Cicero that he should
go to Egypt and endeavour to effect a reconciliation between the king and his subjects, and his own personal
inclination would have led him to accept the employment.
He had long desired to visit Egypt, where his intelligent
mind thirsting for knowledge would have found so much to
interest him ; and he hoped that his countrymen might learn
to value him more by his absence, and that he might thus recover his popularity, which he felt was on the wane. But he
was deterred by the reflection that he could not consistently,
or without loss of self-respect, accept the mission from men
to whose policy he was so strongly opposed, and he feared
that he might stand lower in public opinion if he consented
to go. In a letter to Atticus, alluding to the subject, he
said, "What will history say of me six hundred years
hence ? That is a judgment which I reverence much
more than the small talk (*rumusculi*) of such men as are
now alive. But let me wait and see. If the offer is
made it will be in my power to decline it, and then I can
deliberate and decide. There will be even some glory in
not accepting it. Therefore if you are sounded on the subject, do not peremptorily refuse it for me."

But it was not necessary to come to a decision. The
tyrannical rule of Ptolemy drove his subjects into revolt.
He quitted Egypt and took refuge in Rome.

Another object which Cicero had rather at heart was to
succeed to a vacancy in the College of Augurs, caused at
this juncture by the death of his friend Q. Metellus Celer.
He confesses to Atticus that this was the only prize by
which it was in the power of the Triumvirate to tempt

him, and with candor adds " *Vide levitatem meam!* See
my weakness!" While he thus wrote, his mind was
struggling between the desire for action and the love of the
calm pleasures of literature and philosophy. "To these,"
he exclaims, "I purpose to devote myself: would that I
had done so from the first! Now, however, that I know
by experience the vanity of those things I once thought
so brilliant, I intend to pay court to all the Muses."

But in the same letter he eagerly inquires after all the
news and gossip of Rome. "Who are to be the new
consuls? Pompey and Crassus? or Servius Sulpicius and
Gabinius? Is there anything new in the way of legislation?
Is there any news at all? Who has the office of the augur-
ship?" It was not offered to *him* at all events, for it did
not suit the policy of Cæsar and Pompey to confer the
honor upon him, and he had to put up with the disappointment for the present.

His next letter is in the same strain. He asks · for
news, but declares that he has no practical object in the
inquiry as if he wished to meddle in state affairs; and he
compares himself to a pilot compelled to disembark from
a ship, the helm of which has been snatched from his
hand. "I wish," he exclaims, "to see the shipwreck of
those men from the shore. I wish, as your friend So-
phocles says,—

> 'To hear beneath the roof with tranquil mind
> The rain-lashed window beaten by the wind.'"[6]

So far however from being tranquil, he was in a state of
feverish anxiety. Whenever a messenger came from Rome
his first question was, "Have you brought a letter from
Atticus?" Once, while at his villa near Antium, when
the answer was "No!" he so frightened the couriers by

---

[6]   ὑπὸ στεγῇ
πυκνὰς ἀκούειν ψεκάδας εὐδούσῃ φρενί.

his cross-examination, that they confessed they had received a letter for him but lost it on the road. Here was a disappointment. All he could do was to write to his friend and beg him to repeat the contents of his missing letter. "If it contained matter worthy of history, let me know it ; if only jokes, let me have them."

In April he left Antium and went to his country residence at Formiæ, intending to return to Antium in May as his daughter Tullia wished to see some games that would be celebrated there. But he afterwards changed his mind and determined not to take her to the show, as he thought it would not look well for him to be amusing himself at a time when he did not wish to appear to be travelling for pleasure. From his Formian Villa he wrote frequently to Atticus, and his letters show the deep disquiet with which he contemplated the state of things at Rome. Pompey had assured him that Clodius had promised in the strongest manner that he would do him no injury; and Cicero told his friend that if the promise was not kept, he would take a fine revenge on that "Jerusalemite" as he contemptuously called Pompey.[7] "He shall feel," he says, "the ingratitude he has shown for all my complimentary speeches ; look out therefore for a divine palinode!" He then goes on : "Merrily and with less noise than I had expected has the revolution been accomplished ; more quickly than it was possible had it not been for Cato's blunders and the perversity of those who allowed the existing laws against tribunician abuse and electoral corruption to be violated, and threw away all the safeguards of the State." But he was determined to defend himself, and if attacked return blow for blow. "Let my country support me : she has had from me I will not

[7] Pompey had taken Jerusalem, and most probably vaunted a good deal of the exploit.

say more than was due, but certainly more than was demanded from me.   I would rather have a bad voyage with
another at the helm, than steer the ship prosperously with
such thankless passengers."   The letter concludes with a
few words in Greek, most likely scrawled by his youthful
son, " Little Cicero sends greeting to Titus the Athenian : "
a salutation which is varied in another letter, thus—
" Young Cicero the philosopher sends greeting to Titus
the statesman."   These little home touches are pleasant
and refreshing to meet with in the midst of the discontent
and sorrow that were preying on the mind of the father.

Formiæ was so far away from Rome that he felt himself
quite out of the world. He complains that in his villa
there—the remains of which are still pointed out at the Villa
Marsana near Castiglione—except from a chance traveller
he never hears anything from Rome, whereas at Antium
he had a letter daily from Atticus.   But if he pined for
news from the metropolis, he was in danger of being bored
to death by country neighbours. They so crowded his
house in the morning that he says it was more like a
public building (*basilica*) than a villa.   There was Arrius
who would talk philosophy with him, and obligingly told
him that he stayed there for the purpose. And then
there was that Sebosus ! He gives such a graphic account
of a visit from these gentlemen that it is worth quoting :
" Just as I was writing post haste to you, in walks Sebosus ! I had hardly got over a groan when, ' How do
you do ?' says Arrius. Is this to get away from Rome ?
What was the use of my escaping from those men there
when I have stumbled upon these men here ? I declare
I will be off

'To my old ancestral hills, the cradle of my race.'[8]

---

[8] In montes patrios et ad incunabula nostra.

In short, if I cannot be alone I would rather have the company of peasants than these town gentlemen."

And there were others equally tedious and tiresome, so that he says in joke this was now a capital opportunity for any one who wished to buy his Formian property—meaning that to get away from such company he would sell it cheap. And yet in the same letter in which he says this he declares that he has become so enervated, that he would rather live under a despotism in the repose in which he was then stagnating, than engage in the struggle of active life with the best hopes of success.[9]

It would be tedious to quote at much greater length from Cicero's correspondence at this period. It is all in the same strain: full of intense dissatisfaction at the state of public affairs. In April, Pompey married Julia, Cæsar's only child, twenty-three years younger than himself, and previously betrothed to Servilius Cæpio. He had divorced his former wife Mucia, for adultery with Cæsar; and now, for the sake of ambition, he actually married the daughter of the man who was the author of his dishonor![10] Such an alliance is without a precedent or a parallel. No wonder that Cicero should fear lest, stung and maddened by the reproaches which his conduct brought down upon him, Pompey, or Sampsiceramus, as he nicknamed him, should grow utterly desperate.[1] Cæsar, in the mean time, pursued his old course of reckless extravagance, and lavished enormous sums on spectacles and games to keep the people in good humour. He was as unscrupulous about the means of getting money as he was profligate in

[9] He describes the feelings of the provincials as greatly irritated against "our friend Magnus," whose name was becoming odious along with that of Crassus "the Rich."

[10] Sueton. Cæs. 50.

[1] Ad Att. II. 14. Sampsiceramus was the name of a petty chieftain in Asia Minor conquered by Pompey.

spending it. He contrived to abstract (Suetonius says, he *stole*) from the temple of Jupiter in the Capitol three thousand pounds weight of gold, and replaced it with the same quantity of gilt bronze. The triumvirate, or rather Cæsar in its name, was already master of Rome, and Cicero declared, with prescient foresight, that a despotism was at hand. "For what," he writes to Atticus in May, "is the meaning of this sudden alliance—this distribution of lands in Campania—this profuse expenditure of money? And if this were the extremity of the mischief it would be too much. But in the nature of things it cannot be the extremity. For what pleasure can they take in these things in themselves? They would never have gone so far except to open a path to farther pestilent designs. Good heavens!" So far as personal feelings were concerned, he said that he was not without a consolation. He used to fear that Pompey's services to his country would, some six hundred years later, be thought to eclipse his own; but now he had no apprehension on that score, so lost and fallen had "Sampsiceramus" become.

With such feelings he returned to Rome in June. Atticus, about this time, went to stay at his country-seat in Epirus, so that their correspondence was still kept up; but Cicero told him that he would, for the sake of caution, sometimes write under a feigned name.

He found the Triumvirate very unpopular, and men gave vent to their opinions at dinner-tables and in society more freely than formerly. Grief and indignation began, he says, to get the better of fear; but yet the case seemed to be well nigh desperate. Never was there, according to him, so infamous a state of things at Rome and so detested by all classes as now. When the Triumvirs appeared abroad they were hissed. Pompey especially seemed the

object of dislike.[2] When Diphilus, an actor, recited in the
theatre a line which was applicable to him, *"Nostrá
miseriá tu es Magnus,"* he was rapturously encored ; and
when he went on with the allusion, signifying that a day
of reckoning would come, the audience vociferously applauded. Cæsar came at the moment to the theatre, and
was so coldly received, that he could not conceal his displeasure ; while Curio, a young senator, then looked upon
as a leader of the Opposition, and as conspicuous for his
hostility to Cæsar as he was afterwards distinguished by
servile devotion to him, was loudly cheered. Pompey
happened to be absent from Rome at Capua, and letters
were immediately sent off to tell him of the disagreeable occurrence. As to Bibulus, he was in immense
favor. After the gross insult and outrage offered to
him by his colleague, he refused to enter the Senate
or appear in public, and in no very dignified manner
shut himself up in his own house, where the Senate,
or at all events some of the senators, used to meet,
and from which he issued edicts and public notices
addressed to the people. These were posted on placards,
and the crowds that collected to read them were so great,
that the thoroughfares were blocked up. He declared all
the remaining days of the year, after the passing of the
Campanian law, *nefasti,* or what, in Scotland, would be
called not "lawful" days ; that is, days in which no
public business could be done. But this was virtually to
abdicate his authority and make Cæsar in effect sole
consul, so that the wits of Rome used to date their letters
and other documents, by way of joke, with the words,
"Julio et Cæsare Coss. ;" and the following epigram was
long current amongst them :—

---

[2] Even now Cicero called him *nostri amores.—Ad Att.* II. 19.

"Non Bibulo quicquam nuper sed Cæsare factum est,
  Nam Bibulo fieri consule nil memini."

"Pooh! Bibulus did nought of late, but Cæsar did it all;
  For the consulship of Bibulus I can't to mind recal."

The people, however, were with Bibulus, and hissed and hooted the Triumvirs. Cicero gives a piteous description of the appearance of Pompey when he mounted the Rostra in July to speak to the multitude. He declares that he could not refrain from tears when he looked at him and saw how he was changed. He was no longer the proud and popular orator, confident in himself and challenging applause, but cringing humbly to the mob, and almost ashamed to utter a word. He compares him to a star that had glided from its sphere. "O, Lucifer, son of the morning, how art thou fallen!" is the sentiment, if not the expression; and he says his grief was like that which Apelles or Protogenes might be imagined to feel if the one had seen his Venus, or the other his Ialysus, daubed and covered with mud. And yet he declares that, although after Pompey's conduct in the Clodian business he had forfeited all claim to his friendship, his love for him had been such that no injury could destroy it.

He took no part in public business at this time. He was profoundly disgusted with the state of affairs—a state in which, he said, resistance could only lead to civil war, and the struggle would end in ruin; and as he found he could do no good in politics, he turned to his old and congenial profession of an advocate. He defended A. Themius twice, and successfully; and afterwards, with Hortensius, defended L. Valerius Flaccus, who was accused of extortion in his prætorian government of the province of Asia Minor. Hortensius availed himself of the occasion to speak in the handsomest manner of Cicero's services as Consul, for which he had a good opportunity, as Flaccus had been prætor during Cicero's consulship. His own speech is still extant.

The charges against Flaccus were supported by witnesses who were sent over from Lydia, Mysia, Caria, and Phrygia, which constituted the province of Asia Minor. They were all Greeks, the descendants of the settlers from Greece who had colonized those countries. The line of defence which he principally adopted was to throw discredit on their testimony; and the speech is curious, as showing the low estimate in which Greek veracity was held at Rome. The argument may be summed up in a single sentence: "Do not believe a Greek upon his oath." Passionately fond as he was of the literature of Greece, he had the utmost contempt for the character of the nation; and here was a case in which his duty to his client called upon him to express it. Whether he was as well justified in praising the truthfulness of his own countrymen as he was in denouncing the mendacity of the Greeks, is another question; but an advocate may be allowed to flatter the vanity of the court he is addressing.

"I say," exclaimed Cicero, "this generally of the Greeks. I concede to them literature; I grant them accomplishments in many arts; I do not deny them graceful wit, acute intellect, and ready speech; and if they claim even more than this, I make no objection; but that nation has never cultivated any regard for the sanctity of truth in giving evidence, and they are wholly ignorant of the force and authority and serious importance of the matter. Whence comes that saying, 'Accommodate me with your testimony'? Is it supposed to be the formula of Spaniards or of Gauls? It is entirely the formula of the Greeks; so that even those who do not know Greek, know the words which the Greeks use in uttering it."

Another passage is worth quoting to show what was Cicero's opinion of the evils of democracy. After describing the checks which the constitution of Rome, in theory at least, imposed upon party legislation, and the care with which the wise men of old had guarded the

State against the effects of mob tyranny, he contrasted this
with the history of Greece :—

" All the Greek republics," he said, " are governed by the rash and
sudden impulses of public meetings. Not to speak of the Greece of the
present, which has long been the victim of its own policy, ancient
Greece, which once flourished in wealth, empire, and renown, was ruined
by this one evil—the unchecked liberty and licentiousness of its public
meetings and popular harangues. When uninstructed men, uneducated
and ignorant, were assembled in a theatre, they voted for useless wars,
they placed turbulent demagogues at the head of the government, and
banished the best citizens from the State."

. But besides attacking the character of the witnesses, he
showed that their evidence was utterly untrustworthy in
its nature. It was made up of resolutions passed by
excited mobs, and was unsupported by documentary
proofs. In some cases the witnesses pretended that they
had lost the documents with which they were entrusted ;
in others, the documents were forged at Rome. For
instance, one of them was sealed with wax, according to
the Roman custom, and not with chalk or Cretan earth, as
was the custom in Asia.[3] The orator concluded as usual
with a passionate appeal to the pity of the jury, calling
upon them to acquit the young man who was accused
before them for the sake of himself, his father, and his
family, and to preserve from ruin and for the service of the
State the heir of a glorious name.

In the mean time Cæsar had been invested by a law
(lex Vatinia),—brought forward and carried by Vatinius,
a tribune of the people, and one of his creatures,—with
the command, for five years, of Cisalpine Gaul and Illyricum,
with three legions. This was an extraordinary appointment, and had been conferred by a special enactment. But
the Senate, fearing that the people would go farther and

[3] For the use of clay seals amongst the ancient Assyrians, see Raw-
linson's Ancient Monarchies, vol. i. p. 331.

ignore them altogether, made a merit of necessity, and themselves conferred on him, in addition, the command of Gaul beyond the Alps, with another legion. They little thought that by so doing they were signing the death-warrant of the liberties of Rome. Cæsar, still anxious to conciliate Cicero, offered to make him one of his lieutenants, and pressed the office upon him, as he himself expresses it, in a very handsome manner. At the same time he had a *libera legatio* given him by the Senate; that is, as previously explained, permission to travel with the privileges of an ambassador: and he hesitated between the two. He seems, however, to have accepted the former—at least, nominally; but he had no intention at that time of leaving Rome. "I do not like to fly," he writes to Atticus, "I wish to fight. I have zealous friends on my side: but I say nothing positively. This to you in confidence."

But a much more important event had just happened. Clodius, now qualified as a plebeian, had, at the beginning of April, announced himself a candidate for the tribuneship, and was chosen in July one of the tribunes for the following year. Plutarch and Dio Cassius both say that he owed his election to the influence of Cæsar, which is extremely probable. And yet at first it seemed as if he was going to turn against his patron. He saw how unpopular the triumvirs had become, and threatened to attack them. But more prudent counsels prevailed. He knew that they were rich and powerful and backed by military force, so that abandoning the thought of opposing them, he resolved to spring upon a weaker prey, and gratify his long cherished hatred of Cicero. Clodius had indeed protested with an oath to Pompey that, if made tribune, he would do Cicero no harm. This promise Pompey had exacted from him, for he declared that he should be covered with eternal disgrace if Cicero was

injured by the man in whose hands a weapon had been
placed by himself in permitting him to become a plebeian.
Pompey, therefore, gave Cicero the most fervent assurances
that he was safe. He told him that if Clodius broke his
word and attacked him, then the world should see that
nothing was dearer to himself than Cicero's friendship.
And did Cicero believe this? He did, and he did not.
" Pompey loves me," so he writes to Atticus ; " and treats
me with affection. ' Do you believe it ? ' you will ask. I
do believe it : he makes me believe it. But we are warned
by precepts both in prose and verse to be on our guard
and avoid credulity. Well! I take care to be on my
guard ; but incredulous of his professions I cannot be."

But whatever might be Pompey's sincerity, Clodius had
no intention of keeping his promise. He spoke to others
in the bitterest terms of Cicero, who no longer disguised
from himself the fact that either by open violence or under
colour of the forms of law his enemy would attack him.
But this gave him at first little uneasiness, and he treated
the matter lightly. He never fully realized the weight of
the impending blow until it fell, and for a time crushed
him. Indeed, he almost courted the attack ; for abstaining as he had done from politics of late, and confining
himself to the duties of an advocate, in which he still
shone with unrivalled splendor, he had recovered much of
his old popularity. His house was thronged with clients
and visitors ; he was greeted cordially in the streets ; men
professed zealous attachment to his person ; and the
memory of his consulship seemed to be revived. Let
Clodius now do his worst : Cicero thought himself more
than a match for him. He had not, with all his experience, realized the truth that

> " An habitation giddy and unsure
> Hath he that buildeth on the vulgar heart;"

and he did not estimate aright the strength and resources
of his adversary.

But he soon changed his tone.   Not long after he had
expressed himself thus confidently, almost defiantly, we
find him writing to Atticus in real alarm at Clodius's
threats, and conjuring him to come to Rome: " If you
love me as much as you certainly do love me—if you are
sleeping, awake; if you are standing, walk; if you are
walking, run; if you are running, fly.   You can hardly
believe how much I rely upon your advice and sagacity,
and more than all upon your love and fidelity.   The
importance of the subject requires perhaps a long detail;
but the intimacy of our souls makes us content with
brevity."

In August, Rome was agitated by the news of a plot
which appears to have been as unreal, and to have been
concocted with as much baseness, as the famous Titus
Oates plot in our own history.   We have seen that Curio
was at this time an active leader of Opposition, and,
according to Cicero's account, Cæsar resolved to destroy
him.   Vettius, a Roman knight who had been useful to
Cicero in Catiline's conspiracy, took upon himself the
disreputable office of a common informer.   He promised
Cæsar that he would involve Curio in the meshes of a
conspiracy, or would at all events accuse him of it.   For
this purpose he affected his society, and when sufficiently
intimate with him, made him the confidant of a plan
which he said he had formed to kill Pompey.   Some
writers say that he professed his intention to kill Cæsar
also, and other leading senators.   Curio immediately told
this to his father, and his father informed Pompey.   The
matter was brought before the Senate, and Vettius was
introduced to the assembly.   At first he denied that he
had had any communication with Curio ; but almost

directly afterwards retracted this statement, and offered to
reveal the truth if his safety was publicly guaranteed.
This was promised; and he then declared that a band of
young men, amongst whom he named Paulus Æmilius,
Brutus,[4] Lentulus, and others, with Curio as their leader,
had formed a conspiracy.   He added that C. Septimius, a
secretary of Bibulus, had brought him a dagger from
Bibulus, to enable him to assassinate Pompey.   This was
rather too much ; and the Senate laughed at the idea of
Vettius getting his dagger from the consul, as if he had
no other weapon for his purpose.   Besides, it was proved
that some time before Bibulus had himself warned Pompey
to be on his guard, for which Pompey had thanked him.
Curio was brought in, and totally denied the charge.
A further proof of its falsity was shown by the fact, that
at the time when, according to Vettius, a meeting of the
young men was held to settle a plan for attacking Pompey
with a band of gladiators in the Forum, at which he
alleged that Paulus Æmilius took a leading part, Æmilius
was absent in Macedonia.   The Senate, therefore, ordered
that Vettius, since upon his confession he had carried a
dagger with a murderous intent, should be thrown into
prison ; and they significantly added a resolution, that
whoever let him out, would act as an enemy of the State.
The resolution and order of the Senate were brought
before a meeting of the people, at which Cæsar, in spite
of what the Senate had ordered, had the hardihood to
introduce Vettius from gaol, and permit him to address
the multitude from the honourable post of the Rostra ;—
a place from which, Cicero tells us, Cæsar, when he was

---

[4] Cicero calls him Q. Cæpio Brutus.   This was M. Junius Brutus, the
future assassin of Cæsar.   He had recently been adopted by his maternal
uncle Q. Servilius Cæpio, and for some time, according to Roman usage,
was known by his uncle's name in addition to his own surname.

prætor, had not allowed Catulus to speak, but compelled
him to stand on a lower platform.   Vettius put a bold face
on the matter, and now accused some of the noblest of the
senators whom he had not previously named, such as
Lucullus, Fannius, Domitius Ahenobarbus, and others;
but he made no allusion to Brutus, whom in the senate-
house he had specially denounced as privy to the conspiracy.   He did not mention the name of Cicero, but said
that an eloquent ex-consul, who lived near the consul,[5]
had told him that the times required a Servilius Ahala or a
Brutus.   This, of course, sufficiently pointed at Cicero.
He afterwards added that Piso, Cicero's son-in-law, and
M. Laterensis, were privy to the plot.   Vettius was immediately sent back to prison; and, notwithstanding the
public assurance that had been given him of personal
safety, he was to have been arraigned before Crassus, as
prætor, on an indictment for attempt to murder; and
Cicero says that he intended, if condemned, to earn a
pardon by making a fuller confession, and implicate more
parties in the conspiracy.   But in the mean time it was
given out that he had destroyed himself in prison.   Perhaps
he had : but his death was as mysterious as were those of
Wright and Pichegru in the Temple when Bonaparte was
First Consul.   Cicero afterwards charged Vatinius the
tribune with having caused him to be strangled ; and, if
this was true, there is little doubt that Vatinius acted on
instructions from a higher quarter.

In giving to Atticus the substance of the above narrative (except as to the death of Vettius, which had not then
happened), Cicero declared that he had no fears for

---

[5] Cæsar was not only consul but pontifex maximus, and as such in-
habited the house of the Collegium Pontificum by the side of the Via
Sacra, apparently just under the Palatine Hill, where Cicero's house
stood.

himself. The greatest good-will was shown to him ; but
he was utterly weary of life. No one was more unfortunate than himself, no one more fortunate than Catulus,
both in the glory of his life and the happiness of his death
before this evil time. However, he kept, he said, his
mind firm and undisturbed, and was determined to preserve his reputation with honor. Pompey told him to be
under no apprehension from Clodius, and in the most
marked manner assured him of his friendship.

While he was at his Antian villa this year he chiefly
studied history, though he declared that nobody was lazier
than himself. He wrote to Atticus that he intended to
make a collection of anecdotes of his contemporaries in
the style of Theopompus ; but he does not appear to have
completed, or, at all events, published the work, which
would have been a most welcome help to our knowledge of
the men of his day. He promised his friend a rustic welcome at his villa near Arpinum, and said that, in the
controversy Which is the best kind of life—the life of action
or the life of contemplation? the former of which was maintained by Dicæarchus, and the latter by Theophrastus—he
thought that he practically sided with both. Certainly,
he says, he had abundantly satisfied Dicæarchus, and
would in future seek happiness more in the bosom of his
family, which not only offered him repose, but blamed him
for not having always sought it.

CHAPTER XII.

THE EXILE.

Æt. 49.   B.C. 58.

W E now come to the most melancholy period of Cicero's
life—melancholy not so much from the nature and
extent of the misfortune that overtook him, as from the
abject prostration of mind into which he was thrown.

We fail to recognise the orator and statesman—the man
who braved the fury of Catiline, and in the evening of his
life hurled defiance at Antony—in the weeping and moaning
exile. He was not deficient in physical courage ; he met
a violent death with calmness and fortitude ; but he
wanted strength of character and moral firmness to support adversity.

The consuls of the new year (B.C. 58) were Piso and
Gabinius, two men whose character Cicero has painted in
the blackest colours. Piso was a near relative of Cicero's
own son-in-law, Calpurnius Piso Frugi, and his daughter
Calpurnia was the wife of Cæsar. He was of morose
aspect, and rough unpolished manners, but dissolute to the
last degree. If we may credit the picture drawn of him
and his colleague Gabinius by Cicero, two such infamous
men never disgraced the office of consul. They were sunk
in the lowest and most monstrous debauchery. He calls
Gabinius in scorn, amongst other opprobrious epithets,
a "curled dancer," and says that Piso might be taken
for one of a gang of Cappadocian slaves. Both had
been strongly supported by Cæsar and Pompey in their

canvass for the consulship. They lent themselves readily to Clodius's wishes, who, having entered upon the office of tribune in December, proceeded with consummate skill to execute his design of crushing Cicero. His first care was to ingratiate himself with the three orders—the Senate, the Knights, and the People. With this view he proposed several laws in the interest of each respectively, and, in order to secure the two consuls, he bribed them with the offer of proposing a special law to the people to confer upon them select provincial governments, instead of letting them take their chance as usual by lot. Piso thus got Achaia, Thessaly, Peloponnesus, Macedonia, and Bœotia; and Gabinius, Syria, Babylon, and Persia. We can well imagine the visions of plunder that rose before their eyes at such a prospect.

Everything was now ripe for the final blow. At a meeting of the people in their comitia, Clodius came forward and proposed the following law:—" Be it enacted, that whoever has put to death a Roman citizen uncondemned in due form of trial, shall be interdicted from fire and water." Cicero's name was not mentioned; but it was a bill of pains and penalties against him; and he called it therefore a *privilegium*—that is, a law not of general but special application. He saw at once the imminent peril in which he stood. If it passed, he was undone; for there was no doubt that Clodius would see it executed to the letter. His only chance of safety lay in exciting the sympathy of the sovereign people, and enlisting their compassion on his side. For this purpose he dressed himself in mourning and went about the streets beseeching the pity of the populace, as if he were canvassing for their votes at an election. The whole equestrian class put on mourning also. All Italy seemed moved at the thought of Cicero's danger. Deputations of

burghers came up from distant towns to Rome to implore
the consuls to protect him. When he appeared as a sup-
pliant in the Forum or the streets, he was accompanied by
large bodies of friends in mourning, for twenty thousand
of the noblest youths of Rome testified their attachment
and their sorrow by changing their dress. As the procession moved along it was insulted and mobbed by Clodius
and a gang of ruffians, who pelted Cicero with stones and
mud. It is difficult for us to realize the scenes of lawless
riot, of which the streets and Forum of Rome were the
witness in those days. They were not unlike the bloody
feuds that raged in the streets of Genoa and Venice and
Verona in the middle ages.

The Senate met and passed a resolution that the whole
house should go into mourning. But Gabinius (Piso
being absent on the plea of ill health) interfered, and, by
virtue of his executive power as consul, prohibited such a
mark of respect. Knights and senators flung themselves
at his feet in vain; and Clodius was at the door with an
armed rabble ready to enforce the consul's order. Upon
this numbers of the senators tore open their robes, and
with cries of indignation rushed out of the senate-house.
Cicero attempted to gain Piso on his side. He went to
his house, accompanied by his son-in-law, Piso Frugi, the
consul's relative, and there had an interview with him.
But it led to nothing. Piso said that Gabinius could not
do without Clodius, and, as for himself, he must stand by
his colleague, as Cicero had stood by Antonius when he
was consul: every one must take care of his own safety.

In the mean time, what was Pompey doing? Where
was the friendship he had so often professed for Cicero—
where were the promises he had made when he swore that he
would defend him against Clodius with his life? Whether
it was from fear or treachery, or both, he abandoned him to

his fate. He had retired to his villa called Albanum, near the
modern town of Albano, about twenty miles from Rome,
not, we may well believe, because he credited the reports
which Clodius and his partisans spread, that his life was
threatened by Cicero's friends, but because he wished to
take no active part in the disgraceful proceedings that were
going on, and to avoid the importunities of the most distinguished men at Rome, praying him to exert his influence
to put a stop to them. But Lucullus and Torquatus and
Lentulus, who was then prætor, and other noblemen hastened to him, and urgently intreated him not to abandon his
friend, with whose safety the welfare of the State was
bound up. Pompey coldly referred them to the consuls,
saying that he, as a private individual, would not enter
on a contest with an armed tribune of the people; but, if
the consuls and the Senate were willing to do so and
called upon him to assist, he was ready to draw the sword.

In the extremity of his despair, Cicero made a last
effort to save himself. He went to Albanum and humiliated himself so far as to throw himself on the ground at
Pompey's feet, who did not even ask him to rise, but told
him as he lay there that he could do nothing against the
will of Cæsar. Plutarch indeed gives a different account,
and says that Pompey avoided the interview by slipping
out at a back-door. But we have Cicero's positive
statement that the scene occurred as I have related it, and
this is, of course, conclusive. What, then, was he to do?
Four courses were open to him, and they were all de-
liberately discussed by himself and his friends. Either he
might meet Clodius in an armed contest in the streets; or
in a criminal trial in the courts of law; or he might
seek safety in flight; or he might commit suicide. Lucullus counselled him to stay, and, if necessary, fight for
his life. His friends were numerous and would stand by

him, if it came to blows; nor was there any reason to fear
that they and their followers would not be more than a
match for the armed rabble of Clodius. This, no doubt,
was the bold and manly course, and Cicero bitterly regretted afterwards that he did not adopt it. But he had
a horror of violence and bloodshed; and it was not in his
nature to act as Cæsar, or Cromwell, or Napoleon would
have acted at such a crisis. Cato, Hortensius, and Atticus,
and his own family advised him to quit Rome, assuring
him that in a very few days he would be brought back in
triumph. As to suicide, all his friends, and especially
Atticus, appear to have dissuaded him from it. From a
Roman point of view, such an act would have been justifiable, for, according to heathen ethics, suicide was preferable
to disgrace.

Cæsar was still at Rome, but outside the walls, having
assumed the command of his army; and Clodius assembled
the people in the Circus Flaminius beyond the gates,
where Cæsar could be present, it not being lawful for him
to remain inside the city now that he was at the head of
his legions. Clodius there publicly asked Cæsar what he
thought of Cicero's conduct in his consulship. He replied
that the proceedings against the associates of Catiline were
contrary to law, as he had repeatedly asserted; but that in
a matter so long gone by and ended, he thought they
ought not to judge severely—he himself always preferred
mild measures. This was all that the most powerful of
the Romans would say on Cicero's behalf, and he was left
to his fate. He had long kept in his house a small statue
of Minerva, who was regarded as the tutelary deity of
Rome, as well as of Athens. This he took to the Temple
of Jupiter in the Capitol, and there dedicated it with the
inscription MINERVÆ CUSTODI URBIS. He then quitted
the city, accompanied outside the walls by a large body of

friends in tears. But he left his family behind, not wishing to involve them in the discomforts of a journey, of
which he hardly then knew the direction or the limit. He
buoyed himself up, however, with the hope—which was
increased by the assurances of his too sanguine friends—
that in a few days he would be recalled back to Rome.

It was about the twentieth of March when he turned
his back upon the city, and the same day Clodius brought
before the people a bill interdicting Cicero (naming him)
from fire and water, and enacting that no one should
receive him in his house within five hundred miles of
Italy. This was the purport of the bill, but the untech-
nical way in which it was worded gave Cicero the opportunity, after his return, of ridiculing the blundering drafts-
man who had framed it. The language of the first sec-
tion or paragraph ran thus:—"Is it your pleasure, and
do you enact, that M. Tullius *has been interdicted* from
fire and water?" instead of enacting that M. Tullius "*be
interdicted*." Now, as the interdiction was the consequence
of, and could not precede the law that created it, it was
manifestly nonsense to enact that something *had* happened
which had not yet taken place. But Clodius cared little for
technical accuracy provided he could pass the measure
which would outlaw his hated enemy, and make him a
homeless and houseless fugitive. It was further enacted
that, if Cicero was seen within the forbidden limits, both
he and all who gave him shelter might be killed with impunity. But, to the honor of Italy be it said, this barbarous clause was treated as a dead letter, and disregarded
by everybody.[1]

An alteration was made in the bill before it was finally
submitted to the vote, and four hundred miles were substi-

---

[1] Poena est, qui receperit: quam omnes neglexerunt.—*Pro Domo*,
c. 20.

tuted for five hundred. The Forum was filled with slaves and partisans of Clodius, many of whom were armed; and in the midst of noise, and tumult, and confusion, the bill passed and became law.

Without a moment's delay it was put in force in all its terrible severity. Cicero was at once treated as beyond the pale of the law, and his property was confiscated. Before nightfall his house on the Palatine Hill was in flames and reduced to ashes. His Tusculan and Formian villas were afterwards plundered and laid waste. On part of the site where the Palatine house had stood Clodius erected a temple, which he dedicated to Liberty; and he pulled down the adjoining portico of Catulus, and built another, to which he gave his own name.

Let us follow the footsteps of the exile. He seems to have travelled slowly, hoping for a time to hear that he was recalled. He left Rome no doubt by the Capuan Gate (*Porta Capena*), and followed the Via Appia, which runs towards the south, as it may still be seen, paved with its large irregular slabs of stone, just as when Cicero passed along it on his melancholy journey. On the eighth of April he was somewhere in Lucania (part of the modern kingdom of Naples), on the road to Vibo, a small town on the coast, now Monte Leone. Here he wrote to Atticus, and begged him to come to him, saying, " I know that the journey is a troublesome one, but my calamity is full of all kinds of trouble." He told his friend that, unless he accompanied him, he should not venture to cross over to Epirus, in case it should be necessary to leave Italy, because Autronius, a fellow-conspirator with Catiline, was then living in exile in the neighbourhood, and he was bitterly hostile to Cicero, as one of the authors of his banishment. He concluded his letter with the words, " More I cannot write. I am so distressed and cast down." His

intention was to go to Sicily, of which Virgilius was
governor, or to Malta; and he proceeded as far as Vibo,
close to which a friend of his named Sica had a farm, in
which he generously received him. It seems to have been
about this time that he had the dream to which he alludes
in his treatise *de Divinatione.* A vision of Marius, with
his laurelled fasces, appeared to him, and asked him why
he was so sad. He answered that he had been expelled
from his country, upon which Marius took him by the
hand, bade him be of good cheer, and ordered one of his
lictors to conduct him to his own monument or temple,
where he would find safety. His faithful freedman, Sallust, who was with him, declared that this betokened a
speedy and happy return.[2]

While he was staying with Sica, a letter was sent to
him from Virgilius forbidding him to cross over to Sicily.
At the same time, he got a copy of Clodius's bill, as
amended and passed, which limited the distance within
which he was not to reside to four hundred miles. This,
however, made it unsafe for him to stay at Vibo, and he
was also obliged to abandon the idea he had formed of
going to Malta. He, therefore, turned his steps in the
direction of Brundusium, the most convenient port for
reaching the opposite coast of Greece. On the tenth of
April he was at Thurii, and wrote to Atticus, telling him
how grateful Terentia was for all his kindness to her, and
describing his own wretchedness. His family had great
need just then of friendship and protection, and, if we may
believe what he says in one of his speeches, and it is not

---

[2] This dream was regarded by Cicero as prophetic, and was supposed
to have its fulfilment in the fact that the decree of the Senate recalling
him was made in the temple constructed by Marius out of the spoils
taken in the Cimbrian Wars, and called on that account *Monumentum
Marii.* We may remember that something of the same kind is said to
have occurred in the prophecy of the death of Henry IV.—

"In that Jerusalem shall Harry die."

an oratorical exaggeration, even the lives of his children were threatened.[3]

On the eighteenth of April he arrived at Brundusium, where he got letters from Atticus earnestly begging him to cross over to Epirus, and stay at his country seat there, in the neighbourhood of Buthrotus. The house was a fortified one, which Cicero admitted would be an advantage, if he took up his abode in it, and he could there enjoy the solitude he sought. But it was out of the way if he adhered to his intention of going into Asia Minor, and was too near the residence of Autronius, who had an armed band of desperadoes with him. He wished to make Athens his place of sojourn; but was afraid that it would be considered to be within the prohibited distance from Italy. In fact, he was sorely puzzled and perplexed what to do. He wrote to Atticus, and told him that his advice and remonstrance prevented him from laying violent hands on himself; but could not make him cease to regret that he had adopted the plan of flight instead of committing suicide.

He did not stay in the town of Brundusium, fearing to compromise the safety of the friendly inhabitants, but occupied for a fortnight a building in the gardens of a Roman knight, M. Lænius Flaccus, who, braving all danger of the Clodian law, afforded to the unhappy exile the shelter of which he stood so much in need. His first letter to Terentia, during his banishment, that we possess is dated from this place, and gives a most melancholy picture of his state of mind. He says that he would send letters oftener to her, but whenever he writes to her or receives letters from her, he is so blinded by tears that he cannot bear it.

"Ah!" he exclaims, "that I had been less desirous of life! assuredly I should have seen nothing, or at all events not much, of misery in life.

---

[3] *Pro Sext.*, 24.

THE PORT OF BRUNDUSIUM.

But if fortune preserves me to the hope of recovering any of the blessings I have lost, I have been less guilty of error; but if these evils admit of no change, still I wish to see you, my life, as soon as possible, and die in your embrace, since neither the Gods whom *you* have most religiously worshipped, nor men whom *I* have served, have shown us any gratitude."

The language of his grief is almost incoherent, and is painful to read. He bursts out :

" O ! lost and afflicted as I am, why should I ask you to come to me? You a woman, weak in health, worn out both in body and mind! Yet must I not ask you? Can I then exist without you?... Be assured of this, if I have you I shall not think myself wholly lost. But what will become of my darling Tullia ? Do you both see to it. I can give no advice. . . . And my Cicero, what will he do? I cannot write more— my grief prevents me. I know not what has become of you—whether you still keep anything, or, as I fear, have been utterly ruined. I hope that Piso (his son-in-law) will, as you write, always remain true to us."

He then alludes to the emancipation of their slaves, and tells her not to trouble herself about them. His wife seems throughout to have acted with firmness and courage, and to have done her best to rouse the drooping spirits of her husband, who had abandoned all hope. He goes on—

" As for what remains, my Terentia, support yourself as you best can. I have lived with honor. I have enjoyed prosperity. It is not my crimes, but my virtue, that has crushed me. I have committed no fault except that of not having lost my life when I lost all that adorns life. But if it was my children's wish that I should live, let me bear the rest, although it is intolerable. And I who console you cannot console myself. . . . Take all the care possible of your health, and remember that I am more disturbed by your sorrow than my own. Farewell, my Terentia, my most faithful and best of wives! and my dearest daughter, and Cicero, our only remaining hope !"

Is it possible to believe that the wife to whom he thus wrote was a jealous, imperious, and bad-tempered woman ? and yet this is what Plutarch, and those who follow Plutarch, would wish us to suppose.

At the end of April, Flaccus accompanied him on board a vessel which left the port of Brundusium, and after a stormy passage, they reached Dyrrachium, on the opposite coast. Here he met with a kind and hospitable reception, for there were old ties of friendship between himself and the Dyrrachians, whose patron he had been at Rome; but he did not dare to remain. He dreaded the neighbourhood of Autronius and other banished or fugitive conspirators, and he was anxious to reach Macedonia, of which, at that time, his friend Cnæus Plancius was quæstor. When Plancius heard of his arrival at Dyrrachium, he hastened to meet him, not only without any of the pomp of office, but dressed in mourning. Cicero took the most northerly route to the province, and the two friends met on the way. They embraced each other silently in tears, their hearts being too full for words; and then Plancius turned and accompanied him to Thessalonica, where they arrived on the twenty-third of May, and where Cicero took up his abode for seven months in the house of his friend.

He wrote to Atticus from Thessalonica, and told him that he intended to follow his advice, and wait until the journals of the Senate for May (*Acta mensis Maiæ*) reached him, that he might know what was done.[4] He bitterly reproaches himself for the blindness of his folly in having trusted a man who had betrayed him, and from subsequent letters he appears to have here alluded to Hortensius; but, at the same time, he throws blame upon Atticus for not having been more sharpsighted than himself. There seems to have been no real ground for Cicero's suspicions that Hortensius had played him false; but it is abundantly clear that for some time he was under this painful impression. We know, however, how completely the feeling passed away, and in what touching language he spake of his glorious rival when he died.

---

[4] This is a sufficiently correct rendering of the word *Acta*. A diary or journal of the proceedings of the Senate was kept, and it is the nearest approximation to a gazette that existed in ancient Rome.

In a letter to his brother, written on the fifth of June, he gave vent to his feelings in a burst of passionate grief:—

"My brother! my brother! my brother!" he begins, "To think that you feared that out of anger I sent a messenger to you without a letter, or that I even did not wish to see you! That I should be angry with you! *Could* I be angry with you? . . . . That I was unwilling to see you! Yes! I *was* unwilling to be seen by you. For you would not have seen your brother—not him whom you had quitted; not him whom you had known; not him whom you left in tears at your departure, when you were yourself in tears—not even a trace of him—not a shadow, but the image of a breathing corpse. And would that you had before this seen me dead or heard that I was dead. Would that I had left you the survivor and heir, not only of my life but of my rank and reputation. But I call to witness all the gods that I was deterred from death by this sole consideration—that all declared that with my life some part of your's was bound up. Therefore I erred and acted wickedly. For if I had died, death itself would have asserted my affection and love towards you. Now I have brought it to pass that though I live you cannot be with me—and I have lost others—and in the perils of my home and family my voice was powerless which had often been a protection to those who were utter strangers to me."

Enough has been given to show the tenor of Cicero's letters at this period, and to make us grieve for the weakness of so eminent a man. Like the roll of Ezekiel, there is written therein lamentation, and mourning, and woe. Seldom has misfortune so crushed a noble spirit, and never perhaps has the "bitter bread of banishment" seemed more bitter to any one than to him. We must remember that the love of country was a passion with the ancients to a degree which it is now difficult to realize; and exile from it, even for a time, was felt to be an intolerable evil. The nearest approach to such a feeling was perhaps that of some favorite under an European monarchy, when frowned upon by his sovereign he was hurled from place and power and banished from the court. The change to Cicero was, indeed, tremendous. Not only was he an exile from Rome, the scene of all his hopes, his glories, and his

triumphs, but he was under the ban of an outlaw.	If
found within a certain distance from the Capitol, he must
die; and it was death to any one to give him food or
shelter.	His property was destroyed, his family was pen-
niless, and the people whom he had so faithfully served
were the authors of his ruin.	All this may be urged in
his behalf; but, still, it would have been only consistent
with Roman fortitude to have shown that he possessed
something of the spirit of the fallen archangel, who
exclaimed—

> " What matter where if I be still the same?
> The mind is its own place, and of itself
> Can make of Heaven a Hell, of Hell a Heaven."

Wieland was so impressed with· this painful exhibition of
Cicero's weakness, that he says that good service would
have been done to his reputation if his freedman Tiro, or
whoever it was that collected and published his letters, had
taken the whole of those he wrote to his wife, to his
brother, and to Atticus during his exile, and thrown them
into the fire.	Middleton mourns over the weakness of his
idol, but, determined if possible to excuse him, says, that
" to have been as great in affliction as he was in prosperity
would have been a perfection not given to man."	But we
cannot accept this view.	In prosperity Cicero was far from
being faultless, although in moral and social qualities he
shone like a star amidst his contemporaries.	But what we
complain of is not that he was not equal to himself in misfortune, but that he fell so far below himself, and showed
a pusillanimity which it is humiliating to contemplate.
And yet it is better that this should be known, in order
that we may appreciate his real character, than that we
should have been imposed upon by the destruction of his
letters, and led to believe that he was something different
from what he was.	For if they had been destroyed, and

we had to depend for our knowledge of his demeanor during his banishment solely upon his speeches and letters after his return, we should form a most erroneous estimate of the facts. There he speaks bravely enough of himself, and would have the world suppose that he quitted Rome, not because he was afraid for himself, but solely out of regard to the public interest; and that he bore his calamity with the same courage he had displayed when he faced the conspiracy of Catiline.

During all this trying period Atticus acted the part of a true friend. He assisted Terentia with money, and devoted himself in every way to the interests of Cicero. He tried to cheer the fainting heart of the exile with hope, and to force him to take a more manly view of his position, but in vain. So extravagant was his grief that people began to believe that his mind was affected by insanity. To all the reproaches of Atticus, who strove by that means to shame him into fortitude, he opposed the magnitude of his ruin, and perpetually contrasted the height to which he had once risen with the depth to which he had now fallen. He entreated his friend to spare him, but he was not so ready to spare his friend. In a remarkable letter written to him in August he accuses Atticus of having allowed his affection to blind his judgment, and with the wayward injustice of a man who is determined to find fault, throws upon him part of the blame that such a calamity had overtaken him. But at the same time he expressed in the strongest terms his sense of his friend's services, and the deep obligation he was under to him. Indeed, nothing can show more clearly the sincerity of the friendship between these two eminent men than the liberty, so to speak, which they took with each other in telling home truths. Cicero did not hesitate to reproach Atticus and Atticus Cicero, when each thought the other in the wrong, with a plainness and frankness which it is more easy to admire than it would be generally safe to imitate. But he wronged his friend when he complained of his conduct with reference to his exile. Never did man find in misfortune more devotion than he found in Atticus and Quintus, and he fully experienced then the truth of the divine and touching aphorism, "a friend loveth at all times, and a brother is born for adversity."

In one of his letters about this time there is a curious passage, which is not very creditable to him. It appears that some speech which he had written against Curio, but not delivered, had, contrary to his intention, got into circulation without his knowledge, and was doing him harm. The composition, however, was careless, and so far it was unlike his style. It occurred to him therefore, that he might deny the authorship. *Puto*, he writes to Atticus, *posse probari non esse meum*, and he begs him to take steps to that effect. So that in fact he was ready to tell a falsehood and disavow his own handwriting in order to escape the responsibility in which it might involve him!

During his stay at Thessalonica L. Tubero, one of Quintus's legates, came there and earnestly advised Cicero to go into Asia Minor, as he did not think him safe so near Achaia, where his enemies were active and powerful. But Plancius persuaded him to remain, although he hesitated long and was in as much perplexity and distress as ever. The letters he received from his friends at Rome urged him not to go further away, and held out cheering assurances that better times were at hand. Sextius, one of the new tribunes elect, his son-in-law Piso, and Atticus, all advised him to stay at Thessalonica, as the aspect of affairs at Rome looked more favorable. Atticus and Varro tried to restore his confidence in Pompey, who had so meanly deserted him in the hour of danger, and they hinted that even Cæsar might be depended upon to assist him. Quintus also did his utmost to encourage and console his brother. But Cicero was like Rachel weeping and mourning and would not be comforted. He again and again reproached Atticus with want of foresight and judgment, and it must have been most painful to that faithful friend to receive his letters, although they did not in the slightest degree make him take offence or relax in his exertions. He continued to supply not only Cicero but his family with money, which he was now able to do more easily, as his rich uncle Cæcilius had died and left him his heir.[5] To add to Cicero's troubles he heard that his brother Quintus had met with the usual fate of Roman governors, and was impeached for illegal administration of his province. His accuser was a nephew of Clodius, and in the ordinary course of things his trial would come on before Appius Clodius, the elder brother of his enemy, who was then prætor elect.

In September Cicero declared his intention of going to Epirus, to the residence of Atticus, and in the bitterness of despair he begged his friend to let him have as much land as would suffice for a burial-ground for his body. The soldiers of Piso, to whom had been assigned the proconsular government of Macedonia, now entered that province, and Cicero in terror quitted the hospitable dwelling of Plancius, and on the 26th of November arrived at Dyrrachium, where he was sure of a respectful welcome.

Let us cast a rapid glance at the events that had happened in the interval at Rome. Much against his will Cato had had an appointment forced upon him by Clodius, which it appears he either could not or did not think it prudent to decline. In June the tribune Ninnius,

---

[5] From this time Atticus assumed the name of Q. Cæcilius Q. Fil. Pomponianus Atticus.

at whose instance the **Senate** had gone into mourning
when Clodius introduced his **bill** of pains and penalties
against Cicero, brought **before the** Senate, with Pompey's
approval, a motion for his **recal.** The Senate unanimously
resolved that the **proposal** should be recommended to the
people in order that a law might be passed. But the
tribune Ælius Ligur, acting under the influence of Clodius,
interposed his veto. The Senate, however, adopted their
usual expedient when they were in earnest. They resolved
that they would transact no public business **until the
consuls introduced** a new motion to the same effect. But
the consuls refused to do this, and matters came to a dead
lock. Pompey communicated through Varro to Cicero
his willingness to serve him, but still insisted that he could
do nothing without Cæsar's consent. **On** the eleventh of
August a plot was discovered of Clodius to murder Pompey, who, in real or affected alarm, shut himself up in his
house and declared that he would not go out until the
period of Clodius's tribuneship had expired. Of the two
consuls **Gabinius** ranged himself on the side of Pompey,
but **Piso** still acted under the influence of Clodius. So
violent and lawless were the times that even the two
consuls found themselves engaged on opposite sides in a
street affray. The *fasces* of Piso were broken, and he
himself was wounded by a stone. But a change of
an important kind was approaching. The new consuls
for the following year had been elected in July, and these
were P. Cornelius Lentulus Spinther and Q. Metellus
Nepos. Lentulus had been ædile when Cicero was consul, and was a warm friend of both him and Pompey.
Metellus had been, as we have seen, the declared enemy of
Cicero when he was tribune, but his brother Metellus
Celer was Cicero's friend, and he did not wish to act in
opposition to Pompey. Atticus also urgently appealed to

his compassion on behalf of the exile, and, as the result
proved, with success. The new tribunes elect, amongst
whom was Titus Annius Milo, were almost all favorable
to Cicero, and when on the twenty-ninth of October a fresh
motion was made by Ninnius in the Senate for his recal
eight of them voted for it. These eight then brought
forward a bill before the people founded on the resolution
of the Senate, but it did not pass. Cicero himself did not
approve of this bill, which did not go far enough to satisfy
him. It provided only for the restitution of his civic
rights and former rank, but made no mention of the restoration of his property, especially of his house on the
Palatine, the destruction of which had much affected him.

Soon after he had taken up his residence at Dyrrachium
the year of office of the existing tribunes expired, and
Clodius, no longer armed with that terrible power, became
once more a private citizen, although of course he still
remained a senator; and before the close of the year both
the consuls Piso and Gabinius left Rome to assume the
government of their respective provinces. The period had
all but arrived which even Cicero had admitted would
allow him to entertain hope. And yet even now he felt
almost as much discouraged as ever. He was disappointed
that Pompey and Cæsar did not declare themselves more
openly in his favor, and on the last day of November he
wrote to his wife in a fit of the deepest dejection:—

"I have received," he says, "three of your letters, which I have
almost blotted out with my tears. For, my Terentia, I am worn out
with sorrow; nor do my own miseries cause me more torture than those
of yourself and yours. But in this I am more wretched than you, who
are most wretched, because the calamity itself is common to us both,
but the fault is my own. It was my duty either to avoid the danger by
accepting an embassy, or resist with prudence and sufficient resources,
or fall bravely. Nothing was ever more wretched, base, or more unworthy of myself than my conduct in this. Therefore while I am
crushed by grief I am also crushed by shame. For I am ashamed that
I was wanting in manliness (virtutem) and resolution to you, the best

of wives, and my dearest children. For day and night I am haunted by the thoughts of your misery and sorrow, and the weakness of your health. But very slight hopes of safety are held out to me. My enemies are numerous, and almost all are envious of me. It was a great triumph to expel me; it is easy to keep me in banishment. . . . That our Piso devotes himself with extraordinary zeal in your behalf, I both myself perceive and everybody tells me the same.[6] May the Gods grant that I may be permitted to enjoy the society of such a son-in-law, along with you and our children! . . . Pray be careful of your health, and be assured that nothing is, nor ever was, dearer to me than you. Farewell, my Terentia, whom I fancy I see, and therefore I am weakened by my tears. Farewell!"

It is a great pity that none of the letters of this affectionate and true-hearted woman have been preserved, that we might have read the outpourings of her heart and seen the way in which she sought to cheer and sustain the broken spirit of her husband. Time, however, has been a ruthless destroyer of female correspondence ; I am not aware that we possess a single letter written by a Greek or Roman lady before the Christian era. The comparatively low estimation in which the sex was held in ancient times made the copyists disregard them, and female authors were unknown at Rome. But gladly would we exchange many a literary relic of antiquity for a collection of the letters of Terentia written to Cicero during his banishment. On the same day he wrote to Atticus and said :—

" But if there is no hope (as I perceive both by your conjecture and my own) I pray and adjure you to cherish with affection my brother Quintus, miserable as he is, whom I have miserably ruined. Protect, as well as you can, my Cicero, to whom, poor child, I leave nothing but the odium and ignominy of my name ; and support by your good offices Terentia, of all women the most destitute and afflicted."

Atticus left Rome in December, and on his way to his country seat in Epirus paid Cicero a visit at Dyrrachium.

And so the first year of his banishment passed away.

---

[6] Piso was this year quæstor of Pontus and Bithynia, but instead of going to his province he remained in Rome, to do what he could for the cause of his father-in-law.

Chapter XIII.

THE RETURN.

Æt. 50. B.C. 57.

THE new year opened auspiciously for Cicero.   From all parts of Italy deputations had come up to Rome to intercede on his behalf.   On the first of January, the very moment after the sacred rites were over with which the consuls inaugurated their office, Lentulus brought forward, in a crowded Senate, a motion for his recal.   His colleague Metellus supported him, and L. Cotta, who had been consul a few years previously, insisted that as the proceedings against Cicero had been wholly illegal and contrary to usage, no fresh law was required to enable him to return.   He proposed that he should be not only recalled, but recalled with distinguished marks of honor.   Pompey, however, was of opinion, and he seems to have been right, that an edict of the people (*lex*) was necessary to give validity to a resolution of the Senate.   For the banishment of Cicero had been ordained by a law passed by an assembly of the people legally convoked ; the enactment was still in force and would remain so until repealed by the same authority that passed it.   The Senate agreed in this view, and a resolution to that effect would have been carried forthwith had not Serranus, one of the tribunes, who had been quæstor during Cicero's consulship, and as he says loaded by him with benefits, not venturing to interpose his veto, forced on an adjournment on the pretext that a night was required for deliberation.   He was entreated by the Senate to give way, and his father-in-law Cnæus Oppius flung himself in tears at his feet in vain. The deliberation that Serranus wanted was soon explained. It was to increase the amount of the bribe he received from Clodius, and the night was spent in adjusting the terms of the bargain. This adjournment led to further delay, and it was not until the 25th of January that a bill for Cicero's recal, notwithstanding the continued opposition of Serranus, was brought before an assembly of the people. But Clodius was as desperate as ever, and attended by an armed band of gladiators, whom he had got from his brother, who was going to exhibit them at a show on the occasion of the funeral of a relative, he rushed into the Forum, and a riot ensued in which blows were struck and several lives were lost. The tribune Serranus was severely wounded, and Quintus Cicero narrowly escaped with his life; indeed he was left for dead on the ground. The consequence was that the bill did not pass, and Clodius enjoyed a temporary triumph.

This affords a strong illustration of the evils of the constitution of Rome. All Italy, the Senate, the two consuls, all the tribunes with one exception, Pompey and Cæsar (who was however absent) the two foremost men of Rome, an overwhelming number of the nobility and respectable class of citizens wished for Cicero's return, and yet the wishes of all were frustrated and their action paralyzed by the violence of one bold bad man. But the explanation is easy. Every Roman burgher had the franchise, and his vote was as good as that of the wealthiest and most powerful citizen. But the lower class of the Roman population was needy and corrupt, and in the tumultuous throng that crowded the Forum or the Circus when the people assembled to vote, there were always numbers ready for a riot or a revolt. There was no true balance of power in the constitution. No law could be passed without an appeal to universal suffrage, and what the sovereign people chose to ordain, even where legal formalities were not observed, had generally the force of law.

When Cicero heard of what had happened on the twenty-fifth of January he was in despair. Before that when the news of the Senate's resolution reached him he had determined, come what might, to go to Rome even though the law for his restoration were rejected by the people. But his resolution failed him when he found that Clodius was still master of the field.

Clodius was impeached by Milo for his illegal violence at the comitia, but his brother, who was prætor, with the aid of Metellus the consul, and Serranus the tribune, threw over him the protection of an extraordinary edict, and he laughed at the courts of law. He relied on his gladiators, and Milo took into his pay a band of the same kind of ruffians to protect himself in case of attack. The Senate again passed a resolution that they would entertain no business until Cicero was recalled. Public letters were despatched in the name of the consuls to the Italian towns, inviting them to send to Rome those who wished well to the Republic and were anxious for his return. Orders were given to all legates and quæstors in any province where he might happen to be, to treat him with respect and afford him assistance; and Pompey also at last strenuously exerted himself in his behalf. To keep the people in good humour, Lentulus gave them their favorite amusement of shows and games; and while they were thus occupied the Senate met in Marius's Temple of Honour and Virtue, and resolved that a bill should be introduced for Cicero's restoration. On the same day a scene occurred in the theatre, which showed how anxious the people were to have him back. The favorite tragedian, Æsop, was acting in the Andromache of Ennius, when several passages of the play were caught up by the audience as allusive to the fate of Cicero, and they testified their wishes by their applause.

But Clodius was able still to baffle the Senate, and in some unexplained manner prevented the bill from coming before the people. It was now the month of May, and the Senate assembled in the Temple of Jupiter in the Capitol, to make another effort for the great object they had in view. Pompey addressed them, and in the course of his speech called Cicero the saviour of his country. A resolution in his favor was again passed in a senate consisting of more than four hundred members, and as the senators afterwards in the course of the day entered the theatre to see the games that the consuls were exhibiting, they were tumultuously cheered by the spectators. On the next day Lentulus, and Pompey, and Servilius, and other distinguished men, harangued the people in the Forum, and as we may well believe, reminded them how long one eloquent tongue had been silent which had so often charmed them in that place. Stringent measures were taken to prevent the interposition of a tribune's veto or any further postponement of the measure. The Senate resolved that whoever attempted *de cœlo servare*, " to watch the heavens," or create obstacles, was an enemy of the Republic, and would be so treated. They moreover resolved that unless the bill passed in five days, Cicero might return with a full restitution of all his rights and honors.

But difficulties still stood in the way. Three of the magistrates, Appius Claudius the prætor, and Rufus and Serranus, two of the tribunes, continued their opposition notwithstanding the resolution of the Senate, and two more weary months elapsed before the bill was brought before the people. At last, on the fourth of August, the good cause triumphed. At an immense assembly of the people voting in their centuries in the Campus Martius, where from the highest to the lowest they flocked in incredible numbers, and where men of the noblest rank acted as distributors of the voting tickets and scrutineers (*diribitores et custodes*), the bill passed with hardly a dissentient voice, although Clodius addressed the multitude, and strove in a last effort to induce them to reject it. They paid no heed to the demagogue, and Cicero was recalled.

He had been kept well informed of what was going on at Rome, and felt so confident that the end of his exile was at hand, that he ventured to leave Dyrrachium for Brundusium on the very day on which the bill passed for his return. The next day he landed in Italy. It was the fifth of August—the birthday of Tullia, his beloved daughter, and she was at Brundusium eagerly waiting to fling herself into his arms. She had just become a widow, her husband, Piso Frugi, who had so nobly stood by his father-in-law in his misfortune, having died a short time before. It was also the anniversary of the founding of Brundusium, the *jour de fête* of the town, and by a curious coincidence it was the anniversary of the dedication of the Temple of Safety there. The good citizens were jubilant with joy, and welcomed the wanderer back with the liveliest sympathy.

Soon afterwards he set out on his return to Rome, which he reached in twenty-four days. The time seems long, but he travelled slowly, detained by the demonstrations of respect and honor with which he was everywhere greeted. His journey was in fact one continued ovation. In the route he took he passed through Naples, Capua, Sinuessa, Minturnæ, Formiæ,—where no doubt he cast a lingering and sorrowful look towards his dismantled villa—Terracina, and Aricia. From every town on the road the magistrates came out to offer their congratulations. The inhabitants crowded round the man in whose safety they had shown such a warm interest. The peasants abandoned their rustic labors in the fields, and brought their wives and families to see him as he passed. And from distant places deputations were sent to meet him, so that the roads were crowded by the throng. It was the gala week of all Italy, and his entry into every town and village on his route was the signal for a festive holiday.[1] But his greatest triumph was yet to come. As he approached the Capitol by the Via Appia in September, the Senate came forth in a body beyond the walls to welcome him. A gilded chariot was waiting to receive him, and on this he mounted outside the gate. The whole population of Rome seemed to have deserted the city, and choked the road and adjoining fields. Well might Cicero say that that one day was equivalent to immortality (*immortalitatis instar fuit*). When he reached the Capuan gate he saw the steps of the temples of Mars and the Muses, which were inside the walls, filled by a dense crowd who rent the air with their shouts—and as he slowly proceeded through the Forum along the Via Sacra to the Capitol,—

> " You would have thought the very windows spake,
> So many greedy looks of young and old
> Through casements darted their desiring eyes
> Upon his visage ; and that all the walls
> With painted imagery had said at once,
> ' The Gods, preserve thee ! welcome ' Cicero !' "

From the Capitol he went, as he says, *home;* but certainly not to his former home on the Palatine, which, as we know, no longer existed, but either to some temporary

---

[1] Plutarch declares that it was no exaggeration, and less than the truth, when Cicero declared that he was carried back to Rome on the shoulders of Italy.—*Cic.* c. 33.

residence provided for him, **or perhaps to the house of a
friend.** Next day he entered **the Senate-house and took**
his accustomed seat.

He rose and addressed the Senate **in a speech, which is
too** florid for modern taste, and too full of compliments to
everybody, including himself.[2] But we must remember
the audience around him, and the **character of the man.**
The intensity of his past sorrow was the measure **of his**
present joy. His sensitive and impressionable mind, **so**
easily elated and so soon depressed, bounded at the thought
of his glorious return; and we must not measure with a
cold and carping criticism the impassioned language in
which the orator poured forth his thanks to the authors of
his safety. The limits of this work will **not** allow **me to**
do more than quote one or two short passages.

After lauding the Senate to the skies, and **speaking in
complimentary** terms **of the two consuls, he passed on to
the delicate topic of his own conduct on the occasion of his
flight from Rome. We may pardon him for giving this a**
complexion **not quite** warranted **by fact. He had retired
in terror at the violence** of Clodius, **and because he wanted**
nerve to follow **the advice of** those friends who **counselled**
him to stay and **fight his enemy with his own weapons;—**
and also **because he had believed that in a few days he**

---

[2] Both this however and the consecutive orations *ad Quirites, pro
Domo suâ,* and *de Haruspicum Responsis,* are pronounced by Orelli
and others to be spurious and made up of tesselated passages from the
speeches *in Pisonem* and *pro Sextio.* Orelli thinks they were composed
ab inepto declamatore, in the early part of the reign of Augustus, and
that much use was made of Cicero's genuine work *de Expositione suorum
Conciliorum,* which, according to Dio Cassius, was written in this year.
Orelli gives no sound reason for this opinion; and, judging from internal evidence, I see no sufficient ground for discrediting them. There
is indeed a suspicious similarity, or rather identity, in many passages
between them and the Pisonian and Sextian orations, but the same objection may be made to the genuineness of those two if they are closely
compared with each other.

would be called back in triumph. Now, however, he sought to justify himself by the plea that his only object was to spare the effusion of blood—and declared that he might have defended himself by force of arms.

"Nor was I," he says, "wanting in that same courage, which is to you not unknown! But I saw that if I had vanquished my present adversary, there were too many others whom I must vanquish also. If I had been vanquished many good men must have perished, both for me and with me, and even after me. I saw that the avengers of a tribune's blood were ready on the instant, but that punishment for my death was reserved for the courts of law and for posterity. I was unwilling when as consul I had defended the common safety without having recourse to the sword to defend by arms my own safety as a private individual, and I preferred that good men should mourn over my misfortunes rather than despair in their own;—and besides, I thought that if I alone were slain it would be ignominious for me, but if I perished with many others it would be calamitous for the State."

He bitterly attacked Piso and Gabinius, the consuls of the preceding year.

"I had heard," he said, "from one of the wisest of men and the best of citizens, Quintus Catulus, that not often had there been one wicked consul, but two never, since the foundation of Rome, except in the time of Cinna. . . . But there were two consuls, whose narrow, low, poor, petty minds, filled with darkness and meanness, could not bear the light of the splendor of that honor, nor sustain nor comprehend the magnitude of so great an office ;—not consuls,—I will not call them so, but brokers of provinces and men who made merchandize of your dignity. Of whom one, in the hearing of many, demanded back from me Catiline his admirer, and the other, Cethegus his cousin—two men, the greatest villains since the memory of man ; not consuls, but robbers, who not only abandoned me, and in a cause too that was public and consular, but betrayed and opposed me, and wished me to be bereft of every assistance, not only from them, but from you and all other classes— of whom one, however, deceived and disappointed neither me nor any one else."

He here alluded to Gabinius, upon whom he next poured out all the vials of his wrath,—describing his character and morals in language to which a Roman Senate might listen, but which is hardly fit for Englishmen to read. I can only glance at some of the charges which the infuriated orator enforced with all the power of his eloquence.

He accused him of ineffable sensuality, and declared that
he prostituted his person to repair his shattered fortunes.

" Had he not taken refuge at the altar of the tribuneship, he must
have been thrown into prison by the number of his creditors,, and his
property would have been confiscated. When a countless multitude
had gone to him from the Capitol and implored him as suppliants and
mourners,—when the noblest of the Roman youths, and the body of
knights, had thrown themselves at the feet of that most filthy panderer,
with what a look did the frizzled debauchee (*cincinnatus ganeo*) cast
from him not only the tears of the citizens, but the prayers of his
country ! When the Senate had resolved to change their dress and put
on the garb of mourning, he, smeared with greasy ointments, in his magisterial robe of office, which all the prætors and ædiles had then
thrown off, laughed at their misery and mocked their sorrow. . . . When
however in the Circus Flaminius, he was introduced as consul to the
meeting to deliver an harangue, not by a tribune of the people, but by
a robber and arch-pirate (of course Clodius was meant,, he came forward—
and with what a dignified appearance ! full of wine, sleep, and lust, with
moistened curls and dressed hair, heavy eyes, flabby cheeks, a squeak-
ing and drunken voice, he, a grave authority ! declared that he was extremely displeased that citizens had been punished without a trial.
Where has the great authority so long hidden himself from us? Why
has the distinguished virtue of this dancer with the curling-tongs so
long been absent from his scenes of licentiousness and riot ?"

He then turned upon Piso, and drew his portrait in
colors quite as black. Piso had, he said, early in life
practised as an advocate in the Forum, although he had
nothing to recommend him except an affected solemnity of
countenance. He had never studied law ; he possessed no
gift of oratory—no acquaintance with military affairs, no
knowledge of mankind, no generosity of mind. As you
passed by him, you might notice that he was rough, unpolished, and morose ; but would not suppose that he was
a sensualist and a villain. He was of a dark and swarthy
complexion, and Cicero proceeded—

" Between this man and an Æthiopian block, if you had placed it
in the Forum, you would think there was no difference—a thing without feeling or taste; a tongueless, sluggish, scarcely human piece of
matter. You would say that he had just been carried off from a gang

of Cappadocian slaves. At home too how licentious! how impure! how intemperate! with his voluptuous pleasures, admitted, not through the front door, but a secret postern."

Afterwards, on the same day, he addressed the people in the Forum in an harangue, which is known as the oration *ad Quirites*. He went over much the same ground as in his speech to the Senate, praising the people as he had praised the senators; and it is curious to observe how he clothed the same idea in different words. Often, however, the passages are identical, and prove, if they are genuine, that both the speeches were carefully prepared and written beforehand, as was the case with most of his orations. And, indeed, it may be remarked in passing, that the Greeks and Romans had no idea that it detracted in the least from the merit of an orator that he had composed his speech. The great masters of the art of eloquence were too conscious of its difficulty and too anxious to succeed to be ashamed to confess that upon this, as upon all other arts, labor and pains and trouble must be bestowed.

It happened that about this time, when Cicero was panegyrizing the people, they, or at all events a considerable part of them, were engaged in a serious riot. A severe scarcity had occurred at Rome, and the price of provisions rose to an exorbitant height. There had been a deficiency in the provinces, chiefly Sicily, that supplied Rome with grain; and the corn-factors kept the grain in their warehouses to take advantage of famine prices. In fact, a famine had begun, and the usual consequences followed. The mob rushed first to the theatre, where the shows and games of the Apollinarian festival were going on, and by tumult and disturbance drove the spectators out of the building. They then proceeded to the Capitol where the Senate was sitting, and, headed by Clodius, with an armed band of

desperadoes whom he had taken into his pay, and drilled
in companies almost like regular soldiers, they attacked
the senators with stones. Quintus Metellus, the consul, his
own brother-in-law, was struck, and he afterwards named
in the Senate two of the men who had thrown the stones.
These were Lollius and Sergius, whom Cicero thus
describes in his speech *pro Domo*, in his fiercest style of
virulent invective. Addressing Clodius, he asked :—

"Who is this Lollius? who not even now is without a sword by your
side—who demanded of you when you were a tribune of the people the
life, I say nothing of myself, but the life of Pompey. Who is Sergius?
the squire (*armiger*) of Catiline—one of his body-guard—the standard-
bearer of sedition—the getter-up of tavern brawls—convicted of violence
—a stabber, a stoner—the terror of the Forum—the besieger of the
senate-house."

The mob was so violent, threatening to burn down the
temple of Jupiter, that many of the senators were afraid to
enter the building, and declared that they did not dare to
deliver their opinions on the subject of the scarcity which
was the question then before the house. Clodius made
use of the famine to calumniate Cicero, and strove to make
the ignorant rabble believe that he was the author of their
distress. In one sense, indeed, he may be said to have
been the innocent cause of it, for there is little doubt that
the price of provisions at Rome was affected by the prodigious number of persons who had flocked to the city from
all parts of Italy, to evince their interest in his safety and
witness his return. But this was not the sense in which
Clodius made the charge, although in any other there was
and could be as little connection between Cicero and the
scarcity as between Tenterden steeple and Goodwin Sands.
He says himself: "As if I had any control over the
supply of grain, or kept corn hoarded up, or had any
power or authority in the matter." But it was believed
by the starving populace, and they shouted his name as

they rushed along the streets, demanding bread from
Cicero, as the Parisian mob demanded it from Marie
Antoinette. Both the consuls summoned him to the
senate-house, from which he had kept away while Clodius
and his ruffians occupied the immediate vicinity. Means
were taken to disperse the mob, and Cicero did not shrink
from his duty like many of the senators, but attended at
his post, and, seeing that the measure would be popular,
proposed a resolution that a law should be submitted to
the people, conferring upon Pompey for five years the
absolute power of regulating the import of grain from all
parts of the world. The resolution was carried; and
when it was communicated to the people, they loudly
cheered the mention of Cicero's name,—a mode of applause
which he says was both foolish and novel.[3] He then
made them a speech out of doors; and as the price of
provisions had already begun to fall—indeed, it fell on the
very day when the Senate first passed a resolution for his
recal, but afterwards rose again—they were kept in good
humour, and there was no further disturbance.[4]

Next day, in a crowded Senate, everything was granted
that Pompey required. He asked for fifteen lieutenants,
and put Cicero's name at the head of the list, declaring
that he looked upon him as a second self. The consuls
drew up a bill in the terms of the former resolution; but
Messius, one of the senators, proposed another, which gave
Pompey extravagant power. It conferred upon him a
fleet and an army, and such command over the provinces
as would have superseded the authority of their respective
governors. One consequence of this move of Messius was,
that Cicero's resolution, which had before been thought by

[3] More hoc insulso et novo plausum.—*Ad Att.* IV. 1.
[4] Cicero frequently alluded to the cheapness and plenty that followed
his return, and interpreted it as a special mark of the favor of Providence.

some to go too far, now appeared moderate enough, and it was ultimately passed into a law.

It has been mentioned that Atticus left Rome before the end of the preceding year. He had not yet returned, and therefore was not an eye-witness of the triumph of his friend's recal. One advantage we gain by this is, that a correspondence between them was kept up; and Cicero's letters are amongst our best sources of information as to the events of the period. In his first letter, giving a short account of his return and the subsequent incidents, he thus describes his position: "for a state of prosperity, slippery; for a state of adversity, good." He admits that he had recovered beyond his expectation his brilliant reputation in the Forum, his authority in the Senate, and his popularity with good men; but his private affairs were in great disorder, and he adds that there were, besides, some troubles of a domestic nature, which he did not like to trust to a letter. We have no means of learning to what he here alludes; but it is probable that it is a hint at some disagreement with his wife, who had behaved so nobly to him in his adversity. He entreated Atticus to come to him, and assist him with his advice, saying: "I begin, as it were, a new kind of life. Already some who defended me when I was absent begin to cherish secret anger and open envy towards me now that I am present. I want you here exceedingly."

His chief anxiety was about the restoration of his property. His house on the Palatine had been destroyed, and on part of its site had been built a temple, dedicated by Clodius, with bitter irony, to Liberty. Clodius had also levelled the adjoining portico of Catulus[5]—a monu-

---

[5] The portico stood on the site of a house which had belonged to M. Fulvius Flaccus, formerly consul, who was put to death as an accomplice

ment of his victory over the Cimbrians—and appropriated the ground, hoping that by the device of consecrating part he might keep possession of the whole. The question was, whether the land could be restored to its former owner ? Having been consecrated *ad pios usus* must it not, according to the same theory that has been advocated in later times, remain for ever inalienable ? The matter was referred to the College of Pontiffs, whose business it was to determine questions affecting religion. On the thirtieth of September, Cicero pleaded his cause before them in a speech known as the oration *pro Domo suâ*, of which he says himself, that if ever he spoke with effect it was then, when grief at his own wrongs and the import-ance of the object he had in view gave point and vigor to his eloquence.[6] It consisted in great part of a narra-tive of events which have been already related, and need not detain us now.

The pontiffs considered the case, and gave their formal opinion as follows: " If neither by a command of the free burghers in a lawful assembly (*populi jussu*), nor by a *ple-biscite*, he who avers that he dedicated the site to religious uses had specific authority given him to do so, and has done it without such authority, we are of opinion that that part of the site which has been so dedicated may, with-out any violation of religion, be restored to Cicero." This, of course, was thought conclusive in his favor, and he received the congratulations of his friends. But Clodius still crossed his path. That indefatigable enemy stopped

of Caius Gracchus. The house was pulled down, and on its foundations Catulus afterwards erected his portico. It stood next to Cicero's house.

[6] I have in a former note mentioned that the existing speech, *pro Domo suâ*, is considered by some scholars not to be genuine. Wolf is of opinion that it by no means comes up to what we might expect from Cicero's praise of it, and Markland agrees with him. My own opinion is that *si non è vero, è ben trovato*. At all events, we need not doubt that it is in many passages a close copy of the original.

at nothing to gratify his hatred. He got his brother
Appius, the prætor, to summon a public meeting, where
he harangued the people and declared that the pontiffs had
decided in his favor, but that Cicero was coming to take
possession by force. He therefore called upon them to
follow him and Appius to defend their own temple of
Liberty.[7] In the mean time the Senate, having received
the opinion of the pontiffs, many of whom were present,
proceeded to discuss it, and were quite ready to pass a
resolution in accordance with it. This was proposed by
Marcellinus, the consul-elect for the following year, and
his motion was on the point of being carried, when Serranus the tribune interposed his veto. What was now to
be done? Here, as in so many instances, legislation was
brought to a standstill by the action of the tribunician
power. Serranus had the undoubted right to exercise
his veto, and, if exercised, it was fatal to the measure.
The Senate, therefore, resorted to the expedient they had
adopted to overcome the same resistance in the case of the
bill for Cicero's recal. They could not prevent the veto,
but they could give it the go-by, and make the tribune
responsible for the consequences. They, therefore, resolved that it was the opinion of the Senate that Cicero's
house should be restored; the portico of Catulus let out
to contractors to rebuild; and the authority of their
order defended by all the magistrates. If any violence
occurred, the Senate would consider that person the author
of it who had interposed his veto. This had the desired
effect, for Serranus was frightened. His father-in-law
flung off his robe, and, throwing himself at his feet, as he

---

[7] In relating this to Atticus, Cicero puts into Clodius's mouth a pun
which is most probably his own. He says that Clodius called on the
crowd to follow him and " defend their *Liberty*," ut suam *Libertatem*
defendant.—*Ad Att.* IV.

had before done on the occasion of the bill for Cicero's recal, entreated him to give way. He asked for an adjournment to the following day, and talked of the necessity of a night for reflection. But the Senate remembered that this trick had been played before, on the first of January, and refused to grant it. At last, however, at Cicero's own suggestion, they agreed to the adjournment.

During the night, Serranus thought better of the danger to which he subjected himself if he persisted in his veto; and next day, when the Senate assembled, he withdrew his opposition, and the resolution was passed. The consuls immediately employed contractors to rebuild the portico of Catulus, and, with the assistance of assessors, they put a value upon the property of Cicero which had been destroyed, including his house on the Palatine and his villas at Tusculum and Formiæ, and for which he was to receive compensation.

He was not at all satisfied with the sums that were awarded for his houses, and declared that even the populace thought them too low. Some, he said, attributed the smallness of the compensation to his own modesty in not making a pressing demand for more; but he wrote to Atticus that the real reason was that those persons he knew of (he does not mention their names) who had clipped his wings, did not wish them to grow again. "But," he adds, "they are growing again, as I hope."

He complained grievously in his letter of the state of his private affairs, and of the cost and trouble of refurnishing his Formian villa, which he could not bring himself to part with nor bear to see. He had already advertised his villa at Tusculum for sale, although he says he could not well do without a suburban residence. He admitted that he had exhausted the liberality of his friends, who had generously assisted him with money during his banishment, and that he was now in difficulties. He added that he had other anxieties of a more secret, or, to use his own word, *mysterious* kind, evidently referring to the same cause of trouble to which he alluded in his previous letter.[8]

On the third of November, Clodius went with a band of his creatures to the Palatine, and drove off the workmen who were rebuilding Cicero's house. They also pulled down the portico of Catulus, which had been already raised as far as the roof, and after doing as much damage as they could to Quintus's adjoining house, by throwing volleys of stones at it, they, by command of Clodius, set it on fire. He had now become utterly desperate; and, knowing that if he was to be tried for his crimes he could hardly make his case worse by further violence, he attempted to murder Cicero in open day. On the eleventh of November, as he was going down from the Capitol along the Via Sacra, which ran through the Forum in the direction of the Capuan Gate, past the spot where, in after years, the Arch of Titus was erected, and where it still stands, Clodius attacked him with his cut-throats. Cicero had a body of attendants with him— indeed, it was not safe for him to go into the streets alone while Clodius was at large—and a combat ensued, in which swords, clubs, and stones were used as weapons, and in the *mêlée* Cicero escaped to the vestibule of a neighbouring house, which his assailants tried to force, but were driven off. The next day Clodius made a regular onslaught on Milo's house on the Germalus, a small hill, or mount, within the city, with a band of men

---

[8] Wieland says it undoubtedly refers to some difference between himself and "his Juno or Xantippe," adopting the unfavorable view of Terentia's character. Plutarch has much to answer for in the case of this calumniated lady.

armed with shields and swords, and carrying lighted torches. He established himself without the leave of the owner in a neighbouring house belonging to P. Sylla, making it, as Cicero says, his head-quarters, or camp, for carrying on the siege. Milo, however, was prepared for him. A body of resolute men, headed by Q. Flaccus, occupied the house, who rushed out and killed many of Clodius's followers on the spot. He himself had a narrow escape, and fled for refuge into the interior of Sylla's house.

This lawless condition of Rome had lasted, with more or less degree of violence, for more than a year. And yet it is of such a state of things that De Quincey, in his determination to say little good of Cicero, and to think no ill of Cæsar, thus writes:—

"Recluse scholars are seldom politicians; and in the timid horror of German *literati*, at this day, when they read of real brick-bats, or of paving-stones not metaphorical, used as figures of speech by a Clodian mob, we British understand the little comprehension of that rough horse-play proper to the hustings, which can as yet be available for the rectification of any continental judgment. 'Play, do you call it?' says a German commentator; 'why, that brick-bat might break a man's leg, and this paving-stone would be sufficient to fracture a skull.' Too true: they certainly might do so. But, for all that, our British experience of electioneering 'rough and tumbling' has long blunted the edge of our moral anger. Contested elections are unknown to the Continent—hitherto even to those nations of the Continent which boast of representative governments. And with no experience of their inconveniences, they have as yet none of the popular forces in which such contests originate. We, on the other hand, are familiar with such scenes. What Rome saw upon one sole hustings, we see repeated upon hundreds. And we

all know that the bark of electioneering mobs is worse
than their bite. Their fury is without malice, and their
insurrectionary violence is without system. Most undoubtedly the mobs and seditions of Clodius are entitled to
the same benefits of construction."

I say most undoubtedly no. What Clodius meant was
murder and revolution, and nothing less, and it is an
insult to common sense to compare his insurrectionary
violence to the "rough horse-play" of an English electioneering mob. He had been baffled by his enemies in
his attempt to gain the consulship, and he seems to have
resolved to become master of Rome by pursuing a system
of terror, which it was disgraceful to the magistrates not
to have put down. He had been protected by Cæsar and
Pompey, for their own purposes, until his fury grew intolerable ; and then, finding himself deserted by every
respectable citizen, he relied solely upon armed force.
He took into his pay a body of ruffians, whom he drilled
like soldiers ; and any one who thought of attacking him
knew that he was likely to forfeit his life in the attempt.
But it is inconceivable that the consuls, or, at all events,
Lentulus—for Metellus perhaps was deterred by the consideration that Clodius was his brother-in-law—should not
have exercised the power they undoubtedly possessed, and,
denouncing him as a public enemy, have employed against
him a military force. Did they believe that he was still
secretly supported by Cæsar, and were they afraid of
offending that formidable man, who was giving proofs
in Belgium and Gaul of his incomparable qualities as a
soldier ?

Clodius was at this time a candidate for the ædileship, and hoped, if he gained that office, to escape with
impunity. Milo, however, as tribune, was determined to
oppose this, and exerted all his energies to put off indefi-

nitely the comitia for electing the ædiles. On the day
after the attack on his house, the Senate met, but Clodius
did not appear. Marcellinus, the consul-elect, spoke
strongly against him; but Metellus, Oppius, and another
senator whom Cicero, writing to Atticus, describes as
"your friend"[9] came to the rescue, and tried to waste
time by making long speeches, and so prevent any resolution from being passed.

Clodius afterwards threatened that, if the comitia were
not held, he would attempt a revolution. Marcellinus,
however, announced his determination to put a stop to
them if they were held, by "watching the sky." Upon
this, Metellus, Appius Claudius, and Clodius addressed the
people in furious harangues. Everything betokened that
a crisis was at hand. The comitia were to be held in the
Campus Martius, and in the middle of the previous night
Milo proceeded to the plain with a strong force. Clodius
did not venture to show himself, and Milo remained until
mid-day master of the field. Metellus, as consul, challenged Milo to put a stop to the comitia if he dared by
giving him public notice next day in the Forum that he
was watching the sky, and told him there was no reason
why he should go to the Campus Martius at night, promising to be at the meeting at six o'clock in the morning.
He intended to play Milo a trick, and get the comitia over
before he had time to stop them. Milo, however, got
there before him, and, as Metellus was sneaking along bye-
streets to the Campus Martius, he came up with him at
the place called *Inter Lucos*,[1] and, using the proper formula

[9] Cicero adds ironically, "de cujus constantiâ et virtute tuæ verissimæ
literæ."—*Ad Att.* IV. 3. It is generally thought that he here alludes to
Hortensius.
[1] This was the hollow space between the Capitoline and Palatine
hills, so named from an ancient grove that formerly stood there. The
natural features of the ground still remain as in Cicero's time.

of *alio die*—"at another day"—prevented the meeting. The consul retired, and so, for the present, Clodius was baffled. In giving an account of these events to Atticus, Cicero says:—

"I am writing this on the twenty-third of November, at three o'clock in the morning. Milo is still in possession of the Campus Martius. Marcellus, who is one of the candidates, is snoring so loud that I, who am his neighbour, can hear him! The vestibule of Clodius's house is reported to be empty, or at all events there are only a few ragged wretches there without a lantern."

Milo now openly declared that he would kill Clodius if he met with him—if not, he would drag him to trial. It is right to remember this, as it throws light upon the nature of the encounter afterwards between these two men, when Clodius was killed. In telling Atticus of Milo's threat, Cicero uses a remarkable expression, which shows how sore he still felt on the subject of his banishment. He says—"Milo has no fear of my mischance, for *he* has never relied on the advice of an envious and perfidious friend; nor is he likely to trust a do-nothing nobleman." Here, no doubt, Pompey is alluded to, for he was the *iners nobilis* to whom more than any other Cicero attributed his misfortune. He spoke cheerfully at this time of himself, and said that his spirits were greater than even when he was in prosperity, but that he was much reduced in fortune. It appears, however, that he was generously assisted with money by his friends, for he tells Atticus that by their aid he had been able, in some degree, to repay his brother Quintus for his liberality towards himself, which had seriously affected his means.

During the month there was a meeting of the Senate, which Cicero describes in a letter to his brother Quintus, and which it is worth while to quote, as it gives us a good idea of the mode in which the Roman Parliament conducted its business.

The two consuls were absent, having left Rome for their respective provinces. It was, therefore, the duty of the tribunes to convoke the Senate, propose motions, and ask each of the senators his opinion in such order as they thought fit. The case would be analogous in the House of Commons if the Speaker, instead of " catching in his eye " one of a dozen members who start up at the same time, and calling upon him to speak, were to address each member in turn, and ask him to deliver his opinion. Certainly the Roman method was more decorous, but the practical difficulty of carrying it out in the House of Commons would be insuperable. Unless *all* were called upon in turn, it would be unfair to those who would be excluded, and the idea of *inviting* six hundred and fifty speeches on any question is too dreadful to think of. It appears that the consuls confined themselves to the principal senators, and always began with those who had filled the office, of consul—the consulars, as they were called. But how the rest were dealt with, and whether any senator might get up and speak without being called upon, is not sufficiently clear.

On the occasion in question the number that met was two hundred, which Cicero calls a more than usually good attendance for the December holidays. They were attracted by a motion, of which Lupus, one of the new tribunes, had given notice on the subject of an apportionment of public lands in Campania. He spoke well, but was listened to in silence. He did not finish till late, and then said that he would not ask for the opinions of the senators, or, as we should say, would not give the house the trouble of dividing, as he did not wish to expose any one to odium or annoyance; but he understood the feeling of the Senate from its silence. Upon this Marcellinus started up, and said that Lupus must not infer from their silence either

approval or disapproval of the scheme, and that, as Pompey
was absent, it was better not to discuss the question then.
Lupus said that he had no wish to detain the Senate any
longer.   But Racilius, another of the new tribunes, rose
and made a motion about the necessity of calling Clodius
and his associates to account in a criminal court for the
late outrages.   He then called upon Marcellinus, the
consul-elect, to deliver his opinion first.   Marcellinus in-
veighed strongly in his speech against Clodius, and asserted
that he would, when he entered upon office, have a list of
jurors chosen by lot by the prætor, in the usual manner,
and that, when this was ready, and not till then, the
comitia for electing ædiles should be held.   He also declared that whoever threw obstacles in the way of the trial
would be a public enemy.   The Senate applauded, but
Caius Cato and Cassius, two of the new tribunes, rose and
spoke on the other side.   Cassius proposed that the comitia
should take place before the trial, but he was almost
clamored down.   Racilius then, having gone through the
magistrates present, asked Cicero first of those who were
not in office his opinion.   Cicero took care to avail himself of so good an opportunity for attacking his bitterest
enemy.   He treated him as if he were a criminal arraigned
at the bar, and in his presence went through the long
catalogue of his crimes amidst murmurs of applause.   Se-
verus Antistius afterwards spoke, and declared that he was
for the trial preceding the comitia.   The Senate was on the
point of dividing in favor of that view, when Clodius rose
and tried his old trick of speaking against time.   He delivered a furious harangue, and complained that he had
been treated by Racilius with incivility.   He relied upon
the same kind of support that the Jacobins of the French
Revolution made use of in the Convention, when the galle-
ries were filled with the Parisian mob, who interrupted the

speakers by their clamor. He had posted a body of slaves
at the neighbouring *græcostasis*—an elevated platform or
place on the right-hand, close to the Curia Hostilia, where
the ambassadors and other deputies from foreign countries
used to wait when they were commissioned to the Senate
at Rome. These raised a tremendous shout, which so frightened the timid senators that in disgust and alarm they
hastily quitted the Senate-house, and the business in hand
was adjourned until the following morning.

At the close of his letter Cicero affectionately warns
his brother, who was going to Sardinia as one of Pompey's fifteen commissioners or lieutenants in the grain
business, to be careful to choose fine weather for his voyage
in the inclement month of December.

His next letter is to Fadius Gallus, a great friend of both
Cicero and Atticus, and an excellent and well-educated
man, who was afterwards one of Cæsar's lieutenants. The
letter is curious as affording us a glimpse of Cicero at
home in his Tusculan villa, suffering from an attack of
dysentery.

He says that, feeling very unwell, and yet, because he
had no fever, being unable to persuade friends and clients
who wished to make use of his services that anything was
the matter with him, he had fled to Tusculum, and there
kept himself so rigidly fasting, that for two days he did not
even drink a drop of water. He had been quite worn out
by weakness and hunger. Of all kinds of illness he
dreaded dysentery most—a disease which, he says, had
brought down upon Epicurus (of whose school Gallus was
a disciple) the contempt of the Stoics because he had confessed that he was troubled with it and strangury, the
latter of which they attributed to licentiousness, and the
former to gluttony. Change of air and relaxation from
business had, however, improved his health. He jokingly

attributes his attack to the sumptuary law, for, as vegetables of all kinds were excepted from it, the Roman epicures used to dress these in such a dainty and appetizing way as to form rich and luxurious dishes; and Cicero had partaken of these so freely at a dinner given by Lentulus, the consul-elect, in honour of the consecration of his son as augur, that he was seized with diarrhœa. "So," he adds, "I, who had no difficulty in abstaining from oysters and lampreys, was betrayed by beetroot and mallows! In future I shall be more cautious;" and he hints that, as Gallus knew he had been so unwell, he might not only have sent to enquire after him, but have paid him a visit.

CHAPTER XIV.

CONFUSION AT ROME — CICERO SUPPORTS CÆSAR —
HIS SPEECHES IN SEVERAL IMPORTANT TRIALS —
DEFENCE OF CŒLIUS.

Æt. 51.   B.C. 56.

THE consuls of the new year were Lentulus Marcellinus, and Marcius Philippus. The first business on which the Senate was engaged, and which occupied a considerable time, was the question of the restoration of King Ptolemy Auletes to his throne. He had, as I have before mentioned, been deposed by his subjects for his tyrannical misrule, and had taken refuge in Rome, where he implored the assistance of the Senate. An embassy was sent from Egypt to Rome to plead the cause of the people against the king. It consisted of a hundred persons, the greater number of whom Ptolemy, according to Dio Cassius, caused to be waylaid and murdered; and of the rest, when they reached Rome, he assassinated some and bribed others.[1] Lentulus Spinther, the consul of the preceding year, who now held the proconsular government of Cilicia, had reason to expect that the honor of conducting back the king would be conferred upon him; but he had a formidable competitor in Pompey, who was very anxious to possess a military command, and who knew that, if the king was restored, it must be by means of a Roman army forcing him upon his unwilling subjects. He did not avow his desire for the appointment; on the contrary, he professed to support the

[1] Dio Cass. XXXIX. 13.

pretensions of Lentulus ; but his friends worked for him. The Senate, however, was by no means disposed to increase the authority he already possessed. He was, by their own act, the absolute master in a matter of vital consequence —the import of grain—and they were afraid of making him too powerful if they gave him also the command of an army. And yet they were unwilling to offend him. The way in which they got out of the dilemma is curious. They persuaded the guardians of the Sibylline books conveniently to declare that it was therein written, that if a king of Egypt solicited their help they were not to refuse, but must not assist him with any great number of men,[2] or they would get into trouble. This settled the matter as regards an army. The only real question was, whether Pompey or Lentulus should have the appointment; but in the result neither of them restored the king. The Senate would have nothing to do with it, and Aulus Gabinius, the proconsul of Syria, undertook the enterprise on his own responsibility, being well paid by Ptolemy for his services.

On the twenty-second of January the comitia for the election of ædiles was at last held, and Clodius came in. Without losing time, he immediately indicted Milo for illegal violence, thus retaliating upon him with the same accusation which Milo had preferred against him in the previous year. In February Milo appeared to the charge, and was supported by Cicero and Pompey. At Cicero's request, Marcellus spoke for him, and the impression made was favorable. The case was then adjourned, and when it came on again Pompey spoke, or rather tried to speak, for him,[3] for the hirelings and slaves of Clodius made such a clamor and uproar when he rose that it was

---

[2] πληθεῖ τινί.—Dio Cass. XXXIX. 15. **Cum** multitudine.—*Ad Quint.* II. 2.

[3] Dixit Pompeius, sive voluit.—*Ad Quint.* II. 3.

almost impossible for him to go on. But he stood his ground, and, in spite of the continued interruption, delivered a long and courageous speech. When he had finished, Clodius started up, but was instantly met with such a storm of derisive shouts from Milo's party that he was completely staggered.

The hooting and clamor lasted for two or three hours, and every kind of abuse was hurled at Clodius. The crowd sang scurrilous and filthy doggrel, which was current at Rome, against him and his sister Clodia. Pale and mad with rage, he turned to his followers in the midst of the uproar and asked them who it was that killed the people with famine. The mob shouted "Pompey!" "Who wanted to go to Alexandria?" "Pompey!" "Whom do you wish to go?" "Crassus!" Crassus was present with no friendly feelings towards Milo. At last the low wretches who supported Clodius began to spit upon their opponents. This made Milo's party furious; and when the Clodians began to press forward, they were attacked and put to flight. Clodius was driven off the Rostra, and Cicero, seeing that he himself was in danger, hastily quitted the place. The Senate was immediately summoned, but Pompey, instead of attending, went home. He had given offence by his disingenuous conduct in the Ptolemy business, and the Senate by no means approved of his covert attempt to get the appointment for himself. He was now in his absence assailed in the Senate by Bibulus, Curio, and Favonius; and Cicero, knowing that this would be the case, with more prudence than manliness kept away; for, as he says himself, he felt that if he was present he could not with decency be silent during the discussion, and feared that if he defended Pompey, he might displease the party of those whom he calls "good men." All this he tells in confidence to his brother, and it is in such letters that we get the real key to his character. He was always anxious to do what was right, but was deficient in moral courage, and too afraid of compromising himself to adopt a bold and decided policy. This caused him to temporize, and, in fact, to *trim*, which more than anything else has injured his reputation with posterity.

Clodius fixed the seventeenth of February for going on with the impeachment of Milo, and on the sixth the Senate met in the Temple of Apollo for Pompey's convenience, as it was close to his house. He was present, and made an impressive speech; but the Senate came to no resolution. Next day it resolved that what had occurred was an offence against the Republic. Cato, the tribune, attacked Pompey in a set speech, and, no doubt with the view of sowing dissension between them, took care to praise Cicero to the skies. He accused Pompey of perfidy towards his friend, and the charge was listened to in silence. It was beyond doubt so far true that Pompey had not made the least exertion to save him from Clodius's law of proscription; but we have no proof that he took any active part against him. Pompey defended himself with warmth, and, without naming Crassus, who, he believed, had instigated Cato to assail him, and was assiduously aiming at his life, he so designated him as to leave no doubt to whom he alluded when he declared that he would be more on his guard than Scipio Africanus, who was murdered by Carbo. So entirely was the alliance between Pompey and Crassus at an end, that he told Cicero pointedly that Crassus, whose wealth was enormous, supplied Clodius with money and supported him in his attacks upon himself, which were now open and undisguised. He confessed that his position was precarious; the fickle populace was almost alienated from him by the mob-harangues continually addressed

R 2

to them;[4] the aristocracy was hostile; the Senate unfavorable; the Roman youth depraved. He therefore began to take active measures for his own protection, and brought into the city men on whom he could depend. But Clodius also was marshalling his forces and increasing the number of slaves and gladiators in his pay. He collected a band of ruffians to be ready when Milo's trial came on. Cicero says that his and Pompey's party had much the advantage in point of strength, and expected a considerable reinforcement of soldiers from Picenum and from Gaul, where Cæsar was all-powerful, and as yet ready to stand by his son-in-law.

It shows how completely dislocated the government at Rome was at this period, and how law and order were beginning to succumb to armed violence, when we find a man like Cicero, who shrank with something like womanish repugnance from the use of physical force, telling his brother that one use that would be made by him and his party of the troops they expected would be to defeat Cato's two bills, the one for the impeachment of Milo, and the other for the recal of Lentulus. It is clear that he was ready to reverse his famous maxim of *cedant arma togæ*, and let arms turn the scale. The times were indeed deplorable, and the forms of the constitution were abused to the most factious purposes; but it was very dangerous to attempt to defeat a bill by an imposing military force, although it would have been quite right to arrest Clodius, and, if he resisted, to fight the battle out in the streets.

But let us turn for a moment from the politician to the man of letters and the advocate. Atticus had arrived in Italy from Athens or Epirus, and was on his way to

---

[4] Concionario illo populo a se prope alienato.—*Ad Quint.* II. 3.

Rome. He had just married a lady named Pilia,[5] and
Cicero wrote to him in February, and begged him to come
and stay with him, and bring his wife, whom Tullia was
anxious to see. He told him that Tyrannio, a distinguished grammarian and friend of Cicero, had made an
admirable arrangement of his library, the remains of
which, after the injury it had suffered during his banishment, were in a much better state than he had expected.
He begged Atticus to send him two of his librarians to
assist Tyrannio in glueing the leaves, and to bring with
them a skin of parchment to make indexes, "which," he
says, "you Grecians, I think, call syllabuses." Atticus
had bought some gladiators, whom it was not unusual for
wealthy Romans to keep and train, for the purpose of
hiring them out to the magistrates, or others who exhibited public games. Cicero congratulates him on having
purchased a capital training-ground, and says he hears
they fight admirably.

He now resumed his more congenial duties as an
advocate, apparently for the first time since his return
from exile: at least I am not aware of any earlier case in
which he was engaged. On the eleventh of February he
defended L. Bestia, who was accused of electoral corruption when he was a candidate for the office of prætor.
The trial took place in the prætor's court in the middle of
the Forum, and was attended by an immense crowd. His
speech, which is lost, was unsuccessful, and Bestia was
convicted. All we know of it is what he tells us, namely,
that he seized the opportunity to preoccupy the minds of
his hearers favorably, with a view to his defence in a

---

[5] Pilia bore Atticus a daughter named Attica, who became the wife
of Agrippa and mother of Vipsania Agrippina, the first wife of Tiberius
and mother of Drusus; so that Atticus was the grandfather of a Roman
empress.

more important trial which was then impending, and in which he was counsel for the accused.

This was the case of Publius Sextius, who was one of the tribunes of the people in the year when Cicero was recalled, and who, perhaps, more than any other man, except Quintus and Atticus, had exerted himself on his behalf. He had been severely wounded by the followers of Clodius in one of the numerous street conflicts that disgraced the city, and had owed his life to the interposition of Bestia. He had also been one of the first to propose a law for Cicero's recal, and had always in the Senate given him the most zealous support. By every tie, therefore, of duty and gratitude, the orator was bound to put forth all his powers to defend him when he was in danger. He seems to have been a man of sullen and unpopular manners; for in a private letter to Quintus, Cicero calls him *morosus homo*, and hints that he had himself cause to complain of the perversity of his temper. He was in considerable peril; for he was arraigned on two indictments: one, in which he was charged, under the Papinian law, with bribery; and the other, a more serious affair, in which he was charged, under the Lutatian law, with illegal violence.

The first step in the trial was the arraignment which took place before the prætor, M. Æmilius Scaurus, in February. Sextius was well defended. He had the advantage of having not only Cicero as his advocate, but also Hortensius. The speech which he delivered has been preserved, and it is one of the most valuable of all his orations; for in it we have a narrative of the events connected with his banishment and return.

The trial lasted, with interruptions, until the thirteenth of March, when Sextius was unanimously acquitted. In a letter announcing the result to Quintus, who had been

anxious that his brother should show his gratitude for
Sextius's services by exerting himself to the utmost, he
said that he had most amply satisfied him on that point,
and that he had cut up Vatinius, who was supposed to be
at the bottom of the prosecution, to his own heart's
content, amidst the applause of gods and men. And yet
two years afterwards he defended this very Vatinius, and
was then as complimentary towards him as he was now
abusive.

In a previous letter to Quintus he told him of the
approaching trials of Bestia and Sextius, and gave a flourishing account of himself. He said that his reputation
and popularity were re-established, and he thankfully
attributed this to his brother's kindness and affection, to
whom more than to anyone else he seems always to have
felt indebted for his recal from banishment. Quintus was
on the point of returning from Sardinia to Rome, and
Cicero tells him that Licinius's house at Piso's Grove had
been hired for him, but he hoped that in a few months
after the first of July he would get into his own on the
Palatine, which was being rebuilt. Quintus's other house,
in the Carniæ, had been taken on lease by a family of the
name of Lamia.

In his next letter to his brother, after mentioning the
acquittal of Sextius and his satisfaction at his own speech,
he gives him some domestic news. Tyrannio was acting
as tutor in Cicero's house to the two young cousins, and
he assures Quintus that his son is making good progress
in his studies. Both their houses were getting on fast,
and he had paid his brother's contractor half of the
stipulated sum. He hoped, therefore, that they would be
next-door neighbours before winter. He then mentions
that he was on the point of concluding a marriage engage-

ment for his daughter Tullia. A year had elapsed since
Piso's death; and the young widow was, in April, betrothed to Furius Crassipes, of whom very little is known
except that he was an adherent of Cæsar, quæstor of
Bithynia, and afterwards, according to Livy, prætor. The
marriage was not a happy one, and her husband, a few
years afterwards, divorced her. From the way in which
Cicero speaks, it seems that he brought about the match,
and very likely, as too often happens when third parties
interfere, there was little affection on either side. He
gave the wedding banquet (we should say, breakfast), and
mentions that his nephew, young Quintus, could not be
there, owing to a slight illness. He tells his brother that
he visited him two days afterwards, and found him recovered, and that he had a long conversation with him on
the subject of the disagreement between his aunt and
mother—Terentia and Pomponia—in which his nephew
expressed himself very kindly. Quintus and his wife, who
had remained at Rome while her husband was absent in
Sardinia, were still on indifferent terms, and she complained to Cicero of his conduct. I will quote one or
two passages from the letter in which he mentions this
to his brother, not because they relate to any matters of
importance, but because it is interesting to see the old
Romans, so to speak, in *deshabille*, and find them engaged
twenty centuries ago in much the same daily routine of
business and amusement as ourselves.

"When I left the boy," he says, "I went to look at your new house
that is building. There were numbers of workmen very busy. I spoke
to Longilius the contractor, and urged him to lose no time. He assured
me that he wished to give us every satisfaction. It will be a capital house;
for I can judge better now than I could from the mere plan. Mine also
will be soon finished. On the same day I supped with Crassipes, and
afterwards was carried in a litter to Pompey's gardens. I could not
meet with Luccieus, as he was absent. I wished however to see him

because I intend to leave Rome to-morrow, and he is going to Sardinia. . . I am building in three places at once,[6] repairing and furbishing up what is left; and I live rather more liberally than I used to do."

This last remark suggests the inquiry how Cicero was able so soon after his return to launch out into all this expense. He constantly complained of being ruined during his exile, and we know from his letters to Terentia that this was no exaggeration. He was obliged to resort to the purse of his friends, who, and especially Atticus, came liberally forward to assist him and his family. And yet we find him, in the year following his return, living in comfort and luxury, and, as we have just seen, rebuilding his town and country houses, which were on an expensive scale. He had, no doubt, received some compensation, but he was much dissatisfied with the amount; and it seems to have been quite inadequate to enable him to rebuild his house at Rome and repair the damage done to his villas. Where, then, did the money come from? At this distance of time it is impossible to say, as we have absolutely no information, and can only guess that he borrowed largely; for we know that he was henceforward almost constantly in debt.

In the same letter he mentions an incident which was considered a good practical joke at Rome. The tribune Cato, who was a man of the Clodius stamp, had bought a body of gladiators and wild-beast fighters — some of the latter from Atticus — and he employed them as a body-guard, without which he never appeared in public. But he found that the keep of these cost him more than he could afford, and he wished to sell them. He was naturally anxious that Milo should not buy them, for they were declared enemies of each other; and he had no wish to increase the force at his adversary's disposal. Milo,

[6] His house at Rome, and his Tusculan and Formian villas.

however, employed a third party to purchase the lot[7] from
Cato as if for himself, and take them away. Cato sold
them without the least suspicion who was the real purchaser. Racilius, then, according to a preconcerted plan,
declared that the men had been bought for himself, and
issued a placard advertising that he was ready to sell
Cato's *family* of slaves. This placard caused great merri-
ment at Rome. The point of the joke was, that such a
gang of prize-fighters should be styled as if they were
Cato's domestic establishment.

Cicero left Rome in April, and spent a few weeks in
visiting his country seats. He was growing more and
more dissatisfied with the state of parties, and found, or
fancied himself, an object of envy and dislike. He had
felt much disappointment since his return from exile to his
beloved Rome, away from which he then thought he could
hardly exist ; and we find him corresponding with Atticus
in a very splenetic mood. He had been writing a work,
which is supposed to have been a poem in praise of Cæsar,
and in which he had recanted some of his former opinions.
He apologizes for not having sent it to his friend, and
confesses that he was rather ashamed of letting him see
the change that had taken place in his views.

His detractors found fault with him for buying a villa
that had belonged to Catulus—meaning, I suppose, to
insinuate that he was not worthy to succeed so excellent a
man—but they forgot, he said, that he bought it from
such a rascal as Vettius. They abused him for rebuilding
his house, and said it would have been better if he had
sold the land, and so put money in his pocket.

He uses, in one of his letters, these significant words,
which are the key to much of his political conduct during

---

[7] *Familiam.* This is the word *invariably* used to denote the domestic
slaves of a Roman family, and is never applied in any other sense.

the next few years. "Since," he says, "those who have
no power will not be my friends, let me try to be friends
with those who have the power." This, of course, alluded
to Cæsar and his party. He goes on : "You will say, 'I
wish you had done so long ago.' I know that you wished
it, and that I have been a regular ass. But it is now
time for me to take care of myself, since I cannot in the
least rely on their friendship."

He sent a long letter to Lucceius, the historian, of
whose works not a vestige now remains, and urgently
pressed him to write a history of his consulship. He told
Atticus that it was a very pretty letter (*valde bella est*) ;
but to us it seems in the worst possible taste. He distinctly asked Lucceius not to confine himself to the strict
limits of fact, but to give a latitude to his panegyric
beyond even what he might think Cicero's actions deserved.

Lentulus Niger, a member of the college of *flamens*, or
priests of Mars, and a great friend of Cicero, had just died.
When he heard the news he wrote to Atticus, and told
him that Lentulus was such a true lover of his country,
that he seemed to have been snatched away by the
kindness of the gods from the conflagration that was
destroying it.

"For what," he exclaims, "is worse than our life? especially mine !
For you, indeed, although you are by nature 'political,' are tied to no
party nor bound to public servitude. You enjoy merely the general
name of statesmen. What grief, however, must I feel? I, who if I say
what I ought about politics, am thought mad : if what is expedient, servile :
if I keep silence, utterly done for and laid on the shelf. And the worst
of it is that I dare not express my grief lest I should appear ungrateful.

"What if I wished to give up and fly to a haven of rest? Never ! I
must rush to the battle. Shall I then be a camp-follower where I refused
to be a general? Well ! so it must be; for I see that this is your
opinion, and I wish I had always listened to you.

"'Well !' you will say, 'Sparta is your lot; do your best in Sparta.'

I'faith I cannot; and I am inclined to excuse Philoxenus, who preferred going back to prison." [8]

Cicero had proposed to write a little work to be called Hortensiana, the exact nature of which is unknown, but it seems to have been intended as a collection of anecdotes or sketch of the life of his great rival in the Forum. Atticus urged him to go on with it, but it was a delicate subject to handle, and he was afraid that he might have to show up Hortensius's faults and make public the umbrage he felt at his conduct towards himself. We have seen that for some cause or other he thought that Hortensius had not behaved well to him. He therefore would not promise to write the work, but said he would think of it.

During his absence in the country several portents had occurred which filled the superstitious minds of the Romans with terror. The college of soothsayers was consulted, and they declared that some deity was offended because consecrated places had been built upon and turned to profane uses. This was too good an opportunity for Clodius to lose. He assembled a meeting and harangued the people pointing out the real culprit. What could be clearer than the meaning of the prodigies? The Temple of Liberty had been pulled down and on its site Cicero was then erecting his new house. The Senate also resolved that the consuls should bring forward a bill on the subject of sacred places.

[8] Philoxenus was a poet of Syracuse, who had the temerity to find fault with some verses of Dionysius the tyrant, and was thrown into a prison called the *Latomiæ* (stone-quarries). Soon afterwards he was released and summoned to court to listen to a new poem of the tyrant. But the infliction was too great: he ran off. "Where are you going to?" cried Dionysius. "Back to the *Latomiæ*," answered the disgusted poet. This reminds us of Voltaire at the court of Frederick the Great. Once when the king sent him some royal verses to revise, he said, "See his Majesty has sent me his dirty linen to wash."

Cicero in the mean time had returned to Rome, and the day after the resolution was passed he was in the Senate and delivered the speech known as the oration *de Harus-picum Responsis*, although, as we have seen, some scholars are of opinion that the one we possess under that title is not genuine.[9]

About this time he was counsel for L. Cornelius Balbus, a trusted and intimate friend of Cæsar, and then serving under him in Gaul. It was not a criminal case, but involved the question of his right to be considered a Roman citizen. For Balbus was a native of Spain, born at Gades (the modern Cadiz), and he had been made a burgher of Rome by Pompey under the *Lex Gellia*. Pompey and Crassus assisted Cicero in the defence, and his speech is still extant.

Shortly afterwards he had an opportunity of gratifying his dislike of Piso and Gabinius, and showing his good-will towards Cæsar.

It was proposed in the Senate that Piso and Gabinius should be recalled from their proconsular provinces, Macedonia and Syria, and that these should be declared to be prætorian, in order that they might be placed in the hands of prætors. It was also proposed that Cæsar should be deprived of his government of the two Gauls, Transalpine and Cisalpine, which were to be assigned to the new consuls elect. Some of the senators wished to make a different arrangement, and give Macedonia or Syria and one of the two Gallic provinces to the consuls elect. When Cicero was called upon to declare his opinion, he rose and made a noble speech, known as the oration *de Provinciis Con-sularibus*, and one of the finest he ever delivered, whether

---

[9] Wolf says that the speech we possess is nothing but an old woman's twaddle expressed in a tasteless, childish style which is hardly Latin. But this is not criticism.

we regard its sentiments or its style. He had a difficult part to play. His long opposition to Cæsar exposed him to the charge of inconsistency if he now supported him; but he vindicated himself with admirable tact, and his reasoning is, I think, conclusive. If, indeed, he could have known what use Cæsar would make of the prolongation of his command, if he could have foreseen that, flushed with victory, he would come back to Rome not as the servant but the master of the Republic, not as Imperator but Dictator, he would have spoken very differently. But who could then lift the veil of futurity and see Pharsalia in the distance? Cæsar was now a glorious soldier, chaining victory to his eagles, and adding new dominions to the State, and it seemed to be in the highest degree impolitic to stop him in the career of conquest and hand over the turbulent and warlike nations of Gaul to some incompetent successor, who might lose all that had been gained by the greatest military genius, with the exception perhaps of Hannibal, that the world had yet seen.

He began by assuring the Senate that he would not allow his private enmity against the ex-consuls Piso and Gabinius to influence his public conduct, and would rest the case for their recal upon their own notorious misgovernment of the provinces they held. He then drew a melancholy picture of their misrule, and after describing it in detail in the darkest colors, asked:—

"Shall we retain these men as governors of our provinces? No! I vote for assigning Macedonia and Syria to the consuls elect—but in the mean time declaring them prætorian, so that the prætors may administer them for a year, and Piso and Gabinius may be at once recalled—otherwise a whole year will elapse, and in the interval there will be nothing but calamity, oppression, and impunity of crime."

He then came to the question of superseding Cæsar. It had been objected by a previous speaker, or rather he himself had been interrupted while speaking with the remark,

that he ought not to be more hostile to Gabinius than to
Cæsar, for the storm to which he had been forced to bow
was raised by Cæsar.   But he asked whether he might not
first reply that he regarded the public welfare rather than
his own wrongs, and if he did so he might justify himself
by the example of many illustrious citizens.   Speaking of
Cæsar he said :—

"A most important war has been carried on in Gaul—the mightiest
nations have been vanquished by Cæsar; but they have not yet been
subdued to the laws. We cannot yet rely upon a firm peace. We have
seen a war begun and, to say the truth, almost finished; but we can only
hope to see it brought to a successful termination, if he who commenced
it continues it to the end. If he is superseded, we run the hazard of
hearing that a mighty war has broken out afresh. Therefore it is my
duty as a senator to be the enemy, if ye will so have it, of the man, but
the friend of the republic. But what if I lay aside my private enmity
for the sake of the republic? Who would have the right to blame me?
Especially since I have ever thought that I ought to shape my conduct
on the model set by the example of the most illustrious men. . . . Can I,
then, be the enemy of a man by whose letters, messengers, and fame
my ears are daily greeted with the names of new nations, tribes,
and places? I burn, Conscript Fathers, believe me (as you give me
credit for it—and as you act yourselves) with an incredible love for
my country. . . . . . Thus my old and constant affection for the republic
reconciles me with Caius Cæsar, and restores him to my favor. Let men
think what they like :—I cannot be the enemy of any one who deserves
well of the state."

"Why," he asked, "should Cæsar wish to stay in his province except
that he might be able to complete for the benefit of the state what he had
begun? You say, forsooth, that the pleasant nature of the country—the
beauty of the cities—the civilization and polish of the people—the desire
of victory—the extension of the bounds of our empire retain him there!
What is more savage than that land? What wilder than those towns?
What more barbarian than those nations? What greater glory can
be desired than so many victories? What can be found more remote
than the ocean? Has he any cause to dread a return to his country,
either from the people by whom he was appointed, or the senate by
whom he has been decorated with honors? Does length of time increase
regret at his absence, and do his laurels, which have been won in so
many dangers, lose by the long interval any of their freshness? Therefore if there are any men who do not love him, there is no reason why
they should summon him from his province. They summon him to
glory, to triumph, to congratulations, to the highest honors in the senate
—the favor of the equestrian order—the affection of the people."

The orator then burst forth into a magnificent eulogy of Cæsar's victorious career. His argument is that Gaul was the most terrible enemy that Rome had to dread, and Cæsar alone was the conqueror of Gaul. Formerly it had been thought enough to repel her attacks, but now she was attacked and vanquished herself.

"Nature," he said, "had given to Italy the Alps as a bulwark, not without a divine providence. For if that access had lain open to the fury and multitude of the Gauls, this city would never have given a seat and home to the mightiest empire. It may now rest secure—for there is nothing beyond those lofty mountains even as far as the ocean which Italy need fear. . . . Therefore let Gaul remain under his guardianship to whose virtue, honor, and good fortune it has been committed."

Nay, if Cæsar himself desired to return to Rome, if he wished to be borne in triumph to the Capitol with all his laurels thick upon him, Cicero argued that it would be the duty of the Senate to keep him there where he might finish what he had so gloriously begun. He then alluded to the honors which the Senate had heaped upon Cæsar, and said that it was wise and politic to bestow them, for thereby they attached him to their order instead of throwing him into the arms of the populace to become an agitator and a demagogue.

The peroration of the speech was as follows :—

"This then is my conclusion. If I felt enmity against Caius Cæsar, I ought at this juncture to consult the interests of the republic, and reserve my enmity to another time. I might, after the example of distinguished men, lay aside my hostility for the sake of the republic : but since there never was hostility, and the idea of injury has been extinguished by kindness—in delivering my opinion, Conscript Fathers, I will, if it is a question of bestowing any honors upon him, consult the harmony of the senate—if the authority of your decrees is at stake, I will keep up your authority by honoring the commander whom you appointed ;—if regard is to be had to the Gallic war, I will look to the welfare of the state—if I may take into account any private obligation, I will show that I am not ungrateful. And I should wish by so doing to satisfy all ; but I shall care very little if perchance my conduct is not approved by those who protected my enemy (Clodius) in opposition to your authority, or by those who will blame my reconciliation with my enemy, although they did not hesitate to be reconciled with one who was both my enemy and their own."

It has been doubted whether Cicero delivered his speech in defence of M. Cœlius Rufus this year or not. The difficulty has arisen from the fact that we find Cœlius put upon his trial during the consulship of Domitius Aheno-barbus and Appius Claudius two years later. But this is got rid of by supposing that he was twice tried on differ-ent charges, and it may, I think, be assumed with cer-tainty that it was about this time that Cicero delivered his well-known oration *pro Cælio*.

The case was this: Marcus Cœlius Rufus was a young Roman knight, a native of Puteoli, who had been one of Catiline's friends, and in his early years made himself notorious, even in that licentious age, for his immoralities. He had an intrigue with the infamous Clodia, the wife of Metellus Celer, but quarrelled with her, and she vowed revenge. He grew tired of a life of idleness and pleasure, and determined to follow the path of ambition, in which he was well qualified to succeed; for he was a man of con-siderable ability and a good speaker. The readiest way at Rome to get into notice was to single out some person of mark and accuse him of a criminal offence. This, of course, was followed by a trial, in which the accuser con-ducted the prosecution and had an opportunity of display-ing whatever powers of oratory he possessed before the people in the Forum. Cœlius, therefore, impeached An-tonius, Cicero's colleague in the consulship, of some state offence, and afterwards prosecuted Atratinus for electoral corruption. In revenge for this Atratinus's son came forward and accused him of suborning assassins to commit two separate murders, and it was then that he was de-fended by Cicero.

The charges were that he had borrowed money from
Clodia to bribe some slaves to murder Dio, one of the
Alexandrian ambassadors, who had come to Italy to oppose
the restoration of King Ptolemy, and that when Clodia
pressed him for payment he had employed a person named
Licinius to hand over a box of poison to one of her slaves
for the purpose of destroying her. The nature of the indictment of course shows that Clodia was the real prose-
cutrix, and as such she is throughout treated and addressed
by Cicero. Middleton says, " In this speech Cicero treats
the character and gallantries of Clodia, her commerce with
Cœlius, and the gaieties and licentiousness of youth with
such a vivacity of wit and humour that makes it one of
the most entertaining which he has left to us." This
is rather singular praise from an English divine, and I
confess I think that the defence is one of the least satisfac-
tory amongst all the speeches of Cicero. If delivered at
the present day in answer to a criminal charge, it would be
thought extremely weak. Great allowance must, however,
be made for the difference between a Roman and an
English trial. Anything like logical severity of proof or
argument seems to have been unknown in the ancient
courts of justice. There were no rules of evidence, nor
specific issues, nor was there any attempt to exclude irre-
levant facts from the consideration of the jury. On the
contrary, it was thought legitimate to urge every con-
ceivable topic which could prejudice them either against
or for the accused ; and of course the latitude of defence
was in proportion to the latitude of attack.

I will give one or two passages from the speech, and
only regret that space will not allow me to quote more.
It will well repay an attentive perusal.

Alluding to the delicate subject of Cœlius's immoralities,
he said that the charge could not make his client regret

that he **was born** with the advantage of beauty. Such accusations **were** scattered **against all** whose person was prepossessing. **But it** was **one thing to** abuse **a man,** another to bring a formal charge against **him.** A charge implied a specific **crime to be proved by** argument and evidence, but abuse **had** no defined object except calumny; **if it** was coarse it **was** called low, if **it** was **witty it** was called clever. He expressed his regret that **this part of** the accusation **should** have devolved upon Atratinus, and that a young man of his age should have been chosen to bring forward general charges of youthful irregularities. But he denied them altogether. Cœlius had been brought up virtuously by his father, and **when he** assumed his manly gown he was placed **under** the immediate care of Cicero himself. "And of myself," **he added,** with graceful **modesty,** "I here say nothing. Let **me be just** what you **think me."** Cœlius, in the flower of his age, was always under the eye of himself, or of his own father, or pursuing **an** honorable course of study in **the** virtuous family of Crassus.

But his intimacy with Catiline was alleged against him. To this **his** advocate addressed himself, **and it must be** admitted that he managed his defence **with** consummate art. If he became a partisan **of** Catiline he only followed the example **of many** others **of** all **ages** and ranks who were led away **and** deceived by the extraordinary character **of the** man. **Cicero** described that character with masterly **power.**

"**Catiline,**" said the orator, "had, **as I** think you all remember, many of the signs, **not indeed stamped** on his **character, but** shadowed forth, of the greatest virtues. **He employed many bad men as** his tools, and yet **pretended to be devoted to the** society of the **best. He** was licentious **but laborious.** He gave **the reins to** his appetites, **and** yet zealously conformed **to the** discipline **of the** camp. Never I believe **was** htere another such **a** monster **upon** earth so made up of contrary inclinations and desires

mutually in conflict with each other. Who for a time was more liked by
more illustrious men?   Who more intimate with baser companions ?
What citizen was once of greater virtues? Who a more dreadful enemy
to the state? Who wallowed more in pleasure? Who was more patient
of labor and fatigue? Who was more greedy and rapacious? Who more
profuse in his bounty?   This excites our wonder in him, gentlemen, that
he made so many his friends and kept them his friends by his attentions
—he shared with all of them whatever he possessed—he was ready to
assist them with his money and his influence, and spared no toil nor
crime, if crime was necessary, in their behalf :—he changed his nature
and adapted it to the occasion. With the steady he was serious, with
the loose jovial—grave in the company of the old, merry in the company of the young—bold in villany with the wicked, and effeminate
with the licentious. With a disposition so complex and various, he had
not only collected round him bold bad men out of every country on earth,
but attracted to him by his simulated virtues many good men also. For
he never could have made his nefarious attempt to destroy this empire, if
the wild growth of so many vices had not rested on the roots of a nature
in some respects gentle and long suffering. This article, therefore, may
be rejected, and you may dismiss from your minds the charge of intimacy with Catiline ; for it applies equally to many, and some even excellent men. I myself, I, I say, was once nearly deceived by him when
he seemed to me to be a good citizen, affecting the society of the virtuous,
and a firm and faithful friend."

In answer to the charge of luxurious indulgence, he
excused it on the plea of youth, and pointed out how many
who had been devoted to pleasure when they were young
became afterwards grave and distinguished citizens. The
defence, in fact, in this part of the case was virtually this :
that it was natural and venial that men should sow their
wild oats provided they kept within certain reasonable
bounds.

At last Cicero came to the real charge with which he
had to grapple; the borrowing money from Clodia to effect
the murder of the Egyptian ambassador, and the procuring
poison to murder her. All the rest, he said, were not
matters for judicial investigation, but were mere calumnious
abuse. Let us see how he deals with the case.

" Of these two charges, I see what is the fountain-head and who is the
author of them. He had need of money; he borrowed it from Clodia ;
and he borrowed it without a witness ; he had the use of it as long as he

liked. I see in this the proof of a remarkable intimacy. Again, he wished to kill her, he procured poison; he suborned murderers, and made all his preparations for the deed. In this I see a deadly hatred following a fierce quarrel. The whole controversy in this case is with Clodia, a lady not only noble but even famous, of whom I will say nothing except for the purpose of repelling the charge. But," he continued, apostrophizing the prætor, "you understand, Cnæus Domitius, with your superior sagacity, that we have to do with her alone; and if she does not say that she lent money to Cœlius, if she offers no proof that poison was procured by him to take her off, I should act wantonly if I were to speak of the mother of a family otherwise than is due to the sanctity of the name of matron. But if setting her aside, the prosecutors have neither charge to make nor funds to draw upon, what else can I, as an advocate, do but meet our assailants with a counter attack? And this I would do more vehemently if I were not checked by remembering the enmity that exists between me and that woman's husband—*brother I meant to say*— *I am always committing this mistake.* Now I will restrain myself—and not go farther than my duty to my client and the case itself compel me. For I never thought that I ought to carry on a quarrel with a woman, and especially with one who has been always considered the general *friend* of all rather than the enemy of any." [1]

Then follows a long passage in apology of youthful immoralities, which Middleton no doubt had in his eye when he speaks of the "wit and humour" with which Cicero treats "the gaieties and licentiousness of youth." It comes to this—that it was utopian to expect the virtuousness of past times in the present age—that to "forswear delights and live laborious days," was not to be expected from the young, and they might be allowed to transgress in the path of pleasure, provided they did not go too far and ultimately reformed. One sentence I will quote as showing the line of argument, and it is not exactly that which we should have expected to find approved of by an English Doctor of Divinity:—

---

[1] It is impossible not to be struck with the art as well as the terrible severity of the whole of this allusion to Clodia. Cicero hoped to induce her to give up the prosecution by the threat of exposing her if she went on with it; and yet he could not resist the temptation to sarcasm at the mention of her name. What exposure could in fact be worse than the charge of incest implied by calling her brother her husband, and of licentiousness, masked under the appellation of *amica omnium*?

"But if there is any one who thinks that youth should be interdicted from indulging in *amours*, he is indeed a stern moralist,—I cannot deny it,—but he is widely at variance not only with the licentious maxims of this age, but also the customs of our forefathers and what was conceded by them. For when was this not done? When was it blamed? When was it not allowed? When was that which is lawful declared unlawful?"

Still we ask what has all this to do with the charge of intent to murder for which Cœlius was tried? Two-thirds of the speech are over, and not a word has yet been said in refutation of it. Cicero, however, perhaps wisely, assumed that his only difficulty was to get rid of the prejudice against his client which his opponents had created, and he had then an easy task. He said, using a nautical metaphor, "now that my speech has emerged from the shoals and got past the rocks, it is all plain sailing before me." He argued that Cœlius could not have got the money from Clodia without telling her the purpose for which he wanted it; and if she knew this she was privy to his design and as bad as himself. But to insinuate that Clodia was privy to the crime was to admit that Cœlius was guilty, and to argue that Cœlius could not have procured the money from her without telling her his object, if he was on such terms of intimacy with her as the counsel for the prosecution alleged, was a fallacy that will not bear scrutiny for a moment.

He passed on, however, to a better point. It was, he said, impossible to believe that a man of Cœlius's understanding, to say nothing of his character, should be so bereft of his senses as to trust his guilty secret to unknown slaves. And then he asks, almost with hesitation and apology, although we should think it was the all-important question in the case,—

"I might, in accordance with the custom of advocates and my own, demand from the accuser what evidence there is of a meeting between

Cœlius and Lucceius's slaves—what access he had to them? If he went himself, what rashness! If he employed another, who was he? I might penetrate all the lurking-places of suspicion : you will find no motive—no opportunity—no means—no hope of accomplishing or concealing the crime—no reason—no trace of this atrocious crime. But all these topics, which are proper to the orator, and which, if I elaborated them, might be of some avail in my hands, with my ability and my practice in speaking, for the sake of brevity I pass over : for I have a most unimpeachable witness in Lucceius, who you well know respects the sanctity of an oath, and who would certainly have heard of such a crime attempted to the ruin of his reputation and his fortunes, and would not have allowed it to pass with impunity."

The deposition of Lucceius was then read, and Cicero proceeded.

" What more do you expect? Can you believe it possible for truth itself to speak differently? This is the defence which innocence makes. This is the language of the cause itself. This is only the voice of truth."

But posterity will judge otherwise. We do not know, and cannot now ascertain, whether Cœlius was innocent or guilty, but assuredly the testimony of Lucceius could prove little or nothing to the point. All he could say would be that *he* had never heard of the attempted crime, and did not believe it possible. He was called to prove a negative which is simply an impossibility. The real defence of Cœlius, according to our notions, and they are those of common sense, consists in the few words that follow, of the force of which Cicero, however, seems to have been unconscious. It does not appear to have occurred to him that the *onus probandi* lay wholly on the prosecution ; they were bound to make out their case by evidence, and if that failed his client must be pronounced not guilty. But, as I before said, logical strictness was unknown in the Roman courts of justice. Rhetorical flourishes were accepted instead of proof, and the most rambling charges, if enforced by eloquence, were sufficient to place a man's life and liberty in jeopardy. In the next passage we find the point on which an English advocate would have triumphantly relied, or rather, if what Cicero says is true, he would not have been called upon to address the jury at all; for the case for the prosecution would have broken down.

"In the facts which are said to have happened there is not a trace of words spoken, or place or time: *no one is called as a witness to prove them; no one was privy to the crime.* But that family where so nefarious a deed is said to have been committed is distinguished for its uprightness, its virtue, and its piety—from that family you have heard an authoritative voice speaking under the obligation of an oath—so that you have to balance in a matter, which really admits of no doubt, which of the two things is most likely—whether that an enraged woman has trumped up the charge, or that a grave, wise, and respectable man has given his evidence with due regard to the sanctity of an oath."

There remained the charge of attempting the life of Clodia by poison. Cicero asked:—

"But as to the poison—Where was it procured? how prepared? to whom given, and where? They say that he kept it at home and made an experiment of its effects upon a slave, by whose speedy death he was assured of its fatal strength. . . . They say that the poison was given to Licinius, a modest and excellent young man, and friend of Cœlius—that an appointment was made with the slaves to come to the Xenian baths—that Licinius was to go there and hand over to them the box of poison. Now here I first ask with what object the poison was carried to that place? Why did the slaves not come to Cœlius at his own house? If such intimacy still existed between Cœlius and Clodia, what cause of suspicion could there have been if one of the woman's slaves were seen at his house? But if ill feeling had arisen between them, if their familiarity was at an end, and a quarrel had taken place—then I say *hinc illæ lacrymæ*, and this is the cause of all these criminal charges. She says forsooth—cunning woman that she is—that when her slaves informed her of Cœlius's nefarious design, she told them to promise him everything; but that the poison might be openly seized when it was in the act of being given to Licinius, she ordered them to appoint as the place of meeting the Xenian baths, where she would send friends to remain concealed who would, when Licinius came, rush forward and take him in the act."

Of course all this was capable of proof. If witnesses had come forward who swore that they were at the baths, as Clodia averred, and had seized Licinius with the poison in his hand, it would have gone a long way to establish

the charge. But it appears that up to the time when
Cicero addressed the jury, no witnesses had been named
who could speak to these facts, and he resorts, as usual, to
presumptive evidence to disprove that of which the prosecution had given no evidence.

"Why," he asked, "did she appoint public baths of all places in the
world for the meeting? I know of no lurking place there where grown-
up men can hide themselves. For if they were in the vestibule of the
baths they would not be concealed; but if they wished to retire into the
interior, they would find it very inconvenient to do so with their clothes
and sandals on. And perhaps they would not be admitted—unless indeed
this influential woman from her habit of using the halfpenny public
baths had become friends with the bathman." As to the witnesses he
ironically said, " they must, no doubt, be respectable men who were intimate with such a woman, and consented to lie in ambuscade in a public
bath for such a purpose."

It was further alleged that they had rushed forward too
soon, and that Licinius escaped with the poison in his
hand; but Cicero treated this as an absurd and impro-
bable story, for it was not likely that men who had been
posted there for the very purpose of seizing him would
have let him slip. The whole thing looked, he said, like
a stage plot, where the hero escapes and at the same
moment the curtain falls.[2]

He then urged, what to us seems the most obvious
remark to have been made at the outset, that the whole
case depended on witnesses, the presumptive evidence
being the other way. In a tone of bantering ridicule he
said :—

" I am anxious to see first the fashionable youths who are the friends
of this rich and noble lady; and next the brave men who were posted
by their female commander in the ambuscade and garrison of the baths.
I will ask them in what manner and where they lay hid—whether it
was in a Trojan horse which concealed so many invincible heroes carrying
on a woman's war."

---

[2] *Aulæa tolluntur*—literally " the curtain rises," but, as is well known,
on the stage of the ancient theatres the curtain was pulled *up*, not *down*.

He concluded by a sketch of Coelius's past life, showing how unlikely it was that he should be guilty of so great a crime. He had faults, but they were the faults of youth, and such as time would cure.

"Preserve therefore," he exclaimed, appealing to the jury, "preserve to the republic a citizen of virtuous pursuits and good qualities, and the friend of good men. This I promise you and guarantee to the state, that his mode of life will not differ from mine—if I may speak of myself as having done good service to the state. . . . When you think upon his youth, think also on the age of his unhappy father who is before you, and who leans for support upon this his only son. . . . . Consent not that the one, whose sun is already setting in the course of nature, shall be crushed by a blow from you sooner than by his own destiny; or that the other, now for the first time blossoming with the leaves of hope and when the stem of virtue is growing strong, shall be overthrown as it were by a whirlwind or a tempest. Preserve the son to the parent, the parent to the son, lest it should be thought that you despised old age in its despair, or crushed instead of saving youth when it was full of the greatest promise. If you do preserve him for yourselves, his friends, and the republic, you will have him devoted to you and to your children, and you, above all others, will reap the rich and lasting fruits of his industry and exertions."

Whatever we may think of the argument of this speech, it had the merit of success. Coelius was acquitted, and the prediction of his advocate was fulfilled. He became afterwards a distinguished man.

Chapter XV.

LETTERS FROM THE COUNTRY—ATTACK ON PISO—
GOSSIP — DEFENCE OF PLANCIUS — POLITICAL APO-
LOGY—DISTRACTED STATE OF ROME.

Æt 55. B.C. 52.

CICERO passed a considerable part of the next year in
the country at one or other of his favorite villas,
amusing himself with his books, or employing his leisure
time in literary composition. We will follow him there,
and see him occupied in more congenial pursuits than
politics, of which he was weary, and in which he met with
little but vexation and disappointment.

His first letter to Atticus is dated from Antium, where
he was attended by his friend's faithful and intelligent
freedman, Dionysius, who assisted him in his studies.[1]
We next find him at his villa near Puteoli (*Pozzuolo*), in
the Bay of Naples. He describes himself as devouring
the library of Faustus, a son of Sylla the dictator, and son-
in-law of Pompey, who inherited an immense collection of
books which his father had got together when he plundered
Athens, and these he kept at his country-seat near Puteoli.
Cicero jokingly adds, that perhaps Atticus thought he was
devouring the good things of Puteoli and Lucrinum, which
was famous for its oysters.

But in the present state of public affairs, he said he had
lost all taste for other enjoyments except his books, which

---

[1] It was a pleasant memento of their friendship that Dionysius, on his
manumission, assumed a name from each of them, and was called in
future Marcus Pomponius Dionysius.—See *Ad Att.* iv. 15.

refreshed and delighted him; and he says he would rather sit with Atticus on the seat in his library beneath the bust of Aristotle than in *their* curule chair (meaning of course the triumvirate, although he is too cautious to name them), and would rather walk with him than with the man (Pompey) with whom he saw he must walk. But as to that walk chance must determine, or Providence, if there was such a Being who cared about it.[2] He begs Atticus to look after his gallery and vapour-bath, and all that his architect, Cyrus, had engaged to do, and press the contractor to use despatch with the building of his house at Rome. He then mentions that Pompey had come to his villa at Cumæ to pay him a visit, and had immediately sent to enquire after him. He was going to see him next morning.

The interview took place, and they discussed the state of public affairs. Pompey was dissatisfied with himself; and the private correspondence of Cicero reveals his real opinion of him, which we look for in vain in the fulsome compliments he paid him in the senate-house. He, as I have before said, never really trusted Pompey, although he undoubtedly liked him, and looked upon him as the chief stay of the aristocratic or conservative party, to which he was himself so strongly attached. He struggled hard to believe that Pompey was the man for the time, but he constantly disappointed him. And yet there was no one else of sufficient mark to be the leader whom Cicero was prepared to follow.

It was a sign of the times that Porcius Cato was

---

[2] Sed de illâ ambulatione fors viderit, aut si qui est qui curet Deus.— *Ad Att.* IV. 10. This might seem as if Cicero were a convert to the Epicurean philosophy of his friend. But most probably he said it only in jest; for there can be no doubt that he believed in the existence of Providence and a future state. See, amongst other proofs, *ad Att.* VII. 1; *de Divin.* I. 51; *de Legg.* II. 7; *de Senect.* 23.

this year defeated in a contest for the prætorship, and
Vatinius, the worthless creature of Cæsar, whom Cicero
had severely handled in his defence of Sextius, was elected
in his stead.   But a still more painful circumstance was,
that a law was actually passed on the thirteenth of May,
on the motion of Afranius, enacting that it should not be
punishable to have carried a prætorian election by bribery![3]
Cicero alludes to this in a letter to Quintus, and says that
the law caused great grief to the Senate.   He adds, that
the consuls, Pompey and Crassus, supported Afranius, and
threw Cato overboard altogether.

It is pleasant to notice the terms of affectionate intimacy on which the two brothers were.   Cicero seems to
have loved Quintus with a love passing the love of woman.
His letters to him form some of the most charming portions of his correspondence, full of playful allusions, the
point of which is however dimmed, and in many cases lost,
by the lapse of nearly two thousand years.

In his next letter to him, he tells him that no muse-
stricken poet takes more delight in hearing his own verses
read, than he does in reading his brother's letters on every
subject public or private, and whether full of the gossip of
the country or the town.   *Apropos* to the question of bringing their friend Marius to his villa, he mentions a practical
joke he once played him.   He was taking him with him to
Baiæ, and he dressed up a hundred men as soldiers with
swords, to follow the palanquin (*lectica*) that conveyed
him.   Marius, who had no idea that he was accompanied
by so warlike a retinue, happened to open the window of
his litter, and when he saw the armed attendants nearly
fainted with terror, to the great amusement of Cicero.

In another letter he expresses his opinion of the poem
of Lucretius, and says it showed little genius but much

[3] Ne qui præturam per ambitum cepisset, ei propterea fraudi esset.

art, a judgment in which we can hardly coincide. Genius alone could have made him successful in dealing with so unpromising a subject for poetry as _Natura Rerum_. It is one of the grandest remains of Roman literature.

To Atticus he wrote in May, and told him he was devouring literature with Dionysius, whom he calls a wonderful man. Nothing he said was more delightful than universal knowledge.[4] He was soon afterwards on his way back to Rome, and begged Atticus to come and dine with him, and bring his wife, Pilia, on the second of the following month, saying that he intended to dine on the first with his son-in-law Crassipes, like a traveller at an inn, and go home afterwards, giving the go-by to the order of the Senate, which required the senators at Rome to attend its meetings, equivalent to what we should term a call of the House.

In few things he took greater delight than in ornamenting his villas, and especially his Tusculanum. He had given a commission to Fadius Gallus to make some purchases for him, which his friend seems to have misunderstood. He bought four or five statues, consisting of figures of Bacchanals, one of Mars, and another sculptured as a support for a table. But Cicero did not much care for statues, his passion was pictures and books; and he wrote and told Gallus that he had given more for them than all the statues in the world in his opinion were worth. Gallus had written to him that the Bacchanals might vie with the group of the Muses which Cicero had previously purchased from Metellus; but he replied—

"What resemblance is there? In the first place I should have never thought the Muses worth as much as you have given—and I am sure all the Muses would agree with me—but they suited my library and were appropriate to my studies. But what place have I for Bacchanals?

---

[4] Οὐδὲν γλυκύτερον ἢ πάντ' εἰδέναι.—_Ad Att._ IV. 11.

You say they are pretty—I know them well, and have often seen them; but if I had approved of them I would have given you a distinct commission to purchase statues so well known to me. For I am in the habit of buying only those statues which do for ornamenting my *palæstra* in the manner of *gymnasia*. But what have I, a man of peace, to do with Mars? I am glad that there was no figure of Saturn amongst them; for I should have feared that those two statues would have got me into debt. . . . I have been putting up some seats with niches against the wall (*exhedria*) in the portico of my Tusculan villa, and I wish to adorn them with pictures. If anything of that kind delights me it is paintings. If, however, I must have the statues, I wish you would tell me where they are, when they are to be sent for, and by what kind of conveyance. For if Damasippus (who talked of buying them) changes his mind, I will find some *pseudo* Damasippus to whom I can sell them even at a loss."

The Damasippus here alluded to, is the virtuoso and antiquary so pleasantly described by Horace in one of his satires, who ruined himself by his dilettante tastes.

If we turn from Cicero's familiar correspondence with his intimate friends to his letters addressed to politicians and statesmen, we are struck by the change of style. When he writes to Atticus, or Quintus, or Terentia, or Tiro, the sentences are short, and often elliptical. He hints frequently his opinion by a word. In fact, the letters are just what we might expect from a man who knows that his meaning will be understood by the friend to whom he writes, however brief and playful or ironical his expressions may be. But when he addresses a *political* friend or acquaintance, his style is stately and elaborate—with long-winded sentences full of profuse compliment. The genius of the Latin language is peculiarly suited for this pompous kind of composition, and hence it is the language above all others adapted to lapidary inscriptions. In a letter to Lentulus, the proconsul of Cilicia, written about this time, Cicero says, with an exaggeration which carries insincerity on the face of it, " I wish you to be perfectly assured, that there is nothing however small

it may be in which you are interested, which I do not hold
dearer than all my own concerns!" But I mention the
letter chiefly to show how he still clung to Pompey. He
declares that so great is his inclination, nay, love towards
him, that whatever is advantageous to him, and whatever
he wishes, seems to him right and true.

Pompey celebrated his second consulship by exhibiting
shows and games of extraordinary splendor. The excuse
was the dedication of a magnificent theatre he had built
upon the model of one he had seen at Mitylene on his
return from the war against Mithridates. It is said to
have been large enough to hold eighty thousand spectators. Some fragments of the immense building still
remain. On this occasion every kind of amusement of
which the Romans were fond was lavished upon the
populace. Stage plays were acted, in which the *mise en
scène* was got up with unusual attention to effect. Broad
farces and pantomimes kept the audience in a roar. Ath-
letes struggled, and gladiators fought day after day—

"Butchered to make a Roman holiday."

Africa sent her wild beasts into the arena—and five hundred lions and eighteen elephants were slaughtered in
what were called "hunts," that lasted for five days. We
can hardly form an idea of the gigantic scale on which
these cruel sports were conducted at Rome, which have
no parallel in modern times, not even in the bull-
fights of Spain. Cicero gives an account of the whole
show in a letter to his friend Marcus, written in a very
splenetic mood. He took little pleasure in anything that
was addressed rather to the eye than the mind, and his
taste was too severe to appreciate as we do the accessaries
of stage scenery. He asks what enjoyment there can be
in seeing six hundred mules on the stage in Clytem-

POMPEY'S THEATRE.

RESTORED BY CAV CANINA.

Vol. i. p. 272.

næstra, or three thousand soldiers in the play of the
Trojan horse, or a crowd of infantry and cavalry in a sham-
fight which so delighted the populace.   He certainly would
not have appreciated the way in which we have of late
years seen the plays of Shakespear brought upon the
stage.   Besides, the actors displeased him.   Æsop, the
famous tragic actor, the Garrick of his day, from whom
Cicero had taken lessons in elocution and delivery—was
growing old.   He broke down in one of his parts, and his
voice failed him.   Then as to the "hunts," what pleasure
was there, he asks, in seeing a poor fellow torn to pieces by
a powerful brute, or a noble animal stricken by a spear?
What would he have thought of a modern fox hunt?   He
says the elephants excited the pity of the crowd, who
could not help feeling that they had something human
about them.   Dio Cassius, indeed, tells us quite gravely,
and with all the simplicity of Herodotus, that when the
creatures lifted their trunks aloft uttering cries of pain,
the spectators thought that they were appealing to Heaven
against perjury—for it was believed that to induce them
to embark on the coast of Africa, their conductors had
sworn to them that they should meet with no harm!

But Cicero had not been wholly occupied with the
shows.   In the midst of them he pleaded the cause of
Caninius Gallus, who had been a tribune of the people,
and was impeached when he laid down his office.   The
speech is lost, but it seems to have been successful.   In
the letter to Marius, in which he mentions this defence, he
complains of weariness of a pleader's task, and says that if
the people were as complaisant to him as to Æsop the
actor, he would gladly give it up.   Formerly he might
decline any cause he pleased, and yet even then, though
youth and ambition spurred him on, he grew tired of the
work.   Now, however, he was plagued to death by it; for

he looked forward to no benefit from his labors, and was
sometimes compelled to defend men who deserved very
little at his hands, at the request of others to whom he was
under obligations.

He had delivered in the Senate a more important speech
a few days before. It is that which is known as *in Pisonem*,—the most savage of all his orations. Piso had been
recalled from his government of Macedonia, and he complained in the Senate of the way in which he had been
attacked by Cicero, who proposed that he should be superseded. This gave the orator the opportunity, which he
eagerly seized, of pouring out on the head of the devoted
ex-consul all the vials of his wrath. The language he
made use of was quite unworthy of his lips, and we can
only wonder that it was tolerated by the senators of
Rome.

He calls Piso a beast, a butcher, a lump of mud, a
gallows bird, a carcase, a monster, filth, and other names
with which it really would not be decent to pollute these
pages. As a specimen of the style, it will be sufficient to
quote the passage with which the speech as it has come
down to us opens; for the original commencement is
lost :—

"Do you now see, you beast, or do you feel, what sort of complaint
men make of your appearance? Nobody complains that some Syrian
from a gang of slaves was made consul. It was not your slave-like complexion, not your shaggy cheeks, not your decaying teeth, that deceived
us. Your eyes, your eyebrows, your forehead, in short your whole countenance, which is a sort of silent language of the mind, betrayed men
into their mistake. This it was that deceived, cheated, and imposed
upon those to whom you were unknown. Few of us had known your
grovelling vices—few, your sluggishness of intellect, your stupidity, and
the imbecility of your tongue. Your voice had never been heard in the
Forum. No one had made the experiment of consulting you. No action
of yours, either military or civil, was, I do not say illustrious, but even
known. You stole in upon public honors by a mistake, by the recommendation given you by the smoke-stained busts of your ancestors, with
which you have nothing in common but your color."

He described an interview which, accompanied by his
son-in-law, Piso's relative, he had with him during his
consulship, in terms which it is hardly possible to quote.
They found him in the morning reeking from a debauch,
and were almost stifled with the fumes that he exhaled,
while he pretended that he was obliged to take wine
medicinally, and drove them away with the most dis-
courteous reply and the most vulgar and offensive
manners. We may remember that when Clodius asked
the consuls at a public meeting what they thought of
Cicero's conduct in the Catiline conspiracy, Piso mildly
replied that he did not approve of cruelty. This was not
forgotten by the orator, and he burst out in a fine passage
of indignant eloquence, which may be compared with the
withering sarcasm of Brougham in that part of his speech
in defence of Williams on a criminal information for a
libel against the clergy of Durham, where he retorts the
charge of hypocrisy upon the reverend prosecutors. The
point consisted in the contrast which Cicero drew between
his own alleged cruelty in proposing that the conspirators
should be put to death which the Senate, and not he,
determined, and the cruelty of Piso in forbidding the
Senate to go into mourning when Clodius threatened
Cicero with proscription.

"What Scythian tyrant," he asked, "did this? refuse to allow those
to mourn whom he was plunging in sorrow! You leave the grief—you
deprive them of its emblems—you snatch from them their tears, not by
consolations, but by threats. But if any of the Conscript Fathers had
changed their dress, not in obedience to a public resolution, but from
feelings of private duty or compassion, it was an act of intolerable
tyranny, by the interdict of your cruelty, not to permit them to do so.
When, however, the crowded Senate had voted for it, and the other
orders in the state had already done it, you—dragged out of a murky stew
to be consul, with that frizzled ballet-dancer of yours—forbade the Senate
of the Roman people to mourn the sunset and destruction of the
Republic."

In the autumn Cicero went into the country, and in the

middle of December was at his Tusculan villa, where he was glad to escape being present at the debate that took place in the Senate about Pompey's and Cæsar's provinces. Pompey had the proconsular government of Spain and Africa bestowed upon him for five years; and Cæsar demanded a prolongation of his command in Gaul for the same period, to enable him to complete and consolidate his conquests. This led to some sharp debates; but ultimately Cæsar carried his point, supported as he was by Pompey, who little knew what a power he was building up for his own destruction. In the letter which alludes to this, Cicero mentions the departure of Crassus from the city to take possession of his ill-omened government of Syria, from which Gabinius had been recalled, like Piso from Macedonia. Ill-omened indeed, it was, in every sense. Ateius Capito, a tribune of the people, at first forbade him to go, and attempted to throw him into prison. Some of the other tribunes, however, interfered, and Ateius then solemnly cursed him, which seems to have had such an effect, that no one of note except Pompey ventured to accompany him outside the walls. Under these gloomy auspices he set out.[5]

Before he finally left, Cicero, yielding to the earnest desire of Pompey and of Cæsar, who urged him strongly by letter to lay aside his enmity to Crassus, had been reconciled to him, and at his express request dined with him in the gardens, or park, of Crassipes, which were outside the city, where Crassus, as clothed with a military command, could not now remain.

The great literary work on which he was engaged this

---

[5] While the army was assembling at Brundusium to embark for the East, a seller of figs was heard calling out his fruit in the street—*Cauneas! Cauneas!*—pronounced probably *Caf'neas*—which the superstitious minds of the hearers interpreted as a prophetic warning—*Cave ne eas!*—" Beware of going !"—Cic. *de Div.* ii. 40.

year was his *De Oratore*, in three books, which he tells Atticus in December he had finished, after long and careful labor, and his friend might have a copy of it. It is one of the most finished and most interesting of all his compositions, and happily has come down to us in a perfect state.

The election of consuls for the new year, B.C. 54, had been put off from time to time until the close of the last, chiefly, no doubt, owing to the intrigues of the triumvirate party, who wished, if possible, to exclude Domitius from the office. But he succeeded at last, and Appius Claudius Pulcher, the brother of Clodius, was his colleague.

We shall see Cicero this year drawing more and more closely to Cæsar, the fame of whose victories kept up his reputation and influence at Rome. Quintus had accepted the office of one of his lieutenants, and left Rome for Gaul.

In a letter to him, his brother says that Appius the consul had summoned the Senate to meet on the twelfth of February, but the cold was so severe that he was compelled by the clamor of the populace to dismiss the meeting. We may remember how, on one occasion, Clodius's mob thronged the *Græcostasis* and steps of the building, and frightened the senators by their shouts. It would startle us to hear that the two Houses of Parliament had adjourned because the crowd in Palace Yard thought the weather too cold !

When Cæsar was consul, he had granted to Antiochus, king of the petty principality of Commagene, the honor of wearing a *prætexta*, or robe of office worn by the magistrates at Rome, which was something equivalent to the gift of the insignia of the Order of the Garter or the Bath by our own Sovereign to a foreign prince ; but the privilege seems to have been limited to a year ; and perhaps the consul had no power to grant it for a longer period.

Antiochus wished to have it renewed, but Cicero laughed
at his pretensions ; and, addressing the senators, asked
them, " Will you, noblemen as you are, who refused the
prætexta to a Bostrenian chief, permit a Commagenean to
wear it ? "

In the letter mentioning this, Cicero says that Balbus
had heard from Cæsar that a packet of letters addressed
to him, including one from Cicero, had got so saturated
with water, that the letter was wholly unrecognizable.
He had, however, been able to decipher part of a letter
from Balbus, sufficiently to make out that it contained an
allusion to Cicero, which seemed to promise something
which was more to be wished than hoped for. There can
be no doubt of Cæsar's anxiety to gain Cicero on his side.
He was the man above all others whose support would
have been invaluable to him. It would have gone a long
way to disarm suspicion of his ultimate designs, if he could
have secured the man who was *par excellence* the
champion of the authority of the Senate, and had a horror
of violence. And no one can blame Cicero for wishing to
stand well with Cæsar, and agreeing with him so far as
was possible without a compromise of principle.

As his first letter was thus practically lost, he sent
Cæsar a copy of it ; and as the proconsul of Gaul had
jokingly alluded to his own poverty, he added, in the same
strain, that he had better not become bankrupt by relying
upon his (Cicero's) purse. He told Quintus that he heard
from all quarters of Cæsar's kindly feeling towards them
both.

He took the opportunity afforded by a letter of introduction, which he gave to his friend Trebatius, an eminent
lawyer,[6] in February, to write to the proconsul of Gaul in

---

[6] This is the same Trebatius whom Horace introduces in his Satires,
ii. 1, as recommending a swim across the Tiber to secure a good night's

a friendly and familiar tone, telling Cæsar that he considered him a second self. He wrote also to Quintus, and said : " I agree with you about Pompey, or rather you agree with me. For, as you know, I have for a long time past been singing the praises of Cæsar. He is, believe me, a bosom friend, and I do not intend to let him slip."

His next two letters are to Trebatius, who had joined Cæsar in Britain; and are worth noticing merely from the passing allusions to the barbarous country of our ancestors. He tells him to beware of the charioteers (*essedarii*) of Britain; and says he hears there is neither gold nor silver there. He therefore advises his friend, if this is so, to get one of their chariots, and come back to Rome as quickly as possible.

In May Cicero went into the country, and spent a couple of months at his Cuman and Pompeian villas. He wrote to Quintus, and told him he was engaged upon his work, *De Republicâ*, which he calls a tough and troublesome task; but if it turned out according to his expectation, the labor would be well bestowed. If not, he would throw it into the sea which he looked down upon as he was writing, and would try something else, as he could not be idle. He said he would look carefully after his nephew, Quintus's son ; and if the boy did not despise him, would act as his tutor, for which he was qualified by attending to the education of his own son. In a letter to Atticus, who had just left Rome, he begs him to give directions that he may be allowed free access to his library in his absence, as he wished to consult some books, and especially the works of Varro, with reference to what he was then engaged upon.

sleep. In another letter Cicero jokes him for being very fond of swimming—*studiosissimus* **natandi**—and yet unwilling to cross the Straits with Cæsar into Britain.—*Ad Div.* vii. 10.

On his return to Rome in June, he wrote to his brother, and told him he had received two letters from him, together with one from Cæsar, full of civility and kindness. He speaks of Cæsar's affection as a thing which he preferred to all the honors which the proconsul assured him he might expect from him; and then goes on—

"I am ardently desirous now to devote myself to him alone, and perhaps I shall do what often happens to travellers who are in a hurry. If they rise later than they intended they make up for lost time, and so arrive at their journey's end sooner than if they had awakened before daybreak. Thus I, since I have so long slumbered in cultivating that person, although you often urged me to do so, will, as you tell me that my poem is approved by him,[7] by my future speed make up for past slowness with my poetic steeds and chariot. Only give me Britain to paint with your colors and my own pencil."

What a pity it is that such a book was never written. A description of Britain by Cicero, from information supplied by his brother, would have been a most interesting work.

As to politics, he adds, that there was at Rome some suspicion of a Dictatorship; and everything was quiet in the Forum—the usual focus of disorder at Rome; but this was a sign of the Republic getting into its dotage, rather than of tranquillity.

Quintus had hardly been able to make out his brother's last letter, on account of the badness of the handwriting, and fancied that he must have been either too busy or too excited by some cause or other to write legibly. Cicero now assured him that this was not the case, and laid the blame upon his pen; for he always took up the first that came to hand, and scribbled away with it whether it was good or bad. But he promised that he would in future use a good pen, well-mixed ink, and smoothed paper.[8]

[7] Perhaps this was the poem *De Temporibus suis*, which embraced the events connected with his exile; or it may have been some panegyric on Cæsar's exploits.

[8] Calamo et atramento temperato, charta etiam dentata, res agetur.— *Ad Quint.* ii. 15.

He urged Quintus to stay in Gaul, where he had a good opportunity of making money and getting out of debt. His advice, in short, was that of Iago to Roderigo : " Put money in thy purse ; follow these wars ; I say, put money in thy purse." He said there was no reason why Quintus should return to Rome, as he had generously offered to do if he could be of use to his brother, or danger threatened him. He gave a cheering account of himself at this period. His morning *levées* were crowded, and he was received with popular applause in the Forum and the theatre ; while, with Cæsar and Pompey on his side, he felt secure against any attack from Clodius. He would soon, he said, be free from debt, if life and health were spared. He drew a melancholy picture of the corruption that was going on at Rome. Four candidates for the consulship were in the field ; and the bribery was enormous. He declared that there never was anything like it. The interest of money actually rose in consequence from four to eight per cent.[9]

He gave the same account to Atticus ; and, as his friend was a capitalist, and, like his deceased uncle, Cæcilius, lent money at usury, he added that he was not likely to take to heart the rise in the rate of interest.

At this time, June and July, he was busily engaged in the duties of an advocate. He had just defended Messius, who had been recalled to take his trial from an embassy on which he had been sent by Appius Claudius, the consul, to Cæsar in Gaul, and was preparing to defend Drusus on a charge of corruptly betraying a case he had undertaken ; and Scaurus, who was accused of embezzlement in Sardinia ;

---

[9] Idib. Quint. fœnus fuit bessibus ex triente.—*Ad Quint.* ii. 15. The usual rate of interest at Rome was *triens*, or a third of an *as*, and this was reckoned by the month (as is the case in India), so that it amounted to four per cent. per annum. The *bes* was two-thirds of an *as*, and therefore *fœnus bessibus* was eight per cent.

and Plancius, who had behaved so kindly to him in his
exile, and who was in Sardinia, now accused of bribery.
He told Atticus that he had before him a list of glorious
titles for his speeches, with so many defences on his hands.
But he was annoyed at the acquittal of Sufenas and the
demagogue tribune Cato, who were both brought to trial
for bribery and corruption. At the same time, Procilius,
who was tried for an attempt to murder, was convicted;
and Cicero sarcastically remarks—" From this we may see
that our stern Areopagites do not care a straw for bribery,
comitia, interregnum, treason, or, in short, the Republic
altogether. To be sure, we ought not to try and murder
the head of a family at his own house, and even that
point is not altogether clear. For twenty-two were for an
acquittal, and twenty-eight for a conviction." Hortensius
defended Procilius, and Cicero was with him, but did not
speak. The reason he gives is, that his daughter Tullia,
who was then unwell, was afraid lest he might come into
collision with Clodius, who conducted the prosecution.
After this, he went on what we should call a special retainer into the country.

The inhabitants of Reate (*Rieti*) had a quarrel with
their neighbours,—who lived at Interamna, near the confluence of the rivers Velinus and Nar (the *Velino* and *Nera*),
and were hence called Interamnates,—about draining the
lake Velinus. For a tunnel had been cut through the
mountains, and the waters carried off into the Nar, the
consequence of which was that the territory of the Reatians
which was called Rosea, and was one of the loveliest spots
in Italy, was left dry; and they now sought to obtain
compensation from the Interamnates. A commission was
appointed, consisting of one of the consuls and ten assessors, to try the cause, and the Reatians had the good fortune to be able to engage Cicero as their counsel. We do

not know the result ; but he tells us that, while there, he
resided with Accius, a Roman senator, who had a villa
in the pleasant Rosea, which he calls Tempe for its
beauty.

On the eighth of July he returned to Rome, and wrote
to Atticus, with an affectation of modesty, that when he
appeared in the theatre, he was received with loud applause.[10] As to the actors, Antiphon, who had been once
a slave, was far the best, but his voice was weak. He also
mentions an actress named Arbuscula as having been very
successful, although we know from Horace that she was at
least once hissed in the theatre.[1]

Writing to Trebatius in Gaul, he tells him that a
friend of his, whose name he pretends he cannot recollect,
has frequently asked him to dinner, but, although he is
much obliged to him, he has not accepted the invitation.[2]
He congratulates Trebatius on being thought by Cæsar an
excellent lawyer, and says that, if he had crossed over to
Britain, he would certainly have found no one there more
learned in the law than himself. Those were not the days of
Cokes and Hardwickes and Mansfields in our island. He
jokes him about the cold of the approaching winter, and advises him, as he was not very well off in military cloaks, to
keep up a good fire, which he might do on the authority
of grave jurisconsults, such as Mucius Scævola and Manilius, if he wanted chapter and verse for it.

The next letter to Quintus was written by an amanuen-

---

[10] Sed hoc ne curares; ego ineptus qui scripserim.—*Ad Att.* IV. 15.

[1] Horace says that Arbuscula, when hissed by the audience, said she
was content with the applause of a Roman knight—

—— Nam satis est equitem mihi plaudere, ut audax,
Contemptis aliis, explosa Arbuscula dixit.—Sat. I. 10.

[2] His real name was Cn. Octavius (see *ad Div.* VII. 16). He obvi-
ously bored Cicero, who did not behave very civilly to him; for when he
pestered him with invitations, he asked him, point-blank, "Who are
you ?"—*Ib.*

sis, which Cicero said was a sure sign that he was busily
employed. He had never, in fact, according to his own
account, been more occupied with cases than now, and at
the most unhealthy season of the year, when the heat was
intense. The climate of Rome in August was never good,
and at the present day is positively dangerous. All who
can get away leave the city to take refuge in the hills,
returning not sooner than October. The wonder is, that
Cicero was able to labor in the courts at all in such an
atmosphere; for he declares that he never remembered the
heat greater. He said that in the afternoon he was going
to defend Vatinius, accused of bribery and corruption in
his canvass for the prætorship, and the same man whom
he had before so bitterly attacked, when he was counsel for
Sextius. But Vatinius, as the reader will remember, was
a fast friend of Cæsar, and Cicero's policy was to oblige
Cæsar as much as possible. His speech on this occasion
is lost, and it is perhaps better for his reputation that it
is so. But he not only defended him as an advocate; he
gave evidence for him as a witness to character. This
was called *laudare*. People must have stared when they
heard Cicero praising Vatinius.[3]

Quintus just then was full of a plan he had in his head
to write a poetical account of Britain, and his brother told
him he had a capital subject. He promised to help him
with some verses, as he had asked for them; but it was
like sending owls to Athens.[4] He was pleased that Cæsar
approved of his poem (either the one *de Consulatu*, or *de
Temporibus*), and the great soldier seems to have criticised
it attentively, declaring that he had never read better

---

[3] Licinius Calvus was the prosecutor; and Vatinius felt his sarcasm so
keenly, that while Calvus was speaking he sprang from his seat and exclaimed, "Must *I* be condemned because *he* is eloquent?"

[4] Γλαῦκ' εἰς 'Αθήνας. A phrase exactly equivalent to ours of "sending
coals to Newcastle."

verses even in Greek—he could hardly have been as fond of Homer as Alexander was—but finding fault with some passages as written too carelessly.[5]

The extreme heat at last drove Cicero away from Rome, and in the beginning of September he went to the cool and pleasant shades of his villa at Arpinum, from which he began a long gossiping letter to his brother, which he did not finish until his return to the city before the end of the month. It is full of amusing details, and we there see the orator and statesman changed into the plain country gentleman, planning improvements, suggesting alterations, and giving his opinion about roads, water-courses, and buildings. On his way he paid a visit to Quintus's villas, called Arcanum and Laterium, with their neighbouring farms, and gave him an account of the progress of the works that were going on. He had bought a farm for his brother at Arpinum, and says he never saw a shadier or better watered spot for summer. It was to be converted into a villa, and ornamented with a fish-pond, fountains, shrubberies, and a *palæstra* or place for gymnastic exercises.

These are trifling details, and may seem hardly worth mentioning after the lapse of nineteen centuries. But, I confess, I think differently. It is pleasant to make acquaintance with the ancients at *home,* and find them engaged in occupations and pursuits similar to our own. It does not lessen our admiration of Cicero as an orator to see him amusing himself as a farmer or country squire ; and it increases our interest in him, and makes us feel better acquainted with him.

---

[5] Cæsar knew the Greek language thoroughly, as did most educated Romans at this period. One of the shortest letters on record is that which he sent in Greek to Quintus, when he was besieged by the Gauls, and almost in extremity : Καῖσαρ Κικέρωνι. Προσδέχου βοήθειαν, " Cæsar to Cicero. Expect help."

Piso had published an attack on him in the form of a
speech, and Quintus had advised him to reply to it. But
he declined to do this, on the ground that no one was likely
to read Piso's libel, and every schoolboy got by heart his
own former oration against him. This is a little bit of
vanity, as is also what he says about Milo. Some one had
written and told Cæsar that Milo had been loudly applauded by the people, owing, no doubt, to some splendid
shows he had exhibited as ædile; and Cicero adds that he
is quite willing that Cæsar should believe that the applause
was great, as was certainly the fact; but he could not
help thinking that some part of it was intended for himself! But if he was a vain, he was also a kindhearted
man. He mentions at the beginning of his letter that he
had left Rome when the autumn games were going on;
but he had given directions to his freedman Philotimus to
secure places at the theatre for his fellow-townsmen from
Arpinum, many of whom came up to Rome to witness the
spectacle.

Gabinius, who, as I have before mentioned, had been
recalled from his province of Syria in disgrace, reached
Rome on the twentieth of September, and, after lingering
outside the gates for more than a week, pretending that he
had claims to a triumph, slunk into the city at night. He
was immediately assailed by a prosecution for having
quitted his province without leave, in order to restore
Ptolemy to the throne of Egypt by force, and four more
were awaiting him, three for embezzlement, and one for
bribery. So that he was in a very unenviable position—
indeed, a miserable and forlorn one, as Cicero calls it.
He told his brother that Pompey was very pressing to
induce him to be reconciled with Gabinius, but in vain;
and he declared that, if he retained his liberty at all, he
never would be. But very soon afterwards he surrendered

his liberty, and defended in a speech no longer extant this very Gabinius, the object of his loathing and contempt. Just about this time, Pompey lost his wife Julia, who was Cæsar's daughter. She died in childbed; and thus, although the rupture did not immediately appear, the last link was snapped which held the two ambitious rivals together. Cæsar bore the sad bereavement with manly fortitude. Writing to his brother, Cicero alluded feelingly to his loss, and said that he would not send Cæsar a letter of congratulation on his late victories in Britain, out of respect for his sorrow.[6]

It seems to have been immediately after his return to Rome that he defended Scaurus and Plancius. Scaurus was accused of extortion in Sardinia, of having murdered by poison one of the natives, and driven the wife of another to save herself from dishonor by suicide. The speech is lost, except a few fragments; but we know that Scaurus got off by a verdict of Not Proven,[7] for the jury were largely bribed. In his defence of Plancius, Cicero put forth all his strength. He was bound by every tie of honor and gratitude to try and save the man who had shown him such kindness in Thessalonica during his exile, and his advocacy of him now was a labor of love. Plancius had been a competitor of Junius Laterensis for the ædileship, and was successful. The defeated candidate of course accused him of illegal practices at the election, and Cicero was retained to defend him. The speech is more than usually interesting from the vivid picture he draws

---

[6] We find that it took in those times about twenty days to send a letter from Britain to Rome, "a despatch," says Middleton, "equal to that of our present couriers by post." The distance can now be travelled in four days.

[7] Drusus, Scaurus, NON FECISSE videbantur.—*Ad Att.* IV. 16. This was the technical expression for that form of acquittal. He was again prosecuted by Triarius for bribery two years later, and Cicero again defended him, but with a different result; for he was then convicted.

of the nature of a popular election, and much that he says
is as applicable in England now as it was at Rome twenty
centuries ago. If space permitted, I would gladly quote
several passages in which he admirably paints its various
vicissitudes, and the capricious fickleness of the voice of
the people, whom the candidate, he said, "tossed as he
was by the tempest and the waves of democracy," must
court if he wished to win, and bear its humors cheerfully
if he lost. His description of the ballot is true to the
letter, and exactly agrees with what Sydney Smith said of
it, that it would bring to pass that which David said only
in his wrath, and make all men liars.

> "The ballot is dear to the people; for it uncovers men's faces and con-
> ceals their thoughts. It gives them the opportunity of doing what they
> like, and of promising all that they are asked."

Of course Cicero took care to allude to Plancius's services towards himself. He drew an affecting picture of a
night they passed in Thessalonica, when they mingled their
tears together, and when he promised that, if he were
recalled from banishment, he would show his gratitude;
but if he died in exile, his countrymen would take care to
pay the debt he owed him. At the close of his speech, he
wept, and so apparently did the jurymen and the accused
before them; for Cicero declared that their tears prevented
him from saying more, and he hailed it as a good omen
that they wished to save Plancius—for their tears reminded
him of those which they had so often shed abundantly for
himself.

Plancius was acquitted. He afterwards joined the side
of Pompey in the Civil War, and during the supremacy of
Cæsar he lived in exile at Corcyra.

We now come to the long and celebrated letter which
Cicero wrote to Lentulus, the proconsul of Cilicia, and
which may be called his Apology for his political conduct.

It deserves an attentive examination, in order to appreciate
the motives that, according to his own account, influenced
him. The case stood thus. He had always opposed—
not so much actively as in spirit and opinion—the union
of parties effected by Cæsar, Pompey, and Crassus, and
known by the name of the first Triumvirate. He saw that
this powerful coalition, in fact, over-rode the constitution,
and went far to establish a Dictatorship at Rome resting
upon popular violence, ever ready to side with the strongest, so long as the mob was amused by spectacles, and kept
in pay by corruption. But he clung to Pompey even
then, although always mistrusting him. He really had an
affection for him as a man, and he was dazzled by his
brilliant reputation as a successful soldier. And, besides,
he seems to have believed that he was the only person to
whom the State could look to make head against the ambitious designs of Cæsar, and that he would be found on the
side of the constitution, if Cæsar or any other enemy
openly attacked it. From Cæsar he stood aloof, and could
not be persuaded to accept any office or honor at his
hands. He peremptorily refused to be one of his commissioners for dividing the Campania lands, and he declined,
though with hesitation, the offer to be one of his lieutenants—a post which Quintus afterwards accepted. He
did not, however, openly oppose Cæsar's bill for dividing
the Campanian lands, and indeed took credit for support-
ing it with an amendment, which he carried, for respecting
the rights of private individuals.

But Cæsar was too long-sighted and politic a man to
break with Cicero. He continued to flatter him, and lost
no opportunity of showing kindness and goodwill to his
friends. In the unhappy affair of his exile, Cicero had
more reason to complain of Pompey than of Cæsar. Cæsar
was at that moment at the head of his legions outside the

walls of Rome, and could not by law enter the city. Pompey, however, voluntarily retired to his Albanan villa, and when Cicero went there and threw himself at his feet to implore his aid, did not even ask him to rise, and coldly said he could do nothing without Cæsar's approval. And he did nothing. Cicero passed twelve miserable months in banishment, and when at last he was restored, he had to thank Cæsar as well as Pompey for the influence they had exerted in his favor. Cæsar, indeed, was absent in Gaul, but he had an active party in Rome; and we may feel certain that if he had been averse to Cicero's return, there would have been enormous difficulty in effecting it. Clodius also had now declared himself the open enemy of Cæsar as well as of Pompey, so that the ill-feeling engendered in Cicero's mind by the conviction that his most inveterate foe was secretly supported by Cæsar no longer existed. When, therefore, an opportunity occurred for testifying his goodwill towards Cæsar, without compromising his own principles, he gladly availed himself of it. This opportunity arose on the question of prolonging Cæsar's command in Gaul, and he made that admirable speech, in which he nobly vindicated to himself the right to lay aside private enmity on account of wrongs inflicted on himself for the sake of the Republic, whose interests, he believed, required that the Proconsul's career of victory in Gaul should not be checked before he had completed and consolidated his conquests. Moreover, he clearly saw how little he could in future rely upon Pompey in a struggle, and the instinct of self-preservation led him no longer to repel the advances of the powerful general, who did not cease to court him, and whose name was a tower of strength at Rome from his popularity with the masses and his fame as a soldier. Nor must it be forgotten that, as yet, there was nothing in Cæsar's conduct to make it criminal in a patriot to join him. Some writers, indeed, like De Quincey, assert, that even in the agony of civil war, *his* was the patriotic side; but, without stopping to examine that question, this plea cannot possibly avail Cicero; for he was unalterably convinced *then* of the contrary. Now however the future lay dark before him; and not the most sagacious politician at Rome could have divined the series of events—blundering weakness on the one side, and unscrupulous ambition on the other—which led to the dictatorship of Cæsar and the overthrow of the constitution.

I have thus briefly recapitulated the facts of the case, as it is necessary to bear them in mind while reading Cicero's own defence. His reasoning is often weak and inconclusive, and disfigured by his intolerable vanity; indeed he seems to have felt half-ashamed of himself whilst writing, and therefore to have taken more than ordinary pains to glorify his achievements; but his defence may be summed up in two words: it was necessary to look out for better support than he had hitherto received, and that support was only to be found in Cæsar. The times were changed, and he must swim with the tide.[8]

Alluding to his appearing as a witness for Vatinius, he said that, as some of the most distinguished men at Rome had chosen to patronize and caress his own enemy—if they had their Clodius, he had a right to have his Vatinius. And he quoted some lines from the Eunuch of Terence, where the Parasite advises the Captain to play off Pamphila against Phædria, which may be thus rendered:—

> " If she names Phædria, do you forthwith
> Begin to speak of Pamphila; and if she says,
> ' Let us invite fair Phædria to supper.'

---

[8] I regret that want of space compels me to omit an epitome of the letter and an analysis of the arguments contained in it. I had written both, but find they would swell the volume to an inconvenient size.

> Do you rejoin, 'Let us have Pamphila
> To sing to us.' If she breaks out
> .In praise of Phædria's beauty, you extol
> The face of Pamphila. In short, my friend,
> Take care to pay her back in her own coin,
> And I will warrant that you tease and fret her."

"Aye!" said Cicero, "and gods and men approve my policy."

As to Crassus, although he had great reason to complain of his conduct, he was not going to gratify the malignity of others by continuing his enmity with him, as though they could never be friends; and both Pompey and Cæsar had urgently intreated him to make up the quarrel. He sums up, as it were, the main points of his defence in the following words :—

"Pray be assured that if I had been at liberty, and things had remained as they were, I would have pursued the same course. For I should not have thought it right to contend against such powerful influence, not even if it had been possible to destroy the supremacy of the most distinguished men in the state. Nor do I think I ought to adhere obstinately to one opinion when things are altered and the wishes of good men are changed, but we must go with the times. For an inflexible adherence to one opinion has never been approved of by leading politicians; but as in navigation it is a proof of skill to trim according to the weather, even if you cannot make the port (although when you *can* make it by shifting the sails it is folly to hold on your course with danger rather than by changing it to arrive at the point you wish), so—although all of us who are engaged in the government of the state ought to aim, as I have often said, at dignified repose—we ought always to aim at the same object, but not always say the same thing. Therefore, as I have just observed, if I had been as free as air, I would not have acted otherwise as a politician than I have done. But when to take this course I am both induced by the kindnesses of some and forced by the injuries of others, I find no difficulty in both thinking and saying, on public questions, what I conceive to be most for my interests, as well as the interests of the state."

The rest of the letter to Lentulus refers principally to the more pleasing subject of Cicero's studies. He promised to send a copy of his speeches which Lentulus had asked for—and told him they were not so numerous that they need frighten him at the thought of perusing them. He would send also his Dialogue *de Oratore*, and his poem in three books on his own Times, which would be an eternal memorial of Lentulus's good offices towards him, and his own grateful acknowledgment. He assured his friend in language which has proved prophetic— although it is not often that a man ventures to speak so confidently of his own name and actions reaching the distant future—that not only Lentulus, but the whole world and posterity, should know that no one was ever dearer or a greater favorite with him than himself.

The canvass for the consulships of the following year was still going on, and the competitors trusted as usual to bribery for success. They were all therefore threatened with prosecutions; and Cicero wrote privately to Quintus, that the question at issue was, whether they or the laws should perish.[9] Three of them, however, Domitius Calvinus, Messala, and Scaurus, seem to have applied to him to defend them—or at all events, he expected to be called upon; for in a letter to Atticus on the first of October, he says : "You will ask me, 'What will you be able to say for them?' May I die, if I know. I find nothing to guide me in those three books (*de Oratore*) on which you compliment me." The position of Cicero as an advocate at this time, was something like that of Erskine at the English bar. Every one who was in legal jeopardy was anxious to be defended by the most eloquent orator of Rome; and this was, according to his own account, one

---

[9] *Aut hominum aut legum interitus ostenditur.*—Ad Quint. iii. 2. This does not mean that their lives were in jeopardy. The punishment for the offence of bribery and corruption was not death but banishment. Notwithstanding the strong conviction here expressed by Cicero of their guilt, we find him a few months afterwards rejoicing that they were for the present at all events out of jeopardy, as the courts could not sit during the days of thanksgiving decreed in honor of Cæsar's victories.

of the busiest periods of his forensic career. Not a day
passed in which he had not to speak for somebody or other
in the courts. His time was so occupied with cases, that
he had hardly a spare moment to write a letter, and he
composed and dictated while he walked.

I have mentioned how Gabinius had been recalled from
Syria, and how he crept into the city alone, and in the
silence of night. As he journeyed towards Rome he pretended that he was going to demand a triumph; and to
keep up the farce, he stayed for a few days outside the
walls, as all were obliged to do who sought the honor,
until the Senate had decided on their claim. For more
than a week he did not venture to show himself in the
senate-house; but by law he was obliged to give an
account of the military state of his province within ten
days after his return—and on the tenth day therefore he
appeared, and made the required report. He was then about
to retire, but the consuls stopped him; and the *publicani*,
or contractors, who farmed the Syrian revenues, and whose
treatment by Gabinius has been already alluded to, were
introduced into the house to state their grievances. This
gave rise to a debate, in which Gabinius was bitterly
attacked, and by none more bitterly than Cicero. Exas-
perated by his taunts, he called him, with a voice trem-
bling with passion, "Exile!" Upon this the Senate rose
as one man, and with indignant shouts gathered round
Gabinius, as if about to inflict summary chastisement upon
him; even the strangers, the *publicani*, who were present,
joined in the clamor and the rush.

Gabinius was brought to trial on the charge of abandoning his province and employing his army to restore
Ptolemy without leave from the Senate. This amounted
to the crime of *majestas*. Lentulus was the prosecutor, and according to Cicero, was utterly unfit for

the task.   Indeed, he did his work so **badly,** that **he**
was accused **of** betraying the cause.   Cicero himself
was strongly tempted to undertake the prosecution ; but
as **he** told his brothers, **he was deterred, because he did**
not wish to come into collision with **Pompey,** who
strained every nerve **to procure Gabinius's acquittal—and**
he had lost all confidence in the tribunals.   **His own** expression is, " **we** have no juries now ;—I dread a failure." [10]
Besides, he was afraid that the ill-will, **which he was con-**
scious too **many** bore towards himself, might **tell** in favor
of the accused, **if** he became the prosecutor.   The result
was, that Gabinius was acquitted by thirty-eight votes out
of seventy.   Cicero congratulated himself that **he had**
taken no part in the trial beyond **that of** appearing as **a**
witness against the accused.   If he had **been the** prose-
cutor, Pompey would have made it, he **said, a** personal
matter—and it would have led to a quarrel between them.
Besides, he **added,** considering Pompey's influence and
zeal, he himself would have been likely to come off second-
best, and **he would have** been like the gladiator Paci-
dianus when matched with Aserninus, and might **(like**
him) have had the **tip of his ear bitten off.   The interest**
which Pompey **took in the issue of** the trial was notorious
to all, and he spared no solicitation nor entreaty to procure
an acquittal.   When the ballot-box, into which the votes
of the jurymen were thrown was opened, and the result
was known, one of them rushed away from the court to
carry the news to him.   Cicero mourned over the verdict ;
writing to Atticus, he declared that the constitution was
utterly ruined, and he could take no pleasure in public
affairs.   The Senate was a nullity, and so were the courts

---

[10] Judices nullos habemus—ἀπότευγμα *formido.—Ad Quint.* iii. **2.** We
might almost fancy that this was the language of an English Attorney-
General advising against a **state prosecution.**

of law. But as regarded himself, he affected a philosophic indifference which he by no means felt. He told Atticus that he had grown too callous to be angry, and sought refuge in his villas, his studies, and his books, the kind of life most congenial to him. If he had only his friend and his brother with him, politics might go to the dogs.[1] He could take pleasure only in private and domestic affairs. As to the impending trials of the consular candidates, he said they would all be acquitted; and added bitterly, that no one in future would be found guilty for a less crime than murder. But this was punished with severity, and there was no lack of cases. Some persons, amongst whom were Pompey and Vibius Pansa, afterwards consul with Hirtius in the year after Cæsar's assassination—had tried to induce Cicero to undertake the defence of Gabinius; but he says, that if he had consented, he would have been undone, and have brought upon himself the general odium felt towards the accused. Sallust told him that he ought either to have prosecuted or defended—on which he remarks, "a pretty friend is Sallust, who thinks I ought to incur dangerous enmities, or everlasting infamy." Besides, all his wishes now tended to quiet and repose. He was heartily sick of the state of things at Rome—and not without reason. The Senate was fast falling into contempt: the legal tribunals were infamously corrupt; and the venal populace sold their votes to the highest bidder. At the time of Gabinius's acquittal there was a terrible inundation of the Tiber. The Appian Way was flooded as far as the Temple of Mars, which stood by the side of the road,—the gardens of Crasippes, which lay along the banks of the river were swept away, and the streets were laid under water. Men thought it was a judgment of Providence on account of the wicked verdict.

[1] Per me ista pedibus trahantur.—*Ad Att.* iv. 16.

It is painful to see how Cicero's want of resolution made him do things which he knew to be wrong. Gabinius, though acquitted on the grave charge of treason, had another prosecution hanging over his head, and his advocate was Cicero. The accusation now was that of improperly receiving money from Ptolemy to restore him to his kingdom, and a criminal proceeding was instituted against him to recover back the amount. There was a struggle who should be the prosecutor, before Porcius Cato, who as prætor, had cognizance of the case, and was not likely to show him any mercy. Memmius, Nero, and two brothers of Mark Antony (nephews of the celebrated orator), all put themselves forward, and according to the usual custom, the point was settled by a *divinatio*. It was decided in favour of Memmius. In mentioning this to his brother, Cicero adds, that Gabinius was hard pressed, and intimates that he would be convicted, unless "our friend Pompey, against the will of gods and men, upsets the whole affair." And yet notwithstanding this, he defended him. He could not resist the urgent solicitation of Pompey; but his efforts were unsuccessful, and Gabinius was convicted and sentenced to banishment.[2] If we possessed Cicero's speech, we should no doubt find him complimenting the man whom he had so often fiercely assailed, and we can well believe that praise from his lips must have had little effect with the jury, who could not have forgotten his former bitter denunciation of the accused.

I have already pointed out the capital distinction between his position at Rome, and the position of an advocate in modern times. He was at perfect liberty to

---

[2] I do not understand how this happened, for the *Lex Julia*, which was then in force, had repealed the punishment of exile on a conviction *de pecuniis repetundis*. Gabinius was afterwards recalled from banishment by Cæsar.

decline any cause of which he did not approve, and he did not undertake the defence of Gabinius as an advocate, but as a *friend*. And he was under no obligation to come forward as a witness to the character of a man like Vatinius, whom he had branded with every term of opprobrium and contempt. Even Middleton admits that his conduct in these two instances is indefensible; and where Middleton gives him up, we may feel tolerably sure that there is little or nothing to be urged on his behalf. He says, "Whatever Cicero himself might say in the flourishing style of an oration, it is certain that he knew and felt it to be an indignity and dishonor to him, which he was forced to submit to by the iniquity of the times and his engagements to Pompey and Cæsar, as he often laments to his friends in a very passionate strain."

The "flourishing style of an oration," to which Middleton here alludes, refers to what Cicero said in his speech for Rabirius Postumus, when Memmius the prosecutor had asserted that the Alexandrian deputies had as good a right to give testimony in favour of Gabinius as Cicero had to defend him.

"No! Memmius," he replied, "the reason of my defending Gabinius was my reconciliation with him. Nor am I ashamed to own that my quarrels are mortal, my friendships eternal. For if you imagine that I undertook that defence against my own will from fear of offending Pompey, you are greatly mistaken both in him and me. For neither would Pompey have wished me to do anything for his sake against my own will, nor would I, who have always held most dear the liberty of my fellow-citizens, have surrendered my own."

These are brave words; but after all we know of the circumstances they cannot be accepted as true.

The next cause in which Cicero was engaged arose out of the case of Gabinius. His client, having been convicted, had to restore the money which he was accused of improperly receiving from Ptolemy. This amounted to ten thousand talents (about two millions and a half sterling), and as Gabinius could not pay the sum, his property was sold. But this was insufficient to realize the fine, and Rabirius Postumus, a Roman knight, was accused of having received a portion of the money that had been paid to Gabinius. He was put upon his trial and defended by Cicero. He insisted that the law against pecuniary extortion (*de repetundis*) did not apply to the knights, being intended only to check the rapacity of provincial governors; and, moreover, asserted that not a farthing of the spoil had come into the hands of Rabirius, who on the contrary had lent money to Ptolemy, which had not been repaid to him, and he would have become bankrupt in consequence if he had not been assisted by the generosity of Cæsar. The result of the trial is not known; but Drumann thinks it probable that Rabirius was convicted and sentenced to banishment, from which he was afterwards recalled by Cæsar when he was dictator.

It is refreshing to turn from the distracted politics of Rome to matters of more pleasing interest. Cæsar, always grand and magnificent in his views, had undertaken two great works—the enlargement of the Forum, and the erection of a splendid hall in the Campus Martius for public meetings. He seems to have commissioned Cicero to assist Oppius, his agent at Rome, in the superintendence of the plans. In mentioning this to Atticus, Cicero speaks of the expense in a tone, which it is easy to see is ironical. He says, "On the enlargement of the Forum as far as the Hall of Liberty, an idea which used to have your warm approval, Cæsar's friends (I mean myself and Oppius—you may burst if you like at my calling myself so) have thought the outlay of sixty millions of sesterces a mere bagatelle." It was necessary to pull down a great many private houses, and of course the owners received compensation. The building in the Campus Martius was to be substituted for the old *Septa* or Barriers, a wooden enclosure open to the sky, in which the people used to meet to give their votes. Cæsar was now erecting an edifice of marble covered with a roof and surrounded by a portico, a thousand paces long. To this was to be added a sort of town-hall (*villa publica*). The general object of these undertakings was no doubt to ingratiate himself with the populace; but a special motive was his desire to eclipse Æmilius Paullus, who had just restored an ancient *basilica* in the centre of the Forum, and was then engaged in building a new one, which Cicero calls a most glorious, and at the same time most popular, work. The one or other of these is most probably that of which the foundations have within the last few years been laid bare by the excavation of the Forum. As the spectator stands on the top of the Senator's Palace on the Capitol, he looks down upon it on the right of the Via Sacra, and sees the paved area with portions of columns, and broken fragments of masonry lying on the surface. The best example of an ancient Basilica is at Treves. It is now converted into an Evangelische Kirche. But it wants the rows of columns which were usually found in these buildings, and which became the side aisles when they were converted into Christian churches.

Trebatius, to whom we have already more than once alluded, was a good lawyer, but a bad soldier. He was clearly out of his element in Cæsar's camp, and was always hankering after the polished society of Rome, which he had left, as was usual with civilians at that time, to serve for a short period in the army. He was also impatient at not making so much money as he had expected in that fruitful field for rapacity, a Roman province. Cicero took him to task for this, and told him that he seemed to think

he had carried to the proconsul a bond for the payment of
a debt instead of a mere letter of introduction from himself.
He frankly let him know that he thought him too indolent
and too disposed to shirk his military duties, nay, went
so far as to say, that in his expectations from Cæsar he
often seemed to be rather impudent. He strongly urged
him to stay where he was, and make the most of his opportunities, serving as he did under an illustrious and
liberal commander, and in a wealthy province. He warned
him also not to take offence if Cæsar did not pay him all
the attention he desired, or seemed slow in satisfying his
wishes; for he must remember how much occupied the
proconsul was, and the difficulties he had to contend
against. And this advice he said he could in lawyer-like
fashion fortify, by quoting the authority of Cornelius
Maximus (whose pupil in civil law Trebatius had been),
for he was of the same opinion. He ends with rather a
stinging joke. "I am glad," he says, "that you did not
cross over into Britain, because you thus escaped hard-
ships, and I shall be spared a narrative of your exploits
there!"

Cicero paid great attention to the education of his son
and his nephew, who in Quintus's absence was entrusted
to his care. He spoke in a cheerful tone of the progress
they were making, and rejoiced in the affection the two
cousins felt towards each other. They were studying
rhetoric under Pæonius, whom he describes as a good and
experienced teacher; but he reminds his brother that his
own method of instruction was more searching and scientific, and he promised that if he took his young nephew
with him into the country he would teach him according
to his own plan. In the mean time, however, the boy, as
was natural, liked better the declamatory style of Pæonius;
and his uncle said that that was his own early practice

and he had good hopes that young Cicero would be as successful as himself.

Quintus had been urging his brother to write poetry—probably that he might use the verses in his own projected poem on Britain, but Cicero said that he had neither leisure nor a mind sufficiently free from anxiety. Besides, he wanted inspiration ;[3] and in all sincerity he declared that Quintus was a better poet than himself. His brother's library wanted a supply of books, and Cicero was doing his best to get them ; but those that were suitable were not for sale; and to make copies a dexterous and careful hand was required, which just then he did not possess amongst his slaves. He promised, however, to speak to Tyrannio, his son's tutor, and give his freedman Chrysippus instructions about it. The letter in which he mentions this was written in October, just as he was leaving Rome for his Tusculan villa, where he was taking his son with him to go on with his lessons.[4] In his next letter to his brother at the end of November, he spoke in a tone of deep dejection. He repeated, that he had neither time nor spirits for poetry, being far too much distressed at the state of public affairs.

"I withdraw myself," he said, "altogether from politics, and devote myself to literature; but I will confess to you what I had especially wished to conceal from you. I am distracted, my dearest brother, I am distracted, to think that we have no longer a republic or courts of justice; and that this period of my life, when I ought to have been in a flourishing position, and in the full enjoyment of a senator's authority, is either tormented by the labors of the Forum, or soothed only by literature at home—to think that all in vain have I followed the advice in my favorite line of Homer—

'Strive always to excel; be ever foremost in the race'[5]—

---

[3] Abest etiam *ἐνθουσιασμός.*—*Ad Quint.* iii. 4.

[4] Cicero *plays* here upon the word *ludus,* and makes a pun which is untranslatable. He says, *ducensque mecum Ciceronem meum in ludum disceudi, non lusionis.* The Latins used the same word for "school" and "play;" but surely the boys at Rome must have thought it a misnomer.

[5] Αἰὲν ἀριστεύειν καὶ ὑπείροχον ἔμμεναι ἄλλων.

that my enemies have partly been not opposed, and partly defended by me—that my inclinations are not free, and I am not allowed even to hate as I like—and that Cæsar has proved to be the only one who loved me as I wished to be loved; or the only one (as others think) who really wished to love me. However, there is nothing in all this to prevent me from finding daily consolation; but my greatest consolation will be your society."

He then, after alluding to the trial of Gabinius, turned to the more congenial subject of books. Tyrannio was too dilatory in executing the commission he had given him to make copies for Quintus's library; but it was a troublesome business. As to Latin books he hardly knew where to apply, the editions for sale were so carelessly copied. He joked Quintus for asking him to send him some poetry.

"What! when you tell me that you have finished four tragedies in sixteen days, can you think of borrowing from another?[6] And are you ready to incur a literary debt when you have written the Electra and the Troas? Don't be an idler, nor suppose that the precept 'Know thyself' was intended only to take down arrogance, and not also to make us sensible of our own gifts. But pray exert yourself, and send me your tragedy of Erigone."

Cicero must have been, as I have already remarked, a very early riser, for he constantly mentions that he is writing his letters before daybreak; and in the next to his brother, dated from his Tusculan villa, he tells him, that he is using a little wooden-lamp which Quintus had got made when he was at Samos, which was part of his pro-prætorian government in Asia Minor.

The insecurity of what we should call the *post* is a frequent subject of complaint with Cicero. Of course there was no post in the modern sense of the word, and it was not every messenger whom he dared to trust, especially

[6] These were most probably translations from the Greek. It is hardly possible that Quintus could have composed four original dramas in little more than a fortnight. Abeken treats them as original works, and calls Quintus in consequence, ironically, *ein gewaltiger Poet*—"a powerful poet."

when he alluded to politics.   In a letter to Atticus, written
at the end of November, he says that he is under some
anxiety whether it will reach him; for his correspondence
touched on so many delicate topics, that he did not like to
employ even his amanuensis.   And certainly the next
piece of news he communicated to his friend was of such
a nature that, if it had not become notorious, and was unhappily too true, he might well be afraid of mentioning it
lest it should prove to be a scandalous libel.   I have
already alluded to a compact entered into between two of
the consular candidates, Domitius and Memmius, with
the actual consuls, which Cicero hinted at in a former
letter, but said it was so disgraceful that he did not venture to be more explicit.   But Memmius himself had now
brought the whole matter before the Senate, and Cicero
communicated it to Atticus.   It is well nigh incredible,
but is too well attested to admit of doubt.   In order to
understand the case it is necessary to bear in mind that,
although the Roman consuls almost as a matter of right
held provincial governments at the expiration of their
year of office, which they looked forward to as a certain
means of amassing money, their position as proconsuls
depended upon a special vote of the people assembled in
the comitia curiata.   They could not by possibility
expect the honor of a triumph, the highest object of
Roman ambition, unless they had previously been invested
with the *imperium* or military authority, and the number
of troops they might command, together with the whole of
what we may call their outfit, depended upon the same
vote.   This was styled *ornare provinciam.*   Now the
existing consuls had got their provinces, but had not got the
imperium nor equipments.   They made, therefore, an agreement with Domitius Calvinus and Memmius that they would
support them in their canvass for the consulships of the

next year, provided that *they* would, if they were elected, produce three augurs and two ex-consuls who would solemnly declare that they were present when a bill for bestowing the *imperium* and outfit was brought forward in the Senate and passed in the comitia curiata of the people, although the whole was a fiction and the Senate had never even entertained the question! And the two candidates agreed to forfeit a large sum of money to each of the two consuls unless they fulfilled their part of the bargain. This compact was formally reduced to writing and signed by the parties. Memmius, however, felt as time went on that he had no chance of being elected. He, therefore, at the instigation of Pompey, made a clean breast of it, and brought the whole affair before the Senate, to the confusion and disgrace of the then consuls Domitius Ahenobarbus and Appius Claudius. It is difficult to understand, not that the parties should have been wicked enough to enter into such an agreement, but that they should have thought the success of such a scheme possible. We cannot even imagine a parallel case in this country with the publicity that attends all the proceedings of Parliament, but it was as if a French minister were to try to get three archbishops and two senators to come forward and swear that they were present when a particular bill was passed, which in fact had never come before the Corps Législatif or Senate at all. The thing is too extravagantly absurd to be supposed possible in France, but it actually happened at Rome, and shows that there must have been some glaring defect in the method of keeping the records of public acts.[7]

---

[7] In old times in this country all bills were in the form of petitions from the Commons, which were entered on the Rolls of Parliament, with the King's answer subjoined. At the end of each Parliament the judges drew up these records into the form of a statute, which was entered on

As may well be believed, the revelation of this iniquitous
bargain between the two men who held the highest office
in the State and two of those who aspired to the same
dignity, caused great scandal, even in the corrupt society
of Rome. Middleton says that the Senate was highly
incensed, and passed a decree "that the conduct of the
parties should be inquired into by what they called a
private or silent judgment (*tacitum judicium*), where the
sentence was not to be declared till after the election (of
the new consuls), yet so as to make void the election of
those who should be found guilty." But this is a mistake.
The resolution as to a silent inquiry was come to by the
Senate in September, before Memmius made the disclosure
in November, and it had reference to the wholesale bribery
that was going on. But it was doubtful whether the
Senate could of its own authority order an inquiry of that
kind to take place; at all events the tribunes interfered,
and instead of acting on the resolution, a bill to the same
effect was brought before the people. Terentius, however,
one of the tribunes, interposed his veto, and the measure
was stopped. The Senate acted in the matter with inconsistency and weakness. It had originally resolved that
the consular comitia should not be held until the bill
passed, and that if a veto was interposed the bill should be
brought in afresh. It now immediately resolved, notwithstanding that the bill had not passed, that the comitia
should be held forthwith. Cicero calls the house an
Abdera (equivalent to our Bedlam), and intimates that he
spoke his mind freely on the subject. But the comitia

the Statute Rolls. But it was found that clauses were thus surreptitiously
introduced which Parliament had not assented to, and at length, in the
2nd year of Henry V., the Commons prayed that no additions or dimi-
nutions should in future be made.—See May's *Parl. Practice*, p. 360-1
(3rd edit.).

were not held nevertheless.   On each day that the attempt was made, Scævola, another of the tribunes, prevented the meeting by "watching the sky," that strange device which put it in the power of any magistrate at Rome to stop the machinery of government according to his mere caprice. And in fact no consular comitia at all took place this year.

In the midst of all this confusion Cicero clung more and more to Cæsar's friendship.   He called it the only plank in the general shipwreck, and was much pleased at the attentions which were lavished upon his brother by the politic proconsul of Gaul.   Quintus was allowed to choose the winter quarters he liked best for his troops, and Cicero says, that if he himself were the commander, his brother could not be better treated.   At the same time that he mentioned this he told Atticus that he was now one of Pompey's lieutenants, and would leave Rome for the province of Spain, which was Pompey's proconsular government, in the following January.   But for some reason he abandoned the intention, and it is certain that he never went to Spain.   Quintus, like Trebatius, had become rather sick of campaigning, and wrote from Gaul in a very grumbling tone.   Cicero took him to task for this, and begged him to remember the object they had in view when he accepted a military command in Cæsar's army. It was to secure for them both his powerful protection, well disposed as he was to support them.   He spoke of him as "a most excellent and distinguished man," and as he wrote to his brother in unreserved confidence, we cannot doubt that at the time these were his genuine sentiments.   Indeed there is generally a remarkable difference between the way in which he writes privately of Cæsar and the way in which he writes of Pompey.   He thought he could rely upon the one much more than upon the other ; and with all his personal regard for Pompey, he felt how weak and contemptible his character was in comparison with that of Cæsar. The ivy grows more naturally round the oak than the poplar, and it is, I think, one of the most convincing proofs of Cicero's patriotism that at the first outbreak of the great Civil War he joined the side of Pompey instead of the side of Cæsar, because he believed that, however feeble as a statesman and incapable as a general, he was fighting in defence of his country against an enemy and a rebel.

He promised to finish a poem he had begun on Cæsar's exploits, and in allusion to a report that a dictator would be appointed, told Quintus that Pompey now professed to repudiate the idea, but had previously told him that he should not dislike the office. "Good heavens!" he exclaimed, "how silly he is, how eaten up by self-love, and impatient of a rival!" His disgust at the state of things in Rome had nearly reached its climax ; but he declared that it produced in him an almost reckless indifference. "I am now," he said, "not even affected by public evils and the licence of bold, bad men, by which I was formerly heartbroken. There is nothing more abandoned than these men and the times they live in. Since, therefore, no pleasure can be found in public affairs, I really do not see why I should fret myself. I indulge in repose, and take delight in study, my books, and my villas, and especially in the society and education of our two boys." It seems that young Quintus, his nephew, was something of a glutton; for his uncle says that he would keep his eye upon him now that his mother Pomponia was away, for he was afraid he would do himself harm by his voracious appetite. He thanked his brother for promising to send him some slaves, no doubt prisoners taken in Britain and Gaul, as he had very few either at Rome or in the country; and begged him to be extremely cautious in writing, as he himself was,—not venturing to mention things that were publicly done in the state of confusion that prevailed at Rome, lest his letters might be intercepted and he might give offence.   He had finished his little epic poem on Cæsar, and said he was only waiting to find a trustworthy courier, lest it should be lost on the road as Quintus's tragedy of Erigone was; which, he added, was the only thing that had not had a safe journey from Gaul while Cæsar had commanded there.   Quintus had begged him to look after the works going on at his Arcanum villa, and Cicero told him that it was more like one of Cæsar's buildings than anything else, fitted up as it was with statues, a *palæstra*, a fish-pond, and a canal. It is quite clear that his brother was making good use of his opportunities in Gaul and getting rich.   But both he and Cicero had a little disappointment just then, as a friend of theirs, named Felix, from whom they had expectations, had died, after having by mistake signed a wrong will, so that they got no legacies.

So ended the year, a year which had seen a great change in the policy of Cicero, and in which he had felt dissatisfied with almost every public man but. Cæsar. To him he had now transferred his political allegiance, and to secure his favor had sacrificed his previous enmities, and I fear we must add his principles.   He could look back with little complacency upon his hollow reconciliation with such men as Vatinius and Gabinius, and must have felt how much he had lowered himself by appearing as their apologist to gratify the wishes of Pompey and Cæsar. And he gained nothing by giving up his independence.

He lost his own self-respect, and his influence in the
Senate and the Rostra declined. Stormy times were fast
approaching, and his was not the hand that could guide the
helm of the vessel of the State through the rocks and shoals
with which it was surrounded.

END OF VOL. I.

LONDON: PRINTED BY W. CLOWES AND SONS, STAMFORD STREET,
AND CHARING CROSS.